CAPWAR EMPIRE

BRANDT LEGG

CapWar EMPIRE (CapStone Conspiracy book three)

Published in the United States of America by Laughing Rain

Copyright © 2018 by Brandt Legg

Cataloging-in-Publication data for this book is available from the Library of Congress.

ISBN-13: 978-1-935070-35-1

ISBN-10: 1-935070-35-5

PUBLISHER'S NOTE

This book is a work of fiction. Names, characters, places and incidents are products of the author's imagination or are used fictitiously. Any resemblance to actual persons, living or dead, businesses, events or locales is entirely coincidental.

BrandtLegg.com

As always, this book is dedicated to Teakki and Ro

And to Blair Legg 1957-2017

CHAPTER ONE

The nondescript oak door, marked only by a standard government brass placard which simply read "B-4," was in the basement level of the Pentagon. Most of the 25,000 workers who spent their days toiling away for America's military inside the world's largest office building had no idea the room even existed, let alone what it was used for. The massive building contained seventeen miles of hallways—the true corridors of power—and seven floors (five stories above ground, two below). However, the few who ever walked across the reinforced threshold of room B-4, would find a staircase leading down to a deeper level not officially acknowledged.

Sixty-one-year-old General Imperia pushed his palm print against the reader, which scanned it to give him access. As he descended the wide staircase, he considered the gravity of the situation, the most serious it had ever been in his more than four-decade military career. He took the last steps and now, on the secret eighth level, walked twenty-five feet to a steel reinforced door. Now the biometric recognition system instantly viewed and matched a grid of his facial data points. The door opened.

Inside he found the only other three people alive who had ever been in the rarely-used room, two of whom were also in their sixties; the other was fifty-five. The four men sat around a large table. Two of them sipped coffee. Only the faint, reliable hum of the vintage ventilation system kept this from being one of the most silent interior spaces on earth.

The stern expressions on their faces gave a sense of the serious problem they faced. Each of them had achieved the highest rank in his respective military branches—Army, Air Force, Navy, and Marines. The "B-4 Group" infrequently changed members, in the case of retirement or death. The ultra-classified enclave had been taking place since the 1950s. However, in all those years, this was the first time B-4 was seriously considering removing the president of the United States by military coup d'état, or whatever other means they deemed necessary.

"Pound stepped over the line," Imperia said. "Going to China . . . do we have any idea how he convinced the communists to stand down?"

"Not yet," the Admiral replied. "Our man at the CIA is working on it."

"They may not know," the Air Force general offered. "What about Colonel Dranick? He was with the president in China."

Imperia grimaced. "I'll see what I can do."

"Regardless," the Marine Commandant began, "Pound is a loose cannon. He's defied the recommendations of his Joint Chiefs, Congress, and virtually any voice of reason in his administration, including the Secretaries of Defense and State."

"We all know the problem," Imperia said. "We're here to find a solution."

"Now that the threat of war has subsided," the Commandant continued gruffly, "the House's attempts at impeachment will not get far. So it's up to us."

"Is there no other way?" the Admiral asked.

"He's dangerous," Imperia said. "Pound has refused to carry out a declaration of war authorized by Congress. He publicly said he would not fight. We cannot have a pacifist and a coward as commander in chief."

"If we indeed orchestrate a coup," the Commandant said, "who are we putting in as president? Certainly not anti-war Vice President Brown!"

"No, I think we can get the Speaker on board," Imperia said. "If we're going to sell this to the American people, it's important that we follow the Constitutional line of succession."

"Agreed," the Air Force general said, eager for a short meeting so his extreme claustrophobia would not be discovered.

The Commandant nodded.

All eyes turned to the Admiral. The men had just proposed treason. A coup d'état, the seizure of power from civilian rule by the military, was something they never would have spoken of outside their tiny circle. Even within the thick walls of the completely soundproof B-4 room, as the conversation turned to planning the coup, the four men barely spoke above a whisper.

"Okay," the Admiral assented. "On the condition that the Speaker of the House is on board."

General Imperia stood. The other three followed suit. "Gentlemen, for the first time in the history of our great nation, it has fallen to us, simple soldiers who have served the country our entire lives, to protect her from the enemy within, perhaps the most dangerous threat to our democracy—a weak leader." He paused and slowly surveyed the faces of his counterparts. "Then we are in agreement. We will remove the president from power."

After each man had verbally approved one last time, it became official. The military would assume control of the government. They would each later adjust to the unprecedented magnitude of this decision in their own ways. Nothing in their careers had ever prepared them for this actuality.

CHAPTER TWO

At the exact same time, two hundred-thirty miles northeast, eighty-six floors above ground, in downtown Manhattan, another meeting was taking place, this one between representatives of the Federal Reserve Board and Titus Coyne, a fifty-nine-year-old billionaire who'd made his fortune on Wall Street. Coyne, one of the most powerful REMies, was privately credited with engineering the 2008 financial meltdown. Although many REMies had contributed to the economic "disaster," Coyne had been the mastermind.

Beginning in the '90s, he'd pushed for the repeal of Glass-Steagall and helped to pass the Commodity Futures Modernization Act, which exempted much of the high-risk trading and new financial instruments from regulation. He was already one of the emperors in the empire, and had the best chance at grabbing the CapStone and winning the final CapWar.

In the newly deregulated environment, he further pushed the limits of the law by leading banks into risky hedge funds and exotic derivatives trading. Coyne created a stew of derivatives, including those backed by an endless stream of mortgages. Banks, hungry for more gains, demanded more mortgages to package, and waded deeper into murky waters by offering interest-only loans to borrowers with poor credit. But his greatest move came in 2004, when he convinced many other REMies to have the Federal Reserve start raising interest rates just as all those subprime adjustable mortgages the banks had sold off to investors were set to jump. His "stew" had indeed become a recipe for disaster.

Coyne's shaggy brown and gray hair, tough-guy good looks, and penchant for wearing $60,000 hand-tailored Kiton suits, added to the aura of fear and charm he'd cultivated for decades. His mafia manners, rare smile, and hard-hitting tactics, had made him a legend on the Street, and even among his fellow REMies, who often referred to him as "the shark." However, although not a banker himself, a better moniker for the shadowy financier would have been "Bankster." Indeed, Titus Coyne was the definition of the word.

As the Fed representatives and Coyne sat in the plush boardroom overlooking Central Park, debating the future of the world economy as if they were writing a script for a new movie, they had one problem: the president of the United States. Typically, it didn't matter who was in the White House, nor which party controlled what branch of government. They all answered to the REMies, "one way or another."

"Pound is trouble," Coyne said. "And now that Vonner's gone, we have no way to control this clod anymore. He belongs to nobody." It was the global elite's worst nightmare, to have a president without a master. Normally they could assassinate him or otherwise removed him from office, which they were working on, but Hudson Pound was proving difficult. In fact, one of their code names for him was "cat." They were beginning to believe he truly had nine lives.

"And, it's worse," one of the bankers said. "Pound has Vonner's money, or at least his son does."

"His son, Schueller Pound, lives in the White House. He's so close with his father, the money might as well be in the president's personal account," another banker added.

"That was obviously part of Vonner's brilliance," Coyne said. "The president wouldn't be able to use the funds while in office due to conflict of interest laws." Coyne looked around the room as if disgusted with everyone there, silently blaming them for the $52 billion in Schueller's hands, which was actually almost $3 billion more than Coyne had. "Vonner was trying to screw us." Even as a child, and certainly as a younger man, Coyne despised being crossed, and always made it a priority to get even. *Always.*

"He did a damn good job," another one of the bankers said.

"Vonner was trying to get the CapStone," Coyne said bitterly. Everyone in the room knew that Titus Coyne had been vying for the capstone for twenty years. He thought he had it in 2008, but Bastendorff, Vonner, and Booker Lipton had all been playing different angles of the same game and diluted the thrust of Coyne's power. "But he's out of the way now, and I think there might be an avenue to use the Pound problem to our advantage."

The bankers all understood that by "our advantage," Coyne meant his own advantage, but they didn't care because none of them had the means, or even the desire to go for the CapStone themselves. By riding with Coyne, they would all get even richer along the way, no matter the outcome of the CapWar.

CHAPTER THREE

Hudson and Melissa, having a rare dinner alone together in the family residence dining room, talked in hushed tones. Hudson laid out the priorities, made easier with Schueller's massive inheritance from Arlin Vonner.

"We've got a real chance now against Bastendorff and the others," Hudson said. "I plan on using our new REMie-sized war chest, and every ounce of power I can wring from the presidency, to bring them down."

"Ironic," Melissa said.

Hudson looked at her questioningly.

"That Vonner gave you both the power and money to destroy what you were convinced he was trying to use for his own gain."

He nodded. "I've been wrong enough times to know that sometimes making a mistake is the only way to get it right."

"Now you're starting to sound like a regular politician."

"It's not doublespeak," Hudson said. "Vonner was as corrupt as the rest, but—"

"I don't think that's true, Vonner wanted to change the empire-system."

"They all want to change it to something that makes the empire favor themselves, but it would still be a REMie-run world, still the damned empire. Vonner talked of giving the power back to the people, yet he didn't do anything about it." He raised his glass of spring water and nodded at her in an unspoken toast.

"He made you president, wasn't that a start?"

"I was another weapon to be used against his rivals. Maybe he'd loosen things a bit, let me do some reforms . . . " He offered to pour her some wine.

She shook her head. "Then why leave his money to Schueller?"

"To screw Bastendorff and Booker one last time."

"I don't think so." She pushed her plate away and leaned back in the antique chair.

"Then why?"

"He believed in you," she said, popping a few fresh blueberries in her mouth. It was Hudson's favorite fruit, and he regularly requested it served for dessert.

Hudson stared at his wife, trying to let her words, which sounded false and foreign, sink in. "I don't know."

"I know you don't," she said quietly.

"We've got to end the Federal Reserve system, radically reform the IRS, put Bastendorff, Booker, and all the other REMies in prison—end the empire!" Hudson suddenly ranted. "We have a chance to remake the entire government. We can get back to what the Founding Fathers wanted, a government actually run by the *people*."

"We are the change," she said, knowing these words always strengthened him.

"Damn right!" he said. "And not just from a financial standpoint, but we can bring home the three hundred thousand military personnel serving outside the US. Eight hundred bases in one hundred and fifty countries—do you know what that *costs?* Nearly a quarter of a trillion dollars a year!"

"I do know," she said, holding up the bowl. "Want some blueberries?"

Hudson smiled and paused. She had heard this countless times before.

"President Pound, you sound an awful lot like a NorthBridge sympathizer," Melissa said with a coy smile.

"If NorthBridge has some good ideas, they're lost in a pool of blood," Hudson replied, turning angry. "The path to change is not through violence."

"Stopping them and the REMies at the same time—"

"Is like defeating Nazi Germany and Japan in World War II," Hudson said. "It can be done."

Melissa nodded wearily, her hopes for a quiet evening dissolving yet again.

"We'll mobilize the people just like we did during World War II," he continued. "And we can make part of the reforms the environmental regulations you want—no material can be manufactured that can't be recycled, fossil fuels will be taxed into oblivion, pollution of any kind will be so cost prohibitive that companies doing it will find alternatives."

"That may be a tougher sale than you think."

"Not if the REMies are in prison," Hudson said. "Preserving the planet and taking care of each other will become more important than profit and greed."

"Didn't you run as a Republican?" Melissa asked, laughing. She liked and agreed with what he was saying, but knew it was the nine minutes talking. She marveled at his change.

"Forget the labels. Democrats and Republicans are both REMie parties. From now on, I'm an egalitarian."

CHAPTER FOUR

For the first time since their organizational meetings some years earlier, Booker Lipton—AKA Washington, Fonda Raton—AKA Jefferson, Thorne—AKA Hancock, AKA Adams, and AKA Franklin were together in one place. They met on a secluded island off the west coast of Mexico, one of many owned by Booker, who collected islands.

"In light of what Fonda has reported about her meeting with Pound, and with Booker's similar experience with him," Thorne began, "I think we can no longer ignore the fact that he needs to be removed immediately."

"No," Fonda objected. "He can still help us."

"He's the one who needs *our* help!" Thorne blasted. "I didn't think he was ever strong enough, but since being dead for nine minutes, he seems even weaker to me. And do I need to remind you that he's alone on a virtual island? Congress hates him, his approval ratings are in the basement, the media treats him like a punching bag, and it's only a matter of time before the REMies figure out a way to actually kill him, yet *again*."

"Then we can wait for them to do the job," AKA Franklin said.

"Perhaps *you* need the reminder," Fonda said. "Congress, the media, and the REMies are who we're fighting. Hudson is fighting the same battle we are."

"No, he isn't," Thorne argued. "He thinks the REMies can be defeated by talk and law." Thorne laughed. "A REMie put him in power, and he still doesn't understand them. He believes wars happen by accident."

"I don't think he does," Fonda said.

"Then he's no good at math, because just off the top of my head, I can rattle off over one hundred million deaths in the last hundred years in wars that the REMies made happen. Does the president think that the REMies, who have long used violence as their main weapon, can really be brought down by love and light?"

"We need him," Fonda repeated, her tone flat and firm.

"I'll tell you who needs him, the twenty-two thousand children under the age of five, around the world, who die every day due to poverty! Ten million kids died before age five last year— that would be like every kid in France and Germany dying in a single year. Can you imagine?"

"I know the damage the REMies' 'empire system' has wrought," Fonda said calmly, while silently thinking that she knew almost all such statistics better than he could ever hope to. *The fool!*

"Yeah, but does Pound?" Thorne asked as he flailed his arms and paced around the large gazebo where they were gathered. "The world spent a trillion dollars last year on weapons. One and a half million children die every year due to lack of safe drinking water and sanitation. Do you know how much it would cost to fix that, to save those kids? About $9 billion. That's how much Americans spent on *cosmetics* last year. Half of what we spend on pet food! Hell, Europeans spend a lot more than that on ice cream!"

"Enough," Booker said quietly, yet it felt like a slamming door to the others. "This isn't your radio show, Thorne."

"The world is so screwed up!" Thorne screamed at the ocean.

"We know," AKA Adams said. "That's why we're here, why we're doing all this."

"Well we're not doing it fast enough!" Thorne said, finally returning to his seat. "I say kill Pound and let Brown have a crack at it."

"No one's going to kill Hudson Pound," Booker said. "At least not if I have anything to do with it." The billionaire was both a REMie and a NorthBridger, but he was also an extremely persuasive and authoritative man. Even Thorne knew the argument was over, at least for now, but the shock jock couldn't resist one final jab.

"So the president is coming after us, wants to stop North-Bridge," Thorne said, staring at Fonda, "but we can't fight back?"

"We have enough to fight," Fonda said.

"More if the president finds out who I am," AKA Adams added. "If he discovered your identities, he'll get mine sooner or later."

"The person who IDed Booker, Fonda, and Thorne is dead," AKA Franklin said. "It's likely with everything going on now, and with what's about to happen, the rest of us who are still incognito will be safe. The president is going to be too busy trying to hold the United States together to worry about our names."

"By the time Pound finds out who you and AKA Franklin are," Thorne said to AKA Adams, "it'll be too late."

"That's right," agreed Booker. "And the reason we risked this meeting is because it's time to enter phase two of the revolution." The billionaire slowly scanned the faces of the other four leaders to be sure they understood the gravity of his statement. "The course on which we are about to embark will change everything. There will be no turning back."

Each person nodded solemnly.

"As you know," Booker continued, "this war against the elites may be lost, but win or lose, the world will be left a fragile disaster area. From this day forward, we will be walking away from life as we know it. Destroying the REMie empire destroys all that we have ever known or counted on . . . which means *all* the rules are about to change."

"So that we cannot predict the outcomes of our own actions," AKA Adams said. "In trying to protect the world from REMie rule, we may destroy that which we are trying to save."

CHAPTER FIVE

Lester Devonshire stood on the top floor of a building housing the west coast offices of Gaston, Gaston, and Wyatt, one of the largest law firms in the country. The thirty-eight-year-old's mood could not be soothed even by the stunning view of San Francisco's skyline and the bay beyond. Lester, a newly minted billionaire thanks to his uncle, the late Arlin Vonner, seethed. Many people would have been happy with a billion-dollar inheritance, but Lester thought he deserved much, much more.

For some impossible reason, his uncle had left most of his fortune to the president's son! And as far as Lester was concerned, Schueller Pound was nothing more than a B-list, wannabe rock star who didn't deserve a bequest of a thousand dollars, let alone fifty-two *billion*.

Lester whirled around, tired of waiting for his "useless" attorney to answer the question. "Nothing?" Lester repeated. "There is *nothing* you can do?"

"The terms of the will are explicit," the attorney said, trying to hide his exasperation. "Should you contest your uncle's wishes, you forfeit *everything*." He enunciated each syllable in the final word. "And, in the event that you were successful in a challenge, then the trust stipulates that all the money is instead to be distributed to the Arlin Vonner Foundation." The attorney paused until his client looked up. "Do you really want to risk a billion dollars?"

"You tell me."

"There seems to be no precedent in any of the case law that supports your claim. Your uncle was very careful in how the document was worded. However, should you wish to proceed . . . " The attorney handed a folder to Lester. "Here's a detailed brief outlining the options and explaining how we would go forward, but I have to advise against it. Any judge is going to look at three salient facts: Arlin Vonner was of very sound mind, you were left one billion dollars, and aside from a list of other relatively minor bequeaths, the balance of his estate went to a blood relative."

"So?"

"There's nothing unusual here, and most probate courts tend to side with the Testator."

Lester, the only son of Vonner's late sister, had actually been surprised that Vonner had left him a billion dollars, since the two weren't exactly close. But as a guy who had hustled for everything he'd ever gotten, he wasn't about to let the possibility of becoming one of the world's top ten richest men slip away without a fight. Lester never minded a battle. He'd won more than he'd lost, thanks in part to his talent for fighting dirty. He actually took pride in constant negativity. He felt it gave him a special edge against nice people—actually, *any* people.

Lester ran several brothels in Nevada, as well as the Cash-O-King Casino, one of the smallest casinos located at the "drab" end of the Vegas strip. The place was famous for its low table-game betting minimums, dollar craps, and dollar black jack. Cash-O-King's cheap, watered-down drinks and few hundred slot machines attracted the kind of low end gamblers who wouldn't last long in the bigger gaming castles. Lester didn't mind the riffraff; all their nickels and dimes had made him a millionaire. The brothels had helped, too.

He was worth eight million dollars, but he'd never stopped lusting after his uncle's epic wealth. Over the years, he'd tried kissing up to the old man every way he knew how, but Vonner never seemed impressed. Still, Lester had long planned to attack the will whenever his uncle "kicked off." He knew he had a good chance because of being the only living blood relative, but that was before he knew about his distant cousins, "the damned Pounds."

The billion had been an unexpected gift. He would have only predicted a nominal amount like a hundred grand or so, but his uncle's generosity only made Lester believe he was entitled to a lot more.

Lester had been working a "big deal" to get into marijuana dispensaries in three states, which included a back-alley line to a lucrative import-export business. Legalized pot was extremely profitable, but the real money was still in the illegal side of the trade. Lester could parlay a billion into three times that much in a few years. He also had his eye on a bigger casino, which, even with his inheritance, was still out of reach.

Although it would take at least six months to probate the will, Vonner had made a shrewd move by including a Payable on Death, or "POD", clause on his main accounts. And by utilizing living trusts, loans, survivorship clauses, corporate transfers, and a host of other legal and accounting tactics, had managed it so that the funds went to Schueller and Lester immediately. Finalization through the probate court was a mere technicality. The estate's structure also made it extremely difficult for Lester to challenge.

Lester angrily shoved several law books from the table,

sending them crashing to the floor. Then he snatched the folder from his astonished attorney, never intending to read it, and stormed out of the office. He also had no intention of paying the legal bill for these "useless leeches." Lester had other connections, ones that didn't care so much about the law.

"I'll get that money one way or another," he muttered to himself as the elevator doors opened, the plan already formulating. By the time he reached the parking level, he was certain that both Hudson and Schueller Pound would have to die. This realization actually caused him to smile, a very rare event.

CHAPTER SIX

The president looked up from the Resolute Desk and smiled as Vice President Brown entered the Oval Office. "Give me a moment," he said, typing another few lines into his laptop and pushing send.

"Of course," the vice president replied. She had just returned from a meeting with a Norwegian delegation at Blair House.

Hudson entered a few more commands into the computer, closed it, slid it into a case which he slung over his shoulder, and then walked over to the built-in bookcase and pressed a concealed switch. A wall panel slid back, revealing a secret door. The vice president looked surprised.

Hudson ushered her inside the small space and led her down the stairs. They came out inside a closet near the president's private elevator. The passage opened into the network of secret tunnels which connected the White House to several other buildings in Washington—escape routes.

"I'd heard rumors about these tunnels," the vice president said.

"They're quite elaborate," Hudson said as they headed down one of the lighted corridors. Beige linoleum from another age covered the floors, and shiny tiles one might find in an old public-school cafeteria gave the walls a cheap, dated look, nothing like the grand appointments normally associated with the office of the president. "I brought you down here because it's just about the safest place," Hudson said, stopping at an intersection. "One where we will not be overheard."

"Are you certain of that?" Vice President Brown asked.

Hudson nodded. "The damned leaks are a bigger problem than the eavesdropping. At least those I can find or defeat with our own electronic devices." Choosing the passageway to their right, he began walking again. "We may have stopped the war with China," the president said, "but that was merely a battle in a much bigger war. You know this."

"The REMies."

"Yes, and they're going to continue to try to kill me. Should that happen, you must be ready."

The vice president stopped and touched Hudson's shoulder. He turned to face her. "Mr. President, I've been ready since inauguration day to assume your duties, but we cannot let that happen."

"I appreciate—"

"No," the vice president pressed. "Whichever REMie succeeds in having you assassinated will win the CapStone. I may become president, but I'll be powerless or dead myself . . . "

"From now on, we can never be in the same building at the same time. We can't let them get us both at the same time."

The vice president nodded solemnly.

"And it isn't just REMies, this is a two-front war. North-Bridge is as big a threat. Not only do they want me out of office by any means necessary, but they're forcing a revolution."

"NorthBridge was against the war with China," the vice president offered. "They exclusively target the tools of the REMies."

"Don't let your anti-war beliefs cloud your judgement," the president said as the corridor curved. "There can be no alliance with terrorists. And never doubt that we will stop NorthBridge. I know who three of their leaders are, and it's only a matter of time until we penetrate their veil of secrecy. Once we identify the rest of the hierarchy, we will cut the head off that snake and stamp out this talk of revolution."

"If you know the leaders, why not engage them?" the vice president asked. "You say we cannot ally ourselves with terrorists, but isn't the priority to shatter the REMies' empire? It's a near impossible task. We could use NorthBridge to help—"

"Celia, I'm surprised you would ever consider working with a group like this. They are at war with everyone who disagrees with them. NorthBridge is using brutal violence to accomplish what could be done peacefully. How can you reconcile that with your long-held position against violence and war?"

"I don't condone their barbaric actions, Mr. President, not for a minute, but I fear that there's only the smallest window remaining to defeat the REMies. If one of them gets the CapStone, we'll be under absolute REMie rule, and NorthBridge will become a legitimate resistance to the oppressors . . . a resistance which will quickly be crushed."

"We'll just have to beat them both," the president said.

"My father always used to say that a person has to know his priorities."

"Wise man," Hudson said.

"Then you know you can't succeed by trying to have two top priorities. REMies or NorthBridge. I don't think we can beat either one of them unless we use all our efforts against one of them first."

"Maybe," Hudson said. "I recall what someone said about the

2016 presidential race, deciding between Clinton and Trump was like choosing between cancer and a heart attack."

The vice president didn't join in Hudson's smile. "North-Bridge may be a heart attack, but the REMies are a cancer, and we don't have much time left."

CHAPTER SEVEN

The president, Melissa, the Wizard, Schueller, and Dranick huddled around the conference table inside Laurel Lodge at Camp David. Not trusting the Secret Service, the Wizard had already used one of his custom inventions to scan for listening devices.

"As you know," the Wizard began, "I've finally retrieved most of the data Crane hid on the DarkNet. There are still one or two lost NorthBridge files, but knowing what we do about Booker, Fonda, and Thorne, it isn't nearly as urgent."

"That depends on who else is part of the terror group," Melissa said.

The president nodded.

"Of course," the Wizard agreed. "However, there's enough information here to keep us busy for a long time with the REMies."

"NorthBridge may destroy us and fracture the country long before we can even get to the REMies," Melissa said harshly.

"Let's hear what he's got," the president urged, placing a hand gently on top of Melissa's.

"The two most dangerous REMies that seem to have the best shot at getting the CapStone are Bastendorff and Coyne," the Wizard began. "The first one—Bastendorff. Not a nice guy. Hands into everything. He likes destabilizing governments, causing famines, small wars, uprisings, and just generally excels at peddling fear."

"I've heard he also likes Legos," Schueller said with a laugh.

The Wizard nodded. "Strange dude, no doubt. Crane also uncovered evidence to suggest Bastendorff hired Kniike, the assassin who tried to off you on inauguration day."

"I keep liking this Bastard-dorf less and less," Hudson said. "Enough proof to arrest him?"

"No."

"I thought not."

"Our other friend, Titus Coyne, is a bit more sophisticated," the Wizard said, "and plays wild financial games. He's like a mad scientist experimenting with the world economy, and he's good at it."

"He's tight with the Fed Chairman," the president said.

"Exactly," the Wizard agreed. "And he orchestrated the largest theft in the history of the world. According to the data that Crane unearthed, nearly $20 trillion has been looted from the US treasury, and it flowed into the accounts and corporations controlled by four dozen REMies, and at least another ninety-eight wealthy elites."

"We don't have $20 trillion in the treasury," the president said.

"Not anymore," the Wizard replied with a wink.

"No, there has never been that much," Melissa said. "So how could the REMies take what wasn't there?"

"They printed money, lent it to the banks, pumped it into the economy—basically just created it from nothing—and now it has to be paid back. They've been doing it for years, not just during the last crisis, but it was usually just a hundred billion here, a hundred billion there. No one ever had the audacity or capacity to move trillions before Coyne."

"How does this go undetected?" the president asked rhetorically.

"They control the politicians, the government, the media, all of it," Schueller answered anyway. "Everything is rigged. They keep spoon-feeding us lies. Did you read Crane's last report? It isn't just Manipulate-And-Distract-Everyone. MADE events are only part of it. The REMies have another trick they use every day called SAD—Scare, Agitate, Divide—and the media fosters it, 'us against them.' Everything is a battle, every crisis is politicized. Once upon a time, we all got along."

"And Coyne may really be the worst of all. His ambitions know no limits. This guy has been after the CapStone for decades, and doesn't care what he has to do to reach it," the Wizard said. "Apparently, on Wall Street, they call him 'the shark,' or 'killer.'"

"It's an unimaginable amount of money," the president said, wondering how they could defeat an enemy with truly unlimited resources. He looked out to the rugged Maryland countryside and thought about President Eisenhower naming Camp David for his grandson, who went on to marry President Nixon's daughter, Julie. Eisenhower, Ike, the Supreme Allied Commander in Europe during World War II, prior to becoming president, had warned of the military industrial complex during his farewell address. He knew what was coming. His successor, John Kennedy, had been the last one to try to rein in the corrupt elites attempting to completely control the world . . . the last one until now.

"And it just didn't start with the 2008 meltdown," the Wizard said, bringing Hudson back. "It's ongoing. That's how they've reached the heights of this insane amount of money.

And Coyne is doing it in dozens of countries. All the REMies are!"

"But the initial bailout in 2008 was something like $700 billion," Melissa said. "I still don't understand how we got to trillions."

"Oh, it's crazy," the Wizard replied. "The REMies have more tricks than Houdini. Even back in 2011, an official report showed the government's guarantees had increased to nearly $8 trillion. Then in 2015, the Special Inspector General's summary of TARP, said the total commitment of government in the bailout was $16.8 trillion. They have so many ways. In 2016, the Pentagon admitted it couldn't account for $6.8 *trillion* of taxpayer cash!"

Melissa squinted her eyes at the Wizard. "You're starting to sound like Thorne. Maybe NorthBridge stole it with their digi-GOLD scheme!"

"He is, isn't he?" Hudson agreed. "Crane and Zackers both showed the terrorists had found a way to shave micro fractions off almost every financial transaction."

"Thorne gets a lot right, and twenty trillion is more than micro fractions," the Wizard said. "Do you know that something like one hundred trillion cells make up your body? Each cell is made up of a hundred trillion atoms, inside them are protons, then quarks . . . it's incredible, the Planck length we're talking about, matter, the density of space, I mean can you—"

"Wizard," Hudson said, narrowing his eyes and briskly shaking his head. "We're talking about the REMies . . . "

"It's the REMies who stole it," Schueller agreed. "That's what they do. The eight richest men own as much wealth as the poorest half of the world's population. How did that happen? It's disgusting when over three *billion* people live on less than $2.50 a day. The REMies are out of control."

"I know," Melissa said. "I just don't want to see your father die for a cause that isn't clear . . . we just need to be sure who we're fighting."

"You're all right," the president said. "The way things work now is a mess. There's too much wealth in the world to have billions in poverty, and billions more working their lives away. It must be changed. But the REMies have cloaked themselves in so much secrecy, so many layers of protections. They have a complex system that only they understand. It's the strength of their empire—"

"And I'm not sure even *they* understand it themselves anymore," the Wizard interrupted. "In the past twenty years, as they've slugged it out for the CapStone, they've lost control of their own system. The emperors are at war with each other."

"Be that as it may, it's up to us to bring it, and them, down. And don't forget for a minute that NorthBridge is presumably trying to bring about violent change. We must follow the examples of Gandhi, Martin Luther King, Jr., Mandela—if we shine light on their darkness, they'll be exposed."

"Cherry Tree," the Wizard said. It was their code name for the plan to illuminate all the REMie atrocities so the masses would see the truth and join the president in throwing out the elites and destroying their false system. "That's how we bring down the empire."

"Right," Hudson agreed. "Along with everything else we've put together, the Kennedy papers we found in the Resolute Desk are going to shock people. Once the people know, they'll turn on the REMies and take back what is rightfully theirs."

"Risky," Melissa said. "It sounds a little too much like the French Revolution when the peasants turned on the aristocrats and royals. Thousands were marched to the guillotine. What do you think the masses are going to do when they learn the truth?"

"There'll be trials . . . " the president said. Although Hudson knew it would be virtually impossible to prosecute anyone over the Kennedy assassination, since the papers JFK had hidden shortly before being gunned down in Dallas were, at best, circumstantial. However, the typed contents with margin notes made in Kennedy's own handwriting made it clear he had the goods on the REMies.

"Forgive me," Melissa said, "but I think that's naïve. Don't you recall what Thorne said during one of the debates? *'Ramener la guillotine,'* bring back the guillotine. He has something like thirty million listeners who are already angry. Imagine when they discover that five or six hundred people have stolen most of the wealth in the world because of a system being controlled by fifty of them."

"They have a right to know they've been manipulated," the Wizard said.

"I'm not arguing that," Melissa said. "I'm merely suggesting we take a prudent approach so the country, and the rest of the world, doesn't wind up in anarchy."

CHAPTER EIGHT

B astendorff had just finished completing an elaborate scale replica of the White House built entirely of Legos when two aides entered the room and informed him that Titus Coyne had met with Federal Reserve officials in New York.

"He's going to get them to raise rates," Bastendorff said. "Coyne wants them to constrict the money supply. I like it. It's what I would do." He adjusted his eyeglasses and dug his fat hands into a large bin of all white Lego pieces, massaging the mass of plastic bricks as if he were molding clay or counting money. "Let's ride on Coyne's battle plan and throw everything we've got at Pound. We'll see if he can handle it."

"The president has handled everything so far," one of the aides said.

"Things are different now," Bastendorff retorted. "Pound doesn't have Vonner to protect him anymore."

"But he does have the new billionaire Schueller Pound and Vonner Security."

"Schueller Pound and VS, are you joking?" Bastendorff said,

his puffy face rolling into a smug, yet annoyed smile. "A kid, and a bunch of rent-a-cops. Somehow I'm not very worried."

"VS did fine against the team we had protecting Rochelle Rogers," the aide added.

"Only because Booker Lipton sent his BLAXers to help," Bastendorff said, his grin changing to a scowl.

"I don't know," the aide began. "A deadhead with fifty-two billion dollars, that kind of crazy would worry me."

"I bet it would." Bastendorff smirked. "I think I've got a lot more money, much more firepower, and definitely more experience than some college dropout and an ex-teacher slash ex-hardware store clerk."

"I'm sure you're right," the aide said, wishing he'd never said a word.

"So am I," Bastendorff replied, pulling his hands from the Legos and heading toward the elevator. The aides followed. "I want to give this guy riots in the streets of every city in America, trade wars, mass power outages, drug runners on the borders, embassy bombings, anti-American demonstrations, political unrest, I might even throw in a natural disaster or two."

"Then we're a 'go' on the NorthBridge plan?" another aide asked.

Make it happen," Bastendorff said.

Dranick, who'd been mostly silent during the meeting at Laurel Lodge, walked along Camp David's wooded path later that day with the Wizard and Schueller.

"We may have to do some things that didn't come up earlier," Dranick said. "On the reservation where I was raised, sometimes the coyote tricks you, and sometimes he helps you, but either way, you are changed."

"What do you mean?" Schueller asked.

"You're Hudson's son, Wizard is his oldest friend, and I consider him my brother," Dranick began. "He's counting on us to support him because bringing down the REMies is too big a task for any single person, even the president of the United States." Dranick stopped and looked back along the path they had come, as if gauging the distance from any of the buildings. "That means we have to do what he can't and protect him from the fallout."

"You mean illegal things?" Schueller asked.

"I prefer the term 'Shadow Ops,'" Dranick replied.

"'Illegal' is a relative term," the Wizard added. "The REMies system is the biggest crime ever. The elites are nothing more than racketeering mob bosses."

"Meaning two wrongs make a right?" Schueller asked.

Dranick nodded affirmatively.

"What do you have in mind?" Schueller asked.

"As the Director of National Intelligence, I present a problem to the REMies," Dranick said. "The DNI, along with the director of the NSA, the CIA director, the Chairman of the Federal Reserve Board, and the handful of other REMie loyalists in key positions, formed a quasi-governmental committee, created policy, and actually ran the country."

"And, by default, the world," the Wizard added, as he stopped to compare two leaves.

"I've got access to all major intelligence, and command of the FaST Squads, and just because they're called 'Find and Stop Terrorists' doesn't mean we have to just use them against NorthBridge . . . "

"Are you suggesting arresting anyone knowingly working for REMies?" Schueller asked.

"I am," Dranick said. "And because most people who work for the REMies don't do it knowingly, yet provide the infrastructure, if you will, to allow the REMies to control us, I'm also proposing we arrest them, too."

"That's a lot of people," the Wizard said.

"Does it make us like Covington, or even the Nazi SS?" Schueller questioned. "I mean, if we go around picking up anyone who is seen as a threat to our agenda—"

"If we don't play rough, I don't see how we can win," Dranick said. "Even playing rough, *really* rough may not be enough."

The Wizard looked at Schueller. "It's a slippery slope."

"But he's right. The REMies have everything," Schueller said. "We should be prepared to do whatever it takes to break their hold."

"Little Dawg," the Wizard said to Schueller, "you talk about the REMies as if they're aliens or something, but remember you're one of them now. What are you gonna do with all Vonner's blood money?"

"I'm going to use every last dollar to bring down the tyrants."

"The three of us are in a unique position," Dranick said. "With Schueller's fortune, Wizard's DarkNet skills, and my access as DNI, we can make the difference. We can actually make the difference and win. By hell . . . we're a triumvirate! I didn't realize it until now—a triumvirate for good!"

"It's true," Schueller said. "He can send out FaST squads to arrest REMies and seize assets, you can use Gypsy to track and uncover their schemes, and with my bottomless supply of cash, I can attack the REMies where they've never been challenged before—the financial arena."

"Agreed?" Dranick asked. "We do what we have to do and keep the president insulated?"

"You mean lie to Hudson?" the Wizard asked.

"*Protect* him," Dranick said emphatically, "while we make sure his goals are accomplished."

"Okay," the Wizard said, "but we stay in touch—daily—and nothing too crazy."

"Famous last words," Schueller said, wondering if G. Gordon Liddy had a similar conversation with John Mitchell, Jeb Magruder, and John Dean decades earlier, leading to the Watergate scandal and resulting in the resignation of President Nixon.

CHAPTER NINE

The president and Fitz sat alone in the Oval Office, wrestling with a strategy to prevent the REMies from destroying the administration. The most difficult decision, as in any major confrontation, was whom to trust. They'd debated for half an hour over who could be brought in, how to frame the battle plan so the enormously complex conspiracy could be put into a believable context.

As the conversation hit another wall, Hudson veered slightly off topic to an issue that had plagued his thoughts and confused him since Vonner had first approached him to run.

"So, Vonner wasn't all bad," the president said, looking at Fitz, who knew the late billionaire far better than he did.

"I should say not. He left you a fortune."

"He left it to Schueller."

"A technicality," Fitz corrected. "Regardless, the man believed you could change the world."

"I'm trying."

"Look, Mr. President, you have a real chance to make history here," Fitz said, pouring more Coke into his tall glass, already filled with cola-ice cubes.

"You should try green tea instead."

"Vonner didn't tell you things because he thought in all your innocence, you would run away and hide. You'd cry like a little boy," he said, and then, looking up at Hudson with the eyes of a sniper, "I *hate* tea."

Hudson made an irritated face. "Vonner underestimated me."

"No, he didn't. You're still not sure. You think it's like in the movies. The hero is honorable and righteous, never does anything wrong and in the end, good always prevails."

"What's wrong with that?"

"After all that's happened, haven't you learned yet? It isn't that simple. Vonner stole, broke the law, crossed a thousand lines, but he was getting it done. He introduced the world to you, he—"

"It isn't that hard to do the right thing, you've just got to know what it is first."

"Exactly, but knowing is the hard part because of every complication. Sometimes we have to do things considered 'wrong' or 'illegal' because, in the end, it makes the right effect."

"Sounds like the ends justify the means."

"When you're taking on REMies—the rulers of the world—and they have every advantage—"

"So, anything goes as long as we're fighting corruption?" Hudson asked, leaning against the Resolute Desk. "I suppose you think Booker is a good guy, too, in spite of leading NorthBridge on a killing spree." The president had only recently told his chief of staff the identity of AKA Washington. Fitz had agreed that they didn't have enough to arrest the African American billionaire, and that he was more valuable to their efforts while he remained free, at least for now.

"Booker and Vonner were cut from the same cloth."

"Vonner hated Booker," Hudson protested.

"No, he didn't hate him, just strongly disagreed with him. Thought his tactics and concepts were wrong. And, as far as I know, Vonner didn't even know Booker was behind NorthBridge."

"Then you're saying Booker's trying to defeat the REMies, so he's also on our side? How do we know it's not another MADE event, a hundred of them?"

"Booker believes that the world, and indeed humanity itself, is running out of time. He's wrapped up in all his Universal-Quantum-Physics and the Inner Movement. UQP shapes his view of the world. He thinks he knows what's coming in the future. Vonner told me about a meeting the two of them had several years back where they tried to enlist each other's help, but they couldn't get on the same page."

"Yet I still maintain Booker is a criminal," the president said.

"Like it or not, NorthBridge may be the key to getting what you want: finishing Vonner's quest."

"You can't have forgotten that NorthBridge tried to kill you," he reminded Fitz.

"Because they thought I was corrupt, or rather that I would corrupt *you*. It appears as if Booker wanted you in the White House all along." Fitz took another swig of his soda.

"Then why not work with Vonner?"

"Because they didn't agree on the overall picture, but that doesn't mean they didn't have common ideas on some issues. They both loathed Bastendorff and Coyne, neither believed the REMie system was sustainable, cracks in the empire—there are dozens of examples. You're just another one."

"Melissa thinks the REMies are too powerful, that there aren't enough people left who aren't under their influence," Hudson said, returning to the original topic and sounding more tired with each word. He couldn't seem to have a positive thought. He knew it, yet could not change his current tempo.

"She might be right, but with Dranick as DNI and the DIRT teams in the FBI, we should be able to find the ones that are trustworthy."

"When?" Hudson asked.

"We've already got the preliminary lists. The deeper pass should be done in the next week." Fitz looked at his glass, unprepared to find it empty. He grunted. "Then we have to figure out how to approach them."

"By the way, too much sugar lowers brain function and ads belly fat," the president said, in the same monotone he'd been using for hours. "Soda contains eleven teaspoons of sugar per can. Cherry Tree depends on getting as many bureaucrats on board as possible."

"I know," Fitz said, staring into the president's eyes for an extra beat. "The deep state can swallow us. It's one of the REMies biggest weapons. They've spent decades building that invisible army of bureaucrats."

Hudson's mind switched to the Wizard. So much depended on his abilities and the team he'd assembled. *Will the Gypsy program be able to find the patterns and links to prove enough of the MADE events? Can the Wizard's group track the transactions and provide ample evidence to allow DIRT to seize major REMie assets?* MADE events were the REMies' best tool used for control.

"Is Schueller going to use Vonner's money in the fight?" Fitz asked, interrupting Hudson's spiraling thoughts.

"He has some pet projects," Hudson answered. "But he knows that ending world hunger, poverty, and cleaning up the environment will all be easier without the REMies, so he's all in . . ."

An aide entered the room. "Excuse me, Mr. President, but we need you in the Situation Room, immediately."

CHAPTER TEN

D ranick, who was in mid-sentence when Hudson and Fitz
entered the Situation Room, turned and addressed the
president.

"The Fed gathering in Jackson Hole just got hit. The Fed
Chairman and at least three governors are believed dead."

"NorthBridge?" the president asked angrily.

"They've already taken credit on their website."

"I thought they were going to cancel the event this year?"
Fitz asked.

Dranick shook his head. "They didn't."

The treasury secretary spoke up. "They tripled security. It
was an armed camp."

The Federal Reserve Bank of Kansas City's annual 'Economic Symposium,' which attracted dozens of powerful financial
players, was held at an exclusive mountain resort in Jackson Hole,
Wyoming. Since 1978, central bankers, finance ministers, policy
makers, economists, and academics had gathered to discuss the
world economy. In recent years, the officials often used the event
to set monetary policy and signal the direction of rates. As a

result, the conference drew all sorts of demonstrators, and had become a media circus.

The images filling the screens before them showed the main lodge building with all its windows shattered. Glass and splintered wood, debris, rubble, twisted steel—the luxurious resort resembled a burned-out village in front of the glorious backdrop of the Grand Tetons and reflected in Jackson Lake, creating an apocalyptic juxtaposition of paradise. The president shook his head. "NorthBridge is too powerful. All the bomb sniffing dogs, electromagnetic checkpoints, and armed personnel in the world are useless against them."

"Yes, sir," Dranick said. "Two incoming missiles, fired from a mobile weapon system vehicle. Here." He pointed to a photo blown up on one of the monitors.

"We've just received word," a general in the room interrupted. "That's a Chinese-made Dragon-1518."

"NorthBridge working with the Chinese?" another general asked.

The president swallowed hard. He didn't need any more fuel on that smoldering fire. "If an ISIS fighter drives a Toyota truck, does that mean he's working with the Japanese?"

"Obviously not," the general responded. "However, the Dragon-1518 is not available on the open market. What's more, it would have had to be smuggled into this country. With all due respect, you may consider China a friend, but I submit that they would always be happy to see instability within our borders."

"General, do not use this terrorist attack as another excuse to reignite tensions between us and the Chinese. This detail does not leave this room," the president said firmly. "Clear?"

"Yes, sir," the general said, barely hiding his bitterness.

"Mr. President," Dranick said, "we've just received confirmation. The Fed Chairman and four Fed governors were, in fact, in that building, and are dead."

Smoke and flames still poured from a portion of Jackson Lake Lodge as everyone in the Situation Room watched first responders bring out bodies. Hudson worried that in spite of his warnings, the media would get the story that the missiles and the vehicle were military-grade Chinese weapons. The only thing he could count on keeping secret in his administration was the source of the leaks. The fragile peace he'd negotiated with China could be fractured by even a small matter such as finding lead in Chinese-made toys again, but if the public learned that the Chinese could be linked to this fresh and brutal attack against Federal Reserve officials on American soil . . .

"Who signed the NorthBridge claim on their website?" the president asked.

"AKA Hancock," Dranick, with a quick glance at Fitz, replied. The president, chief of staff, and DNI Dranick were the only three in attendance who knew the true identity of AKA Hancock. All three were now silently questioning the decision to let the three NorthBridge leaders go.

The president read the statement attributed to AKA Hancock, whom he knew as Thorne:

It's impossible to control the world without the central banks. Everyone who seeks to dominate the masses knows there is only one way to do this: you must have control of the monetary system. We have struck against the Federal Reserve once again in an attempt to cripple and bring light on this dark force. These are not ordinary criminals, they are the slick public face of the greedy elites who steal our wealth, productivity, and freedom; who pretend to be honest and legitimate. They are neither. In the face of their paralyzing control over our government, we are left with no choice but to remove them by force. They can be sure, we will not stop.

CHAPTER ELEVEN

I mmediately upon leaving the Situation Room, the president went to his private study off the Oval Office and made a secure call to Fonda Raton.

"You just murdered the Chairman of the Federal Reserve and four Fed governors!" Hudson blasted as soon as she answered.

"I did nothing of the kind. I've just baked a blackberry pie."

"Do you think you're amusing? What about the seventeen injured, three of whom were hotel workers who had nothing to do with the Federal Reserve?"

"I don't think I have enough pie for all of them."

"You do know these people have families? I knew the Fed Chairman, and his wife. I've met their daughter. You've destroyed these people. Their blood is on your hands!"

"Mr. President," Fonda said in her most charming voice, "I really don't know what you're talking about."

"This isn't the way to do what you're trying to do," Hudson said, ignoring her denials. "Are you going to just kill everybody you don't agree with?"

"I beg your pardon, Mr. President, but are you accusing me of something?" Fonda asked, still using her sweet voice. "Or, are you charging me with something? Should I expect a FaST squad to show up? Should I hire a LAW-yer? Is the NSA listening?"

"If I knew where to find you, there would already be a FaST squad at your door. Rest assured that they're looking for you." But part of him admired her and NorthBridge for doing what he could not.

Wouldn't I kill Bastendorff if I had the chance? Is there really a way to do this peacefully?

He wrestled with the moral and ethical questions, his past as a soldier, the nine minutes . . . the inner conflicts made it so that occasionally he didn't recognize his own thoughts. He wanted the REMies empire crushed as badly as Fonda, but, regardless, he wasn't ready to go public with their names.

"Tell Booker and Thorne that lawyers won't be able to help any of you. And as far as the NSA, this is a secure line."

"Ha! There's no such thing as a secure line. You ought to know that by now."

Hudson momentarily felt a wave of panic, not sure if the Wizard's SonicBlock Drive really was more effective than whatever current gadgets Booker had been selling to the NSA. But then it didn't really matter; he had no choice. If they were listening, they were listening.

It's not like the REMies think I'm their friend.

"You're going to get caught."

"No, we won't," Fonda countered. "You have no idea what you're up against."

"None of what you're doing is helping defeat the REMies."

"I can't say I'm upset that we've lost some Fed officials who've been stealing from the American people, turning them into nothing more than indentured servants for the sickeningly extravagant lifestyle of the elites," Fonda said. "But I can't say I had anything to do with it."

"Perhaps you aren't aware that Thorne has already claimed responsibility for you."

"You're mistaken. I read the statement, it was signed by AKA Hancock."

"Dearest Fonda, Thorne *is* AKA Hancock."

"Amusing thought. Regardless, I am pleased that we have one fewer, or in this case, *five* fewer criminals in the world. You know as well as I do that the Federal Reserve and all the central banks are the biggest weapon the REMies use against us. It's good to see them suffering for a change."

He knew Fonda couldn't admit that Thorne was Hancock, but at least now she knew he knew. "I'm just going to appoint a new Chairman," Hudson said angrily.

"Go ahead. The replacement will likely suffer the same fate, and then you'll send in another one, and another, until there's no one left willing to take the job."

"We'll protect them."

"Like you can." Fonda laughed. "Anyway, Mr. President, I guess you don't know yet, but here's how it works with the Fed. The Federal Reserve Board decides on their own people, including who will be the Chairman. Then, they tell the president whoever it is. The president just repeats what he's told."

"We'll see about that," he said defiantly, but knew she was right. The REMies had decided he was to be president. They would make sure the Fed was run by someone they wanted and trusted. "What's next, the IRS? Because they're a big REMie tool as well."

"Don't worry Mr. President," Fonda said as if soothing a disgruntled customer. "I'm sure that NorthBridge will eventually get to the IRS. Do you have any other suggestions?"

"Dammit, Fonda, if I have to fight the REMies, the Washington political establishment, NorthBridge, *and* you, so help me, I'll do it!"

"Don't become the distraction, Mr. President," Fonda said. "That will ruin everything."

"What does that mean?"

"Hudson, think for a minute . . . *you're* still here."

Fitz walked into the room. The line went dead at the same time.

The timing unnerved Hudson. *Did she* know *Fitz was here?*

"Mr. President, there's a report on one of the news sites claiming that the Chinese government was involved in the Jackson Hole Fed attack. They're reporting that China's intelligence service, the MSS, has been backing NorthBridge. Another site has picked up the story and gone so far as to suggest that NorthBridge isn't an American domestic terror organization at all, that it's actually part of the MSS."

"Damn leaks!" the president said. "Get Dranick out there to make the denials. Kill this story *now.*"

"We'll try," Fitz said, and left.

Hudson leaned back and put his feet up on the desk, thinking about the lives lost, and wondered what those people were seeing. Was it like his nine minutes? He knew from Paul Grayson that everyone had a slightly different experience, and in this case, he wondered what the encompassing truth in all of them was.

Even though he knew the attack had come from NorthBridge and was not a MADE event, the REMies were still spinning it. It reminded him of something Rahm Emanuel, President Obama's chief of staff, once said: "*You never want a serious crisis to go to waste.*" The REMies were using MADE and SAD to rekindle the fires for war. He scribbled words on a classified report about the Saudi Royal Family. Manipulate-And-Distract-Everyone – Scare Anger Divide.

The REMies are winning. If they kill me, the only thing that has a chance to stop them is NorthBridge . . . That must change.

CHAPTER TWELVE

E ven before Vonner's attorney, Kensington "Kensi" Blanchard, made the introductions, Hudson could tell he liked the top operative of Vonner Security, Tarka Seabantz. As their eyes met, he immediately had the sense they would trust each other. He also detected anguish, a fierce determination, and one more thing. Hudson couldn't explain it, maybe it was because he knew she had saved his life so many times, but he believed she would always be loyal. Loyalty was perhaps the rarest of all commodities he had discovered since becoming president.

Hudson and Schueller stood near a cliff overlooking the Potomac River on Vonner's estate with Kensi and Tarka. The late billionaire had changed all of their lives, and in one way or another, had been responsible for their fates intertwining at this moment. Although he did not plan the meeting, he made it happen.

"Thank you," were Hudson's first words to Tarka.

"For what?" she asked.

"For everything," Hudson said, smiling, "but I guess especially for Inauguration Day." He paused and looked at her carefully. "And for Rochelle."

"There's still a lot to do," she said, swallowing the pain of who she lost that day, how much Bastendorff had taken. "We're still going to do it, aren't we?"

"Yes," he said. "We damn sure are. And I'm counting on you to help us."

A servant came out with a tray of mugs and hot tea. Hudson thanked him and waved him off, saying he would take care of it. Hudson poured tea for everyone.

"If you're going after Bastendorff, count me in." Tarka turned from Hudson to Schueller. "And you're the new boss?"

"Well, Dad's really the boss," Schueller said, taking his first sip from a steaming mug.

"But he pays the bills," Hudson said, smiling.

"As my father said, Bastendorff is on the top of our list, but it's a long list, so make sure you tell us anything you need."

"I've got a list, too," she said with no hint at humor. "And the first thing on it is my old boss." She had declined the tea while remarking on Vonner's taste in scenery.

Hudson looked surprised. "Vonner?"

"Vonner may have provided the funds for operations, but my old boss was a man named Rex Lestat."

Hudson looked at Kensi.

"Delicious tea," she said, smiling, and added, "Rex was Vonner's right-hand man, and a bit more than that, I'd say."

"He's a 'fixer,'" Tarka said. "The best you've ever seen."

"We've got lots of problems," Schueller said. "We could sure use a fixer."

"Where is he? What happened to him?" Hudson asked.

"Mr. Vonner left Rex very well taken care of," Kensi said. "I can tell you where he is, but I'm not sure he'd be interested."

"Rex will be *very* interested," Tarka said emphatically.

"What makes you so sure?" Hudson asked.

"Because Rex ordered me to kill David Covington."

Hudson looked quickly from Tarka, to Kensi, to Schueller, wondering if even having this conversation put him in the same category with NorthBridge. The woman had just confessed to assassinating the former Director of National Intelligence to the president of the United States.

"But Vonner denied that," Hudson said slowly, his mouth dry, as he worried about a hundred implications of what he'd just heard. He walked over to the railing, leaned on it, and sighed heavily. "The river never stops," he whispered quietly while grasping for a reality to cling to in that moment.

"Vonner knew nothing about it," Tarka said. "In fact, he didn't think it was a good idea to even fire Covington, let alone kill him."

"So this Rex Lestat guy was operating autonomously?" Schueller asked.

"Rex has a brilliant mind," Tarka began.

"Off the charts brilliant," Kensi added.

"That's why we must have him on our team. He knows more about Bastendorff and the world elites than anyone, and he navigates the DarkNet like a rat in the sewers."

"Interesting analogy," Schueller said.

"I'm not good at stuff like that, but what I'm saying is that without Rex, I don't think beating the REMies will be possible."

Hudson turned to Kensi again, who motioned to him for a refill. Schueller stepped in and poured for her.

"Thank you, Schueller," Kensi said. "Yes, Mr. Vonner found Rex absolutely indispensable."

"Do you know about the DarkNet?" Tarka asked Hudson.

Hudson thought of the Wizard, Crane, and Zackers, about how much of the battle had already been fought over the Dark-Net. The Wizard had told him that the only way to bring down the REMies empire was to get at their system through the Dark-Net. It was there that access to the secrets, hidden money, and links to the MADE events could be found. The modern CapWars, which had become so incredibly massive, began and ended on the DarkNet.

Hudson nodded. "Yes."

"Then you should know that if the DarkNet is nighttime, then Rex is a vampire king. He owns it." Tarka's eyes flashed as she said those words.

"Then we'll need to get me in touch with him immediately," the president said to Kensi.

"Let's look at this list of yours," Schueller said to Tarka. She handed a sheet of paper to Schueller, he showed it to his father, and they both looked back at her. Neither one recognized much of what she'd requested, but Hudson suspected it was weapons and technology.

"This kind of advanced equipment . . . " Hudson began. "How much of it is supplied by Booker Lipton companies? I understand he helped you out with Rochelle."

Tarka nodded. "Booker may have been one of Vonner's chief rivals, he even called him his enemy, but Booker Lipton is no enemy of mine."

CHAPTER THIRTEEN

S chueller's $52 billion inheritance had caused a media frenzy as the president's son was declared the world's most eligible bachelor. "I've had to hire two fulltime employees just to handle all the mail," he told Melissa during one of the rare times they could simply chat quietly one on one. They were on the upper White House veranda of the Truman Balcony, a place Melissa liked to escape to often, no matter the weather. They looked over the rush hour traffic of Constitution Avenue at the Washington Monument, a magnificent sight. Beyond that was the Jefferson Memorial, Melissa's favorite place in all of DC. She never tired of looking at it. She didn't know the reason why it drew her, but it always calmed her somehow.

"Business proposals?" she asked.

"Yeah, and people needing operations, others wanting me to save their home from foreclosure, and marriage proposals. Hundreds, every day."

"I bet," Melissa said, laughing. "Women from all over the world would love to marry you."

"And men, too," he said. "I bet at least ten percent are from men. The other day I got a letter from an eighty-nine-year-old woman from Sarasota, Florida, asking me to marry her. Too bad for all of them I already have a girlfriend."

Schueller had put Vonner's money to work on many fronts. Perhaps his most ambitious projects centered around food, energy, and healthcare. All three areas fit into his liberal ideology, however, he was also influenced by his father, the president, and his stepmother, the first lady. His spending was also a three-pronged approach to preparing for the collapse of the REMie empire. Their corrupt system, although oppressive, was still a system, the idea being that if the overthrow of the REMies didn't go precisely as planned, disorder, on a massive scale, would ensue.

"If the economy collapses," Schueller said to his father during an early meeting regarding what to do with the inherited fortune, "and even if it doesn't, it'll certainly be a mess for an undetermined period of time. At very minimum, weeks, probably more like months, maybe even years. Just feeding the billions of people who live in a non-agrarian society will be almost impossible."

It was one of Hudson's biggest concerns, and a primary reason why he opposed NorthBridge. "We've got to hold the empire-system together long enough until we can replace it with a new basic and fair one," the president had said on many occasions. "No food means riots, roving gangs, absolute bedlam."

"Anarchy," Schueller added. And thus was born his plan to get people to grow their own food. Billions were funneled into his new foundation, its mission to "put a garden in every yard." Modeled after the Depression era Civilian Conservation Corps, the Free Food Foundation quickly hired and trained more than a hundred thousand workers, with plans and a budget to add at least another two hundred thousand. The small 'armies' went from town-to-town, helping people set up successful gardens in their yards and in under-utilized public spaces. Elderly people unable to do the physical work in their yards were partnered with youth who had no yards. Schools were brought on board, as well as church and community groups. FFF provided free seeds, garden tools, and supplies, in addition to continual training and support. The Foundation's goals were lofty—one hundred million gardens planted in three years.

Melissa became the public face and driving force behind Schueller's garden in every yard initiative, although FFF had its own director. Schueller and his stepmother worked closely on the massive project. The popularity of the program and its economic impact helped increase the first lady's appeal and added to the many reasons why her approval ratings were typically twice as high as her husband's.

Increasingly, the 3D surveillance system had been the subject of protests from college students and fringe groups, yet the main-stream media gave almost no coverage to the demonstrations. The 3D cameras were everywhere.

At the same time the "digital-eyes" became increasingly intrusive, they became less visible. Through technological advances and miniaturization, the units were almost impossible to detect. Unbeknownst to the public, many of the cameras were also equipped with telescopic lenses and telesonic microphones.

"They can hear as well as see," the Wizard, alarmed, had told the president.

"I know," Hudson replied. He'd learned the fact only a few weeks earlier during a President's Daily Briefing. Hudson had asked why it was necessary and where all the data went. All he got was intel-double-talk and unsatisfactory answers. He wanted to cut that part and curtail the program in general. However, it would require an act of Congress to make it happen.

A breakthrough came when the Wizard discovered a way to hack into at least part of the system. The Wizard and the Vonner Security teams began using 3D to track REMies, corrupt politicians, and trace media contamination by the elites. Meanwhile, Dranick, in his role as Director of National Intelligence, was using the 3D system to zero in on NorthBridge.

"If we can't make it go away," Hudson had said, "at least we can use it for a good cause."

"Who decides what's good?" the Wizard asked. "And where does it end?"

Schueller had purchased an old mansion on Hunter Mill Road in Oakton, Virginia, about a thirty-five-minute drive to DC, depending on traffic. The Wizard moved in and immediately transformed the place into a technology center from which to monitor everything the REMies did. Vonner Security had already turned the new Hunter Mill tech center into a fortress, but even so, when the president arrived via Marine One for a secret meeting, all agents were on high alert.

Hudson had invited Granger Watson, a man many considered one of the smartest people on earth. The Wizard suggested Granger because in assembling a team of hackers and coders to run their hidden tech-center, every time they encountered a challenge none of the brainiacs could figure out, Granger's name always seemed to come up.

"He's about a billion times smarter than me," the Wizard told Hudson. "If anyone can figure out a way to prevent Armageddon once we knock out the REMies 'central-bank-debt-tax' empire-system, it would be him."

"Okay, but hasn't he worked with half the REMies? How can we trust him?"

"The question is, 'how can we not?' Granger is a technology fanatic. He sees it as a way to liberate the world from work. He's called the financial system, 'the slave trade.' Believe me," the Wizard said. "He's one of us."

CHAPTER FOURTEEN

G ranger Watson arrived precisely three minutes early, which was his habit. A chauffeur opened the door of the latest Tesla model, and out stepped the awkward looking "life engineer," as he called himself.

Granger tried to dress as if he were an ultra-cool Hollywood star—ten-thousand-dollar-suits, four-hundred-dollar-T-shirts, the most expensive tennis shoes, etc.—but none of that could hide the fact that he looked like a scarecrow. His tall, lanky frame and thinning hair screamed geek, and he actually *was* a super-geek, he just never wanted to look like one. A long source of personal frustration came from his inability to grow a beard. Granger had such long fingers he'd often said if he'd had a hundred dollars for every time someone told him he should be a concert pianist, he would've been a wealthy man. In fact, he *was* wealthy. Not REMie-wealthy, but estimates of his worth ranged between fifty and a hundred million dollars. Yet, he could have been far richer if he'd wanted.

He'd never pursued a fortune. Instead, Granger sought to expand his, and, therefore human, knowledge in a vast range of topics. A known expert on everything from block chain and crypto-currencies, computer algorithms, intrinsic patterns in nature such as bird migration, whale and dolphin languages, the honeybee colony collapse disorder, to robotics, artificial intelligence, quantum computing, space exploration and colonization, and other far-flung esoteric fields.

The eccentric Granger refused to ever reveal his exact age, saying, "The calendar has nothing to do with how old one is or isn't." However, his Wikipedia profile listed his age at fifty-five. In that time, he'd authored more than two hundred research papers, seventeen *New York Times* bestsellers on topics ranging from dyslexia occurring in ants, to hydroponic gardening in the lava tubes on Mars, to life in the unexplored ocean depths. He also held more than nineteen hundred patents in a diverse range of industries such as solar energy, nanotechnology, the hyperloop, space elevator, and many in computer-related areas. Granger had even composed several symphonies after he developed a program which could take all the works of Mozart, Beethoven, Tchaikovsky, Bach, Wagner, Grieg, and several other composers, then extrapolate the patterns, techniques, frequencies, and "intent" of the greats and merge them together. He then used the tool to create compositions that were essentially a "collaboration" of the musical geniuses of the ages. The works had been so well received that most major symphonies had performed and/or recorded them, netting Granger millions in royalties.

The president had left the White House just before sunrise. Since it was a late summer Sunday, and Congress was in recess, it would be a good day for his absence to attract less notice. After brief introductions and small talk, the president, the Wizard, and Granger sat on a large sundeck surrounded by woods, discussing the reason they'd invited him there. Agents were stationed everywhere, and in the fortress-like atmosphere, eavesdropping-deterrents were as important as security, with sound deflectors and spatial-borders ensuring they could not be overheard.

"Before I get into things, I want to thank you again for coming, and for agreeing to my request for absolute confidentiality," the president said.

"When your president asks . . . " Granger said.

"We need your help," the president began, "with solving a massive corruption issue."

"More than an 'issue,' actually," the Wizard said. "There are a group of global elites—"

"You're, of course, referring to the REMies," Granger said, standing up and beginning to pace. He could rarely sit still for more than a couple of minutes.

Hudson was not surprised someone of his intellect knew of their existence, but wondered how familiar he was with the REMies' deep control over society. "Yes."

"What can I do?" he asked, watching a blue jay and a cardinal land on a nearby dogwood tree.

"We need systems to be designed which can be used to go after them," the Wizard said.

"And go after their assets as well?" Granger asked, still with his back to them.

"Are you aware of their role in world events?" the president asked, getting up and joining Granger at the railing.

"Quite aware," Granger said. "I've done work for several of them."

"Really?" the president asked, looking at the Wizard with raised eyebrows.

"Of course. Everyone has done work for them, but not many of us have done it knowingly," Granger said, pacing to the other end of the deck, spotting some of the various Vonner Security and Secret Service agents around the property. At the same time, he worked out camera angles of the surveillance system. "Seems there's a gap in your grid, just there," Granger said, pointing. "Someone could come in undetected from the woods in that section."

Hudson and the Wizard followed his hand and looked at the trees, then back at the cameras, but they couldn't see the weakness. "I'll report it," the Wizard said.

Granger nodded. "How far are you going to go to find and stop the corruption?"

"All the way," the president said.

Granger faced the president. "Do you know— Forgive me, but can I speak freely?"

"Of course."

"You're crazy," Granger said. "Haven't you been shot enough? How many times do you think you can escape death?"

"It must be done," the president said.

"It cannot be done without collapsing the world economy, and I mean crumbled into dust, nothing left except the zombie apocalypse."

"That's why we need you, to help make sure that doesn't happen," the Wizard said.

Granger wandered to the other end of the large deck, gazed out across the expansive lawn, then suddenly jogged down the steps and kneeled in the grass.

"Is he praying?" the president mumbled.

"Nah," the Wizard replied. "He's an atheist."

Hudson walked down to join the genius. The Wizard followed.

"Ants," Granger said, not looking up.

Hudson rolled his eyes. "What did you do for the REMies? And which ones?"

"It will almost certainly need to collapse," Granger said, his face inches from the ground. "I must insist that it not be propped up by artificial means. The risks—well they're astronomical, but if we replace one faux system with another, there cannot be freedom."

"Then you believe it is possible?" the Wizard asked.

"I agree this will be painful and possibly catastrophic," Granger said, turning his attention away from the ants and back to the president. "You must get the Chinese on board," he added in an inviolate tone, looking into Hudson's eyes with great intensity.

"I think that's possible," the president replied.

"Hmm, you're more confident in the communists than I am."

"Wait," the Wizard said. "You're agreeing to help us, and you *do* think it's possible to take on the REMies?"

"Yes, yes," Granger said. "But I have no idea if it's possible to actually do this. Certainly, they cannot be surgically removed. That is to say, the patient must die—the economy, the structure, everything. A year ago, this would not have been survivable, but now, with AI, the block chain, satellite internet, mobile devices increasing in capabilities and decreasing in cost, digiGOLD . . . yes, there is a confluence of technology and events . . . exciting, most exciting!"

The Wizard smiled. The president maintained a serious expression. "Who, and what did you do for the REMies?" Hudson repeated.

Granger gave him a crooked smile. "We're still speaking candidly, so I might ask you the same question. Arlin Vonner, a top REMie, put you in the White House, left his fortune to your son. If I were a gambling man, which I am, as a matter of fact, I'd wager that those men over there were Vonner Security, and possibly his "REMie" money paid for this old mansion. However, I'm willing to overlook your deep REMie ties."

The Wizard laughed. "Dude's got you, Dawg."

"I still need to know," Hudson said.

"I'll get you a list," Granger said, "but answer me this. What is a day of human life worth?"

"What's that got to do with anything?" the Wizard asked.

Granger's eyes locked onto Hudson's. "He knows," Granger said.

Hudson nodded.

"Titus Coyne: I did a currency exchange/volatility marginal shifts system for him that I believe ultimately wound up as the master system used in currency fluctuations, manipulations by the International Monetary Fund and the Central Banks," Granger said, pacing the deck again. "Booker Lipton: I developed many aspects of the Three-D surveillance system. Karl Bastendorff: I created a program that can convert almost any object, person, or building, into scale plans and detailed instructions for LEGO bricks."

The Wizard burst out laughing. "Bastendorff is a real piece of work!"

"Piece of something," Granger said. "I've also done minor work for Gates, the Koch brothers, the Newhouse brothers, Soros, DuPonts, Kinder, and Euller. It'll be on the list."

"Okay," the president said. "Then you can help us with the Federal Reserve and Three-D?"

"Mr. President, I can help you with everything. I know how the whole thing is wired."

"What thing?"

"The REMie system. It runs the empire," he said, smiling. "Assuming you don't mind the risk, I have an idea on how we can bring it all crashing down."

At that moment, both the cardinal and the blue jay landed on the railing and pecked at something in Granger's hand.

After Granger Watson left, the president and the Wizard reviewed their encounter with the man some had called a tech-mercenary.

"Do you really think we can trust him?" the president asked. "I ran everything we could find on him through Gypsy," the Wizard replied. "It said he leans anti-REMie."

"Leans?" the president echoed, raising an eyebrow. "Is that enough?"

"We have to gamble. He's the only one who might be able to design the new system. Otherwise, even if we manage to beat the REMies, when their empire collapses, the mess will be too big to fix."

CHAPTER FIFTEEN

The president blocked off an hour at seven each morning for a week to meet with Fitz, Melissa, and Vice President Brown in the Oval Office with the goal of reshaping the government. "If we can destroy the REMies empire-system, we must be ready to show what will replace it," Hudson had told them.

The first session started ten minutes late, as there had been a NorthBridge attack. They'd crashed the entire computer network of JPMorgan Chase.

"What a disaster," Fitz said as he walked in the room, holding his morning Coke.

"Good morning," Melissa said cheerfully to the chief of staff.

"That's a matter of opinion," Fitz replied with mock grumpiness. "Booker's sending a message by going after the largest REMie bank."

"We don't know that Booker is calling the shots with North-Bridge," the president said. "There are at least five leaders, and we know only three of them. We also don't know how their power-sharing is structured."

"True," Fitz said, "but they chose the sixth largest bank in the world."

"That's because the four largest belong to our friends, the Chinese," the president replied. "The fifth biggest bank is Mitsubishi in Japan, seven is HSBC in the UK, eighth is BNP in France . . . "

"You've been studying your banks," the first lady said with a laugh.

"I have." Hudson smiled. "I'm trying to figure out a way to stop the REMies without wiping out the global money supply and shattering the economy in a way that will make the worldwide depression of the 1930s look like the good old days."

"The only shot at that," Melissa began, "is to get China to prop up the money supply."

Fitz, who was sitting next to her on the sofa, frowned. "That's never going to fly. They'll use the crisis to take over."

"Take over what?" she said. "One third of the top twenty-two banks in the world are Chinese. Four are American, and they're all controlled by the REMies. In fact, all the others are in some way owned, controlled, or compromised by the REMies. So what happens if the REMies are shut down?"

"Cryptocurrency," the vice president suggested.

"Like Bitcoin or digiGOLD?" Fitz asked. "To run the *entire* global economy?"

"It might work," the president said. "Granger Watson has been looking into it."

"Smart guy," Fitz said, raising his eyebrows.

"The smartest," the president said. "Okay, now the fun stuff. I plan on proposing that we bring all our troops home."

"From where?" Fitz asked.

"Everywhere," the president answered. "I'm talking about the 300,000 military personnel serving outside the country. I want to close all the bases—"

"The Pentagon will *love* you," Fitz said sarcastically. "They're still seething from your decision to stop the drone bombing."

Melissa closed her eyes, knowing all too well what sermon was coming.

"People think I did that because of my near death experience," the president said, "but it was about the REMies. You want the smoking gun to convince the American people the REMies are in charge? George W. Bush, as a candidate, said he didn't believe in nation building, unnecessary foreign entanglements. Obama, a total anti-war candidate, won the Nobel peace prize less than nine months after taking office. Trump had spoken against it for years prior to running, he didn't want anything to do with Afghanistan, and yet they all changed. Each bombed more than the one before. Obama hit seven countries, showering more than fifty thousand bombs just in his last two years, and ten times more drone strikes than Bush. Trump did even more! Why?" The president leaned against the Resolute Desk and hit his fist into his hand. "Why do they betray their beliefs, their promises? I'll tell you why. Something or someone made them change. These weren't minor flip-flops to please a large constituency, they were doing what they were told. A REMie had a talk with them."

"Preaching to the choir," Melissa said, trying to get him back on track.

"Anyway, closing the bases and bringing the troops home will save us hundreds of millions a year," Hudson said. "And the REMies will hate it."

"Congress will never go along with it," Fitz said.

"Yeah, well, I'm the commander in chief, and they'll have lots of other things to worry about."

"Such as?"

"Environmental initiatives," Melissa said. "The causes of global warming don't matter, it doesn't even matter if it's real.

Those debates waste our time. The bottom line is we don't want to pollute this beautiful planet. No one is in favor of pollution. If we all stop arguing about global warming and just seek to end *all* pollution, global warming becomes a totally moot point."

"I like it," the vice president said.

Fitz shook his head in dismay and opened another Coke. "I guess you've decided not to seek reelection . . . at least as a Republican."

"Way too soon to talk about that," Hudson said.

"And we're just getting started," Melissa added. "We're going to launch solar power initiatives to finish off fossil fuels once and for all by heavily taxing them to subsidize the clean alternatives. Plus mandatory recycling, legislation that nothing can be manufactured unless it can be recycled . . . "

"Fun," Fitz said sarcastically. "Why not tax sugar to subsidize healthcare?"

"Great idea!" Melissa said, pointing to his soda.

"I was joking!" Fitz moaned.

"I'm not," the president said. "We need to address healthcare and the obesity epidemic. The richest nation on earth ought to be able to provide the best healthcare to its citizens, and fund it with a fair tax system."

"You do know Washington is a company town?" Fitz said. "You'll never get away with this stuff."

"We will, because the REMies won't be able to stop us if they're not in charge anymore. We can give the people what they want."

"They don't *all* want this."

"That's like saying they don't all want peace," the president argued. "But that's only because the media makes them think war is necessary. Every person on earth wants peace, good health, a chance to build a happy life."

"And the REMies have robbed us of that," the vice president said.

"Do you have any other radical reforms in mind?" Fitz asked.

"Taxes," the president said. "It's finally time we create a whole new system. Fair and simple. I favor the system developed by University of Wisconsin Professor of Economics, Edgar L. Feig. It's called the Automated Payments Transaction Tax, or 'APT.' It would remove the need for all other sales and income taxes, and impose a single, tiny tax rate on each and every transaction in the economy. The APT tax rate would be three tenths of one percent on each transaction. Look into it. I think it's brilliant."

"Really amazing," Melissa said. "Check out the website, apttax dot com."

"You think you can get all this to fly?" Fitz asked. "You think people were shooting at you before . . . " Fitz threw his arms up in exasperation.

"I'm just trying to get us back to where we should have been all along without the REMies," the president said.

"Congress will eat you alive."

"Especially when I push for a constitutional amendment for term limits for senators and House members." The president smiled. "Do you know the difference between a career criminal and a career politician?" he asked, repeating a joke Crane had told him.

"No," Fitz said, shrugging. "What's the difference?"

"I was hoping you could tell me."

CHAPTER SIXTEEN

The president had recalled seeing Rex on one of his visits to Vonner's McLean estate, but things were different now. Vonner was dead, Schueller lived in the grand home overlooking the Potomac River, and Rex had become a critical missing piece in the master plan to destroy the REMie empire. Schueller's estate, as it was now called, seemed the logical place to meet. Security had been added to the other side of the river, which would make an ideal sniper's nest.

Rex felt right at home there. In fact, he had lived and worked there, as he had traveled with his former employer. After introductions from Tarka, the president began with a series of questions about the REMies. Tarka remained mostly silent as Vonner's former lieutenant fielded Hudson's inquiries and talked strategy. The humid evening begged for a thunderstorm that wouldn't come. The three of them walked the cliff overlooking the river as Secret Service agents trailed a fair distance away. The president pressed on the one issue that he felt would prove whether Rex could be trusted or not.

"Tell me about Covington," the president asked, looking directly at Rex after stealing a side glance at Tarka.

"Covington was about to put an irrevocable hit on you," Rex said, looking at the five small blue dice in his hands rather than at the president.

"Really? I'm not some Mafia Don," the president responded. "Who would take that hit?"

Rex snapped his hand closed around the dice. "You do know Covington was behind the Air Force One attack, don't you?"

"Yeah, he had an elite squad of special ops trained for covert missions as part of his role at DNI. There was no oversight, no mission these guys wouldn't take on, but it still boggles my mind that American servicemen could be compelled to carry out an attack against their commander in chief."

"I don't think you understand the CapWars, and how the soldiers are trained," Rex said, now rolling a pair of red dice in his left hand.

"Are you telling me they're brainwashed?" the president asked.

"No, in fact, their training is much closer to the truth than what most high school and college students are taught," Rex said. He put a cigarette between his lips. "Mind if I smoke?"

"Yes, I do," the president replied.

Rex stared at him for a minute, surprised. He took the cigarette out of his mouth, put it back into the silver case, and slid it into an inside pocket of his jacket. "The soldiers are taught about the CapWars. Not by name, but they're educated about the power struggles and shown the true dangers of the world."

"Dangers like extremists?"

"The REMies aren't worried about the extremists," Rex said, as if the president had said something foolish. "They create the extremists, that's easy stuff . . . al-Qaeda, ISIS, Boko Harem,

Hezbollah, Hamas . . . the REMies make them, or at least foster the circumstances that give birth to these kinds of organizations, and then trade off the fear and instability. You've heard of SAD?" The president nodded. "Scare Agitate Divide."

"Right, that's their standard formula, that and the MADE events, Manipulate-And-Distract-Everyone. It's so damned easy to distract people. 'Hey, look a sex scandal, now what about a celebrity divorce, oh let's argue about which bathroom to use, or what patriotism is.' Sorry, I digress." Rex shifted some dice in his coat pocket. "It's the regular-joes who concern the REMies, the unpredictable masses. Of course, they've developed quite a matrix to control the bulk of the population, but increasingly there are those on the fringes who see through the scam, and even more who know something isn't quite right, but can't quite figure it out."

"So they train these special ops to kill average Americans?" the president asked, still trying to figure out how these soldiers would shoot their own president or their fellow Americans.

"First, they aren't all from here," Rex said, abandoning the translucent red dice for orange ones in another pocket. "Some in the unit are American, but not the kind who vote for you. They're ones who think their country's been stolen by some fill-in-the-blank scapegoat. The rest are mercenaries, working for great pay and uncaring about who or what the target is."

"Where are they now? Since Covington's dead, who's directing them?"

"I've lost track. My guess is someone in the NSA has them on a leash, but ready to deploy."

An aide brought out a tray of fresh lemonade. Schueller thanked her.

"Deploy? To where?"

"Wherever they're needed to bring chaos, or silence a critic,"

Rex said, smiling as if he'd just picked a rich man's pocket. "You don't still seriously believe the president of the United States is the most powerful man in the world?"

"Maybe, maybe not," Hudson said. "But I guess I'm still trying to figure that out for sure, and maybe you two are going to help me get that final answer."

Rex looked at Tarka, then out to a stand of large oak trees, then back to the president. "I can already tell you the answer is no. You're not the most powerful person in the world. Far from it. In fact, you don't even rank in the top one hundred."

Hudson nodded tentatively. He did know his authority was limited, but the myth of the influence of the presidency that he'd grown up with, that history had perpetuated, still held sway with him to some extent, and he needed to find enough power to make it true. "What happened with Covington?"

"As I said, he was about to have you killed. He also had a plan to simultaneously destabilize several nations around the world, and . . . " Rex laughed while quickly checking the numbers on the two orange dice in his hand. "Covington was trying to convince some of the REMies to let him be the next president."

Hudson stood, aghast, at the arrogance of his late nemesis. "How did you learn this?"

"That's what I do," Rex said. "Vonner, more than any other REMie, appreciated that the real power lies in knowing *everything*. You're trying to do the same thing with your Gypsy program."

"How do you know about Gypsy?"

"I live on the DarkNet, Hudson. I've been watching your guys watch through Gypsy for some time."

Hudson wondered who else knew, but wanted to finish. "Did Vonner or you order Covington's hit?"

Rex glanced at his dice. He'd added a gray one to the two orange, then cautiously checked back over his shoulder at the Secret Service Agents. "Vonner didn't know about it. Vonner was a tough guy, but too careful sometimes. Covington needed to go away. He was much higher up on the totem pole than you. Once he sought authorization to have you killed from a powerful REMie, something had to be done immediately, or you wouldn't be here talking to me now."

"Who was the REMie?"

"Titus Coyne."

"You're sure?"

Rex shot him a disappointed look, as if the president had just insulted him. "Coyne wasn't going to approve the request, but Covington had already decided to do it anyway and deal with the consequences later. You may scoff at the possibility of an irrevocable hit, but there are people in the world who can make things happen, whether it be the death of a president, the resignation of a pope, or the collapse of a major corporation. Nothing is what it seems," Rex said without any drama or flare. "It's all a damned illusion. None of us is really free."

"Do you know what Vonner's endgame was?"

Rex squinted at the president. "Does it matter?"

"It does to me," Hudson said. "I'm president because of him. I want to know why."

"And you want to know if I can be trusted," Rex said, looking at the president, and then at Tarka.

"That, too," the president admitted.

"Vonner wanted to break the REMies' hold. Maybe not as radically as you and I would like to see it shattered, but he was attempting to bring reality into the system. He meant what he told you, at least in a broad sense."

"What do you mean?"

"Vonner believed you could help, the old man thought you were the real deal, but he knew that your boy scout sense could get in the way. He lied to you, and anyone else, when necessary, to achieve his aims, but his heart was in the right place."

"And you?" the president asked, sensing there was a lot that Rex was leaving out about Vonner.

Rex stared at Hudson as if trying to understand the exact meaning of the question, maybe working out his answer. "I've seen too much to have kept my heart intact." Rex pulled out his silver cigarette case, withdrew one of his hand-rolled smokes, and lit it. "Can you trust me? Probably not. But I've saved your life a few times. I'll likely do it again. But the bottom line, Hudson, is can you do this without me?"

"Then you'll join the team?"

Rex shook his head. "Teams are dangerous things. I'll work the DarkNet for you, run Vonner Security . . . " He glanced at Tarka again. "Of course, she'll do the heavy lifting there. But no team. Just you to me."

"Okay," the president said, reaching out his hand.

Rex shook it, exchanging a hardened look with Hudson.

"Out of curiosity," the president said as their hands slipped apart, "what's with the dice?"

"Odds, numbers, patterns, everything in the universe turns on the sequence of multiples of digits . . . " he answered absently, as if talking to himself.

Hudson half laughed. "You need to meet the Wizard, maybe even Granger."

Rex looked at him questionably.

"The Wizard is my oldest friend. He runs Gypsy."

"The guy in San Francisco?"

"Right, but I thought he was untraceable."

"I don't know his exact location, but I had it narrowed down to a few square miles before he moved."

Hudson smiled, impressed with both the Wizard and Rex.

"But if I find him," Rex added, "he'll be dead within days."

"What?" the president asked, instantly alarmed.

"I'm not the only one on the DarkNet trying to find him. I'm just a day or two ahead of the enemy," Rex said. "They'll kill him the second they find him . . . just like they did Zackers and Crane."

CHAPTER SEVENTEEN

General Imperia and Colonel Dranick walked along the even trails of Long Bridge Park in Arlington, Virginia. The two men, not wanting to attract attention, were not in uniform. Although it was unlikely they'd be recognized, even their security details wore casual clothes. As they waded through the humid air, the pair of military men spoke in hushed tones, occasionally finding their words drowned out by the planes taking off and landing at nearby Reagan National Airport.

General Imperia purposely stopped at a point which provided a clear view of the Pentagon, a building the career military man, who'd been an orphan, considered his only home. "Colonel Dranick," he began, "we need to count on you with this. I'm sure you'll agree that things can't be allowed to continue as they are."

"I have to say, I'm surprised," Dranick replied. "You must be aware that the president and I served together. We're old friends."

"Of course we know that. It is for those very reasons we've approached you." Imperia eyed him carefully. "You may be a friend of the president, but you're also a soldier, a Green Beret, a *patriot*. You know what's at stake here. Hudson Pound is not up to the task of running this country at this, or, for that matter, any other, time."

"I doubt if anyone would be able to handle the job with the elites trampling all over each other to see who can take the most chips off the table, grab the most power—"

"That's not the current discussion," Imperia interrupted impatiently. "We're going to remove Hudson Pound from office. You're his friend. That's why you will help us do this." Imperia's left hand started to shake, he held it firmly to his side until it stopped.

"I seem to be missing the logic," Dranick said.

"Look, this isn't some banana republic. We're not going to murder Hudson and drag him through the street. We're looking for an orderly transition of power."

"To the vice president?" Dranick asked. "Or to you?"

"Colonel, I'll remind you that you're addressing a superior officer."

"President Pound is the commander in chief. He's my superior officer, and your superior. Orderly transition of power, like our Constitution prescribes? I don't recall the Founding Fathers making provisions for a coup," Dranick said in a heated whisper.

"Easy, soldier."

"General, you're suggesting a military coup that would, for the first time, subvert the constitution, fracture our democracy, and remove the president of United States—a man duly elected by the people—"

Imperia looked at him incredulously. "Save me the civics lesson, son. You and I both know Pound was not duly elected by anyone. He was appointed and anointed by Arlin Vonner, and now we've got a problem because Vonner isn't here anymore, so there's no control." The general paused as a jogger trotted passed.

"Pound is waffling and making an unholy mess of things. The Chinese own us, NorthBridge is taking over. He's not even willing to authorize drone strikes on ISIS, al-Qaeda, or other international extremists. Look around—the country is in shambles. We're *rudderless*. This downward spiral must stop, and we are going to stop it."

"Still . . ."

Imperia let out an exasperated gasp. "Try to understand we're not talking about subverting the Constitution or overthrowing the government. This is one thing, and one thing only—preserving the Union."

"I understand," Dranick said quietly. The situation had left him fearing for the future of the country, and those feelings had only increased since he took over Covington's job as Director of National Intelligence. He'd been trying to root out corruption ever since he came to Washington, but it was everywhere, so deep that the rarest things in the Capital had turned out to be truth and fairness.

Dranick began walking again. Imperia hesitated a moment, looked back at his security detail, and then followed Dranick. After several steps, he caught up with the colonel.

"You know this is the right course," Imperia said.

"Forgive me, general, but I haven't had weeks—or has it been months?—to adjust to this idea. Hudson Pound saved my life. I'm not happy with the prospect of betraying him."

"This is not a betrayal, this is your chance to return the favor. If we don't remove Hudson Pound from office, he will surely be assassinated. It'll be ordered by one of the elites you referred to earlier, or NorthBridge will finally get him, and . . . there are others." The general looked over toward the Washington skyline. "We're offering you a chance to save your friend, a chance to save the country."

"When we first met," Dranick began, "you referred to a committee. Who exactly is authorizing this?"

"I assure you, Colonel, that the highest-ranking officer within each branch of the military has decided with unanimous consent that this is the best and only course of action to defend our nation from enemies both domestic and abroad."

"I want to meet them," Dranick said. "At the Pentagon."

"Impossible," Imperia snapped.

"Why? If what you say is true, and that you have unanimous consent from all the branches of the military, it shouldn't be too much to ask for me to hear from them. You're proposing an illegal act to remove our president by force, and asking me to cooperate and assist in that action, based only on your word?" The path before them was littered with cherry blossoms, crushed beneath the hundreds of feet walking the well-known park.

"My word, Colonel Dranick, is worth all the stars on my shoulder." Imperia waved at his upper arm as if he were in uniform. "My word is representative of my lifelong career serving this country."

"I respect that, general, I really do. But I cannot, in good conscience, go forward with your plan without looking into the eyes of the other leaders who have decided this course of action is the best course of action."

Imperia looked gruffly into the colonel's face for a long time, as if his stern military glare would make Dranick change his mind. Yet, after half a minute of an unblinking returned stare, the general acquiesced. "Very well then. I'll arrange it."

The following day, Dranick found himself in the lowest level of the Pentagon, in a room he never knew existed. The simple marking,

"B4", on the oak door did not prepare him for the gathered tradition, power, and resolve that awaited him. General Imperia and the other three men explained to him that he was the first nonmember of the B4 committee ever to attend a meeting of their group, a committee which had been charged as the corps of last resort to protect the nation.

Dranick sat silent for more than thirty minutes as the B4 men, whose storied careers matched the high points of the last half-century of American foreign policy, made their case. The military leaders presented all the arguments and evidence they themselves had used to reach their decision.

At the conclusion, they asked him if he had any questions. The presentation had been so persuasive that Dranick only had one.

"What will become of us if we fail?"

CHAPTER EIGHTEEN

The leaks had plagued the Pound administration from day one, but had become increasingly more problematic with each passing week. Recently, the Wizard used the Gypsy program to search out patterns in an effort to isolate the sources of the disclosures. Not surprisingly, Gypsy immediately assessed that the leaks were a pro-REMie platform. However, its list of potential suspects proved unhelpful, as it included the president himself, most of his closest aides, and even family members. They had tried on two earlier occasions to set traps for the leakers with false information, but were frustrated when those stories never made it out.

"This all means the leaker is definitely you," the Wizard had said once to Hudson.

Hudson was not amused, but promised not to tell himself anything too sensitive in the future. The humor belied the seriousness of the issue as the REMie controlled media continued to attack him relentlessly. Even a former member of the Trump administration said President Pound suffered a far more hostile relationship with big media than Trump had.

Hudson called a summit of this top advisors at the Florida beach house. Before the others arrived, he and Melissa walked alone, barefoot, in the soft surf in luxurious, bathwater-like temperatures thanks to the Gulf Stream.

"We have everything in place," the president said. "The Wizard and Granger are making incredible progress toward the electronic digital ends of the plans for Cherry Tree's release." Hudson thought about his plan, conceived through inspiration from the first president.

George Washington had given the power to the people. *That's what I'm going to do,* Hudson thought. *Cherry Tree will show the world the truth about the REMies, and the illusion of freedom they've created with their greed.*

"That's the most important," Melissa agreed, "but it's also the riskiest. They have to get it right. What about using Vonner's media assets to broadcast across the internet, radio, and television as soon as Cherry Tree launches?"

"Great idea," Hudson said. "I'll get the Wizard on that. He and Schueller are already preparing for a massive blitz on social media—ads and 'organic' posts." Hudson picked up a sand dollar and handed it to her.

She smiled. "If we screw up Cherry Tree, or the economy collapses, this may be what we use as money in the future."

"Don't joke," Hudson said. "I already have enough trouble sleeping."

"I'm well aware of your sleeping patterns, or the lack thereof."

Hudson nodded with an apologetic expression and checked the time. "The others will be here soon. I want to make sure you're up to speed. Dranick is working with the FBI director utilizing DIRT—you know, the highly classified equivalent of special ops inside the FBI that only the Director and I know about."

She nodded.

"He's also pulling in significant resources and personnel from the intelligence community. DIRT is vetting each person from the other agencies to be sure they can be relied on."

"We still have a problem," Melissa said.

"A million of them."

"Don't be so cynical." Melissa pushed him into a lapping wave so that his shorts got splashed.

He laughed, picked her up, and pretended he was going to toss her into the ocean. But he had to put her down quickly as his injuries from the assassination attempts reminded him he wasn't twenty anymore. She kissed him, took his hand, and they resumed walking up the beach.

"It's crucial we identify the rest of NorthBridge leadership before we announce Cherry Tree," she continued. "We have to know who's coming after us in the REMie platform so we can neutralize them in some way. No luck locating Booker, Fonda, or Thorne?"

"Not so far," the president said, still catching his breath. "It's incredible she's still posting her stories online. Thorne is still broadcasting his daily show and Booker is still running his infinite empire, too."

"That just shows the power of the REMies if Booker can protect them and elude detection. Imagine going after dozens of REMies. It's so risky, Hudson."

"I know, I wrestle with it constantly. Am I going to be responsible for sending the world into absolute anarchy and destruction, or am I going to be the one to give it back to the people?" Hudson walked over to dry sand and sat down.

"Do the people really *want* it back?" Melissa asked, joining him. "Will they even know what to do with it? What if the empire-system that the REMies have created over the past hundred years has worked because it's the best way?"

Hudson shook his head and lay back in the sand, propped up on his elbows.

"What if you do all this and the REMies come back stronger than ever, or somebody just like them fills the void, someone worse?"

"Now who's being cynical?"

"It's a dangerous time," she said, looking desperately out to the ocean, as if she might see an answer there.

"I have to try."

"The REMies thrive on crisis," Melissa added, still caught up in the drama. "What if they just turn the chaos in the aftermath of Cherry Tree into another MADE event? You heard what the Wizard said at the last meeting, '*Bringing down the REMies empire might not just destroy the economy, it might destroy everything.*' You've got to decide if it's worth the risk, and you have to decide soon."

He pulled her down into his arms and held her in a long embrace, ending in a gentle, enduring kiss. "Don't worry," he whispered. "We're going to show the world who the REMies are, and what they've done."

Melissa kissed him back while reminding herself not to say one more word.

CHAPTER NINETEEN

Titus Coyne sat in a room with the new Chairman of the Federal Reserve Board and three Fed governors. "I don't give a damn how risky it is, we've got to push interest rates higher."

One of the governors held up a thick stack of papers. "The current economic climate cannot—"

"Screw the data," Coyne interrupted. "Higher."

Another governor pointed to her laptop. "We've taken them as high—"

"*Higher,*" Coyne demanded. They'd been raising rates for a year, but it wasn't fast enough for him. He'd been pushing them to do more for months, but the bombing slowed his efforts. Now, several within the Fed were getting scared.

The Chairman stood. "Titus, this is dangerous. The mess could be impossible to clean up."

"We have got to torture this economy," Coyne said slowly, as if talking to a five-year-old. "President Pound needs to be tested and pushed further, and the population needs to be more distracted and strapped."

"We may wreck it," the Chairman said, referring to the economy. "The entire thing."

"Better us than Pound," Coyne said. "He wants it to come down, then by God we'll bring it down!"

While on the beach waiting for the others, the president and first lady continued their discussion. They moved to a circle of beach chairs that had been set up so all could at least have a sense of basking in the sun, enjoying the view and salty breeze while their minds searched for answers. Someone brought out platters of fruit and placed them on a table which already contained glasses, pitchers of iced tea, and water.

"Rex and Tarka are rapidly increasing the size of Vonner Security," Hudson said. "Booker has built a formidable private army called the BLAXers. Vonner tried for years to keep up with Booker's growth, almost like a corporate arms race."

"What is Booker planning on doing with his army?" Melissa asked, sipping tea.

"Fitz suggested one of the reasons Vonner was so against Booker was that he didn't trust why anyone would have such a large 'private security force.' That is absolutely the question. 'What is he going to do with that army?'"

"What are *we* going to do with it?" Melissa asked quietly.

"Do you mean Booker's army, or Vonner Security?"

"Both."

"It'll be difficult to avoid using them for a war with Booker and the other REMies."

Melissa looked at him skeptically, concerned.

"We have no choice. It's no longer a world where it's country against country. Now it's company against company, and unfortunately the REMies control all the largest corporations and have a loose alliance that's only going to strengthen once we really start going after them."

"But how do you reconcile this with what you experienced in those nine minutes?"

"I don't." Hudson kneeled down, scooped up a handful of sand, and let it slip through his fingers. "There's no way I can make sense out of any of this. I don't know how to be president at this time knowing what I know about the REMies' control over the world, while understanding what I know to be true about life and death. I'm just doing the best I can." Hudson looked distressed.

"What's wrong?"

He shook his head, looking as if he were enduring great pain.

"Talk to me."

He shook his head again. "Somewhere in the conflicts and the contradictions . . . it's there . . . tearing me apart."

She took his hand.

"I know the truth, and what I must do," he said. "And that's the reason I'm president now . . . to do this. I must stop the REMies."

Melissa hugged him.

"Their empire is totally unsustainable," Hudson continued. "If we don't stop them, the rich will keep getting richer, and everybody else will keep getting poorer. The world will be more depleted of its resources, the environment further damaged . . . It's riskier to allow the REMies to continue than it is to risk destroying everything in the process of trying to stop them."

CHAPTER TWENTY

F itz, the Wizard, Schueller, and other close advisors joined the president and first lady. Most of them wore shorts and sunglasses on the warm October day. The vice president attended via a secure digital hook-up, since she and the president were never in the same place at the same time. Fitz smiled when an aide showed up with a small cooler full of Cokes.

The Wizard gave them a brief update on Gouge, their childhood friend who had been horribly injured in the same fire that burned his father alive.

"Gouge is suffering bad," Hudson said after listening to the description. "He's still never been able to speak."

"He never will," the Wizard said sadly. "Gouge isn't in that tortured body anymore. It's total agonizing pain. He needs to fly into the stars."

"Why didn't you move into Vonner's big Potomac estate instead of that old mansion out in Oakton?" Melissa asked the Wizard after a mournful silence.

"I couldn't live in a house where a REMie used to live," the Wizard said, stroking his goatee and re-tying his ponytail. "The energy would be all wrong. Where I am now, a documentary filmmaker once lived with his wife, five kids, and a bunch of dogs. That's the kind of flow I want around me. You know, the atoms, on a quantum level, are always present, that's why you sometimes feel weird in a hotel room. Maybe something bad happened there, or someone mean recently stayed there. I can't imagine the vibe at the White House. Wow, talk about some cosmic energy and karma—"

"Back to the subject at hand," the president said, tilting his head at the Wizard.

"Dawg, it's all one." The Wizard winked, putting his fingers at the outside edges of his eyes and stretching the skin so he looked even more Korean. Then he bowed his head and went off in a made-up dialect like an old, wise, Zen master before getting serious again. "Okay, this is what we need to be looking at. It goes along with your Automated Payment Transaction Tax proposal, and gives us the best chance at surviving a collapse of our current monetary system."

"Is Granger on board with what you're about to tell us?" the president asked.

"One hundred percent," the Wizard replied, reaching for a cluster of grapes. "So the dollar, and just about every other currency in the world, is what's known as 'fiat currency,' legal tender that's backed only by the authorizing government's promise that it's good. As you know, money used to be backed by gold, silver, or something else of value, but those are inconvenient for governments who need money to fund wars and other follies."

"The last hundred years, starting with World War I," the president added, "this planet has experienced almost constant conflict and war, and massive spending on weapons. It's no accident that all this coincides with the existence of central banks, including the Federal Reserve. Countries used to fund wars from their accumulated treasury of gold, but once the REMies figured how to create a system where they could add money into the economy at will, war became easy to fund. They built their empire that way."

"My point exactly," the Wizard said. "They create money out of thin air and stick us with the debt. That's why NorthBridge went after the Fed in Jackson Hole; they want to bring about the end sooner. The Federal Reserve system will end because cryptocurrency is coming. The Fed has no place in the future. Paper money, are you kidding? Digital transactions are everything, but they're still based on dollars that the REMies control."

"They can't control cryptocurrencies?" Melissa ventured.

"Right," the Wizard agreed. "No one can. It's decentralized, meaning it's impossible to hack because it's contained on so many servers, it's transparent, and the amount is fixed."

"Yeah, but what is it backed by?" Fitz asked.

"Did you see that!?" Melissa shot up. "A pod of a dolphins, jumping." They all looked, talked about it for a moment, and then continued.

"Agreement," the Wizard said. "Which is more than the Federal Reserve notes we use are backed by. With Bitcoin, there will never be more than twenty-one million created."

"Wouldn't we need more at some point?" Fitz asked.

"No problem, it's infinitely divisible. And digiGOLD has a similar structure. The transparency lets the market decide the worth, unlike our dollars, which come with interest owed to the Fed every time they create one and put it into circulation. No automatic interest with cryptocurrencies, and, best of all, no middle men. No need for banks in that case."

"Then we strengthen the top three cryptocurrencies in advance of launching Cherry Tree," the president said, "so that if the REMie central bank system collapses—"

"Not 'if'. Rather *when* it collapses," the Wizard corrected.

"Noted," the president said. "*When* it collapses, the world will already have an alternative in place. End of empire."

"Right. An alternative that will eventually come anyway," the Wizard said matter-of-factly.

"And all those transactions will be digital," Vice President Brown said. "Making it simple for the APT Tax to be shaved off each transaction."

Schueller rose and began pacing. "It sounds good, but can't someone—the REMies, NSA, Nigerian hackers, anyone—access it and see every dealing a person has? Couldn't someone with the right sequence of key strokes wipe out your entire savings?"

"Not really," the Wizard replied. "There are safeguards, and specifically the blockchain—"

An aide jogged across the beach and whispered into the president's ear. Hudson's face fell, and he stood up. "We have to go. NorthBridge has attacked again."

CHAPTER TWENTY-ONE

As they headed to the motorcade, the president relayed what he'd learned. "There's been some type of EMP attacks on *The New York Times* and the NBC buildings in New York. NorthBridge also hit *The Washington Post* building, the Fox News bureau in DC, CNN in Atlanta, and the Los Angeles Times."

"NorthBridge claimed responsibility?" Fitz asked.

"Oh, yes," the president answered emphatically.

Fitz, staring into his phone, took over the conversation. "AKA Hancock, also known as Thorne, said on the NorthBridge website that they could have taken out all broadcast networks, including the internet, but preferred to have some reporting to continue."

The president, first lady, Schueller, and Fitz piled into The Beast. The others followed in various vehicles.

"Yeah," the president said. "What Thorne really means is Fonda didn't want the Raton Report not to get out, and Thorne wanted to protect his show."

"True," Schueller said, "but they're also taking out the mainstream media, or what we all know as the REMies' propaganda division."

"That doesn't give NorthBridge the right to attack and kill people," Melissa said.

"No fatalities," Fitz corrected, his face still buried in the screen. "That's the thing with EMP, or an electromagnetic pulse. It fries the electronics, everything that needs power is toast."

"The Wizard told me just before we left that no one has ever successfully used EMP weapons in this way before," Schueller said. "It's scary that they can target certain buildings."

"ABC News is reporting neighboring buildings were also impacted," Fitz said. "Experts believe it will take months before those companies are able to recover, if ever. They lost all their digital data, and NorthBridge took out virtually all their broadcast facilities—dozens and dozens of locations hit simultaneously."

The president took a call from Dranick. "The intelligence community and military were stunned by the sophistication of the attack, and are in full panic mode," the colonel reported to Hudson. "We aren't confident we could withstand a similar attack on military and intelligence targets."

"Incredible," the president said.

"Mr. President," Secret Service Agent "007" Bond interrupted, "they don't want you flying back on Air Force One. An EMP could take you right out of the air."

"What plane do they want me on?"

"No flying."

Hudson shot him an incredulous look. "The hell with that! If Booker Lipton wants me dead, he could have done it before now."

"It's unlikely they have the technology to do it anyway," Dranick said through the phone.

"How unlikely?" the president asked. "We didn't even think they could do what they just did."

"This is a whole other level," Dranick said. "We would have difficulty—"

"It doesn't matter," the president argued. "We're going back on Air Force One!"

During the flight back to Washington aboard Air Force One, and in between updates concerning the latest NorthBridge attacks and the media's attempts to recover and report, Hudson pushed his plans to radically reform the United States government and financial system. The Wizard, and other advisors, had rejoined the group prior to takeoff. They continued discussions about cryptocurrencies replacing central banks, and APT replacing income, sales, and all other forms of taxation. The Wizard and Fitz would work together to appoint a secret commission that would refine the post-Cherry Tree plans for implementing the two new systems.

"We'll be ready to launch Cherry Tree very soon," the president began. "For the first time, the masses will see just what the REMies and other elites have done; how peace and prosperity have been stolen from a trusting population; how MADE events and SAD tactics have been used to control them." SAD offended him even more than the MADE events. Scare Agitate Divide pitted people against one another, and stole the chance for society to evolve to a higher place.

"I can't wait for that day," Schueller said.

"I can," the Wizard said. "No matter how prepared we think we are, the REMies are bigger, smarter, faster . . . richer."

"But they're *wrong*," the president insisted. "They are wrong."

"Of course," Schueller agreed. "But after the Kennedy papers . . . I mean, Dad, he may have been planning to do the same thing we are, his own version of Cherry Tree. Obviously, the internet didn't exist back then, but he still managed to accumulate proof of the REMies' MADE events, frauds, and schemes. My question is what was he going to do with it?"

"*My* question is who betrayed him?"

CHAPTER TWENTY-TWO

Hudson took a risk and arranged a call with Fonda Raton. Their communications had been limited since Crane made the discovery of her identity as AKA Jefferson. Because she was a criminal and a fugitive, each time he had contacted her through a "back channel," even though her reason for being underground had not yet been disclosed. Melissa and Fitz had repeatedly pressed him to declare Booker, Fonda, and Thorne as the leaders of NorthBridge, but he and the Wizard still believed it would be counterproductive at this stage.

"We have FBI DIRT units and other intelligence sources looking for them," the president had told Melissa after the EMP attacks on the media.

"We still need to find out who the other AKAs are, especially Adams and Franklin, because NorthBridge is doing your dirty work," Fitz had said.

"I beg your pardon?" the president had snapped, clearly bothered by his chief of staff's implication.

"You're happy to allow NorthBridge to go after REMie

targets. They're doing what you can't or won't do. It's convenient, isn't it?"

Hudson reflected on the conversation as he sat in his private study, waiting for the call from Fonda. He had denied the charge from Fitz, but even Melissa seemed to believe there was more than a little truth in it. Hudson had to admit to himself that NorthBridge was helping his war against the REMies. In fact, so far NorthBridge *was* the war. The president had fired their man Covington and averted a REMie-planned war with China, but not much else. In addition to regular blows against the elite's establishment, NorthBridge was giving the REMies a taste of their own medicine. The terror attacks had to be a major distraction to the forty-eight billionaires who ran the world. For the first time, they had to face an unknown enemy.

And what will happen after *Cherry Tree, when seven billion rise up against their evil?*

Fonda came on the line. "I thought I might be hearing from you," she mused.

"You have to stop."

"I thought you understood the rules," she said. "Stop what?"

"NorthBridge, NBC, Fox, CNN . . . "

"Hmm, do you believe those are fair and objective sources of news? Or are they the mouthpiece of the elites? C'mon, Hudson, the REMies *own* them."

"I'm not arguing that, but your methods."

"No one died."

"Not this time."

"NorthBridge appears to be very careful about that. Then again, there's collateral damage in any war," she said impatiently. "And you need to realize that NorthBridge is just getting started. What's more frightening is that the REMies have hardly begun to fight back. The real war is about to explode, and then counting the bodies will be the least of your worries."

"Fonda, you know what I'm trying to do here."

"Same as us."

"Maybe, but your way is not—"

"Do you know how many people have tried to tell the truth, who knew all or part of the REMie lie, and did all they could to show it to the world?"

Hudson thought of Zackers and Crane, but she didn't let him answer.

"*Thousands!*" Fonda blasted. "And they paid with their lives. So just imagine what a great day it was when a person, an honest, thoughtful, intelligent man, landed in the White House, a president who's a real hero for a change. And when you discovered the game, you decided not to play it. Can you conceive what that means? All the men who occupied the Oval Office before you for a hundred years were in on it! And you were, too, in the beginning, playing Vonner's perfect every-man candidate. But you became an illusion within the illusion, and instead you decided to break the game."

"I'm trying," Hudson said.

"Hooray! But it's too big, you can't do it alone," Fonda said. "Remember when I told you not to become the distraction? That's because each passing year, as the REMies' schemes and corruption grew larger and larger, it became more difficult to conceal their greed and treachery, meaning more people saw it, or might. So they gave us bigger and bigger MADE events. *Everything* became a distraction. People thought Trump was so bad? He was nothing, just another front man, yet another giant, appalling distraction, and the people fell for it. Every. Single. Day! And it wasn't just Trump! All the politicians before and since have played their part as either unwitting accomplices to the game, or bought-and-paid-for actors in it."

Hudson realized she would not listen. He'd wasted his time.

"You're telling me what I already know," he said, raising his voice. "I will *not* help you."

"Then act like you know it. I'm sorry you died, but don't let those nine minutes blind you and cost us everything. Leave NorthBridge alone. You *can't* stop them. Worry about REMies instead. You wanted to be president, use the few strings you have. Give us authentic realism. Don't help us. Don't try to stop us. Just *show* us!"

CHAPTER TWENTY-THREE

Perhaps Schueller's favorite multibillion-dollar undertaking was Zero-cost Alternative Power, or "ZAP." It was another dual-purpose enterprise created to provide energy in the event that the infrastructure and power grid were devastated during the chaotic transition from the existing REMie empire-system, to the new fair and free system. At the same time, ZAP would help the environment, and allow consumers to access free power.

Schueller had shifted billions into ZAP. Tens of thousands of employees were put to work installing solar and wind power installations. The president also spoke on the importance of solar energy for the environment, and asked Congress to pass new legislation that would include bigger tax breaks than ever before for the implementation of alternative energy systems. Meanwhile, ZAP would pay the price of installing new roofs made of solar panels by companies like Tesla, above and beyond what a normal roof would cost.

ZAP worked with well-known tech entrepreneurs/visionaries, such as Elon Musk and Granger Watson, to develop technologies that would incorporate solar panels into vehicle roofs and hoods, as well as small energy-producing wind turbines into the front grills. Schools and parks were given grants from Schueller to add solar and wind into their facilities and campuses. Already, more than seventy-thousand schools had added both ZAP power generation and FFF gardens. Schueller had publicly stated that ZAP hoped to be on *every* roof by the end of the next decade.

"The more roofs," the president said privately to his son, "the less chance of a bloody revolution when the REMies eventually fall."

Hudson, frustrated by his failed attempts to convince Fonda to see things his way, had been trying to call Booker in the days since the journalist had lectured him. Unable to reach the pivotal billionaire, he contacted Linh, the leader of the Booker-backed Inner Movement, hoping for some help.

"I'm glad to hear from you," Linh said over the SonicBlock-protected video chat. "I've been worried."

"*That* worries me," Hudson said. "The last few times you were worried about me, someone ended up trying to kill me."

"It doesn't take any special abilities to know that you're a man in great danger," Linh said. "However, some threats are more serious than others. I'm sorry to say that those you trust the most might present you with the greatest difficulty."

Hudson was not in the mood for more prophecy, veiled threats, or vague mystical terms. "I appreciate your concern, Linh, I really do. However, what I need most from you is help reaching Booker. Can you assist with that?" Hudson thought she looked aged. Her silky black hair had a few threads of grey now. He wondered how she managed the stress of it all—or maybe she didn't.

She looked at him with a mixed expression, one of sadness. "I don't know where he is."

Hudson wasn't sure he believed her, but at the same time, a nagging question surfaced. "It seems curious to me that you would associate with such a man."

"There are things you don't know about him, or me," she said. "Many things you don't know."

"I know that Booker is one of the leaders of NorthBridge," the president said sternly, lowering his chin and softening his gaze. "A terrorist organization that uses violence to achieve its objectives and has killed many people with no regard for the rule of law—or, in your world, no regard to the law of karma."

"Did you want to discuss karma with me?" she challenged, watching him.

"N-no," Hudson stuttered, then half smiled, interlaced his fingers, and leaned his handsome face on them. He let out a sigh. "I do not. I'm simply interested if you're going to defend him."

"He can defend himself. But I will tell you this, I don't agree with the methods of NorthBridge. I've made that clear to Booker on many occasions."

"Yet you take his money?"

"My opposition to NorthBridge and his support of the Inner Movement are not mutually exclusive," she said.

Hudson found her impossible to argue with. Not because she didn't listen, but because he would not. This fact troubled him. Prior to his near death experience, he didn't believe any of the "new age nonsense" that she did, but after those nine minutes, he understood what the Inner Movement was about, and as instantaneous as his transformation had been after his "death," he was having extreme difficulties in applying it to his daily life. There was a part of him that was still refusing to believe what he knew, rejecting anyone or anything which would continue to shake that foundation.

Yet, in those moments of awareness, he understood that he was trying to push it away. It would take time and contemplation to discover how to blend the truths he had absorbed in death into what he was destined to accomplish in life.

"Could you get a message to him?" Hudson asked. "Would you urge him to contact me?"

Linh nodded. "And will you do something for me?" She didn't wait for an answer. "When you do all the *possible* things you'll do as president, will you never stop dreaming of what is thought to be impossible?"

With these words, she instantly appeared younger, incredibly beautiful, magnetic. His earlier impression seemed absurd now.

Her simple request, the intonation of each syllable, as if presenting a beautiful flower, or whispering a sacred secret, took his breath away.

He nodded, not knowing what to say that wouldn't seem cheap in response.

CHAPTER TWENTY-FOUR

L ater that day, Booker called the president's private cellphone while he was changing in the residence.

"How's my timing?" the billionaire asked.

The president thought of asking him if he knew he was in the residence. It could have been a coincidence that Booker had reached him in a rare moment when he was alone, but Hudson had an eerie feeling Booker knew his every move.

"Perfect," Hudson said, checking the SonicBlock. "Thanks for calling."

"Believe it or not, I'm one of your biggest fans."

"Booker, you're a charming man, that's for sure, but you're the most powerful force within the two groups I'm trying to destroy, so forgive me if I have trouble believing you."

"Fair enough, Mr. President. Then what can I do for you?"

"Make my job easier. If you really want to help me, shut down NorthBridge and join my plan to end the REMie empire."

"The problem is you don't understand my motives, you can't see what I'm trying to do. Vonner poisoned you—"

"I'll tell you what I see," the president interrupted. "You're one of the wealthiest people in the world, a top REMie, the CapStone within your grasp. You're the major manufacturer of specialized military weapons and surveillance equipment, and yet with all that power, you choose to start a revolution against your government. What don't I understand?"

"You're only seeing things from Vonner's perspective. Let me explain it from another angle, okay?"

"I'm listening."

"Vonner and I had different approaches. He was much more conciliatory than I am. I need the CapStone, but not for my own power—"

"What else is the purpose of a CapStone if not to obtain power?" Hudson picked out a shirt, then put it back.

"Of course, that's what the CapStone is—ultimate absolute power. This may sound silly to you, but I need it to save the world."

"You know what they say about absolute power?" the president asked. "It corrupts absolutely." He chose a blue shirt.

"If Bastendorff, Coyne, Miner, or one of the others get the CapStone first, we're doomed. *Absolutely* doomed."

"And that means you can do whatever you need to do to get it?"

"The CapStone isn't some relic, it's control. In some ways, it can never be won," Booker said. "But for a period, it can be held, and one of us will be in total control. That needs to be me."

"Because your cause is the noble one?"

"Yes. REMies aren't normal people. They're the one percent of the one percent. No rules apply to them. They cannot be arrested. It's difficult for the average person on the street to fathom a million dollars and what that can buy, but a billion? Impossible. Now make that *hundreds* of billions. With every billion added comes connections, power, and control. It multiplies exponentially. You might be beginning to see some of that with your son receiving Vonner's money, but my point is that for all your good intentions, you won't be able to stop the REMies through legislation, law enforcement, prosecution, or negotiations. There's only one way to stop them, and that's by force."

The president sat down on a stool in the large closet. "What if you're wrong?"

"I am not wrong," Booker said.

"But you don't know."

"I do know."

"How?"

"Because I have near infinite wealth at my disposal. I wield more power than all the presidents, kings, and rulers in the history of the world *combined*. I've seen things you cannot begin to imagine. The world is at a precipice. Those with a limited view are missing the obvious. We have little time left before freedom becomes just a word with forgotten meaning."

The president considered for a moment that Booker was on the insane side of eccentric, but decided to give the man who had achieved so much the benefit of the doubt.

This guy is a whole lot smarter than me.

"Can you give me a little more to go on? Show me some facts."

"That would require our spending quite a bit of time together. Unfortunately, with you being president of the United States, and me being sought by the *government* of the United States, that is not possible. But ask yourself, Hudson, how come you cannot find me, or stop me, or any of the people I protect?" Booker paused.

The president did not respond. Hudson stood and ran his hand over his suits, hanging in color order.

"You know the world is a disaster, you've said it yourself. Everything is out-of-control. The human race has become just that, a race against each other; a race no one can ultimately win. We need each other."

"Then we should be the change we want to see," Hudson said, paraphrasing Gandhi. "We should work together. This is the last time I'm going to make the offer."

"No," Booker said. "There's no time. The REMies must be stopped now, and you can't do it with words alone."

The call ended a few minutes later, leaving the president more frustrated than ever. He knew in some respects that Booker was right, but he could not condone an illegal war, an armed rebellion.

He decided to order the FBI to release the names. By this time tomorrow, the world will know Booker Lipton, Fonda Raton, and the shock jock Thorne, were all AKA terrorists.

CHAPTER TWENTY-FIVE

B astendorff glared at his two assistants as they typed on keyboards, listening to his commands. "There's not enough turmoil," the overweight billionaire said while wiping duck fat from his fingers. Several plates of food littered his desk. "I want a wave of crime sprees in American cities, and not just ordinary crimes. How about gang wars and people tossing stuff off overpasses, lots of random killings in high-end shopping districts. Let's have the people screaming for President Pound to do something."

One assistant was typing notes, the other was moving money into previously set-up (and often used) slush fund accounts in the United States.

"Of course, Pound won't be able to help much, because he'll have his hands full with NorthBridge and the craziness going on with all their foreign bases," Bastendorff said, scooping up an éclair.

"Craziness?" an assistant asked.

"Pound wants to shut down all the US military bases around the world," the billionaire responded. "Can you imagine? Just think about all those Pentagon generals . . . oh, it's too good. I couldn't have planned this better. Booker Lipton has so much money to lose if they cut back on defense as much as Pound wants, and then there's Titus Coyne. He wants the bases open because he has plans for those bases in the CapWars, thinks he can use them to help get the CapStone. See the loveliness here?"

Neither assistant answered.

"In this case, we're happy to assist our friend, President Pound. See where I'm going?"

"Craziness at the bases," one of them replied.

"Exactly," Bastendorff said, smiling as if he'd just placed the last brick in a five-thousand-piece Lego set. "Let's get some of those servicemen and women in trouble at US bases in Germany, Japan, South Korea, Italy, Turkey, Bahrain, and hell, every base you can think of."

"Trouble?" one of his subordinates asked for clarification.

"I mean get them accused of rape, peddling secrets, bar fights, I don't care, just make trouble for the administration. I want all those countries giving Pound headaches."

Bastendorff had a large and capable network of operatives around the world in numbers comparable to Vonner Security and Booker Lipton's BLAXers. However, he was more willing to use them in devious and ruthless ways. Bastendorff budgeted between one and two billion dollars a year for such operations. Other REMies thought him reckless, but had grown accustom to his twisting and outrageous acts, and regularly packaged Bastendorff's follies as Manipulate-And-Distract-Everyone events. Many REMies had profited considerably by shadowing Bastendorff's moves and using them to consolidate power and achieve their own goals. Several REMies also manipulated Bastendorff's MADE events to enhance their own, more conservative, MADE events.

Even though Vonner was dead, Bastendorff was still fighting

a personal CapWar with him. Bastendorff lived in a perpetual state of infuriation that Vonner had put Hudson Pound in the presidency, then left the bulk of his fortune to Schueller Pound. His outrage that Hudson was still in power in Washington, without direct REMie control, drove the bloated billionaire to take greater risks at obtaining the CapStone. What power President Pound had was now unchecked. The most reckless REMie was willing to act in an extremely brazen manner, even by his standards, to strip the Pounds of everything. Those who had worked with Bastendorff the longest knew there was something different this time; not just a vendetta against Vonner, not just trying to teach the Pounds a lesson, not just trying to win another CapWar.

Karl Bastendorff was scared.

"I want to start seeing this stuff on the news tomorrow," Bastendorff said to his assistants. "Will that be a problem?"

"We should be able to make that happen."

He may have appeared to be a belligerent slob, grossly overweight, playing with children's toys, seemingly spoiled and crass, but a man like Bastendorff, who other REMies called "the Grinch," could not have risen to such a level, accumulated the enormous amounts of wealth, possessed incredible power, without being smarter than people thought—and he was *much* smarter. Bastendorff might actually have been one of the smartest REMies, and he knew they were all in danger. He had tried unsuccessfully to convince them of imminent catastrophe. He had implored them to join forces to have Hudson eliminated. All of his own efforts had so far failed, however, he still had ongoing operations underway toward that end. But Pound had also proved to be smarter than originally believed, and that fact raised Bastendorff's blood pressure every time he thought of it.

The president had protected himself well, cleaned out rogue Secret Service Agents, put his man in at DNI, and somehow managed to find the clean agents in the FBI. Vonner had also ensured that it would be difficult to remove Pound. He left many procedures in place and networks to protect the president even after his own death. This wasn't just shutting down another problem, not just another obstacle in his path to the CapStone. Bastendorff knew he was also trying to save his own personal fortune, and keep the REMies in power.

"Any luck getting Walton on board?" an assistant asked.

"No. These idiots don't get it, and, of course, they don't like me. They know I'm close to the CapStone."

Unfortunately, Bastendorff was so disliked by most of his fellow REMies that although he had been working the phones for weeks, he'd been having difficulty getting anyone to see the urgency. Even those who *did* realize the threat Pound posed were unwilling to sign on to his radical plans. Instead, some launched their own initiatives in order to stop the president, while others didn't believe Pound would get very far since no one else ever had.

"Fool!" Bastendorff barked after another call with a noncooperating REMie. "That's okay, this young president is soon going to have more to deal with than he can possibly imagine. Between NorthBridge, the Chinese knowing his weakness, our plans, and all the other REMies coming at him in various ways, this guy isn't going to be facing a crisis a week, he's going to be dealing with one every hour! The empire strikes back!"

CHAPTER TWENTY-SIX

During a video chat the president, the Wizard, and Granger, discussed a new threat.

"Ever hear of Lester Devonshire?" the Wizard asked from the old mansion in Oakton, Virginia, where he and Granger had been working with little rest for days.

"Yes," the president answered from his private study next to the Oval Office. "Vonner's attorney mentioned him. He inherited a billion dollars from Vonner."

"Right. He's Vonner's closest blood relative, and it seems he's met with attorneys about challenging the will."

"Too late, it's settled," the president said.

"I know, but he's not a nice guy. The only reason I know about him is because Gypsy spat out an alert on his activity."

"Which is?"

"It's vague so far, but the guy owns a beat-up casino, some Nevada brothels, and has a bunch of pawn shops, among other seedy ventures and shady activity. Also, he seems to be investing big into the legal marijuana industries in Californian and Oregon."

"So? Now he has a billion dollars to play with. Maybe he'll upgrade into international trafficking or money laundering."

"Or really go legit and get into politics," Granger joked.

"This guy is no joke," the Wizard said. "He's had someone looking around the DarkNet. Based on the footprints, my guess is Lester is looking to smear your reputation—blackmailing and sordid accusations."

"Do I have a reputation to protect?" Hudson asked in mock surprise. "There certainly isn't anything to blackmail me about."

"Dawg," the Wizard said in a serious tone, "it's a real threat."

"Okay, I don't mean to make light of it, but Wizard, there are *a lot* of threats, aren't there?"

"Yeah," he said quietly. "I'll keep an eye on him."

"Thank you," Hudson said. "Now, Granger, how are we looking on the new structure?"

"The new financial system, based on the blockchain—"

"Sorry, I'm still not a hundred percent clear on how the blockchain works . . ." Hudson said.

Granger smiled patiently. "Every transaction—a purchase, a funds transfer, real estate, whatever—is represented as an information block across the internet. It's instantly scrutinized by every party on the network. Assuming it's verified, it will be approved and added to the chain, which records a permanent record of all transaction. It all happens in seconds, and cannot be erased, altered, or hacked because of the transparency and redundancy."

"Amazing," the president said. "What about the APT?"

"The Automated Payment Transaction Tax is sliced off of every transaction, a tiny fraction, also part of the permanent record," the Wizard answered. "We shrink the IRS down to a few thousand employees, same with Social Security, because it all becomes automated, efficient, and fair."

"But we have a way to go," Granger said. "The REMies have

such a tight grip on things right now. They're using cameras from the Three-D system, which, as you know, are everywhere now. Back in 2018, the last time they did official estimates, the number was one hundred million surveillance cameras in the US. It's at least six or seven times that now."

"Two cameras for every citizen," the president said sadly.

"But what the REMies *do* with all that data, compiled by the NSA and other secret agencies, is what's really terrifying," Granger continued as he leaned against one of the eight huge white Roman columns at the edges of the sweeping brick veranda. "The REMies are going way beyond MADE events. They actually distort reality."

The Wizard took over. "It's insane, Dawg! Seriously, they've got artificial intelligence going that you could have a conversation with and not know it isn't human. It's easy for them. They have tens of millions of fake profiles on social media, but you couldn't tell if you looked at them if they were your Facebook friends, even if you messaged them. It's suddenly like, 'what is reality, man?'"

Granger flashed the Wizard a quick, incredulous look and resumed his explanation. "They are into disinformation," he said. "Not just individual REMies, but organized, state-sponsored campaigns as well. It's extraordinary. We have competing networked propaganda moving the dial on what people feel strongly about, what they support, what they buy, who they like and dislike. What's crazy is it's impossible to tell it's happening. The social media companies lost control of it a long time ago. All they care about is monetizing your life, which plays right into what the REMies and other bad actors are trying to do."

"The REMies are also using these systems to manipulate public opinion," the Wizard added. "Not just for MADE events, but for every moment of our lives. Dawg, it's been a long time since a democracy existed."

"You see, it's not just fake news sites, but many other, much more subtle things," Granger said.

"Like mind control," the Wizard said. "Imagine if you could use the same formula to turn the world, raise its consciousness, bring on the enlightenment!"

"Every single day this stuff gets stronger—artificial intelligence, machine learning, bots, spiders, algorithms, trend targeting, mechanized false content."

"Mechanized false content?" Hudson echoed. "Guys, with all due respect, I think you ought to get out and take a walk in the woods. Really, re-fresh the negative ions."

"They can create video with manipulated audio and visuals," Granger warned. "There is a total erosion of truth."

"And the tech companies?" the president asked, walking to a window, eyes following a few birds in their flight across the sky.

"They're controlled by the REMies, or completely overwhelmed by them," Granger replied. "And even the sites that are independent have been targeted by the agents of disinformation and digital paramilitaries."

"You stopped a war with China," the Wizard said to Hudson, "but that was old-school. The future is now. We're being bombarded by information warfare. It's cyber war, and America no longer owns the advantage of the most tanks, carriers, and nukes."

The president knew his old friend was right. In the internet-era, US brute force wasn't enough to bend the will of reluctant governments around the world. A handful of good hackers with computers could change history. It was that thought that had kept him from releasing the NorthBridge names. Hudson still wasn't ready to play that card. He might yet need Booker Lipton and the other AKAs. The enemy within could be the only ones able to hold the gates shut from the outside invaders.

CHAPTER TWENTY-SEVEN

During the next several months, the administration continued to have issues with leaks, especially once the media companies that had been hit by NorthBridge began to recover. The networks and major papers seemed to come at President Pound with renewed vigor, as if it was *his* fault NorthBridge had targeted them.

However, leaks were a minor concern compared to the other problems which plagued the country. A new crisis appeared almost daily. Crimes sprees in Philadelphia, Detroit, and Houston, and gang violence across Los Angeles and Chicago gripped the nation, all of it on a scale unprecedented before, and all of it happening simultaneously. A wave of "overpass attacks" in Los Angeles and a copycat in Atlanta were the latest. Someone had been tossing things off overpasses, already killing three motorists and injuring a dozen others across the two cities. No suspects had been arrested yet.

At the same time, the Pentagon had been besieged by international incidents stemming from military personnel finding their way into trouble in seven different countries. Two Marines raped a local girl in Italy. Four Army privates killed a German Muslim outside of a bar in Germany. At a base in Japan, an Airman was charged with attempted murder. Incredibly, a young naval officer was charged with robbing a jewelry store in Bahrain. Worst of all was an espionage ring in South Korea involving three enlisted men. Demonstrations had not only been staged in the five countries where the events had occurred, but had spread to nineteen other nations where America had bases. Chants of "Yankee go home!" "We don't want no NSA, CIA, USA!" and "War Machine can't fix this!" rocked crowds as large as three hundred thousand outside American bases around the globe.

"It's a coordinated attack," the Wizard told the president during an emergency meeting with Dranick, Fitz, the FBI Director, the Secretary of Defense, the Secretary of State, and several other top national security advisors.

"Of course it is," the president said. "The domestic crime sprees could be a result of the breakdowns caused by the steady NorthBridge attacks."

"Law enforcement is spread perilously thin," the FBI Director confirmed.

"But eleven military personnel going bad in five countries within weeks of each other?"

"No, I mean all of it," the Wizard said, meeting the president's eyes. "The domestic, military, *and* embassy issues."

The State Department had also been the victim of scandals at three embassies in different countries that ran the gamut from embarrassing to dangerous. The first included underage prostitution and pornography in Saudi Arabia. On the heels of that came allegations of selling secrets in Belgium. The third, involving smuggling and money laundering, had just come to light in India. Early indications were it could be the most massive of the three.

"Gypsy?" the president asked quietly.

The Wizard nodded.

Several questioning looks from those gathered went unanswered.

"NorthBridge?" the president asked. The leading theory in the administration had been that the domestic terror organization had been involved in at least some of the mayhem. Attacks by NorthBridge had lessened during the period, and many saw it as their way of keeping the pressure on the government while taking it off of the outlawed organization.

"Who else benefits from wearing down law enforcement resources and distracting the administration?" Fitz ventured.

"Karl Bastendorff," the Wizard said.

"The billionaire?" the Secretary of State asked in astonishment.

Most of the cabinet had not been made privy to the REMies plot since they were undoubtedly part of it, knowingly or not.

"Colonel," the president said to Dranick. "Want to handle this?"

Dranick knew that even though it was phrased as a question, it was actually an order. "Of course. We'll match it with what we already have on Bastendorff and report back next week."

"In the morning," the president corrected.

Dranick nodded. "The morning, then. If you'll excuse me."

The president nodded and continued speaking as DNI Dranick left the conference. "Now, exacerbating all these problems is the fact that even before we get a chance to take action, our plans are often leaked to the media."

"It's become an epidemic," the FBI Director added.

"Although it is unlikely to be any of you in this room," the president continued, "should I read the name of reclusive billionaire Karl Bastendorff in the *Washington Post* tomorrow, or see any mention of him on CNN, you better believe each of you is going to be arrested, charged, and dragged before investigators. One. By. One." Hudson scanned the collected faces and registered the shock, indignation, and outrage on each one. "Understand?"

After a round of affirmative nods and yeses, the president continued. "Good. Thank you." He made eye contact with each of those gathered. "Now, portions of classified reports, which included details leading up to and surrounding the situation at our embassy in Saudi Arabia, were released to the *New York Times*. This has caused us more embarrassment. It should be noted that all those involved deny any wrongdoing. Innocent until proven guilty—ring a bell? And we should all remember that this could easily be a set-up by any number of bad actors."

"We're seeing the same pattern with these leaks, Mr. President," the FBI Director said. "As you know, there were even more serious leaks relating to the South Korean spy investigation."

"How are we supposed to stop espionage when we can't stop the leaks?" the president asked. "Get it done."

"What about the domestic crime situation?" one of the advisors asked. "The country's internal bleeding makes us extremely susceptible to external threats."

"We're asking Congress for more emergency funding to put additional police officers on the street," the president answered, "and I've ordered the FBI to move resources and increase manpower in the cities most affected."

"If this goes on," the Secretary of Defense said, "we may have to send in troops. Boots on the ground in Los Angeles, Chicago, Houston . . . that would change things in a hurry."

"Maybe the Pentagon will take my proposal to bring *all* the troops home seriously now," the president said.

Everyone looked at him for a silent moment of tense confusion.

"Either way, there will be no tanks on Main Street," the president said. "Not on my watch."

CHAPTER TWENTY-EIGHT

That evening, Hudson had dinner with Melissa, Schueller, and the Wizard in the residence dining room. The White House chef prepared a gourmet vegan meal. Hudson, once a big meat and cheese eater—one of his favorites had been a bacon cheddar cheeseburger, with extra bacon and extra cheese—had, without explanation, immediately eliminated all of that from his diet after his nine-minute death.

"Nice work today," the president said to the Wizard.

"Thanks, Dawg," the Wizard said. "I thought the Secretary of State was going to have a heart attack when I laid it on Bastendorff."

Melissa raised an eyebrow.

"I used today's national security meeting to put the fear of God into those attending. We're trying to plug up these endless leaks." Hudson looked across at a portrait of George Washington and thought of Cherry Tree. "We're running out of time," he said, mostly to himself.

"You don't really think the leaker could be one of them, do you?" the first lady asked.

"It could be any of them, or several of them. According to the computer models from Gypsy, it could even be one of us in this room."

"That's crazy," Melissa said.

"I wish it were one of us," Schueller said. "That way we could get the media to believe anything we tell them."

"Don't think we haven't tried that," the president said. "The problem is they aren't on our side. They only run stories that fit the REMie agenda. Anything that counters that, any semblance of real truth hinting at the conspiracy, just gets ignored."

"They sure do like to cover NorthBridge," Melissa said. "Even when there aren't any attacks, they rehash the old ones and talk about the lack of progress. They're relentless."

"NorthBridge is the ultimate SAD story, as in Scare, Agitate, Divide," the president said.

"It's a good example of how the REMies turn something they didn't have anything to do with into a MADE event," Schueller added.

"Remember, Booker is a REMie *and* head of NorthBridge," Hudson said. "Coincidence? I think not."

"Then why haven't you exposed him yet?" Schueller asked.

"Because it's too important to know who AKA Adams is," the president replied, stating what had become his primary reason for delaying the announcement. At the same time, he didn't want to admit that allowing NorthBridge to peck away at the REMies had been more effective than anything his administration had done against the corrupt elites. "I wish the media would help us. Maybe they could use some of their investigative reporters to actually investigate and find the identities of the other AKAs, instead of finding fault with everything I do."

"The REMies control the media," Schueller said.

"I know," Hudson said. "That explains why they badger me, but not their inability to identify the NorthBridge AKAs."

"Why is Adams so important, and Franklin, too, right?" Melissa asked.

"Because NorthBridge operates on a decentralized leadership system," the Wizard answered. "So, if we get Booker, Fonda is in charge. We get her, Thorne takes over. Take him out—"

"AKA Adams steps in. After that, it's Franklin," the first lady finished.

"Right," the president said. "Even now, we have decent intel that certain leaders make decisions without full agreement from the leadership, meaning Booker may order them to bomb the Federal Reserve Bank, and Fonda might not even know about it in advance. Or, she may order the leak of a whole bunch of classified material without checking with the others."

"They did that during the campaign," the first lady said. "Remember all the opposition research that prompted several candidates to drop out of the race?"

"Yeah," Hudson said, adding another helping of Brussels sprouts to his plate. "We think that's why different AKAs sign the statements on their website. The one who ordered it, claims it."

"But, Dad," Schueller began, "couldn't there be ten more AKAs that have never made public statements? So even if you get Adams and Franklin, then somehow find Booker, Fonda, and Thorne, couldn't a whole new crop just take over?"

"That's possible," the president replied. "But we don't think so."

"Let's say you figure out who AKA Adams and Franklin are," Melissa said. "How do you know you can find them? And what good will it do when you haven't even been able to locate Booker, Fonda, and Thorne?"

"We're making progress on that," the Wizard said. "Recently, our team has managed to isolate some of their tracks on the Dark-Net. There have been digital fingerprints and coded footprints discovered belonging to Thorne and Fonda."

Melissa's eyes widened and she smiled. "Impressive."

"Then what?" Schueller asked.

"It won't be long until we're able to triangulate their position, so to speak," the Wizard responded.

"Meaning?" Melissa asked.

"If the cyber gods are with us, we'll know right where they are," the Wizard said. "Then boom, boom, boom, we got 'em."

Melissa took a bite of some daikon and winked at Hudson. "Nice work," she said, pointing her fork at him. "How was this made?" She pointed to the food. "I've never liked radish, but this is incredible."

"I'll ask the chef," the president replied. As for tracking the AKAs, that's all Wizard and Granger, but it's a little too soon for congratulations just yet."

"Maybe," the Wizard said. "But give us a couple more days."

CHAPTER TWENTY-NINE

A n article on one of the major online news sites speculated that the young billionaire, Schueller Pound, seemed intent on quickly spending every last penny of the fortune he's inherited from Arlin Vonner, citing a burn rate of more than a billion dollars a month. One commentator joked, "Perhaps the president's son has some inside information on the coming end of the world, and he's trying to spend it all first."

The current fuss had been caused by yet another one of Schueller's ambitious billion-dollar ventures. This time the focus was on healthcare, and he had the help of his sister, Florence. The president's daughter had put her nursing career temporarily on hold to head up what Schueller had dubbed "Medical Emergency Details," or "MEDs." The idea was that in the event of a breakdown in essential services following a natural disaster, civil unrest, or any other unforeseen situation, the population should be able to take care of all but the most serious medical problems themselves.

MEDs hired thousands of doctors, nurses, and other health practitioners. Their objective was two-pronged. First, small teams of medical professionals fanned out across the country and began training anyone interested in first aid and medical basics, all the way up to triage and minor surgery. The second aspect of the MEDs' mission was to respond to actual disasters. Teams of medical personnel remained on call. MEDs also had helicopters, small planes, four-wheel-drive vehicles, and medical supplies staged at strategically located facilities around the nation and in more than sixteen other countries.

The American Medical Association (AMA) immediately initiated lawsuits against Schueller and MEDs in thirty-two states, claiming it amounted to a program to teach people to practice medicine without a license. Schueller, undaunted, added an army of attorneys to MEDs' payroll. It was another extremely well-received enterprise across the general population.

"Giving control of healthcare back to the people," Schueller said, "is long overdue."

He also pledged to find a way to make health insurance affordable.

"Do health insurance companies really need to collectively make tens of billions in profits while people struggle to pay for doctor visits, hospital stays, and medicine? There must be a better way, a *fair* way, and I'm going to find it."

Fitz entered the Oval Office, interrupting a meeting with several members of Congress, their aides, and representatives from two large environmental groups. After apologizing and informing them the meeting would have to be rescheduled, he quickly sent them away.

"What is it?" the president asked as soon as they were alone, fearing another NorthBridge attack.

"How well do you know Mandy Engbert?" Fitz asked.

Hudson stared blankly at his Chief of Staff. "I don't recall ever hearing the name before. Who is she?"

"Are you certain? Because she's just told a story to a cable news channel that you sexually harassed her during your work on the school board back in Ohio."

Hudson sat back in his chair with a puzzled expression on his face. "I've never sexually harassed anyone in my life. I've never heard of this woman. This is obviously just somebody looking for publicity or money."

"If she wanted money," Fitz began, "she would've approached you or your attorneys before going public."

"No one's going to believe her. It's not true. Just have the Press Secretary issue a firm denial," the president said, waving his hand dismissively. "There's no way they can prove this because it didn't happen."

Fitz looked skeptical. "I believe you didn't do it, but I don't believe it will go away as easily as you think."

By the end of the next day, it was clear that Mandy Engbert was part of something bigger than just a woman seeking publicity. Three more women came forward—one claimed an affair, another charged sexual harassment and unwanted advances, and the fourth alleged victim said Hudson raped her. All four were light on details, two of the women had retained the same attorney, and all were the subject of intense media attention. Wall-to-wall round-the-clock coverage delved into the sleazy claims and the supposed seedy and scandalous past of the president.

The first lady, who had been at the United Nations women's conference, was pelted with questions upon leaving the function. Even without talking to Hudson yet, she forcefully announced complete belief in Hudson, adding that she thought everyone else should also believe him. When a reporter fired back and asked if she was calling the four women liars, Melissa calmly answered, "I was raised to not talk badly about people. But if they're saying that my husband did something, and he's saying that he did not, I'm saying that I believe him, and you can draw whatever conclusion you think is appropriate."

That evening, alone in the residence, Hudson repeated what the White House spokesperson had already said. "I don't know these women. None of it is true, and I have no doubt that this is a REMie hatchet job."

"It seems a bit weak for a REMie MADE event," Melissa said, showing absolutely no signs of doubting Hudson. "I would think the REMies would've been able to produce photographs, physical evidence, video recordings . . . you know their game. They can create anything."

"Then who?" Hudson asked, sitting on an antique, blue upholstered chair while taking off his shoes. "I've got the Wizard on it. He's already put all the names and data into Gypsy. Hopefully something will turn up."

"Is it even worth wasting the computer program's capacity on this?" she asked.

"It's dominating the media, and I don't think it's going away anytime soon. In fact, I wouldn't be surprised if more accusations hit tomorrow. It could be a good old-fashioned political enemies' crucifixion. You know there are plenty of people in the Senate and Congress in both parties who despise me. Or any of the REMies could've taken it upon themselves. I don't know. But I think it would be helpful to know where this is coming from."

"It's certainly a distraction."

"Fonda Raton always warned me not to become the distraction," Hudson said. "Now I am, and anything that makes me less effective is a real threat, especially as we get closer to launching Cherry Tree."

"The timing is troubling," Melissa said. "People may disagree with you, but if they know they can believe in you, than we have a better chance of succeeding. This is an attack on your credibility and nothing else."

"Yeah, 'which office do I go to, to get my reputation back?'"

Sitting in his penthouse office in Las Vegas, Lester Devonshire watched a bank of five televisions. The media was on fire with speculation and accusations about his distant cousin, Hudson Pound. Not since Bill Clinton's Monica Lewinsky days had a president been subject to so many lurid news stories. As a candidate, Donald Trump had somehow survived the Access Hollywood tape, and other incidents that would have sunk any other person running for even a low-level political office. It still astonished Lester that Clinton and Trump had weathered those storms, and he intended that President Pound would not make it through this scandal. Lester was running the "side-show" like a business. He tossed a pillow at one of the screens when the White House spokesperson denied the accusations.

"Just wait!" Lester shouted at the television.

There would be more women coming forward tomorrow, and more the next day. Even if it wasn't true, he planned on burying Hudson in so much sleaze and filth and innuendo that people would begin to *think* it was true. He'd learned the trick from his uncle, Arlin Vonner—repeat a lie long enough and the people will eventually believe it. And in this case, he was counting on the public's cynicism: "*If so many people are saying the same thing, it must be true. Why would all those women lie?*"

Yes, he thought, *I could have been a great REMie, if only the Pounds hadn't stolen my inheritance.*

CHAPTER THIRTY

"**M**elissa goes everywhere with the president until this scandal is cleared up!" Fitz barked the order like a man frustrated by never-ending problems, just before the roof caves in.

Hudson wasn't about to argue; he missed his wife. Since their marriage at the start of the campaign, they'd spent more time apart than together. She had been an effective and popular campaigner, and her connections from her days with the National Governor's Association gave her contacts in all the state capitals. Once she became first lady, she travelled tirelessly, pushing the president's agenda, and had managed to attend most meetings structuring the president's planned "radical reforms." Her schedule became nearly impossible after Schueller inherited Vonner's fortune because he'd begged her to head FFF, his Free Food Foundation.

Despite Hudson's denials and lack of proof, the media was in full feeding-frenzy mode, and the public, who had become somewhat jaded by sex scandals, couldn't seem to get enough of this one. Although Hudson wanted to ignore it and proceed with Cherry Tree preparations, his top advisors insisted on a family trip. Melissa, Hudson, Schueller, and Florence boarded Air Force One and flew to Ohio.

During the flight, the Wizard updated Hudson on the pre-war-efforts against the REMies.

"We unearthed communications between Covington and Titus Coyne," the Wizard said. "It turns out that Coyne had been Covington's superior—in the shadows, I mean."

"And I guessed Bastendorff was his REMie controller," the president said.

"Actually, you originally thought it was Vonner controlling Covington," Melissa reminded him.

"Right," Hudson said, feeling a little guilty. "Then once I figured out that wasn't the case, I set my suspicions on Bastendorff."

"He's easy to blame for *everything*," the Wizard said.

"True, but Coyne is a more formidable foe."

"Dawg, we push into the ancient energy of the lost, like fallen empires," the Wizard said. "Do you know what I mean? If the cold is what it was, then we have to see the warm sun, a star rising across the dark abyss. That's how we'll know. If we feel its apparent imprint already occurring—"

"Okay, Wizard, you lost me," the president said.

"Where?" he asked.

"Way back there, a long time ago . . . "

"Don't worry, Dawg, you're still here, you just don't realize it. I promise you'll eventually catch up to yourself."

"Take another bong hit, Wizard," Melissa said, laughing.

"Oh, I don't need outside stuff to get me into the dream realm of *reality*."

"I know," Melissa said, laughing harder.

"The Wizard doesn't do drugs," Hudson said, "but I might need to start so I can understand him."

"Nah," the Wizard said. "You've been places." He eyed Hudson closely. "You remember more than most of us, you know what I'm talking about?"

A silence hung for several moments until Melissa changed the subject. "Then without Covington, does Coyne still have access to NSA and FaST squad files?"

"I think so," the Wizard replied. "Dranick should hunt that down for sure."

A man brought them fresh beverages.

Hudson sent a secured message to the DNI. "Having such a trusted friend as the Director of National Intelligence is going to make all the difference," the president said.

"The REMies have to be going crazy with Dranick running intelligence," the Wizard agreed. "I hope he's got extra security."

"He does," the president said. "Vonner Security covers him twenty-four-seven. But they know I'll just put in another loyalist, so I think the bigger risk is the REMies working around him using underlings and the Deep State."

A little later into the short flight, the Wizard asked to see the president alone and announced that he'd discovered who had killed all the men who had raped Rochelle and murdered her brother.

"Who?" the president asked, knowing the same person had burned down the tire shop with Gouge and his father inside. Whoever was responsible for the retribution killings had also caused the slow, painful death of Gouge—whose funeral they were on their way to attend.

"It was Torland Rogers," the Wizard whispered.

Hudson's face registered shock. "Rochelle's younger brother?"

"Yeah," the Wizard said quietly. "He's forty-two now."

"Damn," Hudson breathed, sighing heavily. "You're sure?"

"Absolutely. What do you want to do?"

Hudson sat silent for a few moments, looking out the window as they flew over the mountains and began their descent into Ohio. Finally, he turned and met the Wizard's eyes. "Rochelle's family has suffered enough."

"But Torland killed Gouge," the Wizard said.

"No, Gouge's father and his buddies killed Gouge thirty years ago. Killed us all . . . "

"You, me, and Rochelle are the only ones who somehow survived," the Wizard said.

"Did we?" Hudson asked, turning back to the window.

Florence had not visited her father since he'd recovered from the Near-Death Experience. She claimed to have been too busy with helping Schueller with MEDs, but the real reason had more to do with her being traumatized by the attacks. Florence felt that every time she traveled with her father, he almost died. It had taken Schueller, Melissa, and Fitz all together to convince her to join them on the trip to Ohio.

Even when Air Force One safely touched down in the Buckeye State, she didn't relax. Not until The Beast pulled up to Melissa's house and Secret Service agents escorted them all inside did Florence let her guard down.

It was a good reunion of all Hudson's siblings. Florence and Schueller caught up with their cousins, aunts, and uncles. Even the Wizard tagged along, having not seen Hudson's family since he'd left Ohio more than thirty years earlier. But the reason for the trip hadn't originally been for the purposes of showing Hudson to be a family man. There was a funeral to attend.

CHAPTER THIRTY-ONE

B astendorff laughed raucously as he watched the reports of the charges against Hudson. "Good ol' President Pound apparently gets his kicks being naughty. It seems he just loves to 'pound' the women." More laughter.

"Do you think it's true?" a top aide asked.

"Hell no, it's not true," Bastendorff replied while reaching for his third glazed doughnut. "The guy's a damn Boy Scout. I wouldn't be surprised if he was a virgin before he married his first wife." He gave another snorting laugh. "No, one of the REMies is doing this to him, and I'd like to know which one." Bastendorff looked at the doughnut lovingly, as if the thrill of it being in his hand was as good as eating it. "Tricky business, this. We could help the scandal out, maybe throw some more dirt his way, but I'm guessing it's one of our friends . . . one who's also going for the CapStone. I don't want to botch this CapWar by aiding the enemy, you know what I mean? So let's get to the bottom of this and see who it is." He stuffed half of the doughnut into his mouth.

"What if it's the Democrats?"

"The Democrats?" he asked around the doughnut. "Are you kidding me? Pound may have started out as a Republican, but now he's more of a Democrat than most of them."

"Either way, wouldn't they rather see an *actual* Democrat in office?"

"I think you're forgetting that Democrats and Republicans are actually the Unity party. Hell, they almost all work for us anyway. Sure, sure, there are some political hacks, small time guys who've gotten through the cracks. A few *honest* smacks have made it into office, but nothing too big." Bastendorff said the word "honest" as if it were something he was allergic to. "Then, of course, there's the citizens. Some of them are more conservative while others are more liberal, but that doesn't have anything to do with Democrats or Republicans."

"I've often wondered why the Americans put up with a two-party system that's never served them."

"It serves *us*. The parties are a perfect funnel for corruption, allows the elites to control things. None of it can be left to the average knots."

"All right, we'll see if we can find out who's behind these women."

"They sure are fun to watch. I bet his wife is giving him some 'second thoughts' and 'what's what' right about now." Bastendorff laughed again until the disturbing thought that Coyne or one of the other REMies going after the CapStone might be gaining some advantage by the sex scandal. "Send Hendley in on your way out. I need an overview on how our mass distraction is going."

Hendley, a tall, skinny, balding man who'd been appointed to oversee the coordinated campaigns of crime waves in America and misconduct by American military personnel at international bases, gave a report to the bloated billionaire.

"Good, I enjoy watching your work on the news," Bastendorff

said. "Let's ratchet things up, shall we? The president is being buried in sexual harassment charges. Dumb sod thinks he'll gain sympathy by escaping off to a family funeral. Pathetic. He hopes that's gonna fix his image, but it won't. I want a few more surprises waiting for him when he gets back."

"You want more women to make some allegations?"

"Not yet," Bastendorff said. "We're trying to find out where all that's coming from, and I'm not interested in helping unless I know it's somebody I *want* to help—which I doubt." He looked at the doughnuts and considered another, but decided against it. "Meanwhile, be ready to pin the sex scandal story on Titus Coyne."

"We're ready to go with the US-China exposé. It's all set up, and will ensnare tourists and businessmen."

"You're tying it all into a bribery and corruption scandal? Making it an international incident with major US corporations, Chinese exporters, bankers, and communist government officials?"

"The works."

"Excellent. Let's keep tensions high between America and China. We may just get that war yet."

"And what about Coyne?" the aide asked. "Won't that help his inroads with the military?"

"He'll have a lot more to worry about soon enough."

Coyne had spent months locked in CapWar combat with REMie rivals. Conventional warfare—with weapons and soldiers—was an aspect of CapWars, but the real battles were fought in the boardrooms, media, manipulating the public through MADE events, and having REMie-owned politicians do their bidding. Coyne, known as "The Shark" and "Bankster," earned his ruthless reputation by destroying the politicians of other CapStone-seeking REMies and pushing MADE events that did serious damage to their businesses.

"Why do you ignore Bastendorff?" the chairman of one of Coyne's banks asked during a strategy session.

"Now that Vonner's dead, Booker Lipton is the biggest threat," Coyne said, while exchange rates, money supply, and commodities prices whizzed by on a giant screen inside his New York headquarters. "He's taking a great deal of our resources right now."

"What about these seven?" the Chairman asked, pointing to another massive monitor which tracked the assets and dealings of other REMies thought to be competing for the CapStone.

"I can handle them," Coyne said coolly. "I need some help with Booker, which I'm counting on the president unknowingly to give." He paused and stared at the constantly-changing REMie data on the screen. "Bastendorff is also very useful in knocking out the others. It may take both of us to finish off Booker."

"And then?"

"Then," Coyne said in a killer's voice, "I'm going to rip that pig apart and bury him under the CapStone."

CHAPTER THIRTY-TWO

The president sat next to the Wizard, doing something he hadn't done in years—sharing a beer with his old friend. The two surviving members of the Tire Shop Gang were alone on the back porch of Hudson's brother, Ace's, modest home. The stop had been kept from the media; nevertheless, security was as tight as always, with dozens of extra agents in the nearby trees.

"I'm sorry it took so long for him to die," the Wizard said. It had only been a few hours since Gouge's funeral. Both Hudson and the Wizard eulogized their life-long buddy, each doing their best to translate feelings into words. Hudson relived some humorous memories because he knew Gouge would want that. He also remembered Gouge's TRUTH tattoo.

A few days earlier, when Ace called and told his brother that Gouge had finally succumbed to the burns inflicted during the tire shop fire, Hudson had smiled, relieved his friend was finally free and out of pain. Then he'd taken a walk in the tunnels beneath the White House and cried.

The Wizard and Hudson sat on old white wicker chairs, staring out into the rolling woodlands, and toasted Gouge with bottles of New Belgium Brewing Fat Tire Amber Ale. They reminisced about the good times, most of which had been lost in the dark shadow of the night Rochelle was raped. It was the first time they'd relived many of those happy days since.

"Gouge would want us to laugh," the Wizard said. "Remember how he always made us laugh?"

"It's hard to laugh when I think of how much suffering he experienced," Hudson said. "Not just at the end, but his whole life."

"But now he's out there in the cosmos, learning all the secrets of the universe," the Wizard said. Then he turned to Hudson and narrowed his eyes. "Isn't he, Dawg?"

Hudson knew the Wizard was not probing about what had happened during the nine minutes, but was seeking reassurance that their friend was in a good place and still enduring.

"He's flying free," Hudson said with a faraway smile. "He's already deep into the next great adventure. Gouge is part of time-less imagination now."

The Wizard nodded, taking a sip of beer. "Yeah, he is," he whispered.

They continued to talk and tell funny stories for quite a while before Hudson brought up Rochelle's brother, Torland, and the wrath he had visited upon those who killed his older brother and raped his sister, Rochelle.

"I've been thinking about it, and I believe Gouge would agree," Hudson said.

The Wizard looked at him, knowing what he was about to say, and nodded.

"We let Torland go . . . " Hudson said.

"Brutal way for Gouge to go," the Wizard said. "But Torland did something that . . . taking out each of the sick monsters who got away with murder and rape . . . in all those years . . . those bastards didn't just rape her and kill her brother, they stole our innocence. Torland didn't avenge just his older brother and sister, he avenged each of us."

"And Gouge paid for our sins," Hudson added, downing the rest of his bottle.

"Putting Torland in jail wouldn't help anything," the Wizard said thoughtfully.

"Leaves us keeping another secret."

"Yeah," the Wizard breathed, as if the shocking idea was occurring to him for the first time.

"I don't think Torland was ever coming for us. He didn't even know we were there that night," Hudson said. "Poor Gouge was just in the wrong place . . . with his father when Torland caught up with the old man. It's wrong, it's unfair, it's nothing less than barbaric and horrific, but so is everything about that night."

"None of us escaped the tire shop unscathed," the Wizard said.

"Time to end it," Hudson said firmly. "Once and for all."

"I'm all in," the Wizard agreed. "Let's not bring any more pain to that family."

Hudson nodded. "It's what Gouge would want now, I'm fully convinced of that, as he looks back at us, and that night, through a cosmic lens."

The Wizard stared at him intently, then nodded. "Okay. For you, Gouge," he whispered, "the tire shop is gone. That night . . . it's time to let it go. We're letting go."

On the flight back to Washington, Hudson thought back on the last conversation he'd had with Vonner.

"I wanted to trust you from the beginning," Hudson had told him. "Why is it I never could?"

"Maybe because you don't trust yourself," Vonner had

replied, and then added, "You probably haven't trusted yourself since you let Rochelle down. It's time you start trusting. Even if you don't trust me, at least learn to trust yourself."

Hudson now realized Vonner had given him good advice. Deciding to allow Torland Rogers to go free was more about forgiving himself than letting Rochelle's brother off.

Hudson closed his eyes to better absorb the important clarity he'd just received. *It's impossible to trust yourself until you forgive yourself. And vice versa.*

CHAPTER THIRTY-THREE

The president quietly and dramatically increased the pressure on NorthBridge. He ordered the FBI Director and Director of National Intelligence to devote even more resources into locating the terror organization's leadership. He also authorized loosening the "rules of engagement" in the war against domestic terrorism. At the same time, he worked with the FBI Director and Dranick to create a new team to specifically target financial crimes by REMies.

A few weeks into his tough new campaign, Fonda Raton posted a blistering rebuke of him on the Raton Report, writing:

President Pound has ordered hundreds of low level arrests of anti-government activists who have no known connection to NorthBridge. Absent any evidence, the administration is engaging in strong-arm tactics normally seen in brutal dictatorships.

Hudson read the post and smiled. *We must be getting close,* he thought, as he continued reading.

Colonel Dranick, the Director of National Intelligence, appears to be an appropriate successor to DNI David Covington, whose tenure as the country's top intel office was marked with Gestapo-like FaST

Squads rounding up thousands of 'enemies of the state,' whose only crime was independent thinking and criticizing the administration.

Fitz knocked on the door to the President's Study, used to finding him there during most unscheduled time. "Have you seen the Raton Report?" the chief of staff asked as he entered.

"'The president, through his attack dog, DNI Dranick, is doing nothing more than what Covington did, in a desperate attempt to keep the public from revolting,'" Hudson read aloud to answer Fitz. "'President Pound thinks throwing the peasants some red meat will keep them from storming the palace gates. We are not fooled—the 'NorthBridgers' they are arresting have about as much to do with NorthBridge as the president's son, Schueller, does. Just because they don't like the current government doesn't mean they are terrorists.'"

"She sounds a little upset," Fitz said, offering a bottle of Coke.

Hudson waved off the soda. "She sounds worried to me."

"Think NorthBridge is feeling the heat?"

"Wouldn't that be nice?" the president mused. "But what bothers me is she published a complete list of arrests. Only about a quarter of them were made public."

"Leaks," Fitz said in a suddenly tired tone. "Could be from DNI or FBI."

"No. Neither had a complete list."

Fitz nodded in frustration.

"We've got to stop the leaks," the president said. "We can't beat NorthBridge or break the REMies if they know everything we're thinking and doing."

"I thought Granger was working on it."

"The data still shows it could be any of us," the president said. "I'm meeting with him tomorrow on another matter. I'll get an update."

"Fonda's also attacking Three-D again."

"Even though Booker profits from it," the president said. "She's pushing the linkability issues—getting everyone riled up. Did you see where Fonda calls me 'President Big Brother' and suggests the Three-D system would be too oppressive for even an Orwell novel?"

"Ignore her," Fitz said, pouring his Coke into a tall crystal glass filled with cola cubes.

"I would if everyone else would. The college campuses are in constant demonstrations, the mainstream media is jumping on her bandwagon—which is incredibly hypocritical since the REMies are the ones who ultimately created and instituted Three-D. The media is happy to hang the blame on me."

"Release Fonda's name as a NorthBridge leader."

The president stood and began to pace. "Not until we get AKA Adams and Franklin. Anyway, the timing is bad. It's possible Granger will give the greenlight tomorrow and we'll be ready to go with Cherry Tree."

"Impressive," Fitz said. "So he's worked out the new economy?"

"As you know, right now the world currencies are connected and leveraged."

"Right, like dominoes. One goes and—"

"If we switch to digiGOLD, it changes the entire dynamic of the economy."

"Isn't NorthBridge the master of digiGOLD?"

"No, they just use it. That's the beauty of cryptocurrency and blockchain based systems. No one is in control."

"Fair and Free."

"Exactly."

"So the Federal Reserve is raising rates, crushing us into another recession . . . "

"Assuming we survive this one long enough to get to Cherry Tree, all that, and the Fed itself, will be a thing of the past."

"Then what?"

"Radical reforms," the president said excitedly. "We introduce them one after the other. Bring the troops home, outlaw pollution, implement mandatory recycling, universal healthcare, start—"

Fitz held up his hands. "I'm in the meetings, remember?"

"I know, I've seen you there. But, Fitz, we're making history here. We're about to fix the world!"

"Doesn't the success of your 'revolution' depend on stopping the revolution already underway?" Fitz asked.

"Maybe," the president said cryptically. "Maybe not."

CHAPTER THIRTY-FOUR

A gent Bond normally gave the president the weekly recap of the most serious assassination attempts every Saturday morning. Lately they'd averaged three physical actions every ten days. In addition, there were nine to twelve credible threats each week, and hundreds of potential situations to investigate. But at least once a month a close call would require an immediate debriefing. The most recent case involved a cache of military grade weapons found in Washington.

"This one worries me," 007 began. "Obviously, we have a perimeter of protection around the White House. We conduct searches, do breakdowns, satellite and drone surveillance, various reconnaissance, and constantly utilize Three-D. It would be very hard for someone to bring any ordnance of size within our perimeters. "

"But clearly not impossible," the president said.

"Right."

"I've read the reports in the past, and I understand how the radius fans out looking for weapons capable of hitting us," the president said. "So what happened in this case?"

"It's a sophisticated operation, Mr. President. Fourteen advanced rocket propelled grenades."

"Advanced?"

"Leading technology—nothing that's available yet. What you might call a 'shoulder mounted smart bomb'," 007 said, sounding as if he were describing the end of the world. "This thing can be programmed with coordinates and launched from a small tripod mount. It's designed for urban single strikes."

"Terrorism."

"Yes, our military experts agree that's its primary function. The weapons can be moved in a hurry, carried, maneuvered, and set up by just one person, and it's even possible to fire from the shoulder. However, in most cases it would be safer to use the mobile tripod." He offered a grave expression. "This thing is equivalent to a tank with legs."

"Where do they come from?"

"We don't know."

"Guesses?"

"Same as yours."

The president nodded, already thinking about Booker Lipton.

"The thing is," 007 said, summoning back the president's attention, "we got there as they were preparing the launches."

"How close?" the president asked.

"Three or four minutes later, and we'd be having a different conversation right about now, and in a different building, or . . . not having one at all."

The president raised his eyebrows. "Good work. Then you have people in custody?"

"There were three suspects. They fought hard. Two of them are dead, one is critical. We lost an agent."

Hudson looked up shook his head. "I'm sorry. Did the agent have a family?"

"He was single."

"Did I know him?"

He gave him the name.

"Yeah, curly brown hair? Damn nice guy." The president clenched his fist and leaned his chin against it. He didn't speak again for several moments. "I want to talk to that piece of garbage you have in custody, whenever he wakes up."

"He's awake now," 007 said. "Not saying zip."

"Take me to him."

"Not a good idea," Bond said.

"Really? Good. Because I'm not known for my good ideas, so my record's safe."

"Sir, I must ask—"

"*Now*," the president said. "As in, *right* now!"

CHAPTER THIRTY-FIVE

Titus Coyne sat at the head of a large conference table, its surface, an oblong white marble slab, covered with papers and laptop computers. The eight other REMies seated around him in the ultra-modern meeting space waited in agitated silence for "The Shark" to speak. The completely glass-enclosed room was suspended by a nearly invisible section of cables above a classic library filled with leather volumes and accented with antique wingback chairs. It was connected to the second floor by four glass walkways, one on each wall. It appeared and felt as if they were floating.

The nine assembled REMies together controlled nearly half of the world's wealth. This was not a normally scheduled meeting. In fact, the nine in attendance had not ever before been in the same room together.

"Gentlemen," Titus began, "by your presence here, you are acknowledging what some of our colleagues are still denying— that we are facing a crisis."

He gazed around the room at their faces. The power wielded by these men, aged between forty-five and eighty-one, was truly unfathomable. The entire world ran on a system that they, and the REMies who'd come before, had created. It existed for the sole purpose of enriching the REMies and maintaining their control over the affairs of the global population. The empire had been built on it.

"For more than a hundred years, we have managed to keep the people in the dark," Titus continued. "With each passing year, we have tightened our hold so that we, fewer than fifty individuals, decide fate and destiny."

"Titus, can you cut through the glory and pride speech?" said one of the other REMies, a silver haired man wearing a dark cashmere sweater, blue jeans, and cowboy boots.

"Yes, yes, we're the greatest emperors the world has ever known," a large Hispanic man wearing gold-tinted glasses and with a long scar on his hand said in a mimicking voice.

"Forgive me," Titus said, "I was merely setting the stage for what I'm about to say. Our power, and therefore our wealth, our very way of life, and ultimately our freedom, is at stake as it has never been before. At a time when we're at our most powerful, Arlin Vonner opened a Pandora's box and put someone into power who's not a reliable friend of the REMies, nor a servant of the one percent. As a result, for the first time in generations, we have an independent man in the White House."

"We all know the situation, Titus," another REMie with thick, dyed black hair said from the other end of the table. "You don't have to convince us. The others who chose not to come may need your speech, but we don't."

"Either our friends don't see the threat as significant, as we do, or they think they can handle it on their own," one of them added. "Of course, in the case of Bastendorff, we simply didn't invite him." He shook his head in disgust, as if talking about a serial rapist.

Titus was used to their impatience. These were men not

accustomed to following orders or being on the defensive. "I appreciate you all coming," Titus pushed on. "I do believe our best chance is by uniting."

"If that's possible."

"Yes," Titus said. "It is no secret that some in this room, including myself, are vying for the CapStone. However, it's time to recognize that the CapWars are what have weakened and exposed us. While it could be debated that one person with ultimate control might give us a stronger position against Hudson Pound, I don't think anybody would argue that working separately, and still competing with each other, hurts our chances and gives him an opening. I'm calling for a truce in the CapWars."

A sudden murmuring swept around the table. Most would admit that Titus, Booker, and Bastendorff had the best chances to win the final CapWar, so it came as a surprise that he was willing to stand down.

"What about Booker and Bastendorff?" one of them asked.

"They can't win if we are unified."

"Is this about stopping Pound, or a new scheme that has you ending up with the CapStone?" the Hispanic man asked.

"Right now, our entire existence is at stake," Titus said, trying to make it sound like a news bulletin. "The CapStone is meaningless rubble if the pyramid beneath it collapses."

"Are you proposing a cartel, then?" another REMie asked.

"Will that work?" the man with the dyed black hair asked before Titus could respond.

"We work together until Pound is out and reevaluate then."

Everyone agreed. None of them trusted Titus, but they knew he was right. Dangerous times . . .

"Pound may seem unstoppable—"

"He seems immortal," the silver-haired REMie in cowboy boots said to nervous laughter.

"As I was saying," Titus continued, "he seems more powerful than he is. This guy managed a *hardware* store."

"I believe he owned a successful *chain* of hardware stores," a bald, raspy-voiced REMie corrected.

"Whatever," Titus said. "He should never have gotten this far. He's no match for us."

"He's managed to stay alive," the oldest REMie in the room, an eighty-one-year-old German, said. "Extraordinary achievement."

"If he succeeds in dismantling the central bank system, puts in place a crypto currency on a decentralized blockchain, and adds his automated payment transaction tax system to that recipe . . . " one of them began. "Well, gentlemen, if he pulls that off, then we're not going to be much more than a useless group of old rich men!"

"And even that is very much in doubt," another man added.

Someone else opened his mouth to say something, but Titus waved his hand to cut him off, and raised his voice. "We may lose our cash and liquid wealth if Pound's proposed 'Fair and Free' system comes to pass. Worse, if an uprising accompanies this transition, which Booker Lipton is trying to make happen, then we'll also likely see our physical assets seized. It must not be overlooked that there's a real chance we'll all wind up in prison."

Several of the men began talking at once until Titus was able to calm them down and regain control of the meeting, at which point serious deliberations ensued on how best to destroy the president's plans.

CHAPTER THIRTY-SIX

The Beast pulled up to the back entrance to the George Washington University Hospital. Agent Bond opened the door and barely missed getting bulldozed as the president jumped out and marched inside. More than twenty VS and Secret Service agents maneuvered to keep up and protect him. Four FBI DIRT agents met the entourage.

On the way over, 007 had explained that the suspect had suffered two gunshot wounds, one in the abdomen and one in the leg. "They expect him to recover, but there's no guarantee."

"Is he still awake?" the president asked the first FBI agent.

The agent nodded. "He's weak, but conscious. However," the agent paused and looked at Bond, "the doctors are very upset about this. One of them wants to meet with you before you see the suspect."

The president looked annoyed. "Where is he?"

"The suspect or the doctor?" the agent asked.

"The doctor," the president said reluctantly.

A couple of minutes later, they were standing in a private waiting room while the surgeon tried to explain that the president's planned interrogation was not only risky to his patient, but also very inappropriate.

"This man is a criminal. He killed a federal agent and was attempting to assassinate the president of the United States." Hudson stared at the man and let the words hang.

"I'm not claiming that he's a decent person," the doctor said. "But he *is* a person, a human who is suffering, and it's my job to keep him alive. If he survives, and is well enough to leave the hospital, then you can chat with him all day long. He'll no longer be my concern. You can try, convict, and then sentence him to death if that's what you want."

"I understand," the president said. "But this is a matter of national security, so I'm going to talk to that man, and if he happens to die while I'm doing it, that'll be inconvenient, but I can assure you I know where he's going."

The president turned and stormed out of the room.

The doctor followed after him. "Mr. President, I must insist."

Without turning around, through gritted teeth, the president said, "Detain him."

A Secret Service agent immediately stepped in front of the doctor. Another stepped up and informed him that he would be placed under arrest and taken to jail should he make any attempt to stop the president.

The corridors ahead were cleared as President Pound and the agents found the intensive care unit where the suspect was being guarded in a private room. The suspect, a battered, twenty-something white guy with a military haircut and athletic build, looked noticeably disturbed when he saw the president enter.

"Do you know who I am?" Hudson asked.

The man nodded and licked his dry lips.

"Good," Hudson said, pulling a chair right next to the suspect's bed. "You tried to kill me earlier today, didn't you?"

The man just stared and said nothing.

"Listen to me you uneducated, neglected, troubled, product of a bad school system," the president ranted in a hushed but firm voice. "You radicalized misfit. Yet another member of the common class tortured by the one percent, confused by the oppressive life you find yourself stumbling through . . . Is it money? Is it the chance to rise above the hopelessness? A moment when you can make a difference instead of wallowing in the damp despair of powerlessness?" Hudson's eyes never left the suspect's. "Do you even *know* what you're fighting for, and why you can't stop the flood of anger that drowns you every morning? Where does the hate come from? You're desperate, aren't you? I can see it on your face. You want out so bad it's impossible not to scream sometimes, but you can't, so you swallow it again, and it mixes with all the other bitter bile that constantly gnaws at you."

The man stared attentively at Hudson, his expression less angry.

"You're going to tell me what I need to know."

The suspect shook his head.

"You killed a federal agent during an attempted assassination of the president of the United States, they're going execute you for what you did today." Hudson softened his tone and expression. "And I'm the only friend you have."

"You aren't my friend. I want a lawyer."

Hudson shook his head. "I don't think you're hearing me." Hudson put his hand firmly on the man's injured leg.

The man winced.

"Sorry, that wasn't intentional," the president said sincerely. "You know what happened to me don't you? I'm sure you heard about the day I died."

The man nodded slightly.

"Those nine minutes . . . " Hudson said, his voice filled with wonder as if discussing magic. "I know where you're going. I learned some things up there—"

"In heaven?" the man asked weakly, sounding almost like a child.

"No. Up there at thirty thousand feet aboard Air Force One."

"What?"

"You tell me what I need to know, I'll tell you what *you* need to know."

The man blinked his eyes and licked his dry lips again.

"Where did you get those weapons? Who sent you?"

"Can you guarantee I won't die?" the man asked.

Hudson shook his head. "Because of you, an innocent man who was just doing his job is dead."

"Then no deal."

"You're way beyond deals. You may not even survive the night, and if you do, it's going to be a whole lot of horrible for the next couple of years. Solitary confinement, shackles, interrogations that are going to seem more like torture, and then you're going to be executed. This life is over. All you have is what's happening next."

"I'm going to hell? *You* go to hell!"

"Where did you get all this hate?"

The suspect glared at Hudson. "You don't understand."

"Maybe not, but I'm all you got."

"I don't *got* you! We're not friends!"

"You're right," Hudson said. "But we're brothers."

The suspect looked confused.

"Brothers," Hudson repeated. "You tell me, and the rest of your life, whatever time you have left, will be easier. But if you don't, you're going to die cold and lonely without knowing what's next. Don't you want to know?"

The man looked at the agents in the room. They stared blankly back. "You aren't gonna tell me nothing. You ain't told no one."

"But I'll tell you." Hudson stared at the man. "Look, I do

understand. I have a pretty good idea of why you hate this much. The world is a mess. It feels like the Hunger Games sometimes. Did you read that book?"

"I saw the movie."

"Well, it's not that bad yet, but it could be. The system is rigged, corruption is everywhere. We're living under a repressive conspiracy that we help sustain, but I'm trying to fix it. You tried to kill the wrong guy. They don't want me to change anything. That's why they want to kill me. You think they bother assassinating people that aren't a threat? You've been working for the very empire that you hate."

The man looked at Hudson and almost smiled. "That's why we're brothers?"

The president nodded. "Lots of us are on the same side, but we don't know it. They divide us our whole lives. They can't let us know that the only real enemy we have is them."

The man thought for a few minutes and finally said, "Okay. Clear the room, and I'll tell you."

"Mr. President, we can't do that," Agent Bond said.

"He's restrained, hooked to a bunch of machines—I'll be okay," the president said, and then added firmly, "Go."

After they were alone, the man confessed the details the president wanted to know. Hudson thanked him, then whispered his side of the bargain. He began with the words, "Don't worry about heaven or hell, those are myths."

Ten minutes later, when the president emerged from the room, the suspect was happily crying.

CHAPTER THIRTY-SEVEN

Hudson used the short helicopter ride from the White House to Vonner's old Potomac River estate to contemplate his next move. Soon they would have to make the decision on whether to arrest REMies and seize assets. It was a daunting prospect which would inevitably lead to negotiations with the elites.

Or, Hudson could choose to simply implement the new system by force.

Neither option seemed palatable, given the thin margin for error. One bad decision, and they'd be in the middle of a bloody revolution with no obvious or quick way out.

As Marine One landed, the president spotted Rex, Granger, and Schueller already talking at "the shack." The shack, one of Schueller's additions, was an enclosed glass structure that allowed them to view the beautiful Potomac River year-round in a temperature-controlled space surrounded by trees and boulders. The structure gave the illusion of being nearly invisible. Both sides of the river had security stations on high alert.

By the time Hudson reached them, they were in the middle

of a heated debate regarding the very subject he'd been thinking about aboard the chopper.

"As you know," Rex said, "we've expanded the Gypsy program quite significantly. I've added all of Vonner's data, including everything VS had. The results have been very impressive. Our next—"

"Mr. President," Granger said as Hudson entered. "We were just going over the new Free and Fair system."

Hudson greeted them and made it clear he didn't have much time. Used to his tight presidential schedule, they all jumped back into the deliberations.

"We've come up with quite a bit on Thorne," Rex said. "Not only do we now know where he is, we also have a profile from Gypsy which seems to indicate he's a little more radical than we previously thought."

"I can't imagine," the president said sarcastically. "Thorne's whole persona is to continually surprise."

"He's a shock-jock," Schueller added.

"Yes. However, these findings, if accurate, and I believe they are, show that he's planning to lead a post-NorthBridge victory."

"What's that mean?" the president asked.

"If the NorthBridge revolution fully ignites," Rex began, twisting some blue dice in his hand, "then whatever happens after, whatever is left from the resulting wars, Thorne plans to be the new leader."

"Our analysis of such an event," Granger interjected, "shows that there'll likely be six or seven regional areas controlled by different groups."

"Thorne plans on initially leading the West Coast," Rex continued, "and then quickly working to unite the other areas under his control."

"That's crazy," Schueller said. "It sounds like a bad plot of a dystopian novel."

"Thorne *is* crazy," Rex said.

"How can he be planning to be some post-apocalyptic dictator, or chieftain, while espousing the return to the Founding Fathers' principles and the US Constitution as his guide?" Schueller asked.

"I think Gypsy has misinterpreted," Granger said. "Artificial intelligence in machine learning built into the Gypsy program isn't perfect yet. It takes all of Thorne's outrageous remarks and applies them in such a way that paints our friend as a madman." Granger laughed. The others couldn't help but join in his amusement.

"Let's hope you're right, Granger," the president said. "If the computer has every inflammatory remark Thorne has ever said, I'm surprised the AI system hasn't overheated and crashed the program."

"He's still dangerous," Rex said.

"Let's move on. Our main concern today is when and how to implement Granger's new Fair and Free system in place of the REMies' unfair and not free system." He couldn't help but chuckle again at his own humor.

"That's exactly why Thorne came up," Rex said. "I've pushed the projections and scenarios out and looked at the pro formas, and it shows that what we might think is the riskiest course, isn't." Rex pulled a laptop computer around so the president could see the screen. "See for yourself. The conclusion is that to arrest and seize assets and forcibly implement the Fair and Free system, while dismantling the central banks—including the Federal Reserve—is the way to go."

"The treacherous approach seems the safest," Granger agreed.

"Are we ready for that?" Schueller asked. "It's going to be violent . . . brutal."

"The REMies are never going to go away quietly," Granger added.

"Maybe not," the president said. "But one way or another, the REMies *are* going away."

On the way back to the White House, ignoring the views that he loved, the president worried about all the risks to unseating the REMies. He felt the urgency, knowing he was lucky to still be alive, knowing at any moment that luck might run out.

They needed to launch Cherry Tree as quickly as possible. However, with all the potential things that could trip them up in the minefield of making Cherry Tree go off perfectly, the leaks worried him the most. Everything else could be planned for, but the leaks threatened to destroy the element of surprise, or worse, reveal their game plan to the REMies or NorthBridge.

Who is it? Hudson ran through all the possibilities again. There were nearly twenty people who had access to all the material that had been leaked. However, it seemed to be more than one person. If so, that meant the list of suspects swelled to more than one hundred.

What if it's Fitz, or the Wizard, or Dranick? Dranick would never betray me. Would the Wizard? No, but he has that crazy Universal Quantum Physics connection to Booker . . . Still, it couldn't be him. I've got to find out who it is!

CHAPTER THIRTY-EIGHT

The B-4 committee met for what they hoped would be their last session prior to the coup that would remove Hudson Pound from the presidency. A large, gold fringed American flag on an eagle-topped pole stood in the corner of the room, three stories below ground level at the Pentagon. The sensor light on a signal-blocking device indicated they could not be overheard. General Imperia began with a review of the charges against the president.

"One: The commander in chief declared that he was a pacifist and would not use force to defend the nation. On your summary, you will see the evidence for the alleged crime as footnotes detailing the occasions on which he made the statements," the general said, scanning the stony faces of his comrades. "We will vote today on the contention that these statements by the commander in chief would, at any time, call into question his ability to lead, disqualify him for his position, and that his own words constitute an admission that he is unfit to carry out his duties as commander in chief. However, in a time of war, as currently exists domestically with NorthBridge and internationally with the war on terror, his statements clearly represent an act of treason."

The other men in the room nodded solemnly.

"Item two," Imperia continued, his impeccable uniform seemingly matching his uptight *I'm-always-right* attitude. "The president's refusal to continue drone operations and bombings in the aforementioned war on terror, which has been part of the country's foreign policy for more than two decades to various degrees, depending on the level of technology, and regardless of which administration was in the White House."

"The Constitution does give him that authority," the Air Force general said.

"True," Imperia admitted. "However, it is our assessment that this dramatic departure from long standing policy weakens the nation and strengthens our enemies. Obviously, the Founding Fathers could never have envisioned the type of war in which we find ourselves with stateless terror groups, so no provision was made for a president refusing to exercise his duties."

The tick from the track lighting blinked. All the men looked up, at each other, raised their eyebrows, then continued.

The explanation seemed to satisfy the general.

"Three: The president's illegal subversion of congressional authority by making an 'eleventh hour' secret and unauthorized mission to communist China after Congress had declared war on the country. Title 10 of the US Code § 904 - Article 104, states that: 'any person who aids, or attempts to aid, the enemy with money, or other things; or without proper authority, knowingly harbors or protects or gives intelligence to, or communicates or corresponds with or holds any intercourse with the enemy, either directly or indirectly; shall suffer death or such other punishment as a court-martial or military commission may direct.'"

"Again," the Air Force general interrupted, "doesn't the president have the authority referred to in the statute?"

"Congress had declared war. The president did not consult with them," Imperia said firmly. "Any other questions?"

The room was silent. The lights blinked again.

"Then if it is this committee's determination that this president is guilty of high crimes and misdemeanors, including treason, the appropriate legal classifications of the above charges leave but one remedy. The president must be removed from power."

"The normal channels are not appropriate in this case," the admiral said.

"Correct," Imperia agreed. "As we have previously discussed, impeachment, though the normal remedy for cases such as this, and the twenty-fifth amendment as another option, are unavailable due to the urgent threats we face. Such public and time-consuming methods would only aid and encourage the nation's enemies further."

The admiral nodded while wishing the room had windows.

"Therefore, it is with absolute resolve and tremendous deference we move forward with the motion to remove President Pound from office," Imperia said, pausing to meet the eyes of the other members of B-4.

Each signaled their approval.

"He'll be temporarily replaced with a military leader until such time that a new election can be held?" the Marine Commandant asked, wanting to confirm what he already knew.

General Imperia nodded. "Yes. Because the vice president is also a devout pacifist, and has shared in and condoned the president's actions in every case, she is also not qualified as a replacement, and due to the chaotic and corrupt climate, we believe it is best to avoid the normal line and succession and, therefore, a military appointment is in order."

"Then we are agreed," the Admiral said gravely. "We will go forward and remove the president of the United States from office for the first time in our nation's history."

"God help us," the Air Force general said.

CHAPTER THIRTY-NINE

Lester Devonshire threw a heavy brass book-end into a glass coffee table when he heard that the two largest news networks were not covering the latest sexual harassment claims against the president. As the shards of glass splintered into hundreds of pieces and landed across the dark hardwood floors, he cussed a storm and swore the Pounds would not enjoy "his money" much longer. One of the networks he knew had links to his uncle's, Arlin Vonner's, former holding. The other he'd discovered was part of Booker Lipton's media conglomerate.

Lester considered the latest bombshell report his best work yet. The accuser was gorgeous, and claimed that she'd grown up a school friend of the president's daughter, Florence.

"I used to go to weekend sleepovers at [the Pound's] house. Her dad [Hudson Pound] would always stay up flirting and teasing with us. He was so handsome. I lost my virginity to him," she said on a TV interview.

"How old were you at the time?" the show's host asked.

"It was the summer before I turned fifteen."

"Then you were only *fourteen*-years-old?" the host asked in an astonished tone, slowly emphasizing "fourteen" as if it were two words.

"Yes," the woman replied, weeping.

Lester replayed the interview. The studio audience, consisting almost entirely of women, was riveted and appalled.

"A spokeswoman for Florence Pound claims she never knew you," the host said. "However, we have located two of your former teachers."

Two older women came on stage. Both took turns talking about Florence and the accuser as school girls. "They were inseparable," one said.

The president's approval ratings plummeted in spite of White House counter claims that neither of the "teachers" or the woman accusing Hudson appeared in any of the yearbooks, and no school system records indicated any of them were actually there during that time.

Many of Florence's classmates and actual teachers came forward to deny ever knowing the woman who made the accusations, or the teachers corroborating her story. However, most media outlets didn't cover the rebuttals and denials. Instead, they replayed earlier claims by other women and the interview of the woman saying she was only fourteen. White House spokespersons insisted all the records had been faked, and that the media was complicit in the character assassination job.

At the same time, another scandal broke that Hudson had plagiarized papers in college. A firm Lester had secretly contracted produced evidence they fed to the hungry media firms, happy to contribute to the takedown of Hudson. Lester had also crafted a grand scheme to go after Schueller next.

"The White House is right," Lester told his right-hand man. "There's no need to hire an assassin to take out the president when the media will do the same thing. And it's a lot more fun to watch."

"But not all the media is playing along," the man said.

"Yeah, it's not like the old days when there were only three or four TV channels and the wire services to feed. Much less control now, but that also has its advantages. The more controversy, the better," Lester said, laughing heartily.

CHAPTER FORTY

The president's travel schedule was the most restricted of any president in history due to the threats arrayed against him. When he did travel, extreme measures had been put in place which far exceeded those implemented by his predecessors. When flying aboard the presidential helicopter, Marine One, three decoys flew in unison, along with four armed gunships.

Due to the difficulty and risks associated with moving the president in the NorthBridge era, Hudson visited the secure Camp David retreat more than any other president. He often felt like a prisoner in the White House, and with limited options, the two thousand wooded acres seemed like total freedom in the wilderness. The thirty-minute flight also gave him a chance to catch up on intelligence reports. Melissa often stayed there for a week at a time, able to accomplish more with fewer distractions. She also felt it caused Hudson to come to the relative safety of Camp David more than he would otherwise.

On this trip, back to the White House, he reviewed the latest summaries from the Wizard, Granger, and Rex. As he read one of the REMies' recent MADE events and looked over Granger's latest revisions to the "Fair and Free" plan they hoped would one day replace the current corruption, he had difficulty concentrating on the financial minutia and complex structures.

A new sexual misconduct allegation had surfaced. This time from a "former Pound Hardware store employee. He didn't remember the woman, and had already checked with his sister Trixie. The accuser had never worked for him, but like the previous claims, the media ran the salacious stories first and asked questions later.

Suddenly the pilot shouted an expletive through the intercom, then yelled, "Brace! Brace!"

Successive explosions erupted in the air around Marine One. From the large rectangle windows, the president watched in horror as two of the decoy helicopters, which had been flying in tandem, spiraled to the ground in flames. More ordnances, threatening Marine One, blazed past.

"We're going down!"

Hudson assumed a crash position, but seconds later the pilot clarified that they'd be making an emergency landing.

"The military is already responding, Mr. President," another official said as they descended rapidly. "Four F-15 Eagles have been scrambled. They're en route at supersonic speed. ETA three and a half minutes."

With all the current chaos and uncertainty, Hudson didn't know if that made him feel any better. He knew there were those inside the Pentagon who were appalled and alarmed by his presidency, some even disgusted at the negotiations with China, the calls for peace, and, of course, his proposed massive defense budget cuts. The Wizard had warned him that assassination attempts could come from inside the Pentagon, either sponsored by REMie controllers, or even independent plots. Yet as Marine

One neared the ground, still taking fire, he knew that the most likely culprits were individual REMies, possibly Bastendorff or Coyne. At the same time, he didn't discount the fact that it might also have been NorthBridge. Both Fonda and Booker had made it clear that NorthBridge was far from a unified body, and even though they had acted in the past with precision and discipline, elements within the increasingly powerful terror group could initiate unsanctioned attacks. Dranick and others had warned that the known NorthBridge leadership—Booker, Fonda, and Thorne—might be losing control of the different factions within the terror organization.

Marine One hit the ground hard, jostling the president. Before he had time to stand, or think what to do next, rough hands of a Marine pulled him up and pushed him toward the door.

"Go, go, go!"

Another Marine clamped a locator bracelet on Hudson's wrist.

"Mr. President, we have to get you away from any target," a different Marine shouted as they moved away from the helicopter.

"Aren't *I* the target?" the president asked breathlessly as they jogged.

Four Secret Service agents surrounded the president. Hudson tried to count all the people shielding him. "Who's attacking?" he asked, shaken. His combat training and experience left him better prepared for this kind of situation than any of the previous attempts on his life. Colorado had also been similar, but his daughter and Fitz's presence changed the priority of that mission.

"We've got to make cover," the Marine ordered.

It could be a rogue unit of NorthBridge, members who had

moved farther to the extremes even beyond Thorne, or it could be a foreign actor—terrorist, or state, seeking to strike a weakened America.

"You're much harder to hit than that big bird there," the Marine answered his earlier question about being the target. "We're moving to the tree line."

There wasn't much daylight left. Hudson estimated ten to fifteen minutes before the twilight would go dark. It was difficult to know just where they were, but it looked to be some sort of rural suburban area.

They made it to the trees. As another chopper landed and six more Marines jogged toward them, he wondered again if the military might have staged the event to take him out. Listening to the cross-talk on the many radios, he ascertained that several more were securing the helicopters. As they stumbled through the trees, Hudson was beginning to think the threat had passed until an explosion shook him. Seconds later one of the Marine's radios crackled with the report that they had lost Marine One. Fortunately, there had been no casualties.

"Where are we?" the president asked.

"Somewhere outside Germantown, Maryland."

"Where are we going?"

"Still working on that, sir. There's a housing development on the other side of these trees," the Marine said while looking into his GPS and urging everyone to move faster.

"The FAA has already cleared a no-fly zone and grounded or diverted all planes within a four-hundred-mile radius," someone else reported.

"Have any other attacks . . . is the vice president safe?" the president asked.

"Yes, sir, Nobel is secure," a Secret Service agent responded, using Vice President Brown's code name.

"Thus far, no other attacks detected," a Marine replied.

The tree line ended at a field, which turned out to be a large backyard in a row of generously spaced McMansions.

"Looks like we found a temporary refuge," the Marine said.

"Do we know anybody there? Are they Republicans?" the president asked, trying to inject some humor to defuse the tension.

"Sir," the Marine began, "we are trying to get you out of harm's way."

"I know that, but who's giving you your orders?"

"I've got standing orders," the Marine responded, moving rapidly away from them toward the house.

"DC is talking in my ear," a Secret Service agent said.

Hudson looked over at his trusted Secret Service agent as if to ask, *Are we okay?*

The agent responded by moving closer to the president and spoke only a few inches from his ear. "As of this moment, the Marines have jurisdiction, but you can change that."

"Mr. President, wait here," another Marine said, halting the group as two Marines ran into the yard and the remaining Marines took perimeters fifteen feet apart. The Secret Service closed in tighter around the president. "Teacher in gauntlet," one of them said into his wrist.

"What's to stop whoever was shooting at us back there?" the president began. "Do we know yet who was shooting at us?"

No one answered.

"What's to stop them from blowing up this house?" he continued. "If we go in there, aren't we a big target again?"

One of the Marines ran back and signaled the group to move across the field.

"Or getting us while we're in the open?" the president persisted.

Still no answers.

Two military jets buzzed overhead at low altitude. "I assume those are ours," the president said. By now he knew he was talking to himself.

Several helicopters could be heard getting closer.

"And I damn sure hope those helicopters are ours!"

CHAPTER FORTY-ONE

B *oom, boom!*
      Someone shoved the president forcefully to the ground.
He hit the cold, damp lawn and his military training kicked in,
instantly rolling and scanning for cover. Old injuries from prior
attacks reminded him he wasn't twenty anymore.

"What's going on?" he snapped in a whisper, trying to see
where the explosion had come from.

Several Marines crouched around. The Secret Service agents
stood with guns drawn. Even after his movement, the perimeter
remained around him. Other Marines continued to move toward
the house.

"We're still trying to track the source," a Marine said. "The
ordnance detonated over the woods."

As fiery shards rained down over the trees they'd just come
through, two agents grabbed the president's arms and hoisted him
to his feet. The three of them kept low as they pushed him
toward the house.

"Move, move, move!"

The president's foot caught in a hose and sprinkler and he

tripped. Before he could even hit the ground, Secret Service agents caught him and supported him upright until his feet found ground again. Seconds later, they were at the home's backdoor that the Marines had just kicked in.

They found themselves in a large kitchen—granite countertops, stainless steel appliances, mahogany cabinets. The agents had Hudson crouch between the island range and kitchen sink while the Marines and two Secret Service agents searched the house. He heard screams and guessed they belonged to the homeowners.

Some poor family, he thought, *just minding their own business, probably watching TV, trying to relax on a Sunday evening.*

A few minutes later a Marine reported back, "House secure."

"What are we dealing with?" one of the agents asked.

"Family of four," the Marine said, making eye contact with the agent and then looking back over his shoulder. "We have them in the basement. Married couple, son—twelve, daughter —nine."

"You didn't hurt them, did you?" the president asked. "They aren't part of this plot."

"They are unharmed," the Marine said. "Their level of involvement is still unknown."

The president shook his head and laughed in annoyed amusement. "We randomly stumbled into this house to seek refuge. We could have gone anywhere. The odds that they're involved are miniscule."

"That's above my pay grade, Mr. President. Smarter people than me solve those problems."

"No doubt," the president said, looking from the Marine to a Secret Service agent. "Take me to talk to them."

"Negative," the Marine said.

"I wasn't asking," the president snapped. "It was an order. In fact, bring them up to the living room."

The Marine looked at the Secret Service agent, the communication clear.

"Yes, sir," the Marine said, turning on his heel and heading back to the basement.

"Take me to the living room," the president said to his agent.

The shaken family marched into the living room a few minutes later.

"I'm extremely sorry for this intrusion," the president said to the parents.

"Oh my God," the mother said. "You're the president."

"Guilty as charged." He turned to the Marine. "You didn't tell them?"

"At first, we thought it was a robbery," the husband spoke up. "Then we thought it was some sort of mistaken identity drug bust or something, then we realized they were soldiers and we didn't know what to think."

"I was flying back from Camp David," the president began. "Someone shot our helicopters out of the sky. We did an emergency landing. Marine One got hit after we were out."

"That's awful," the mother said.

"We aren't sure who's shooting at us or where they are. That's about right, isn't it?" he asked, looking from the Marines to the Secret Service agents for confirmation.

"Oh my God," the mother repeated. "Then we're all in real danger."

"I'm afraid so," the president said. "However, you can be assured that all manner of assets possessed by the mightiest military on earth are converging on this spot as we speak." He reached out his hand toward the woman. "We'll be okay."

She held his hand for a moment and looked into his eyes as if thinking, *This man never dies.*

The president shook the father's hand. "I'm truly sorry about this intrusion and about how you were treated. Sometimes my security team is overzealous." He asked the son and daughter their names as he shook their hands. "We're going to get out of your way just as soon as we can, and we'll see to it that you get a new back door. I'm not sure why they couldn't just knock, but they've got a tough job. Apparently, a lot of people don't like me."

The president quietly told an aide, who had been in a trailing group and just caught up with them, to be certain the family was invited to the White House. "Also send them flowers from the first lady and myself," the president added. "And make sure a crew gets here to do permanent repairs."

"Yes, sir," the aide replied.

It wasn't long before a military Black Hawk helicopter landed on the front lawn. Seven others hovered above. With efficient precision, the president was whisked away. On the flight back to the White House, he was informed that two "adversarial" helicopters and a makeshift ground base from where the missiles had originated had been destroyed.

"Has NorthBridge claimed responsibility?" the president asked.

"Not yet," the commander on board told him.

Hudson didn't think they would. Although the operation reminded him of the attack during his campaign in Colorado, which had been ordered by someone in NorthBridge, he didn't believe that Booker, Fonda, or even Thorne would be looking to take him out right now. But he had to admit that he didn't know about the other NorthBridgers.

We've got to find out who AKA Adams is before NorthBridge turns this into a full-scale revolution.

CHAPTER FORTY-TWO

The first lady and Schueller had flown back to Washington as soon as they were informed of the attack on the president. They'd been attending a Free Food Foundation event in North Carolina. The media reported the news almost instantly as the nation stood once again gripped with fear that the president might be killed, and if NorthBridge could reach him, then no one was safe.

Florence and all of Hudson's siblings phoned him even before he'd landed back in DC, and in the coming days the White House was inundated with well wishes from across the country and around the globe. Countless world leaders sent their concerns and congratulations that Hudson had survived yet another horrible assault. Mexico and Canada promised continued full cooperation and new efforts to assist in apprehending NorthBridgers on their side of the borders.

However, within hours it became clear that NorthBridge had not been responsible for this latest attack. Information gathered by the Wizard and Granger showed a broken but likely trail leading back to Bastendorff. Not enough to prosecute or go public with, but the substance made it clear that NorthBridge hadn't been involved.

"There's another possibility," the Wizard had told him. "It's real esoteric, even Granger thinks I'm crazy, but there's something in the cycle of data that could mean this is actually a double frame, kind of a dual reality . . . "

"In English, please," the president had said.

"Someone might have made it look like Bastendorff was trying to make it look like a NorthBridge attack."

"Who would do that?"

"Only another REMie," the Wizard had said. "I can't prove any of this yet, and may never. The DarkNet is deep with secrets and mystery, but the truth is swirling in there somewhere, buried by bits and bits under infinite encryption. The military might have even been involved. That was high-end hardware."

"Granger said it definitely wasn't NorthBridge, but are we sure?" Hudson had asked, suddenly concerned.

"Ahh, you're thinking it could be a triple frame."

"I'm so paranoid."

"For good reason . . . nothing is ever sure during the CapWars."

Colonel Enapay Dranick, as Director of National Intelligence, also briefed the president every day on the latest threats and intelligence gathering efforts. With the NorthBridge threat, the growing number of other "counter-groups" emboldened by NorthBridge's "success," and increased REMie activity, in addition to all the normal crazies, it was always a substantive and very often disturbing meeting.

"Mr. President," Dranick began. Although addressing his old friend by his formal title, the DNI spoke in a relaxed manner.

"Yesterday Three-D picked up this man," he said, showing a photo. "Turns out he's an employee of Titus Coyne."

Hudson knew 3D captured virtually every American every single day, so waited for the reason why this was news. The 3D system had become incredibly invasive, penetrating some of the most private spaces and intimate moments.

"And we also got film of this woman who works for Karl Bastendorff."

Hudson realized where this was going even before Dranick told him the rest. "They were meeting?"

"More than meeting," Dranick said, showing him more footage of the two subjects entering an expensive hotel together.

"Very interesting," Hudson said. "And I assume Three-D picked them up in the lobby again?"

"Yes," Dranick said. "And in the hall on the fourteenth floor. Then we switched to cell phone captures." He pointed to dual image streams presented on a split screen. "We got both of their phones linked. The pictures aren't great because of the angle of the phones most of the time. However, fear not, we do have audio. "

"I don't have to watch them have sex, do I?" the president asked.

"No, and you don't have to listen either. Although it was quite a performance," Dranick said, winking. "Let me fast-forward through this part . . . here we go."

"*Bastendorff is going after the president,*" the woman could be heard saying. "*All the trouble on US bases around the world, the exploding domestic urban crime . . . he's making it happen.*"

"*Titus is playing the same game—raising interest rates, and all those corporate layoffs. He's also manipulating stocks,*" the man replied.

"*Pound's already overwhelmed by NorthBridge,*" she said.

"*Soon he may wish he hadn't come back after his nine-minute exit.*"

"*If things get much worse in this country, someone will find a way to send him back again . . . this time for a lot longer than nine minutes.*"

"Interesting timing," the president said. "You saw the data on Bastendorff and my Marine One mishap."

"Yeah," Dranick said. "He doesn't like you too much."

"Obviously that REMie must think I'm a threat. We must be doing something right." He pointed back to the screen. "That was a good grab. It'll be interesting to see where this leads. We needed a break like this."

Although Hudson appreciated the intel, he was still uncomfortable by how it was gathered. One of the first things he'd learned as president was that the public had absolutely no privacy anymore. Post-9/11 legislative changes, such as the Patriot Act, allowed the government to intrude on every aspect of the lives of its citizens. What little privacy remained had been fully eroded by 3D. People had grown accustomed to cameras in Walmart parking lots, at intersections, ATMs, convenience stores, and slowly accepted them into more and more of their lives.

Hudson's thoughts drifted, as they often did, when faced with the reach of the REMies empire. *Even after Edward Snowden told the world that the NSA could listen and watch us through our phones, computers, and televisions, the people hardly seemed to notice,* he thought. *And now the government and their contractors can see every aspect of our lives—they know who we're talking to, who we're seeing, where we're going, the keystrokes on our computers, how much is in our banks, what we spent it on and where, whether we've been naughty or nice.*

"We're going to track them," Dranick said. "Coyne and

Bastendorff hate each other. They obviously have no idea that two of their top people are messing around."

"Unless it's a set-up."

Dranick nodded. He'd already thought of that possibility and ruled it out due to the nature and circumstances of the encounter. "Eventually we'll have a talk with them."

The president gave his old friend a hard look. "Enapay, we're running out of time."

"We sure are."

CHAPTER FORTY-THREE

The president stood overlooking the Potomac River at Vonner's picturesque estate, as he had many times with the late billionaire. However, now the estate belonged to Schueller, and this time he was there with Kensi, Vonner's former attorney, Senator Sheri Bennett of Hawaii, and a congressman from Vermont. As he turned, he caught the glint of binoculars from across the river and assumed it belonged to his security detail, since they routinely worked both sides of the Potomac when he visited.

Kensi had brought the three of them together because Vonner had put each of them in office. The senator and congressman had been hand-selected and financially backed by the late REMie. Like Hudson, they were also independent of the empire, which made them the rarest of politicians on Capitol Hill. They also shared a common goal to end the REMies empire-system.

They waited as Hudson stared out at the great river, churning muddy rapids. His mind continually reevaluating everything he had ever thought about Vonner, the man who had put him in position to bring down the empire.

And yet, what would have become of Vonner if he'd still been alive when I succeed?

Finally, Hudson spoke. "I don't understand why he didn't just tell me. Vonner knew I didn't trust him, how come he couldn't convince me?"

"As you know, Arlin Vonner was a complicated man," Kensi replied, standing in front of the three political leaders. "It's a hard thing to wrap your head around . . . that a tiny group of incredibly wealthy people had built an invisible empire that not only completely controls the world economy, but also initiates or manipulates virtually every major event, including wars, scandals, and the rise and fall of our politicians." She swept her arm at the three of them. "Then you discover that the person who helped you gain your own power was one of the 'emperors.' It's understandable that it would be hard to trust a man like that, under the circumstances, when he was both your most important ally and one of the most powerful among your enemy. But I'd bet that he tried to tell you the truth—that he wanted to end the empire. I know Arlin Vonner had a plan for each one of you."

Hudson nodded, recalling election night, when Vonner had assured him that he wanted to bring down the REMie empire, that he'd chosen Hudson and put him in the White House to do just that.

How sure and arrogant I'd been, thinking that I knew a better way to go about getting the REMies than Vonner did, a man more familiar with the REMies' empire than anyone, a man who had accumulated astronomical wealth within that system.

Hudson shook his head, disappointed in himself, wondering how much he could've learned from Vonner, how much further along they'd be if he'd just followed the old man's timeline . . . and trusted.

But that was over now. The meeting today was to see how much help the senator and congressman could offer in getting through some of the anti-REMie legislation he needed as part of his radical reforms.

"Right now, your programs are all dead on arrival," Senator Bennett said. "As you know, most of those in the Congress are controlled by various REMies."

"Of course," Hudson said, then he paused. Vonner had also chosen them. Kensi had said they were trustworthy. He needed every friend he could find. Hudson took a deep breath, and then for the next half an hour, outlined the Cherry Tree plan. He held nothing back.

"Bold," the senator said when the president finished.

"It's risky," the congressman said. "But if Cherry Tree works, and the REMies' lies are made public, the voters may well demand action."

"That's what I'm counting on." Hudson had chosen not to tell them about the Kennedy papers, which he was counting on to add some emotional spark to the release.

"I know a number of senators who would love to see the REMies empire crumble," the senator said. "Even though they benefit from the corruption, they see the damage."

"Likewise, I could name dozens in the House who might not have full knowledge of the REMies web, but would be willing to vote for real reform."

"There are many politicians who lean away from the elites. We can target them, have a mass campaign ready to flood them with voters from their home states as soon as Cherry Tree goes."

"We've got a list, already building, of politicians to include in the first wave," the president said. "In addition, there's a plan where the most corrupt senators and members of Congress would be charged and prosecuted by the FBI on day one."

"The FBI has been fully infiltrated by REMies," the senator said.

"We know," the president replied, knowing the squeaky-clean DIRT teams were already accumulating evidence. "That part will be handled."

"Going after the FBI, too?" the congressman asked. "Brave."

"Cherry Tree is a huge operation," Kensi said, having been fully briefed. "Gather public support, get the friendly politicians on board, kick out the corrupt ones, and scare all those in the middle into doing the right thing. Arresting REMies, seizing assets, and at the same time introducing the most radical financial, political, and governmental reforms in American history . . . "

"And it might work," the president said.

"Depending on how far NorthBridge goes," the congressman added. "If the country is in the middle of a revolution and all order breaks down, the people won't give two hoots about the crimes of the elites. They'll be too busy trying to find food and medicine."

"That's why we're moving soon."

"When?"

"Soon," the president repeated. "I'm sure you understand, even if I knew exactly when, I couldn't say. But you'll get at least thirty minutes notice."

"By God, I think you might pull this off," the congressman said, looking admiringly at Hudson.

"If you live long enough," the senator added.

Suddenly Schueller came running across the lawn. "Dad! Dad!" His face didn't look happy.

CHAPTER FORTY-FOUR

The president, suddenly surrounded by aides, began moving toward Marine One even before Schueller could finish his account of the coverage he'd seen online. A suspected North-Bridge attack on Minton Micro, a California-based computer chip maker, had instantly captured the world's attention, as the initial explosion and resulting carnage had all been broadcast live on the internet. Hundreds of millions of smartphones showed the horror and graphic details.

"They've gone too far," the president said, slapping a file folder down on the Resolute Desk as he entered the Oval Office immediately upon his return to the White House. "I suppose this is in response to my stepping up the pressure against NorthBridge. I swear it, we're going to release the names this time."

Schueller, who'd flown back to Washington with him, quickly scanned the room to see who else had heard his father's statement. "Is that wise?" he asked quietly.

"Mr. President," an aide began before Hudson could respond to Schueller, "Minton Micro has Defense Department contracts."

Hudson wasn't surprised. "NorthBridge always has a reason. The terror group's ruthless campaign against the REMie empire knows no innocents."

"Mr. President!" Schueller said sternly, while leaning close and motioning toward the cabinet members and other non-inner-circle aides in attendance behind him.

Hudson, caught by his son's use of his formal title, quickly reined in his emotions and nodded at Schueller. At the same moment, Hudson's private phone rang. He couldn't believe Fonda Raton had the nerve to call right then. "I need the room cleared," he said to Fitz. "*Now.*"

"Ladies and gentlemen, we need to move this to the Situation Room," Fitz began. "The president will join us there . . . " He turned back to Hudson, who held up his hand, indicating five minutes. "In a few minutes."

Absently, he automatically returned Schueller's wave as his son followed the others out of the Oval Office. Hudson hit a command icon on his phone which would put the call on extended ring and stole a quick glance at a screen, displaying the latest information on the Minton Micro attack, before accepting Fonda's call.

The brutal attack on the chip maker had left six hundred and twelve employees killed and more than nine hundred injured. NorthBridge, which had usually been so careful to avoid unnecessary casualties, had seemingly changed the rules. Their website initially claimed responsibility in a post signed by AKA Franklin, but the page had since been taken down. NorthBridge had issued several denials on their website and through media channels. Hudson suspected the group's leaders had not anticipated the amount of bloodshed and public outcry, and were now attempting to distance themselves from the bad PR. The mainstream media hadn't bought into their reversal, and still blamed the terror organization, noting that NorthBridge backpedaled only after public opinion turned on them. InstaPolling had already shown that NorthBridge's support among the public was collapsing.

The president quickly stepped behind a panel in the Oval Office wall and hastily descended into the secret tunnels to take the call.

"It's a set-up, Hudson," Fonda said as the president opened the line. "This catastrophe is a false flag. Someone inside the deep state has done this with REMie backing to discredit NorthBridge."

"I don't think NorthBridge needs any help being discredited," the president said while wandering the tunnels beneath the White House. He had taken to this habit as soon as he discovered the passageway from the residence. Another narrow staircase which led to the subterranean labyrinth from the Oval Office had become one of his favorite retreats. He was perfectly safe, and nobody knew he was there other than two of his most trusted VS agents who followed him into the "underground."

"Ask yourself," Fonda said, sounding more angry than desperate. "Why would NorthBridge attack a computer chip maker?"

"You tell me," the president said, thinking of the DoD connection.

"Minton Micro is owned by the Chinese," Fonda said.

Hudson hadn't previously known that, but wasn't sure it should change his mind. He walked slowly along one of the main corridors as his security detail kept their distance. All known entrances to the secret tunnels were also guarded by his elite team, consisting of VS and approved Secret Service agents.

"The Chinese," she repeated. "Who wants bad relations between the US and China more than the REMies? More than the deep state? They haven't given up on the idea of war. They look at your victory in Beijing as just a delay, not something that will stop the war."

"Come on, Fonda, that's a stretch. How is some terrorist organization blowing up a Chinese-owned computer factory going to start a war?"

"That factory doesn't just make chips for video games, children's toys, and cheap phones," she said. "Minton Micro manufactures communications and military grade hardware and equipment—the brains *and* workings."

"Well then they're one of Booker's competitors," the president said. "Now it all makes sense."

"Be serious! Booker doesn't blow up his competitors. He knows how to beat them the old-fashioned way." Fonda fell silent for a moment. Hudson started to say something else when she continued. "REMies get a three-for," Fonda said.

"A what?"

"One: they knock out a risk posed by certain things that firm was manufacturing. Two: at the same time they cause tension between the US and China. Three: the big score—they get to discredit their great enemy, NorthBridge. Three-for-one quick bombing."

"The problem is," the president began in a somber tone, "you cannot be trusted, Fonda. Even if what you're saying *is* true, I simply can't believe you anymore."

"Then check it out. Launch an investigation."

"Oh, don't worry about that. There'll be lots of investigations," the president said. "But you and I both know that'll take a long time before we learn the truth."

"Or what they're *calling* 'the truth' these days," Fonda said in a flat tone.

"Here's some advice for you; if you don't want to get blamed for blowing things up that you say you didn't blow up, then just stop blowing things up."

"We. Did. Not. Do. This."

"It's not too hard to think NorthBridge is responsible, since every few weeks you do something just like this."

"No," Fonda said. "Review everything that NorthBridge has ever done. Put it into your computer program that finds patterns. Your friend, the Wizard, ought to be able to help you with that."

Hudson wasn't surprised she knew about the Wizard and the Gypsy program. Still, he felt exposed. Fonda always knew too much. He silently wondered who AKA Adams was, and why AKA Franklin kept the lowest profile, then shivered in the dimly lit section of the tunnels.

"You'll find that the Minton Micro attack doesn't fit any of the others NorthBridge has done."

"What about NorthBridge taking credit?"

"A simple hack."

"Northbridge can't be hacked."

"*Anyone* can be hacked. Who do you think controls the internet?"

The Empire, Hudson thought.

"NorthBridge would not have attacked that plant," Fonda continued, "and you know it. It's the REMies and if you go on letting everybody blame NorthBridge, then you're aiding the REMies and they'll get away with it. That means you're not only helping them win, but you're also a coward."

Hudson stared at his phone in disbelief. "How dare you call me a coward! I'm here in front of the world risking my life to fight the REMies while you and your friends hide behind aliases and bombs! Why don't you think about who's *really* the coward here."

"Oh, I'm sorry," Fonda said sarcastically. "Are you really out there in the public fighting the REMies? I don't see you giving speeches about who the REMies are, what the REMies are doing, or how you're going to stop them. I don't see any of that. You seem to be doing an awful lot of hiding yourself."

"History will judge," Hudson said. "History will judge me, and history will judge NorthBridge."

"Most of the history you know was written by the REMies."

"There have been some notable exceptions," the president corrected. "Historians attempting to tell a straight account of history, Howard Zinn for one—"

Fonda sighed an interruption and continued her lecture. "As far as what people in the future will read about what happened during this time, I can tell you one thing: if they are allowed to read about it at all—the *truth* of it, I mean—it will be only because NorthBridge was here, and NorthBridge did what had to be done in order to save the future."

"NorthBridge may just be a vehicle Booker's using to win the CapWar," Hudson snapped. "You may think you're part of some great cause, but don't forget Booker is a REMie. Perhaps you're just part of a massive MADE event."

"Did Vonner tell you that?" Fonda shot back. "Just like he told you that Trump was a mistake? When, in fact, Trump *was* the massive MADE event."

"What are you talking about?"

"There was a group of REMies who decided their best chance at winning the CapWar was to put in a giant disrupter, a distractor . . . a bull in a china shop. Trump was perfect. Remember, each MADE event has to *trump* the one before as the public becomes immune to scandals, and the latest crisis is boring after twenty-four hours. They gave us an actor, a CIA man no one liked, but that was payback, a young governor who couldn't keep his pants on, a president's son just in time to handle 9/11, a handsome and eloquent African American, and then how could they top that? By then, the internet and twenty-four hour news cycle, the instant and viral social media, and all the polarization they had created, meant the perfect choice was reality TV."

"You're off-topic."

"*No, I'm not,*" Fonda said, as if spitting the words. "Trump was a while ago, but remember what it was like? Every day another outrage, another scandal, another tweet, another *distraction.*"

"We were talking about Booker."

"No," Fonda said, "we're talking about the truth, and the truth is your vote doesn't count. The truth is you really aren't free. The truth is a bigger lie than you can believe. And the truth is you believe it anyway."

"The truth hurts," Hudson said. "Especially when it lies . . . "

"That may be the truest thing you've ever said," Fonda said slowly, and then, lowering her voice to a whisper, added, "Goodbye, Mr. President."

As he raced up to join the gathering that hopefully Fitz was keeping going, Hudson puzzled why Fonda had even bothered to make the call.

Did I miss something?

CHAPTER FORTY-FIVE

D ays after the Minton Micro attack, the president, flanked by a large security detail, walked the winding path through a heavily wooded section of Rock Creek Park in Washington, DC. The two-thousand-acre sanctuary sometimes seemed almost invisible in the bustling capital city.

Eventually, he found Tarka seated on a pile of large carved stones, which looked as if they'd been haphazardly stacked there by ancient giants. His agents spread out and took positions among the trees and slabs of carved rock.

"What is this place?" the president asked.

"It's called 'The Capitol Stones,'" Tarka responded. "Back in 1958, during renovations of the US Capitol Building, the architect stripped these old stones from the project. Some of them date back to the 1700s, before the burning of Washington. Apparently, it was illegal to sell or dispose of the historic stone, so . . . " Tarka waved her arm out to the ruins.

Hudson looked around at the piles of sandstone, marble slabs, and granite blocks, some ten or twenty feet high, many at least partially covered with moss and lichen, an effort by the earth to reclaim what was once her own. Some of them had ornate carvings, etched letters or numbers, decorative curls and scrolls.

"It seems a strange decision to have just abandoned them here," the president said, eyeing her. "Also, an unusual meeting place."

"Absolute privacy," Tarka, the head of Vonner Security, said in a tone of combined experience and confidence.

Hudson walked between two massive stacks into a long alley. The thick foliage and aged white and gray stones made him feel as if he were discovering ancient Mayan ruins in a central American jungle.

Tarka, having already explored several times, followed the president.

"I need you to do something," Hudson said, stopping at a panel detailed with eagles and carved leaves. He handed her a printed list. "Can you put together teams to shadow and protect these people?"

"I don't understand," Tarka said, scanning the page. "You want me to guard REMies? It really wouldn't hurt my feelings if these people landed in harm's way."

"NorthBridge is no longer content to attack REMie institutions," the president said, a tinge of anger in his voice. "Now they're targeting the REMies themselves."

"By assassination?"

"We uncovered a NorthBridge plot to take out Titus Coyne."

"These men all have their own adequate or better protection teams," she said.

"Yes, they do, but not up to the level of Vonner Security, and not with our access to intelligence. I'd like you to personally head up the team that gets assigned to Coyne."

"What about Bastendorff?" she asked, pointing to his name on the list. "Isn't he more important?"

"Yes, but as far as I know, you don't want Coyne dead."

She looked at him with her best puzzled expression.

"I know that given the chance, you would kill Bastendorff yourself," Hudson said, tracing his fingers over the talons of a stone eagle. "Too tempting."

Tarka nodded quietly. "What about you?" Tarka had not been providing the president with round-the-clock protection as she did when Vonner was alive, but it was still her primary mission, and she was never far away. This new assignment would take her around the globe and definitely be a distraction.

"Thanks to your efforts, we have an incredibly deep and talented VS force." He gazed at her with sincere appreciation. "Between Colonel Dranick and Agent Bond, we've also created a locked and truly impressive Secret Service detail . . . one we can trust."

"I understand," she said. "I know that Rex, the Wizard, and Granger Watson have significantly increased the digital and electronic safety nets around you, but still, with NorthBridge, the REMies, and all the usual nut cases, you're the most targeted man on earth. I think you need me here."

"Not if REMies start dropping like flies. Then we won't just have a Civil War in this country, we'll have an all-out global war between the one percent and everyone else."

"Aren't we heading to that anyway?" Tarka asked as they rounded a corner and came face-to-face with some kind of marble gargoyle half covered in dry leaves. "And would that really be such a bad thing?"

"I have this debate continually," the president said. "If we aren't painfully careful, absolutely meticulous, in how we break the REMies' empire, the result will be anarchy." Hudson brushed some of the leaves off the mythical stone creature. "The system is extremely fragile. Even if we do nothing, it could all collapse under its own weight with the wrong news story, or a financial domino falling at the wrong time. No, NorthBridge is being reckless, and they can't be allowed to push us to the brink."

"Forgive me, Mr. President, but isn't going too slow also risky?" They both knew she had earned the right to be blunt and question his methods. He would not be alive if not for her.

Hudson wasn't surprised at her question, and he understood the meaning between the lines. "You mean, can't we just kill the forty-eight key REMies over a weekend and pick up the pieces from there?"

She couldn't help but smile.

"On some days, I'd like to do just that," he admitted. "But however tempting that course might be, not only is it morally wrong, it would crash the empire instantly, resulting in pandemonium so severe that we would be unable to climb out of it . . . the end of the world."

She nodded, unconvinced, but committed to following orders. "Okay," she said. "But at least promise me you'll keep an open mind."

"Believe me, Tarka, after all I've been through the past few years, all I've got left is an open mind."

After the meeting, Tarka immediately expanded VS operations and coordinated with Rex, Granger, and the Wizard, on a strategy to protect the most important REMies. The Wizard had already been using the Gypsy program to track the REMies and overlay their movements and meetings with transactions and MADE events, so making the transition from surveillance to protection wasn't that difficult.

However, in spite of their efforts, three fairly well known REMies died during the next month. All three deaths were ruled as various natural causes, but VS investigations, as well as information from the DarkNet, contradicted those official findings. Hudson didn't need any of the Wizard's back channel facts to tell him that NorthBridge had successfully assassinated three REMies, or to know that more "natural" and "accidental" deaths were planned.

An overt attempt had been made on Titus Coyne's life, which Tarka and her team were able to prevent. Thus far, Bastendorff had been able to insulate himself from any direct attacks, but Hudson was worried it would only be a matter of time before more REMies fell and the world would begin to notice the "coincidence," shaking the markets, creating panic, and causing the remaining REMies to resort to incomprehensible tactics to save their empire.

CHAPTER FORTY-SIX

F itz caught up to the president in his private study prior to a Cabinet meeting. "Did you see the NorthBridge statement?"

"Reading it now," the president said.

It is time that we examine what we want to be as a nation and as a people. NorthBridge began originally to return us to the ideas set forth by the Founders of this country. We had hoped that through elections and education, our organization would be able to remind people that we don't have to be liberals and conservatives, Republicans and Democrats. None of those labels matter. What does matter is our pursuit of happiness, and that we use our precious freedom to take care of one another and our planet. Life is not a competition, it is a combination.

"Seems like an effort to rebuild their shattered reputation after Minton Micro," the president said.

The news of the attack on the California chip maker had hit while the president was in the middle of seeking support from members of Congress concerning his secret radical reforms for the government. NorthBridge had immediately been blamed for the horrors, but in recent days, Dranick and the Wizard had discovered evidence suggesting it had been a REMie operation, just as Fonda had claimed. Either way, it had been an awful distraction, and further delayed the planned Cherry Tree launch.

"Keep reading," Fitz urged as he opened a Coke.

However, there are those within NorthBridge who believe returning to the core constitutional values of America would take too long, or that it would be impossible to regain what was lost more than a century ago. And how was it lost? It was not. It was stolen from us by a group of elites—the 1% of the 1%—some of whom you read about in the business pages, some of whom remained hidden in the anonymity that allows them to rule from the shadows. What they all have in common is a lust for wealth and power that is limitless and unmatched by any definition of greed. These people seek to increase their wealth and control by any means necessary. They have manipulated and stolen the truth for so long that most of us have a hard time recognizing what is real and what has been created by this group known as the REMies.

"Wow," the president said. "Has any media picked this up yet?"

"None of the REMie-controlled main stream media," Fitz said. "But a few indie news sites are hyping it."

There are factions within NorthBridge who chose to utilize violence to incite a revolution to wake up the population to what is happening, to take it from beyond the fringes of conspiracy and shadow and paranoia to the light of day . . . to the mainstream. Those factions inside our organization have won more times than not. However, we have tried to minimize the loss of life and violence while still sending a clear signal to the REMies that we are not going to stop. We have always believed that eventually public opinion and knowledge would move in the right direction so that the REMies would no longer be able to hide.

I am one NorthBridger who stands for nonviolence. I'm sorry for every blast, every bullet, every act that has harmed another human life in the name of NorthBridge, yet I do not discount our progress. Please, we need you to join us, because it is only with the people that we will have enough power to stop the REMies. Don't be afraid. Through 3D and the NSA surveillance of your phone calls, Internet usage, and social media activity, the REMies have created a police state far more sinister than Orwell's worst nightmare. But because there are so many of us, and so few of them, we can win. REMies may have the dollars on their side, but here's a little secret: those dollars aren't worth the paper they're printed on. I ask that you join the resistance, and even if you won't join us, start questioning everything . . . especially authority.

Signed AKA Adams

"My God, AKA Adams has practically launched Cherry Tree for us!" the president exclaimed, getting up and looking out the window as if there might already be demonstrations in the streets. "We've got two choices now. We can either bring out Cherry Tree tomorrow, or delay it even further."

"The problem is, if we do Cherry Tree now," Fitz began, "it's going to look like we're endorsing NorthBridge."

"Exactly, but we can at least see what kind of momentum

they get," Hudson said. "If people respond to this, it could pave the way for our launch."

"That's certainly the most prudent approach," the chief of staff replied, stirring his soda as though it were a mixed drink. "Let's give it a few days, see what happens, then reevaluate."

After the Cabinet meeting, the president returned to his study and contacted the Wizard and Granger, instructing them to find out, once and for all, the identity of AKA Adams.

"This person is obviously the moderating force in North-Bridge, and that's who we need to talk to," Hudson told them. "If we can find out who it is, we might have a way in. Make it your top priority."

"Do you really want to work with these terrorists?" Melissa asked that evening in the residence.

"I don't think we have a choice," Hudson said. "And at least Thorne, Fonda, and Booker are known entities in the world. I know who they are. I know them *personally*. I think this will help."

"But can they be *trusted*?"

"Fonda once told me that no one could be trusted."

"Telling."

Hudson nodded. "The final investigation is going to show that NorthBridge didn't do Minton Micro."

"But they've done plenty."

"True, but this is a messy business."

"That's an understatement," Melissa said, massaging

Hudson's shoulders on the edge of the bed. "But why did AKA Adams come out with this now? It sounds like they know about Cherry Tree and want to undermine it."

"Adams may legitimately be tired of the attacks. Fonda has told me several times that there is extreme diversity within NorthBridge. Adams might be going rogue and trying to stem the violence by changing NorthBridge's direction from the outside."

"Or it's a publicity stunt because of all the fallout from Minton Micro."

"Maybe," Hudson said, falling back into her lap and wondering, not for the first time, if AKA Adams might be Linh, the leader of the Inner Movement. "If Adams really is the voice of reason, then we have to talk to her."

"Her?"

"Perhaps Adams is *you*," he quickly said, pulling Melissa on top of him.

"Wouldn't that be convenient?" she said, laughing.

"I can't stand what NorthBridge has been doing, but I can no longer deny that getting them on board with us could make all the difference." He pushed himself up on the bed. "I'm not sure we can beat the REMies while still fighting NorthBridge, but together . . . and Adams may have just given us the opening."

"As long as it's not a trick," Melissa said.

CHAPTER FORTY-SEVEN

The following morning, the idea of making a secret alliance with NorthBridge seemed even more imperative.

Fonda's been right all this time, he thought, *suggesting we needed each other to break the REMie empire.*

But instead of contacting Fonda, he called Linh.

"I need the truth," he said while walking among the trees on the west side of the south lawn. It was one of his favorite places on the White House grounds, an area where he didn't feel as much a prisoner. He often meditated there.

"Of course," the leader of the Inner Movement said, as if nothing else were possible.

"Are you AKA Adams?"

The silence lasted so long that he was at first convinced he'd been right, and then wasn't sure she was still there.

"Hello?" he said.

"I'm sorry," she said softly. "I'm just extremely surprised you could imagine me part of NorthBridge."

"Only after I saw the statement by AKA Adams denouncing the NorthBridge violence—"

"Don't forget those nine minutes. Don't waste the second chance you were given," she said, her voice still quiet, yet full of reverence. "You think the REMies have created this world, so out of balance in the last hundred years . . . it's started long before that. We've been lost for millennia. Now we're at this moment in history, and you have a chance . . . your words can show the people not just about the wrongs, but of the hope, not only pointing to all the darkness, but actually point them toward the light."

"Okay," he said. She always made him feel like he could do better, as if the cheapness of politics was weighing him down. He spotted Fitz coming through the trees. "I'll do my best."

"I know," she said. "And I'm sure you can count on AKA Adams to help."

"Then you know who Adams is?"

"So do you."

"I need a name," he said firmly, then added more gently, "*Please.*"

"I wish I could help, but that is not my story to tell."

"It's important," he pressed.

"Very."

Fitz was standing in front of him now.

"When you change your mind, you know where to find me," the president said.

"Look within," were her final words.

"What?" Hudson snapped at Fitz.

His chief of staff ignored his boss's mood. "We need to talk."

The president began walking back to the White House, his mind still distracted with speculating who AKA Adams was. As soon as he was done with Fitz, he'd contact the Wizard.

We have to find Adams and Franklin, we need to talk to them.

"The American public is being asked an awful lot from you Mr. President," Fitz began. "Even before your election, you claimed to be an outsider, yet you were backed by one of the wealthiest and most influential insiders there was. Arlin Vonner and all his baggage came with you into the White House."

"What's your point?"

"You stood against NorthBridge, with their attacks on your fellow candidates, the assassinations of your rivals, and finally you endured the repeated attempts on your own life. The people mourned for you when you died. Then, like Lazarus, you rose from the dead and came back to life!"

The president was hardly listening.

"After all of that, you opposed a popular war and somehow managed to hang on to their trust, or at least some of it, just a little longer."

"Are you going anywhere with this, Fitz?" the president interrupted.

"I am," he said, smiling and taking a sip of his Coke as if it were life-saving medicine. "And you've led the country through the most tumultuous time in American history, even more frightening and divided than the Civil War. I think even you'll admit that fact, based on where we are now, the scale of the country's problems in relation to its size."

"Are you writing my eulogy?"

Fitz would not be hurried. "The voters have forgiven you of all that. Even when their patience has grown thin with your inability to stop NorthBridge and the violence that has escalated throughout your term, even when a dozen or more women accused you of sexual harassment and misconduct dating back decades, you managed to keep their faith and hold on to some surprisingly positive numbers in your approval rating. You also got past all of that at the same time you've been pushing for radical changes in the way we all live our lives."

"*And?*" the president asked, showing the impatience he was feeling in the way only he could do—with a forced smile, his good looks accentuated by fiercely piercing blue eyes.

"If you go forward with Cherry Tree, from the shaky ground on which you stand, I don't believe they will go with you."

"What are you talking about?"

"It's too big. You know the old line 'it is easier to fool people, than to convince them they have been fooled?' Don't you see, Mr. President? That's exactly where we are. You're going to try to convince the American people that all this time, all their lives, and their parents and grandparents before them, has all been a lie. You simply cannot convince them they have been fooled."

"We have proof."

"What is proof anymore? Artificial Intelligence can photoshop reality so well that none of us can even be sure who we are."

"They'll know the truth." He stopped close to a large tree and put his hand on its trunk.

"No one wants to be told that they've been manipulated, especially when you try to explain how the whole system is just part of an empire controlled by a few dozen wealthy families. The people aren't going to go there with you. They won't want to believe it, and don't forget it's almost impossible to believe. At the same time, the media will be calling you crazy. Everybody will be against you—the media, the banks, the politicians, the teachers, the business community. *Everybody* is going to show that you're wrong, that you're a conspiracy freak. They'll claim that you're just making excuses for your failings. The timing is wrong. You. Have. To. Wait."

CHAPTER FORTY-EIGHT

The president broke his schedule and flew to the Hunter Mill mansion to confer with Granger and the Wizard.

"Fitz thinks Cherry Tree is DOA," the president said as the three men took advantage of the beautiful summer morning and walked outside. More than twenty VS and Secret Service agents were nearby, most of them invisible. "He thinks the REMies are just hoping I go public, then they'll pounce to totally discredit me. Fitz pointed to how the media buried AKA Adams statement about the REMies, and how politicians and business leaders made the claims into a joke."

"It doesn't matter," the Wizard said. "We're inside."

"Wait a minute." The president stopped and grabbed the Wizard's arm. "You're telling me you hacked into the CIA and NSA computers?"

Getting "inside" had long been a goal of the Wizard, going back to the early days with Zackers. Crane had also worked on the project, which certainly contributed to the murder of both hackers.

The Wizard smiled, looking gaunter than ever, his black hair pulled back into a stringy ponytail. He seemed to have developed a twitch on his left eye, too much Red Bull or something.

"I'm the president, I can just request the information that's in there."

"You don't really believe that, do you?" Granger asked as they walked the worn footpath along the edge of a deep creek in the woods that bordered the house.

"No, not anymore," Hudson admitted. "What did you find?"

"Stuff that will show the REMies to be the evil scourge that they are," the Wizard said. "We've got three occasions over the last fifty years, and four more over the last sixty, when the US military developed plans that were approved at the highest levels that would use special teams to commit acts of terrorism within the borders of the United States."

"To what end?" the president asked, already knowing the answer.

"The purpose was to convince the public to support illegal and unnecessary wars," Granger replied.

"It wasn't too long ago when this would've surprised me," the president said, "but I recall documents being released during the Trump administration that referred to Operation Northwoods. The Joint Chiefs of Staff had created that plan in the early 1960s with the intent to blame Cuban terrorists for attacks on Americans that would actually be conducted by secret US military units. The idea was to find a reason for the public to support a war against Cuba. Apparently, Kennedy decided not to go ahead with the false flag operation. Perhaps the idea of having our special ops units kill innocent Americans didn't sit so well."

"And the mainstream media, always a REMie tool, buried the story when those documents came to light fifty-five years after the fact," Granger said. "It should have been front page outrage."

"Obviously the military, the CIA, and the REMies were not

happy with Kennedy," the Wizard said, letting the implications of his statement hang in the air.

"There've been dozens of other times when they've done similar things; committing atrocities and then blaming the attacks and other incidents on someone else. you can see them detailed in the reports." Granger paused and looked at the president carefully.

The president sensed that Granger was struggling with information. "What is it?"

"The most significant occurrence of their dark strategy . . . was carried out in September 2001."

The president stared at Granger. The brilliant technologist never took his eyes from Hudson's. He only nodded.

"My God," Hudson said, looking over at the Wizard and thinking about how Schueller's wildest conspiracy theories had been true.

"We can also directly link the CIA to propaganda against the American people, beginning with a plan known as Operation Mockingbird, when the intelligence agency gained and exercised control over the media in a decades-long grand effort to sway public opinion and collect intelligence on our own citizens."

"I've heard of Operation Mockingbird," the president said. "The Church Committee, led by Senator Frank Church, exposed and ended the program."

"Only after some leaks," Granger said. "That was merely a cosmetic move. Most of their actions were never revealed, and they certainly never stopped. It goes on to this day. We have the evidence. The CIA has influence at hundreds of media outlets. The Agency internally creates bogus news stories to fit their narratives and objectives and distributes them with reporters who are either on-board with the program, or those who believe the news is legitimate. Then it snowballs as those reports are cited by other media outlets or picked up by the wire services."

"Fake news is real," the president said.

"Out of control real," the Wizard said. "We're way down the rabbit hole, Dawg. There's no way to figure out where we are in the alternate reality generated by the faux stories, because it's like a fictitious report causes ripples that become true . . . facts created from fiction. Things made true because of lies."

"So are the REMies controlling the media, or the CIA?" the president asked.

Granger shook his head. "Do the REMies control the CIA? Do the REMies control the media? Does the CIA control the media? Rhetorical questions, all with the same answer."

"The answer being we're screwed," the Wizard said.

"I've got proof of MADE events that have started wars from the Gulf of Tonkin to weapons of mass destruction."

The president looked down the steep bank of the creek, lost in thought. "We've got to put all of this into Cherry Tree. Can you have it fully authenticated so nobody can question it? If the American people see what's been done to them, they won't let the REMies stay in power for one more minute." *Fitz is wrong. After so long without the truth, the people crave it. It's water in a desert. They know something's wrong.* "They just need the truth."

"Absolutely." Granger stepped close to the edge and almost slipped, but the president grabbed him and hauled him back up. "Thanks," Granger said. "That's a slippery slope. A damn slippery slope."

The three friends all laughed.

"The thing is," the president said, turning serious again, "it's not just America. The REMies have done this to the whole world. And we have to make sure the whole world turns on the REMies at the same time. They must find no refuge."

CHAPTER FORTY-NINE

The president's phone rang. He glanced at the lit number and groaned in disbelief.

"Unbelievable . . . it's Fonda Raton."

"You're not going to take it?" the Wizard asked as the three were heading back to the mansion where Marine One was waiting to return the president to the White House.

Hudson pressed "Accept" and said, "Where are you?"

Fonda laughed. "Nice try." I just called to give you a chance to comment on the Mandy Engelbert story. Of course, it's a lot more than Mandy, isn't it? Maybe you could help us, because we're having a tough time keeping track of just how many women you've harassed, abused, damaged, or whatever."

"I thought you were a terrorist," Hudson said, "and here you are pretending to be a journalist again."

Granger rolled his eyes.

"Cute, very cute," Fonda said. "But I didn't call *just* about the bogus womanizing story."

"I certainly hope not."

"It's the CapWars," Fonda began. "In case you haven't

noticed, the REMies are out of control right now. They're desperate. The elites all sense this is the final CapWar, and you, Hudson, are the main obstacle."

"I know all this."

"No, you don't," she said emphatically. "We're out of time. There are REMies actually trying to take the CapStone by monopolizing the world's food supply. Others are attempting to control all the pharmaceuticals. They've been working for years on these schemes and have made great progress in getting greater numbers of the population to depend on those pharmaceuticals. Booker has uncovered a REMie-backed group called the 'Aylantik'. They're planning a plague, a worldwide pandemic."

"Why would they do that?" he asked, keeping his voice determinedly calm.

"It's a lot easier to control three billion people than seven billion," Fonda answered.

Hudson stared stunned at Granger and the Wizard, who could both hear the conversation. He might not have believed her if not for the information they'd just given him about the CIA killing Americans in order to further REMie objectives. Now he felt sick. *Can I stop these people in time? With their limitless power?* Lately he'd been wondering if the only reason he was still alive is that it served one of the REMies' schemes in the CapWar against the others.

"Are you there?" Fonda asked.

"Yes, I just don't know if I should believe you."

"Fair enough. You don't have to. Just look into it. Have your brain trust there prove me right or wrong. But it's true," Fonda said, pausing taking a deep breath. "You still make the mistake of thinking of the CapWars as normal, conventional wars. This isn't one country against another with militaries and rules of engagement. CapWars are more complex than that. *Way* more. The opponents work together at the same time that they fight each other. It's extraordinary. You've never seen anything like it. We're all pawns in their game. The mighty emperors will do anything to control the empire. *Anything!*"

"I'm trying to stop them."

"I know you are, but you aren't doing a very good job," she said, her voice brimming with resignation. "You're not even on the same playing field as they are. You think truth can beat them, but truth doesn't exist in their world. Bastendorff will create some horrific, damaging MADE event with somebody—another REMie, say Miner—and at the same time he'll be plotting against Miner with Gates or someone else. Their first objective is to consolidate control for the REMies, and then, within that, their next first objective becomes to consolidate control for themselves. It's all happening at the same time."

"It's all insane," the president said. "The REMies all need to be in prison, and I will put them there one by one. They're just people, subject to the laws and arrest like everyone else."

"Not really."

"It may be harder to catch them because of their power and resources, but they still count on rigging the system to protect them, and I'm not rigged."

"The best thing you've got in your fight is Booker Lipton," Fonda said.

"Yeah," Hudson said dryly. "There were two good REMies, Vonner and Booker, and now there's only one." His sarcastic tone was beyond bitter. "I don't buy it. There's no such thing as a good REMie."

"Tell that to Schueller," Fonda said. "Or is he too busy counting Vonner's money to talk?" She didn't wait for an answer. "I'm going to keep helping you whether you want or deserve it."

"You know what they say, with friends like you—"

"You'll thank me one day. Now, I better go." She added

sarcastically, "Before someone traces this call," and then she was gone.

Hudson looked back to Granger, who was smiling, obviously amused.

"What's so funny?"

"How she drives you crazy."

"I don't think that's funny."

"Only because you know she's right," Granger said, "and you don't want to admit it."

"No such thing as a good REMie?" the Wizard asked. "You and I were both wrong about Vonner."

The president voiced what he'd been wrestling with for some time. "You think we should form an alliance with NorthBridge?"

Granger nodded.

"It would have to be so secret that it could never leak," the Wizard whispered.

"That's impossible," the president said, thinking of the leaks that had plagued him since he'd gotten into office.

"There might be a way," the Wizard said as they reached Marine One. "But we'll need Tarka."

CHAPTER FIFTY

Titus Coyne strolled into the Oval Office as if it was his own living room. "Love what you've done with the place," he said, smiling in a full charismatic assault.

The president shook Coyne's hand across the Resolute Desk and returned the smile. "I plan on staying a while, so I might as well make it suit my style." Hudson had made only minor changes to the Oval Office's décor, certainly not enough to be noticeable or out of character for the historic room, but he played along. "Great desk though, huh?" the president said, knocking on the hard wood. "Lots of secrets."

"I'm sure," Titus said. "Would you mind terribly if we had our little chat while strolling the grounds? I always find the Oval Office so stuffy, don't you?"

Hudson looked at the fifty-nine-year-old billionaire and couldn't help but laugh at his insulting charm. They'd only met once before, at a banking conference where the president was speaking while still a candidate. Coyne had said to Hudson then, "*I'm not really sure why Vonner's wasting his time with you.*

Aren't you a construction worker, or something? Isn't he worried that you might win?"

"Titus, that's a nice suit. What'd it cost?" the president asked. "I'm guessing three times what my annual teacher's salary was back in the day."

"You weren't a teacher too long, were you?"

The president ushered him to the door leading outside. "When I told Fitz I would be meeting with you today, he asked me to say hello to 'the old shark.'"

Coyne smiled as if complemented, but his eyes registered insult.

"But I didn't want to insult you," the president added. "I always thought you preferred to be called a 'Bankster.'"

"Yes. Yes, I do," he said, as if amused. "I asked to see you today because I'm a little concerned that some of my friends have been, how should I say it, *dying* lately."

"Friends?" Hudson was about to say, 'I didn't realize you had any,' but decided the sparring had gone on long enough.

"Yes." Titus went on to name five REMies who'd been killed in the previous six weeks.

"I'm not sure why you're bringing this up with me. Certainly I'm aware of their deaths. They were all prominent business leaders, and correct me if I'm wrong, but weren't the causes of deaths listed as various accidents or natural causes in each case?" the president asked as they entered the Rose Garden. "Admittedly, the timing of five such powerful individuals dying so close together does seem remarkable . . . "

Coyne stopped and stared at the president. "Please, Mr. President, you're not an idiot. Vonner, who could also be added to that list of dead, would not have chosen a fool. Although, depending on his objectives, which were always a bit clouded in cocktails as far as I could see, he managed to get you into power, and you've certainly caused a lot of trouble in a short time, so perhaps he was more sober than I give him credit for."

"No doubt."

"Good, then let's not pretend that those deaths are anything other than what they are. NorthBridge is removing REMies."

"You do realize that I've been trying to stop NorthBridge?"

"Of course you have." Coyne half smiled. "I'm sure you mean well. It's just hard to tell that you've been doing anything at all with NorthBridge, what with all their successes and all your failures."

"Titus, are you asking for my help, or are you just here to offer criticism?"

"I think both of us would agree it's not a good idea to have some of the most prominent people in the world just all of a sudden drop dead one by one, or in groups."

"Really? Are these people truly friends of yours?" the president asked. "Because you're going for the CapStone. Wouldn't fewer REMies around mean less competition?"

"Competition has never been a problem for me. You see, money begets power, and power begets more money. It's a lovely little circle."

"Nothing little about it," Hudson said sharply. "Maybe we should talk about MADE events."

"What? Are you wearing a wire?" Titus asked, patting the president's shoulders, and then smiling as a nearby Secret Service agent moved closer.

The president waved the agent off. "I doubt you'd be concerned about a wire. We both know in the current environment you and your kind are impervious to those types of tactics."

"My kind?" Titus echoed indignantly. "As if I'm some type of creature?"

"Exactly."

The REMie flashed a fake smile. "Which MADE event do

you want to talk about? Or are you insinuating that REMies dying are MADE events?"

"I'm surprised the REMies aren't turning them into MADE events. Or are they too scared? Maybe they're finally afraid of something."

"Fear is our business," Titus said, admiring a large white rose.

"That's the problem," the president replied.

"The problem is NorthBridge. *They're* the distraction. And it's Booker Lipton who's using them."

"Why?"

"For the CapWar," Titus said, as if it were the most obvious reason possible. "I think Arlin Vonner and Booker Lipton sat down on the beach of one of Booker's islands and concocted this whole thing."

"You've lost me."

Titus looked at him with contempt. "NorthBridge, you, the REMie take down plan . . . It's always about distracting people and getting them not to look behind the curtain to see the real power, right? That's the game, and it has always worked. Sex scandals, mass shootings, terrorism, foreign threats, financial bubbles—those are the big ones. Booker and Vonner just went nuclear and turned the empire in on itself."

"They hated each other."

"So? Everyone hates everyone until there's money to be made. Is Vonner even dead?"

Hudson was surprised at the question. He'd often wondered if Vonner's death had really been from natural causes. At the time, Kensi, and later Rex, had both assured him they believed it was not an assassination. But in light of the rash of REMie deaths lately, he'd rethought that position and wondered if perhaps Vonner was just the first in this final volley of the CapWars.

Is Booker really trying to wipe out his competitors so he can gain total control? Or is this part of NorthBridge trying to save the world from the REMies' empire?

But Coyne's proposition that Vonner might not really have died seemed ludicrous.

Titus was staring at him, as if reading his mind. "Mr. President, you should know by now that nothing is what it appears."

"It doesn't make sense that Vonner would leave all his money to Schueller and fake his death."

"Ha, you think Vonner only had, what was it, $50 billion? No wonder you think you can beat us. It would be impossible to even make a run at the CapStone without at least ten times that much!"

Hudson couldn't hide his shock. *REMies worth half a trillion dollars? If that were true . . . and what about the rest of Vonner's money?*

"But—"

"Yeah, but," Titus said, laughing. "The complexities here dwarf whatever you could imagine." He studied the president for a moment. "Do you really think we're worried about you and your rag-tag group of choir boys? You're nothing but a few fleas. I don't even remember your name half the time."

"Titus, you don't impress me."

"Likewise, but ask yourself this: why didn't Vonner warn you about NorthBridge? He had to know they were coming. REMies don't wait for accidents or surprises. But I understand this is all beyond your capacity, so I'll help you out. These things are *years* in the making. He might have been watching you since you were in college, maybe made some of your breaks along the way, like a fairy godfather. But he knew you'd be president, and he knew NorthBridge would be threatening to break the country apart. Why did he do that and then die, leaving you with enough money to think you could actually do something?"

"You're grasping here," the president said, trying to pretend his head wasn't swirling. "Oh believe me, I understand that if I look back at the history of the past century, it's littered with MADE events, most of which I thought 'just happened.' But now I know they were contrived by your ilk, and even if that weren't the case, it all happened as a result of artificial MADE events, the repercussions of which the REMies used to make even *more* MADE events. Aren't you guys exhausted? Terrorist events, mass shootings, corporate scandals, sex scandals—you *creatures* have no shame. You'll twist anything for profits and power."

"Are you done with your speech?" Titus asked with an impatient sigh. "I don't care about your outrage and elementary understanding of how we keep the world running. I just want the killing to stop."

"You, yourself, just said I haven't done much about North-Bridge, so what makes you think I can stop these killings?"

"I'm telling you right now that if you *don't* stop them, and I mean *immediately*, then—"

"Then what?" the president snapped, stepping toward Coyne.

"The REMies—surely you must know this—we're not the sweet and gentle group of philanthropists that we may appear to be. We have all the money, all the weapons, and all the power. You don't want us to turn our attention away from the CapStone and each other, because we will. Do you know what that would mean?" He turned, glaring at the president, and moved in even closer, so that their faces were only a few inches apart. "We'll turn all of our fury upon NorthBridge, and you, and anyone else who thinks we can be overthrown. Believe me, Hudson, you don't want that."

"Overthrown? You all really do think you're emperors, don't you?"

"This isn't a game! This is the way the world works. It's survival of the fittest. Darwin wasn't just talking about lizards and snakes, he was talking about REMies in the human survival story of evolution."

Hudson pushed a finger into Coyne's chest. "I'm going to bring you down, Titus. I'm going to take every last dollar you have, even if it's a trillion. Then I'm going to put you in prison, and do you know what I'm going to do next?" He didn't wait for an answer. "I'm going to come and visit you in your six-by-eight cell and remind you of this conversation."

"We'll see," Titus growled.

"You know, I used to wonder how you all could keep everything secret, how no one knew about the REMies' control and CapWars and the whole CapStone conspiracy. But then I figured it out. People *do* know. The REMies just do such a good job at labeling anyone who puts the pieces together as a conspiracy nut, a crackpot, or paranoid, that they make people afraid to speak out, and if someone *does* start taking them seriously? Oh, well sorry, the brakes fail on their car, or whoops, they have a sudden heart attack, or something even more creative. But if you think you can threaten me that way, you're wrong. Your days are numbered whether NorthBridge assassins get you, or the FBI comes knocking on your door. One way or another, you're almost out of time, so enjoy your caviar and gold goblets full of champagne, or whatever it is you do, because the people are going to take all of it away."

"You're a fool, Hudson. A tiny little fool."

"If you're so rich and powerful, why can't you REMies figure out how to protect yourself and others from the big bad North-Bridgers?"

"I gave you a chance," Titus said. "Just remember, I offered you this." He began walking away. "And we're not talking nickels and dimes here. This is about all the tea in China, *everything*, reality-bending amounts of money—trillions and trillions upon *trillions* of dollars. What would you do for that kind of power?

Ask yourself, and then imagine people willing to do whatever you come up with, a thousand times that to a magnitude of ten. It's over, and you never even understood."

Coyne snatched a rose off one of the bushes and stormed away.

Hudson didn't move for quite a while. He wasn't sure he could. When one of the agents started to approach, he willed himself to wave and began walking back toward the West Wing. He felt as if the ground was moving beneath him.

CHAPTER FIFTY-ONE

"This is a risky meeting," Thorne said as the leadership of NorthBridge met in an old farm house in rural Virginia. The property had a private airstrip, was close to the nation's capital, and had lots of privacy. "I don't know why we couldn't have done this over a secure video feed like usual."

"The Pentagon has recently put into service some new technology that is providing them a work around," Booker said. "I'm not sure where they're getting this equipment. It's not from me. If I had to guess, it would be from Titus Coyne, but either way . . . "

"I didn't know he owned any defense contractors," Fonda said.

"As far as I know, he doesn't," Booker said. "But he's got connections. I think it's a consortium based out of Germany. It may even be Russian technology. I've got people trying to figure out the sources. However, none of that really matters to this meeting. Right now, the time has come. We have to decide."

"Are we going to launch this revolution?" Fonda asked.

"Yes," Booker said. "Overthrow by force. All out efforts. No peace."

"I think it's too soon," AKA Adams said. "We should give the president a little more time."

"It's no surprise you're siding with him," Thorne said. "Can you imagine what he's going to do when he finds out your true identity?"

AKA Adams frowned. "I'm still hoping he won't ever find out."

"But if all hell breaks loose," Thorne said, "there's a much better chance he's going to discover who you are. And what the hell were you thinking, releasing that statement on peace, naming the REMies, asking for help?"

"I have the right to speak under this banner," Adams said.

"You shouldn't," Thorne said. "Not *that* garbage. It weakens the movement!"

"We've been through this. The post did no harm," Booker said as a trusted servant brought in refreshments. Booker typically downed two smoothies, which he called "concoctions," a day. This one, a yerba mate power smoothie filled with one of his special blend of herbs, was a favorite.

"It may have even brought Hudson closer to joining us," Fonda said, sipping a cup of tulsi and ginger tea.

"I'm not anxious for the president to find out who I am either," AKA Franklin said, "but we're wasting our time talking about that. We've already agreed it's best that he doesn't find out who Adams and I are. So, if he does, we'll deal with that then, but in the meantime, that's not what we're here to debate."

"I'm just saying, Adams is against the revolution only because of the entanglements with Pound and the risks of all that not only being exposed—"

"The entire administration could unravel," Franklin said. "We could bring down this government."

"Isn't that what we *want* to do?" Thorne asked.

"I don't think Adams is concerned only with that," Fonda

said. "What we set into motion is going to mean the deaths of thousands. If it's handled improperly, that number will swell to hundreds of thousands. And if the REMies fight back, and we know they will, then we're looking at *millions* dead because of what we decide in this room right now. So let's forget all about the reasons why we think what we think. Adams has opposed the violent side of this revolution since the beginning, unlike you, Thorne."

"The risk of loss of life hasn't stopped *you* from ordering some violent activities," Thorne said to Fonda.

"Why are you so antagonistic, Thorne? We're on the same team. We've come a long way. We would never have been able to get this far if not for the diverse contributions we all bring to the table."

"Everyone, please," Booker said, moving his hands across the table. "Enough."

"I tend to agree with Adams," AKA Franklin said. "It's a critical time. I think we can give the president a few more weeks."

"Of course you do," Thorne said. "I don't know why we all had to risk getting arrested to fly here. I could've told you how each one of you is going to vote. Adams and Franklin, as always, want to wait. Fonda and I are willing to go ahead, although she reluctantly." He smirked at her.

Fonda returned his smirk.

"And how will I vote?" Booker asked.

"You're always a tough one to read," Thorne said. "But I believe you think the time is now. That's why we're here."

Booker nodded. "It's an extremely difficult decision, but my fellow REMies are in a panic like they've never been before. All of them have increased their security as a result of the deaths of now seven of their members. That makes it nearly impossible to reach any of them, although we continue to try." He glanced at Thorne. "We have reason to believe that the military is growing restless with the president, and perhaps most importantly, due to our actions over the last several years, there are a significant number of organic groups rising up, or preparing to defend themselves—preparing for some sort of apocalyptic event."

"Like a full-fledged revolution," Thorne interrupted. "It's at the boiling point."

"And you've stirred that fire," Adams said. "You and your hundred billion listeners, or whatever it is. You've made sure to incite them all."

"That's my job," Thorne said. "I tell them the truth. It's not my fault that it infuriates them. The public was asleep for too long. Don't get mad at me for trying to wake them up."

"The ramifications are difficult to calculate," Franklin said. "But AKA Jefferson is right, there could be millions dead. I believe that is most likely to occur. But beyond that, we will certainly see the complete breakdown of society. As you know, the president is working on a plan he calls 'Fair and Free' to replace the REMies' central-bank empire-system. It's a very strong, logic-based proposal that I believe can work."

"Logic . . . of course you do," Thorne said.

"*However,*" Franklin continued, ignoring Thorne, "Fair and Free has little chance to succeed if it's smothered in the ashes and blood of this brutal revolution."

"I see those risks and consequences," Booker said, "but if we don't act now, the REMies, or the military, will make a move. I think we need first mover advantage."

"*Millions of deaths* . . . we're batting around these statistics like we're talking about the stock market," Adams said. "These are *real* lives. These are friends and neighbors, innocent citizens who have no idea what's coming."

"They have no idea because they've been asleep," Thorne said. "They've chosen *not* to see."

"They are going to *die*," Adams said. "We all know you don't care about that, but I think we need more time to see if we can find a way to do this without losing millions."

"Don't tell me I don't care," Thorne said. "I've been the only one, from the beginning, who's been doing this out in the open, unlike the rest of you, who're afraid of retaliation, assassination, or arrest. I'm going to lose people I love, too, and I love this country, and it's going to be destroyed. But we have to act."

"We will," Booker said. "I'm sorry, but we have to be the first, or we can't win."

"Win?" Adams said. "No one will win."

CHAPTER FIFTY-TWO

Tarka, who was in Europe shadowing one of the Rothschilds, handed her assignment off to a team of VS agents and immediately flew to New York, where she met with the Wizard and Granger. The three of them spent hours on the DarkNet and devised a plan. Her history with Booker during the Rochelle search and rescue would be critical to the success of this new mission, perhaps her most important one ever: how to form an alliance between the most wanted terrorists in the world and the president of the United States.

Later, after the Wizard personally briefed the president on the plan, Hudson called in his chief of staff.

"You win," the president began. "We're going to wait two more weeks on Cherry Tree."

"Really?" Fitz asked. "Why the change of heart?"

"I think you were right about the timing. Plus, Granger needs a little more time to get Fair and Free finished."

"I know he's one of the smartest people in the world," Fitz said as the two men sat in the President's Study, "but can he really create from scratch a system not only to replace the entire world economy, but at the same time design it to survive a total collapse of the REMies' empire?"

"Yeah," the president said casually. "He's actually mostly finished already, just needs to fine tune some things."

"Well that's great," Fitz said. "Still, I don't see conditions improving enough in two weeks to launch."

"Because people still won't want to hear it?"

"Partly."

"Don't worry, conditions will change," the president said, knowing that an announcement about NorthBridge would have seismic effects. Yet, without knowing the source of the leaks, he couldn't risk telling Fitz the details.

"Care to elaborate?"

"Not right now, but I need you ready with radical reforms. You have to be prepared to push the whole agenda in a week."

"You just said we had two weeks."

"Everything is fluid, and we only get one chance. Understand?"

"Not entirely."

"But you can do it?"

"Yeah," Fitz said, "but you're still going to have to figure out how to get Congress on board. You can't twist enough arms to make them move on your proposals."

"Don't worry, by then they'll be desperate to follow anyone with a plan."

Fitz gave him a strange look. "You're leaving me out of the loop . . . why?"

"Because you're part of the plan," the president said. "Do you trust me?"

"Of course," Fitz replied. "The question is, do *you* trust *me?*"

"That's not a question at all."

CHAPTER FIFTY-THREE

G ypsy had produced gigs of data showing all the women were lying about Hudson, but other than the former Vonner stations controlled by Schueller, the media ignored the data. Still, they got enough of it out there that the fury was dying down. Melissa had also mentioned in numerous speeches standing behind her husband, including one event where she laid it out bluntly: "Although sexual harassment and sexual assault are despicable acts, and most women making these types of accusations are genuine and to be believed, in some cases, there are other motives behind the charges. In the case of my husband, President Pound, these claims are entirely false, and the women making them are liars paid by enemies of the president." She then named each woman and announced that they were going to be investigated by the FBI.

Lester watched the speech with disdain. He had told none of his staff, nor the sleazy private investigators he employed, what he hoped to accomplish—destroying the president's reputation. But many of them had reported being followed in recent days. In some cases, their offices and homes had been "rifled and tossed."

The PIs had sworn it wasn't the FBI closing in on them, it was someone far worse.

"Mafia?" Lester had asked, knowing he could probably handle that situation.

"I wish," one of the PI's had said. "No way, these guys could only be with one outfit—BLAXers."

"Who the—?"

"Private corporate army," the PI said, as if he were talking about vampires. "They don't play."

"What corporation?" Lester asked, sure he had heard the name 'BLAXers', before but couldn't place it, and he certainly didn't see how they could be more trouble than the FBI or mafia.

"Booker Lipton," the man answered. "And if you've pissed off that guy, then we're all screwed."

Schueller saw less of his father, as he now had his own large staff helping to oversee billions of dollars. His three public projects – the Free Food Foundation, Zero-cost Alternative Power, and Medical Emergency Details, had each become massive multi-billion dollar foundations, which moved on their own momentum and no longer required his daily attention. Most of his time was currently focused on a number of expensive and secret anti-remit measures.

He considered his most important project to be recruiting young candidates who believed in freedom and intellectually accepted that the REMies' empire was wrong. Along with Granger, he'd developed a comprehensive screening process. The program saw potential applicants increase dramatically after AKA Adams' anti-REMie post.

The idea was to get honest candidates to run for different offices, from local to national. He'd already been quietly working with a number of campaigns, and was outspending REMies. Granger, in advance of the new Fair and Free system, helped develop strategies with cryptocurrencies so that in the post-empire world, elections would be publicly funded in order to eliminate a major source of corruption.

Prior to the Minton Micro attack, NorthBridge had been attracting many disenfranchised members of society who, even without understanding the dynamics of the REMie empire, knew something was wrong—so wrong they were willing to join a revolutionary movement to stop it. That was one of the reasons the REMies blamed the attack on NorthBridge, to stem the flow of members and sympathizers joining the fight against the elites. They also wanted to push back into the China tensions and punish the firm that wasn't "playing ball." As with everything the REMies did, there were multiple layers of reasons and hundreds more smaller considerations and ramifications, all carefully plotted and designed.

Schueller, hoping to attract those same people drawn to NorthBridge's cause to the peaceful side of the revolt, had enlisted social media experts and speakers to make content for YouTube, PoseUp, Facebook, Pathfind, and Twitter. They produced sophisticated ads and videos offering solutions counter to what NorthBridge was offering. But the efforts were slow compared to the numbers the terror group was attracting. As the progress continued at its frustrating pace, Schueller warmed to the idea of a collaboration with NorthBridge, something Granger had been pushing for months. When Hudson told his son that some kind of collaboration was on the table, Schueller had been relieved.

"NorthBridge is attracting a lot of people again," the president whispered to Schueller as they stood under the stars at the Potomac estate. "Booker was able to get information out there that proved NorthBridge had nothing to do with the Minton

Micro attack." Hudson paused to point out the constellation of Orion to Schueller, as he had done hundreds of times for as far back as they both could remember.

"I listened to the recordings," Schueller said. The audio captured a REMie ordering the attack and the false flag to make it appear NorthBridge did it, and even the hack to their site claiming responsibility. The REMie had died of an apparent brain hemorrhage the same day the evidence appeared all over the internet.

Suddenly they heard footsteps. Hudson immediately crouched, grabbing Schueller. His heart pounding, they held their breath. "Over there," Schueller whispered, pointing to a stand of trees. Hudson caught a glimpse of a point, sighed, stood up, and muffled a laugh. It was another buck, with many points of its antler. Schueller started to hum, and then sang the chorus of a song he'd written. Hudson joined him, and together, arm in arm, they walked back to the house, singing in hushed voices under a magnificent sky. Their mood and actions belied the reality that these two men were desperately working for peace, for a vestige of what human potential is really about, for a fair and free world.

The FBI's DIRT unit was investigating, and indictments were expected on many underlings of the man on the recording, but Hudson knew the REMies' owned the judges and prosecutors and the case would fall apart in that rigged system and go away. Still, it was a crack in the empire, but the fact that it had been Booker who'd caused it rather than the president made the point even stronger that it was time to find common ground.

Hudson lowered his voice again. "If Tarka can pull this off, this won't be the last crack. We'll launch Cherry Tree with NorthBridge backing, and then ... "

"We don't just get the CapStone. The whole damn pyramid comes down."

CHAPTER FIFTY-FOUR

Dranick had agreed to help General Imperia's B-4 Committee. It had been a difficult decision, but he viewed his betrayal as an act of loyalty. Removing Hudson from office was the best way to save him from certain death. Beyond that, as a patriot, Dranick believed the best hope for the country to survive the chaos engulfing it was a strong leader with the backing of the military. That was certainly not Hudson Pound.

Dranick did get one concession in an effort to ensure that the government would be restored to a democracy as soon as was possible. General Imperia was neither surprised at his request, nor hesitant in granting it; Colonel Enapay Dranick would become the vice president as soon as the military assumed power. He took no pride in the fact that he'd be the first Navajo to hold the high office. Dranick knew history would likely vilify him as a Brutus. However, he believed he could help protect the country from remaining under military rule longer than necessary.

General Imperia had assured him that the B-4 committee, which had policies dating back to its founding that prohibited any of the members of the group's leadership assuming the presidency, wanted civilian rule brought back as soon as the threats were neutralized and order reestablished. In addition to Dranick as VP, B-4 had selected the current Chairman of the Joint Chiefs of Staff, a well-known and popular military figure, as the next president. In his role as Director of National Intelligence, Dranick had been organizing squads of CIA, NSA, and other intelligence agencies operatives to assist in the actual coup—now codenamed "the incident." They had carefully selected thousands of troops within the ranks of the military, and hundreds of officers to ensure that any reluctance or resistance that might initially arise during the incident would be quickly quelled. Documents had been drafted detailing the reasons for the takeover and outlining the regulations during the military's reign. Another report showed how a transition back to a democracy would work and what a post-military-controlled-government would look like. After the incident, the materials would be made public through controlled media outlets.

It all seemed meticulously planned; they'd thought of every-thing. *What could go wrong?* Dranick thought. *Everything.* He believed General Imperia and the others when they stated emphatically that this was a temporary measure. Like him, they were all patriots, and each was very uncomfortable with what they were about to do. But it had to be done.

At perhaps their final assembly before the incident began, Dranick muttered to himself, "We're about to destroy our democ-racy in order to save it." It was only his second time in the B-4 underground conference room at the Pentagon. He thought of the closed space as a dungeon, which made him feel uneasy, or at least that's what he told himself. If pressed, he might've said it was the treacherous power of the men—less like authority and more like contagion—that bothered him. But even that would not have been accurate. B-4 members weren't the issue, his own conscience was.

He'd wrestled repeatedly with the decision. *Am I doing the right thing? Will Hudson ever understand? Is there . . .*

"Colonel Dranick?" General Imperia's deep, sharp voice snapped him back to attention. "Your report."

Dranick stood, cleared his throat, and began detailing the plan. They went over it repeatedly, every aspect reviewed tirelessly, step-by-step, computer-generated, Artificial Intelligence-derived scenarios and responses. Interactive charts showed which divisions of which branch of service would act, where, and when. A separate, specialized strategy was in place to seize control of the media, including the Internet. Dranick questioned the need for strict curfews and automatic searches, but Imperia would not yield on any points.

The following day they would bring in the Secretary of Defense. They expected his cooperation. The militarization of local police forces around the nation would make their task of moving large numbers of troops around the country quickly much easier. They expected pockets of resistance, and had long-prepared tactical procedures in place to handle them. "Swift force," General Imperia called it. "Zero tolerance for any would-be challenges. Order must be maintained to minimize casualties."

"We must penetrate his inner circle of security," General Imperia said, referring to the president's hand-picked VS and Secret Service details who had so far been impenetrable. "Colonel, that's your area. How are we coming?"

"As you know," Dranick began, "the president, more than any of his predecessors, has taken charge of his own safety. He uses both private VS and ultra-vetted Secret Service agents. He's rarely exposed."

"And we do not, I repeat, we *do not* want to be killing US Secret Service agents."

"Nor the president," Dranick said.

"Of course not," General Imperia agreed.

"I have some ideas," Dranick said. He'd given that aspect of the coup a lot of thought. He knew it was where his greatest violation of trust would come.

Hudson, in response to the NorthBridge attacks and the REMie threats, had closed his security window and inner circles very tightly. The president knew everything about every agent. He had Vonner Security agents watching the Secret Service, and the Secret Service likewise watching the VS. He rarely met in person with people outside his circle, but when he did, Dranick always knew. Dranick, as one of the president's oldest and most trusted friends, combined with his role as DNI, had complete security access.

"There are three dates in the next ten days when I believe we would have our best chance to take the president into custody without bloodshed to his security detail or bystanders," Dranick said, pointing to his laptop screen, displaying the dates and locations.

They all agreed, after reviewing different options, that Camp David would be ideal. Troops would be waiting, agents would be replaced, the president would be relaxed, comfortable, and feeling his most secure. Camp David was a military base. Camp David was the perfect site for a coup d'état.

"I'll, of course, be at Camp David that weekend," Dranick said. "Along with Chief of Staff Emmitt "Fitz" Fitzgerald, and the first lady, which is convenient, since they'll also need to be detained."

"At the same time, the vice president will be in Washington," the Admiral said. "We'll summon her and the other cabinet members to the White House, where they'll be notified and held."

"Officially, all upper level members of the administration will be placed under house arrest," General Imperia said. "All except the Secretary of Defense and the Secretary of Interior who will, by then, be on board."

"The internet and media?" the Marine commandant asked.

"We hit the kill switch on the internet the instant the president is in custody," General Imperia said. "Simultaneously, we'll have teams hit every major newspaper. NorthBridge has already weakened several of our targets, but we'll finish the job. Broadcast media will be easier to handle because we control the airwaves, spectrum, and satellites."

The conversation soon switched to what they called "the wildcard"—the possibility that the public could not be convinced that the charges against the president and the threat to the nation were severe enough to warrant the military's actions.

"We've got scenarios ready," Imperia said. "The public can be scared easily. They get virtually all their information from the media. They believe what they're told. It's sad how easy they are to manipulate. However, in this case, it allows us to achieve our objectives."

"If you're talking about embellishment," Dranick said, "I'm not really comfortable with that.

"We're simply painting a picture, telling a story that already exists with brighter colors, fancier words," General Imperia said. "He met with the Chinese, they cut a deal, war was averted, a war that was days away. It must've been some agreement. We don't know everything that was in that pact. It could've been anything. We're merely speculating, and maybe by then we'll have additional evidence. But if he's seen as colluding with the Chinese, nobody could deny that he needed to be removed immediately."

"We shouldn't do anything that makes him look as though he did something wrong."

"That's the whole idea," General Imperia said, barely

suppressing a smile. "And it's only a backup. We only use this information after the coup has taken place, if there's any trouble."

"But—" Dranick began to protest.

"Can you imagine the chaos and horrific violence and the uprisings that would occur if our actions aren't seen as entirely necessary?" the admiral asked.

"Hundreds of thousands of casualties in order to regain order," one of the other members said.

"And if that happens," Imperia said, "we'll have to resort to even more drastic measures . . . none of us wants that."

CHAPTER FIFTY-FIVE

The first lady had been traveling the country for weeks in an attempt to personally visit contacts and governors of all fifty states. Her assignment was to ready them for Cherry Tree, radical reforms, and the new Fair and Free system without actually telling them what was coming. The impossible task had been made easier with data and intelligence gleaned from the Gypsy program. Granger and the Wizard had sought information on each governor, their staffs, and other key elected officials. Her mission was more to gauge who could be counted on in the days following Cherry Tree.

"I'm optimistic," she said while checking in with Hudson one night after meeting with the governor of New Mexico.

"That's great," Hudson said. "We had written off the entire Southwest."

"Obviously Texas and Arizona are impossible," Melissa said in a tone that meant they really were. "The REMies have a firm grip all the way down to county officials in both states, but I think we can count on Oklahoma and probably New Mexico."

Part of their plan was to arrest any governors, lieutenant

governors, state attorneys general, and on down the line, who might impede the implementation of Fair and Free. The charges would be based on evidence being collected by the Gypsy program and 3D system. Dranick had been funneling intelligence to the DIRT unit at the FBI for months. The president had a good idea who might abandon the REMies, and who would not. They'd also discovered a small number who were already independent of the elites.

"Where to next?"

"California."

"The big prize."

"Yeah, REMies own the state, and their reach goes deeper into the state legislature there than anywhere else, but I have some strong contacts. And you saw the intel; I think we can get as many as one-third to come our way."

"You're amazing. Tired?"

"I'm too exhausted to think about being tired."

"Want me to fly out and join you?"

"Yes."

"I wish I could, but I can't."

"I know."

"I'll see you in my dreams."

"Every night."

Granger and the Wizard showed up at the White House unannounced, and were waiting for the president in the Oval Office when he got out of a meeting with Congressional leaders.

"Twenty minutes," the Wizard said.

The president looked at his secretary.

"I don't see how . . . " she said, exasperated, knowing she'd have to make it work. "We're already thirteen minutes behind.

The treasury secretary is waiting with the SBA people, and then the Florida delegation about the hurricane efforts," she said without referring to the tablet computer in her hand. "Then the Central American strategic session, and that was already going to be tight, and the German chancellor arrives in three hours . . . "

"State Dinner tonight," the president said to the Wizard and Granger. "Want to stay?"

His secretary looked startled, certain that this would create a whole new set of logistical problems.

"Drop the Central American thing," the president said. "As you said, we need more time for that anyway."

He didn't wait for a response as he ushered his guests outside onto the South Lawn.

"Didn't mean to wreck your day," Granger said.

"Truth be told, I was hoping to pass the Central American meeting onto the vice president anyway." He smiled.

"Dawg, you do know you're the president, and don't have to meet anyone you don't want to, right?" the Wizard said.

"Shows how much you don't understand about my job," the president said. "And you heard her, I'm already thirteen minutes behind, so what's the urgency?"

"Remember our suspicions about the REMies' influence on the internet and social media?" Granger asked.

Hudson nodded.

"Dawg, it's the biggest scandal of the ages," the Wizard blurted out. "It's like, carbon dioxide is only a tiny fraction of the Earth's atmosphere, but if it wasn't there, the plants would die and the oceans would freeze. We'd all be dead."

"And this is the REMies fault?" the president asked, confused.

"I think what Wizard is trying to say is that what we've uncovered is earth-shattering," Granger said. "Facebook and

Google, as well as several other social media and internet companies, are complicit."

"With the REMies?"

"With everything," the Wizard said.

"It appears that from the earliest days of some of the largest social media and tech companies, REMies and members of the Deep State were involved," Granger explained. "They were designed to mine data, and . . . " he paused and met the president's stare, "these platforms were created for control."

They had long known that the REMies, and their proxies in the US intelligence apparatus, used the internet to track and profile the general population, but what Granger and the Wizard were saying went well beyond that. The companies, the very internet itself, had, from the beginning, been part of the CapStone conspiracy.

"They gave the people the greatest toy of all: freedom, convenience, the whole world in the palm of their hand—the internet," Granger said. "But what they really gave us was the ultimate prison," he bent down and picked up a small pinecone, "where they watch everything we do and record our every thought through our searches," he said, turning the pinecone between his thumb and forefinger, "the sites we visit, how long we stay, what we read, and the social networks, who our friends are, what we like—"

"And the worst part," the Wizard interrupted, "is we think it's made our lives better and easier, but it's just made it easier for them to control us."

"But that's not really the worst part," Granger added. "The evil in their grand digital plan is that it's a feedback loop." He crushed the pinecone in his hand and inhaled deeply.

"Meaning?" the president asked.

"They've got these massive computers that utilize artificial intelligence to show each of us a customized view of the world,"

Granger said as he put the crushed cone in the president's hand and motioned him to take a breath.

The president held it to his nose and inhaled. The scent of earth and pine dominated, but a slight aroma of vanilla came through. "Nice," Hudson said.

Granger nodded as if they'd just shared a great secret and then continued. "You know how when you search for the price of a Makita cordless drill, and then for the next week or whatever, all you see are ads for Makita and other power tools?"

"Yeah."

"They do that with *everything*," Granger said. "They show you headlines in a certain order, news stories written especially for you. The artificial intelligence and algorithms are incredible."

"Are you saying that whenever anyone goes online, they're actually surfing through one giant MADE event?" the president asked.

"Is reality still real when it's constructed from only a select portion of the facts?" the Wizard asked. "The truth becomes a lie when enough of it is omitted or rearranged."

"Every search someone does on the internet is restricted and filtered based on the user's profile, every news story is biased depending on the reader, even the order in which one sees social media posts is directed by the system," Granger said. "It's all instant, it's accurate, and more complex than you can comprehend. To answer your question, yes, anything you view on a connected device is part of the empire's order to Manipulate-And-Distract-Everyone."

Granger mentioned to the president in parting not to forget that scent.

CHAPTER FIFTY-SIX

For the next several days, the president and his inner circle continued to work on an enhanced version of Cherry Tree to include an alliance with NorthBridge. However, his closest advisors were divided over the idea to include the terror organization in their fight against the REMies. Even those in favor of pursuing that strategy had their doubts, and everyone wondered if it would even be possible.

Yet the prospect of the social media giants and massive tech companies providing back doors and even direct channels to the FBI, CIA, NSA, and a host of other secret agencies, including countless international players because of the global scope, added a drastic new urgency to the cause. With the knowledge that the Deep State could sway public opinion and control the citizens with such covert methods, Hudson's battle against the empire suddenly became impossibly more difficult.

"We have to get Booker to go along with Cherry Tree," the president said on an infinite-encrypted call with the first lady.

"That would be a big secret to keep," she said. "The president joining the most notorious terror group in the world."

"There's no choice."

"Just think about the leaks," Melissa said, her voice heavy with concern. "Cherry Tree may have a better chance without NorthBridge than with them."

"Slim or none," Hudson said. "Slim with them, none without them, is how I see it."

"It's not just the leaks you have to worry about. The Three-D system is going to pick up the first breaths of your revolt against the empire . . . and then we'll find out how strong

their wrath is."

The president returned to the old Hunter Mill Mansion, where Vonner Security had now installed underground surveillance stations to supplement the already heavy security. He sat with the Wizard on the front veranda during a hard rain.

"Where's Granger?" the president asked, used to seeing him whenever he came to what had become the nerve center of their strategic and intelligence gathering operations. They had forty-nine dedicated staff working on Gypsy and other programs to prepare for the move against the empire.

"Traveling."

"Where?"

"I'm not sure. He said it had something to do with Fair and Free. He might have had to go back to California to meet with the cryptocurrency specialists."

The president nodded. "It'll be ready, right? The APT tax system and the conversion to digital currency? Because that's the key. Without an economy and a way to fund the government, we'll descend into anarchy in about three days."

"It'll be ready," the Wizard said. "But, Dawg, we have a problem."

The president looked at his old friend expectantly, bracing himself for what was an hourly occurrence—another crisis to deal with.

"Tarka can't find Booker," the Wizard said.

"She can't find him, or he won't see her?"

"He's disappeared. It's like he's in hiding," the Wizard said. "We know he owns a lot of islands, but I'm beginning to think he has a few that are quite literally unknown. Or . . . I mean, we would *know* if he's dead. It's just so strange, not a single digital footprint that we can attribute to Booker exists now."

"He's alive. They're getting ready for something big," the president mused. "Dranick told me hours ago that they're picking up signs of NorthBridge activity on an unprecedented scale."

"NorthBridge, not Booker . . . Either way, you think they're going to the next level?" the Wizard asked.

"Dranick says the intelligence community has just begun planning for a 'revolution strike,' a huge, coordinated campaign simultaneously hitting major cities in all fifty states."

"That would bring an end to law and order instantly— complete chaos, government response would be overwhelmed . . . "

"Anarchy."

"Then we might be too late," the Wizard said.

"If we can't get to Booker, then the only other hope is to find Fonda."

CHAPTER FIFTY-SEVEN

Hudson had not been back to Oregon since the Air Force One attack that had briefly claimed his life. He found a poetic irony that his first trip back there was to declare a particularly beautiful section of the coastline a national monument. Due to the severity of the potential threats arrayed against his plans, he might have cancelled, but he had one final hope of finding Booker, and she was waiting in Oregon.

"I'm preserving a small, but sacred, slice of the universe," he told his daughter, Florence, who had been on the plane that fateful day and helped save his life. She'd returned too, as part of the healing. "People think I'm doing it to erase the horrors of what happened to me," Hudson continued, "but nothing bad happened to me. For the thirty-one people who died protecting me, and all the others who suffered injuries, it was a terrible and tragic day. For me, it was spectacular beyond all imaginings. I glimpsed eternity, and saw that we are all there."

After the dedication speech, Hudson met with Linh, the leader of the Inner Movement, who had also attended the ceremony. She'd long campaigned for the designation of the area. For years, her organization had sought protection for numerous remarkable natural places around the globe. Critics of the president claimed that followers of the Inner Movement believed the area held spiritual or mystical significance. The media created a small controversy over the matter before it was quickly eclipsed by the mounting troubles in the American cities, overseas military bases, and sexual misconduct allegations against the president.

Hudson and Linh, flanked by more than twenty security personnel and several Secret Service Counter-Assault Teams, walked the rugged trail along the cliffs overlooking the Pacific Ocean. Waves crashed and swirled onto the giant rock monoliths before washing onto the sand far below.

"Thank you for this," Linh said gesturing her hand to the scenic area in which they were walking.

"Don't believe everything you read," the president said with a sly smile. "I know you pushed hard for this monument, but I would've done it anyway. And, to be honest, I don't mind having a monument in the state where I rose from the dead."

"Thank you just the same."

"I wanted to talk to you today. I'm troubled." He smiled again, mostly to himself. "I guess that's an understatement."

She laughed.

"Extremely, deeply, in-way-over-my-head-troubled would probably be a better description, and even then . . . "

"I think you're doing just fine in spite of all the distractions," Linh said, gently touching his elbow.

"Thank you," the president said. "Your friend, Booker, has been causing a lot of these problems. I know you said before that you don't get involved in that part of his life, but I've heard you speak about everything being connected, about us all being one. How do you reconcile that with what Northbridge is doing?"

"We don't have control," Linh said thoughtfully. She stopped and stared out at the ocean for a moment, and then looked back at

Hudson. "The connection doesn't mean we are all doing the same thing or are all in agreement. It's quite the contrary. It's as if we are one giant organism, moving together, and yet we're held back by our own desires and ego, foolishly believing that our own thoughts are correct, even when they are not. Slowly, we will all realize that with all our differences and unique approaches, each of us is right, and we all have the answers within us, the same answers just differently expressed."

Hudson felt a little frustrated, as he often did when speaking with Linh. He could sense her sincerity, yet her words always seemed evasive, and rarely did her responses help resolve any of his concerns. "I sometimes wonder," he began, and then paused to rethink his next statement. "Just the other day, Granger Watson, the futurist and technologist—"

"Yes," Linh said. "I know who he is."

"Brilliant mind, and really has a handle on what's in store with all the computers, technologies, and artificial intelligence taking over our lives. He was telling me that in as little as twenty or thirty years, computers will have completely taken over and control our lives."

"The REMies and other elites in the big powerful corporations are pushing forward for profits, as they seemingly know no limits to their greed," Linh said as a pair of butterflies flitted nearby. "The super-rich don't care about the risks of pursuing ever more profits. As with tobacco, oil, and all kinds of other damaging products, they'll invariably ignore the long-term risks for short-term gains."

"Exactly. There's so much money to be made with artificial intelligence, self-driving cars, smart homes, all kinds of nano and computer applications in healthcare," Hudson said, while momentarily distracted by watching her watch the butterflies dancing in the sun. "They can send micro-robots inside our bodies to look for and repair trouble. These little machines will go after viruses and clean out our arteries, whatever. They can manufacture replacement body parts. All sorts of amazing break-throughs. I don't know, it all sounds like science fiction to me, but it just keeps happening. Every day you read about something else . . . " He stopped.

Linh was staring at a magnificent lichen and moss-covered tree; an enormous, healthy sentinel on the Coast. For a minute, he thought she might hug the tree. But she just looked out at the horizon and took a deep breath. "I'm listening," she said.

"When I was running for office, so many people asked, 'Why would we elect this nobody, this inexperienced former school-teacher and hardware store owner? Why would we elect him to be the most powerful man in the world?' And whether I was the right one for the job isn't the point, but then I got into office and discovered that I really had so little power. Almost none, compared to these titans of industry, the elites, the CEOs of the billion- and trillion-dollar companies. *They* have the power, and I wonder sometimes if it's even possible to take it away from them and return it to the people, or will the machines just take over anyway?"

"I think you worry too much," Linh said. "Even if you don't believe in a higher power, I think it's difficult to deny that there's a force when millions of people, maybe even billions of people, all want the same thing and all push in the same direction. That much desire creates a force, and that force can move anything. So your job isn't to change everything, it's to get everybody heading in that direction, and the rest will happen by itself." She smiled at him.

He nodded.

"And I'm not sure why you're so concerned about artificial intelligence and computers taking over the world, but some days it certainly seems like that's already happened," Linh continued, smiling. "Nevertheless, the future is bright. The machines, no matter how advanced and magical they appear, do not possess a soul, and never will. Therefore, they can't eclipse humans. But what they will do is allow us to focus on what is truly important by taking over all the mundane tasks and chores which will free up so much time and energy for us, that we'll then be able to look inward and find so much more power within ourselves than we could ever imagine. That's when we'll move to the next level."

Hudson looked at her silently for several moments. "Thank you for that," he said, feeling better. "I hope you're right. Now, I have a favor to ask you."

"I don't know where he is," Linh said before Hudson could speak.

"Who?"

"You need to speak with Booker," she said softly.

"Yes, but how—"

"I think it's too late, but I will do my best to get word to him."

Melissa stole a few hours to travel up from California to join Hudson for what seemed to both of them like mere minutes before he left Oregon. He had a dozen people still trying to get word to Fonda. All the usual numbers and channels to her and Booker no longer worked.

Hudson knew at any minute NorthBridge could strike, and Cherry Tree would no longer be an option. The prospect of a bloody war between NorthBridge and the REMies with his administration caught in the middle gnawed at him, as if he were being pursued by a pack of hungry wolves from one direction and a pride of lions from the other. He and Melissa made love as if the world was ending, because they knew, one way or another, it was.

CHAPTER FIFTY-EIGHT

Dranick was waiting for Hudson as Marine One touched down on the White House lawn. The two old friends immediately went to the Situation Room, where they sat alone, discussing the intelligence-gathering efforts of the 3D surveillance system. They'd been utilizing the NSA's "big brother" camera network to gather information on the REMies.

"There's so much chatter," Dranick began. "NorthBridge, foreign terrorists, a dangerous array of bad actors . . . and they all appear to be zeroing in on this time period. Clearly they perceive the country is vulnerable."

"We're not that weak," the president said.

Dranick gave him a doubtful look. "Are you sure? There are those in the Pentagon who are gravely concerned."

"The Pentagon? Sometimes I think they're as big a threat as the REMies, or NorthBridge."

"I'm not sure about that," Dranick said. "There are those in the service that are probably part of the conspiracy, but overall I think the military wants to protect the country."

"You know, people always say it's impossible to keep a

conspiracy secret, but what they don't understand is that almost all the ones involved in the conspiracy don't even know it's a conspiracy. The workers at the CIA, NSA, the Department of Defense . . . they all believe they're helping the country by protecting Americans from 'bad people' seeking to do us harm, but those workers are victims of the same conspiracy that they're part of without even knowing it. They're actually trying to protect the country from themselves. Incredible. The REMies have woven an endless and reality-distorting web. Damn them."

"Yeah, these are insane times. But if we stop the REMies . . . " Dranick paused.

"What is it Enapay?" the president asked, sensing his friend was troubled.

"The chatter," he said. "There are groups—Omnia, the Aylantik, Mirage, TechTrains, branches of the REMies, and others, it's hard to say how many. Even your friend at the Inner Movement has a revolutionary faction known as Inner Force. I feel like any moment, one spark and the world erupts into a splintering revolution that leaves us all vacant, wasted, dead."

"I'm so glad you're so optimistic," the president said sarcastically, patting his old army buddy on the back. "We'll get through it."

"I think you need to throw a bone to the Pentagon," Dranick said. "I don't think they trust you."

"Of course they don't trust me. I don't trust *them*."

"But if everything is about to explode, they're the ones who will keep the peace."

The president looked at his friend carefully and nodded. "Okay, I'll set up a meeting with the Defense Secretary. We'll have a little chat to make sure everybody's one big happy family."

"Good," Dranick said, visibly relieved. "I think that's the smart move right now. Cherry Tree?"

The president nodded again. "Yeah, I think we can launch on

Monday. Melissa has us in good shape with the states, and Granger has given us a green light on Fair and Free." Hudson looked at one of the blank screens across the room and thought about Booker. He knew Cherry Tree had a better chance if NorthBridge was on board, but if he couldn't find Booker or Fonda over the weekend, it would be crazy to *not* launch, since all indications were that NorthBridge was about to blow the country apart. He had to launch before they did. "You know time is working against us. Every day we wait, it becomes riskier."

"Didn't Fitz talk to you about selling it? The REMies won't let your message out."

"We've got all Vonner's media properties already loaded up and ready. The Wizard has almost completed a plan to take control of the unfriendly media—"

"You mean you're going to nationalize the media?"

"No, nothing like that. Although, I wish I could," the president said. "Instead, we're just going to take control of their signals for a few days to make sure our content is seen by their audiences. Then we'll hand it back to them and let them rip everything apart."

"So, the people are going to just believe all this?" Dranick asked. "I've been knee deep in it for more than a year and I'm still not sure *I* buy it."

"We've been in almost constant wars for the last hundred years. Really, when you think about it, we've just been butchering each other, raping the planet, and exploiting the people. Everyone feels that, though they may not want to believe it," the president said in anger, "I've been told that the people have been too brainwashed to get it, but I think they already know. All they're waiting for is for it to be acknowledged, and when they see our proof—"

"You simplified it, right?" Dranick asked.

"Yeah, it's pretty slick, but easy to understand. And remember, everyone has lived through this nightmare. They know we're not on the right track, that something is definitely not right—too many people left out, too much suffering, having to just work and work and work . . . that's not living. I really don't think we're going to get much resistance to the story we're telling. The truth has a way of smoothing out all the kinks and wrinkles, because the truth is the truth." The president stared at one of the monitors showing violent demonstrations taking place in Chicago. "Whenever I speak of truth, I'm reminded of the words of Martin Luther King, Jr.: 'I refuse to accept the view that mankind is so tragically bound to the starless midnight of racism and war that the bright daybreak of peace and brotherhood can never become a reality . . . I believe that unarmed truth and unconditional love will have the final word.' His statement gives me hope for Cherry Tree."

"Let's hope you're right," Dranick said, looking at him very seriously. "Otherwise, I believe we'll have a fierce reckoning with unintended consequences."

CHAPTER FIFTY-NINE

I t had taken three days to arrange the video call with Fonda. During that time, Hudson had reluctantly delayed the launch of Cherry Tree.

"You look well, Hudson, for a man who's cheated death so many times."

"Thanks, Fonda, so do you," the president said. "You're a difficult woman to get ahold of."

"By design, my friend. Wait, *are* we still friends? I keep forgetting. Let's see, you've been trying to arrest me and put me in jail forever. Maybe we aren't friends."

"My own party doesn't trust me. I was never the most conservative Republican, but—"

"But now you're more like a Democrat," Fonda finished.

"I'm a liberal conservative, or conservative liberal," Hudson said. "Shouldn't we all be?"

"No. The REMies have conveniently made two parties—everything is a contest, everything's us against them. We've been trained to root for our favorite team and not even look at the other point of view."

"We're close to the brink, Fonda. I wanted to try to bring NorthBridge on board with our plans one more time, for the good of the country."

"Good of the country?" Fonda said, a strained tone in her voice. "There's no country to talk about. At least not in the way you mean. There hasn't been a country in your or my lifetime. We're a corporation, my dear—"

"Fonda, I didn't go to all the trouble of tracking you down to hear another one of your rants," the president said.

"My rants? I haven't even begun . . . I can't believe people trust politicians with money. In the first place, you can't trust politicians with *anything,* and yet we've given them a blank check for more than a hundred years."

"Are you even capable of having a discussion?"

"I keep ranting because I've been covering these 'stories' for decades and watching the last shred of truth get swallowed up in the elite's MADE world. Did you ever stop and ask what drove someone like me to join the movement? None of us were radical terrorists, but we knew the truth, and saw no other path forward."

"A dangerous path," the president said. "Leading to what?"

"I'm just so disappointed in you, Hudson," she said quietly, with sincere regret.

"You are? What would you have me do? I've tried to get investigations and independent counsels to look at the CIA director, NSA overreach, Covington, banking, Bastendorff, Coyne, Booker, and all the other REMies. Each seem to have their own people in the government. The Senate and Congress belong to the REMies. I can't get anything done. The deep state bureaucrats, corruption everywhere, the damned leakers, and all the lobbyists and influencers—the REMies have rigged the game."

"Poor, poor, Hudson," Fonda said. "That's been my point all along. Nothing you've tried has worked. You've been beating your head against the wall. That's why you need to allow North-Bridge to take care of things."

"There is an order—"

"Order? Yes, there is . . . Titus Coyne is behind the Fed interest rate hikes, wreaking havoc on the economy with their false system—inflationary booms and busts, yanking everybody around. The constant control by the one percent. Ha! Isn't it amazing that there hasn't been a revolution already when the one percent hold almost all the wealth? Why aren't the ninety-nine percent screaming bloody murder and rioting in the streets? I'll tell you why—because they've been so manipulated and brain-washed for so long, they seem to think it's a good idea trusting a bunch of greedy banksters with the whole economy. And not just that, who thinks it makes sense to put for-profit corporations in charge of their healthcare? Don't they know it's in a corporation's best interest to screw you? Why would they—"

"You're ranting again."

"*Somebody* has to. You know what they've been doing, and you just watch them go on and continue to do it. You're too polite—"

"Maybe I've gone too slow, maybe I messed things up, but that doesn't mean *your* way is right."

"Oh Hudson, don't worry. The country survived Richard Nixon, Bill Clinton, and Donald Trump. It'll survive Hudson Pound." Then her expression turned delightedly mischievous. "The question is will *you* survive with your apparently aggressive sexual appetites?"

"Those accusations aren't true, and you know it."

"Wait a minute, are you *denying* those charges? Yes, a president must be trusted, like when Ronald Reagan said, and I quote, 'We did not, I repeat, did not trade weapons or anything else to Iran for hostages.' Or when Bill Clinton told us he 'did not have sexual relations with that woman, Miss Lewinsky.' Is that what you're saying? Oh no, no, no, wait, we *trust* the president. I remember Richard Nixon said, 'I'm not a crook.' Or that time Bush senior told us to read his lips, 'no new taxes.' What about Obama promising we could keep our health plan? I could go on and on. *All* presidents lie. Why are *you* any different?"

"The truth is all I have."

"Then tell it, damn it!"

"I'm about to."

"I know you are, but can you get it past the media? The REMies have used the media to spoon distractions, gossip, and scandal to the public for so long it's like junk food—"

"We've got the media covered, and we have a few people in Congress who are on our side," Hudson said.

"And I can name them," Fonda said, rattling off the names accurately and in alphabetical order. "They aren't enough."

"They're a start," the president countered. "Now we need NorthBridge to stop the violence."

"No."

"How can someone as smart as you not understand that we can achieve much more with huge peaceful rallies and more of the data dumps? Terrorism is polarizing; we need unity."

"Twenty years ago, your plan might have worked."

"We've got Vonner's media properties ready to spin the message our way. With Booker's assets, we could—"

"There isn't enough time. There's too much corruption, Hudson, you know that."

"Damn it Fonda, I need NorthBridge to end the violence and put the organization's force behind the agenda we both believe in."

"So you can launch Cherry Tree?"

"I assume Thorne filled you in on the plan? I never would've told him had I known he was AKA Hancock."

"We didn't need Thorne to tell us about Cherry Tree."

Her statement unnerved him. Booker supplied the surveillance state with most of their tools; it was horrifying to think about what that man knew. Hudson wondered if there was anywhere to hide, anywhere to find privacy anymore from the government, the NSA, CIA, FBI, and all the secret alphabet agencies no one has ever heard of and the elites who control them.

"We're going to show the American people."

"Don't do it," Fonda said. "Don't launch Cherry Tree yet. You aren't ready."

"I never said when we were going to launch."

"Even if we didn't already know you were about to, I think your latest timeline calls for the initial launch to take place today." Fonda squinted at him, as if to drill her point home and twist the knife a little deeper. "We have so many ways of learning your plans, but your call would have told me that you're close anyway. This is a last-ditch effort to get us on board because you know that Cherry Tree is a long shot."

"It'll work." He thought of the Kennedy papers that had been hidden in the Resolute Desk. That story alone would add to the outrage that the REMies had controlled and killed for generations . . .

"You're counting on the brainwashed sheep to wake up all at once when you show them your horde of facts and figures, assorted colorful charts, and a passel of extreme claims. It's too much for them to comprehend, and they'll be unwilling to believe."

"We'll see."

"And then what do you think, that the REMies are going to run? Take a deep breath and get real. They're going to get all their people to call you a conspiracy nut. They'll say that you were brain-damaged during those nine minutes. You'll be impeached if you're lucky, dead or imprisoned if you're not."

"Dammit, Fonda, I am *begging* for your help!"

"I know you are. And you have no idea how much I've already helped you." She paused. "But what you're asking for now is something I cannot do."

"What does it cost NorthBridge to stand down and halt the violence and attacks for a few months to see if Cherry Tree can take root?"

"The revolution," Fonda said. "It'll cost us the revolution."

"Why?" Hudson looked at her and suddenly gasped. "Oh . . . of course. I don't quite have the intelligence network North-Bridge does, but I should've figured it out. You're going to switch to open warfare mode . . . *before* Cherry Tree, aren't you?"

She smiled, secretly pleased he'd figured it out. "It's too late to stop it."

"Fonda, what if you're wrong? Do you really think the country can handle this revolution that you have planned?"

"I told you before, there is no country."

"There won't be after you get through with it!"

"We're going to give it a transfusion," Fonda said. "Other-wise, the patient is dead."

"Do you want to talk to *me* about being dead? Do you want to talk to *me* about coming back to life?"

"No, I don't."

Hudson shook his head, glaring at Fonda. "I don't know why I thought you'd help, but I did."

"You were right to think," Fonda began. "Believe it or not, I'm your biggest fan. Yet perhaps your greatest failing is you were unable to convince me that your way was the correct path, and I share a similar fault in my inability to bring you onto our path. But Hudson, I truly hope at the end of the road that we're both still standing, and we wind up at the same spot."

They stared at each other in silence for a long moment. "Are you sure?" Hudson finally asked.

Fonda nodded slowly. "Are *you* sure?" she asked.

"I see no other way." Hudson knew he could be wrong, but he thought he had a better chance of being right than NorthBridge.

"Then I'll see you at the end of the road."

Hudson pushed a button and terminated the connection.

CHAPTER SIXTY

Even before the president could get all the key people together and give the final order to launch Cherry Tree, he knew it was too late. He read the intelligence report coming across his laptop screen at the same time images were beginning to show up all over the media.

"This is crazy," Schueller said as his father told him what was going on, in between reading and watching live updates. Mass demonstrations in several cities against government corruptions had apparently started spontaneously. At the same time, dozens of terror strikes had taken place which appeared too small to be attributed to NorthBridge—bank branches, 3D cameras, offices of multinational corporations . . .

"It's a perfect storm," the president said.

"Is it planned, or is it snowballing from the first city?"

"NorthBridge is obviously moving," the president said. "These are coordinated attacks designed to raise the level of anger toward the establishment and the REMies. They're also doing a damned good job at continuing their reign of terror against me in order to make my job impossible."

"Real revolution?" Schueller asked.

Hudson thought back on his conversation with Fonda. "Absolutely," he said as he answered a call from the Wizard.

"NorthBridge went without us," the Wizard began. "Should we launch Cherry Tree?"

"Not in all this mess," the president said, putting the call on speaker so Schueller could hear.

"We may miss our chance," the Wizard replied. "In the background of all the NorthBridge noise, and potentially caused by it, are dozens of organic movements springing up—militia groups, disenfranchised poor, minority populations—anyone with a gripe against the empire, they're rising up and taking advantage of all the unrest."

"Can we stop it?" Schueller asked. "It looks like it's getting out of hand really fast."

"No," the president said. "Northbridge has been building for this moment for years. Booker Lipton is one of the smartest people on the planet. He hasn't left anything to chance." Hudson pressed a button on his desk and asked his secretary if the first lady had arrived. She informed him that Melissa was on the premises.

"I thought Melissa was in New York," Schueller said.

"She was," the president said. "It's not safe out there right now. I sent for her as soon as the trouble started in Los Angeles."

"The demonstrators seem well funded," the Wizard said. "Printed signs, transportation, megaphones, public address systems. And the other groups doing the attacks all have plenty of resources—arms, intelligence, vehicles, everything they need. Gypsy's picking up patterns, connections. We don't have enough data points yet, but I'm guessing that within a few hours we will, and then Gypsy will show it all pointing back to NorthBridge."

"Booker fooled us into thinking NorthBridge was something other than what it really is," the president said. "They aren't just terrorists occasionally hitting a REMie target and leaking data revealing the crime and corruption of the elites. NorthBridge is just the tip of the iceberg. The revolution was always just under the surface, but we only saw the danger on top."

"I've done a lot of research on Booker," Schueller said. "I wanted to know why Vonner saw him as such a threat. Ever hear of Mansa Musa?"

"No," the Wizard said.

"Mansa Musa Kieta I," Hudson said. "The wealthiest black person in history. Emperor of the Mali empire from 1312 to 1337."

"Impressive," Schueller said. "But did you know that estimates of his wealth put in today's dollars peg his worth at about $400 billion? That's more than John D. Rockefeller, the Rothschild family, a lot more than Bezos or Gates. So he's not just the richest black person in history, but the richest person *ever* . . . except for one."

"Booker?"

"Yes," Schueller said. "If the facts came out, they would show that Booker is actually the richest black person, or person of any race, ever. Vonner estimated Booker controls somewhere between half a trillion and a trillion dollars in assets."

"Your point?" the president asked.

"How can we beat that?"

"No," the Wizard corrected. "How can the rest of the REMies beat him? Combined, they have even more wealth than that. His war is against them, not us."

"Yeah, but we get crushed in the middle," Schueller said.

Melissa and Fitz entered the Oval Office from different doors at almost the same time.

"Situation Room," Fitz said as the president and first lady shared their first embrace since Oregon. "Looks like the world's ending," the chief of staff added.

Hudson and Melissa shared a fast glance filled with the dialogue of a hundred conversations before quickly heading for the Situation Room.

CHAPTER SIXTY-ONE

The Situation Room, crowded with the most senior members of the administration, buzzed with activity. The screens streamed live footage of trouble spots from around the country. Even with the reports he'd been hearing, the images on the screens shocked the president. The Chairman of the Joint Chiefs of Staff and the director of the FBI took turns briefing those gathered on the horrific events.

"NorthBridge, various militia groups, sympathizers, copycats, and other fringe elements have launched coordinated attacks on sixteen American cities," the FBI director said.

"This is quite an escalation for NorthBridge," DNI Dranick added, motioning to the screens. The giant monitors showed sections of Manhattan, Los Angeles, Houston, Chicago, Miami, Philadelphia, and Detroit in flames. Other parts of the same cities either had massive demonstrations or were engulfed in riots. Additional metro areas such as Wichita, Des Moines, Indianapolis, Reno, and Baltimore were not yet burning, but coping with massive rioting, looting, and other forms of civil unrest.

"Mr. President, we are not yet able to rule out involvement

from foreign governments or international bad actors," the Chairman of the Joint Chiefs of Staff said.

The president stared back at the screens, and then around the room. "This is an unprecedented attack. Regardless of who's responsible, there can be no doubt that this is an act of war." He scanned the faces of the generals as he continued. "In the history of our nation, we have never experienced an assault of this scope, this level of magnitude. We must and *will* act swiftly to stop this aggression."

General Imperia spoke up first. "Mr. President, this may be the start of the Civil War NorthBridge has been promising, it may be the largest and most coordinated terror attack in world history, or it may be a devious and well disguised attack by one of our enemies. China or Russia would be the only ones capable of something of this scale, perhaps Iran. But I see little choice on how to respond."

"Tanks in the streets?" Hudson asked, shuddering as he uttered the words.

"Mr. President," the Chairman of the Joint Chiefs continued, "we must declare martial law immediately, and then pray that we have enough tanks to restore order. General Imperia is our point-person on martial law. He's prepared for just such an emergency as this. Please hear him out."

For twenty tense minutes, they debated the unthinkable— declaring martial law across the United States of America.

"Martial law is not a pick-and-choose type of proposition," the president said. "If we do this, it means the suspension of all constitutional rights—no freedom of the press, freedom of speech goes out the window, no right to assemble. We could even prevent people from going to their chosen house of worship. I do not take the thought of such actions lightly."

"Mr. President, with all due respect," General Imperia said, "if we do not declare martial law in the next few hours, I fear constitutional rights will be the last things on the minds of Americans. They won't be worried about losing their right to speak, they'll be worried about losing their right to live."

"Mr. President, the situation is deteriorating," one of the cabinet secretaries said.

"Look at Dallas." Imperia gestured to the monitors depicting block after block of the city in flames. "Chicago." The images looked like a war zone and were hardly recognizable as a major American city. "Los Angeles, Manhattan, Brooklyn, Philadelphia." The footage was astonishing. Bodies in the streets, explosions, fires, screaming mobs running from other screaming mobs. Police and National Guard overwhelmed. "How can you look at all of this, and even hesitate?" Imperia asked.

"Because I know what has caused this."

"NorthBridge is to blame for this," the Chairman of the Joint Chiefs said. "We are at war."

Hudson shook his head. *It's not NorthBridge,* he thought. *It's the damned REMies—Bastendorff, Coyne, and the others—who've caused this.*

"My God, look at Detroit," the FBI director said. They all turned to the monitor where she was pointing. It looked like San Francisco during the 1906 quake. Total devastation—ten ground zeroes.

"I'm not even sure we can save that one," General Imperia said.

The president was silent for a minute. The mood in the room grew increasingly uncomfortable. General Imperia looked at the Chairman of the Joint Chiefs and Dranick almost imploringly, but Hudson didn't notice.

"Fitz, I'd like a word," the president said, then stood up and left the room. Fitz followed him into a separate, secure, soundproof meeting room two doors away. The president looked at his Chief of Staff somberly. "You agree with them, don't you, Fitz?"

"Mr. President, there's no choice. Kissinger once said, 'The absence of alternatives clears the mind marvelously.' You have to do this. You have to do it *now*."

"Can I trust you, Fitz?" the president asked in a desperate tone, as if his life depended on the answer. "Forgive me, but I've never been entirely sure of your loyalty, and I can no longer afford those doubts."

Fitz looked at him with an expression of half-anger and half-hurt.

"You can't blame me for asking," the president said. "After all, you came via a REMie plot."

"And so did you, Hudson," Fitz said, not addressing him by his formal title for the first time since the election.

"True, but I still need an answer."

"I've always wondered how someone as smart as you can constantly make the same mistake," Fitz said.

Melissa knocked on the door and entered the room. "You look like two boxers about to come to blows. Did you forget you were friends?"

"Are we?" the president asked.

Melissa looked surprised for a moment, but shook it off. "Regardless, you need to get back in there. "I think we just lost Portland."

CHAPTER SIXTY-TWO

The president stared at Fitz, trying desperately to decide, once and for all, if he could trust the man that Vonner had placed inside his campaign with the sole purpose of monitoring and manipulating him.

"He planted you to make sure I did his bidding."

"Hudson," Melissa said.

He held up his hand. "The sum total of our military and intelligence wisdom is in the Situation Room. I think they can handle things without me for another minute."

Hudson and Fitz had been through a lot, beginning with a marathon campaign, the primaries, the attack in Colorado. The president had learned to rely on Fitz and considered him a friend. Fitz had been a competent chief of staff; his intelligence, humor, and political instincts were equally important to Hudson. He liked him very much.

Now that Vonner was dead, there seemed to be a liberation between Hudson and Fitz, a lightness that hadn't been there before. Yet the president still couldn't let his guard down, because all along he had known that Fitz had been spying on him for the old man, and he might still be working in some way for the REMie agenda. There was a high possibility that Fitz was one of the leakers, if not the primary source for the media. Gypsy had indicated many times that the leaker was somebody in the inner circle, but now in the face of the greatest crisis he had ever faced, in fact, the greatest threat to the nation since the Civil War, he had to finally decide if he could count on Fitz.

"You tell me right now, Fitz, are you going to back me no matter what I do? Privately we may disagree, we can yell, shout, cuss, and debate, but in the Sit Room, the cabinet room, or in the press room, I need to know that you have my back no matter what, and that your advice is always going to be objective and unbiased; that you are not serving the REMies or any other agenda floating around out there against me."

"I know you think because Vonner chose me to run your campaign and to be your chief of staff, that I was somehow on the other side, but damn it, he's *dead!*" Fitz snapped. "You've learned a lot since we started, but when he died, you discovered a lot about what was really going on. Vonner could've done anything with that money, but he gave it to you and Schueller, not just because you're related—hell, if he just wanted to enrich a relative he could have given everything to Devonshire. And it wasn't just so you would continue his work, but so that you would finally know the truth, and the truth is he was always on your side. He did everything to put you in a position to change the world, to make history, to take it back from the REMies. He knew better than anyone how corrupt things are. You still don't know all the things he saw and knew, about what really happens in the world and how corrupt things are, because you've been brainwashed in the same conditions as the rest of us. You grew up with the pressures of society telling you how it was, reading their fake history, listening to their fake news, and reacting and reeling and suffering through every single MADE event the REMies shoved down our throats. You *still* can't see beyond that brainwashing. Sure, your intellect can get you past a little bit, but there's a part of you that still thinks that votes matter, that the banks are keeping your money safe, that wars have to be fought every few years to keep us safe.

"Vonner didn't have that filter. He knew the *truth*, and he tried to show you. It's time for you to step up and take it all the way—*finish* what he was trying to do. In order to do that, you have to completely acknowledge that he was on your side, and if he was on your side, then I've always been on your side, too. That's the truth. The real question is, do you trust yourself to be the kind of president that you always thought there should be, that you always thought there was?"

Hudson stared at Fitz for a moment. "Yes. When this all started, I had no idea what I was getting into because you're right. I believed it was all real. I recall thinking that if somehow, impossibly, I got elected, then maybe the history of it, the presidency, the White House, would imbue special power and I'd be able to rise to the occasion and do the job. But to wade through this corruption and filth and fight every bit of the establishment and have the media constantly pecking at me, the plots of the bankers and the NorthBridge revolutionaries and enemies on so many hidden fronts setting minefields and traps because they know what I'm trying to do, and they must stop me . . . No, I wasn't up to that task. I'm man enough to admit it. But they *killed* me," his voice cracked, "and I came back from the dead to do this. I've learned, and I've fought through the scars and the lies and the corruption, and I'm ready." He turned to Melissa. "When I look at those burning cities, knowing what the REMies and North-Bridge are willing to do in this war . . . with the future of freedom at stake . . . I know I'm ready now, especially knowing that the two of you are with me."

"Glad to hear it," Fitz said, reaching to shake Hudson's hand.

"Then let's get back in there," the president said, moving toward the door.

"Wait, what are you going to do?" Melissa asked.

"It's a tough call," the president said, looking back at them. "At first I wasn't sure. But then I realized it's a much simpler choice. If General Imperia wants me to declare martial law, then that's exactly what I'm *not* going to do."

CHAPTER SIXTY-THREE

The president, Fitz, and the first lady returned to the Situation Room. However, instead of sitting, the president paced back and forth in front of the screens. Portland, Oregon, had become an apocalyptic scene. State and local police, along with national guard troops, were vastly outnumbered, and had been completely overrun by competing mobs. The city was in flames.

"Get the Army in there immediately," the president ordered.

"Are you declaring martial law?" General Imperia asked.

"Tell me what martial law would look like, General Imperia. How will the American people react? Our citizens own more than three hundred million guns. Do you really think they're not going to shoot back? You don't think we're going to incite the paramilitary revolution that NorthBridge *wants* if we declare martial law?"

"With all due respect, Mr. President, the screens behind you sure seem to indicate that we've already got that bloodied revolution they want."

"Then we're running out of time, General. Tell me your plan."

Fitz made eye contact with the president, but said nothing. General Imperia stood and pulled up a screen by pushing a button on his laptop. "The first thing we need to do is deploy the military to *all* the major cities. And be assured that three hundred million handguns and hunting rifles with the occasional assault weapon are nothing more than slingshots against the arsenal of the United States' Military."

"That won't stop them from trying," the president said. "There'll be a lot of bloodshed."

"The population will not resist," the general countered. "They will welcome the return of law and order as this violence spreads." He motioned to the monitors.

"How long are you proposing we keep martial law imposed?" the president asked.

"That will depend on the situation. If in the first few hours, if we do see any resistance, then we can implement the Beta-Pi plan."

"The Beta-Pi plan?" the president asked.

"Beta-Pi is a plan we developed in the last fifteen years," the general said. "It, uh—"

"It's the Department of Defense's blueprint for implementing martial law in the United States under situations where the public might resist the idea," the Chairman of the Joint Chiefs interrupted.

"Wait a minute," the president said. "We actually have a plan to declare martial law when it wouldn't be obviously necessary?"

"Mr. President, the Pentagon has a plan for every eventuality, or possible occurrence, that involves our mission—which is to protect the citizens and interests of the nation. We can't afford to wait until something is happening. *Inaction* during a crisis is dangerous," General Imperia said, pausing to steady a trembling hand as he looked back at the horrors on the screens. "The military plans for everything years in advance."

"Of course," the president said, feeling silly for even asking. At first, he was outraged that they would be planning for martial law, but then, as he thought about it, he would've been outraged if they had *not* been. The REMies had made him too paranoid. "Please continue, General."

"Operation Beta-Pi has many variables, but its basic premise is informing the population of the pandemic."

"But there is no pandemic," the president said at the risk of sounding foolish again.

"Of course not," the general said, a slight trace of impatience in his voice. "But our studies have shown, and logic dictates, that the population will comply most with martial law if they believe we are protecting them from a pandemic."

"But will they believe a pandemic on the heels of these riots?" some official asked.

"It doesn't seem out of the question," the general continued, "that NorthBridge would take this opportunity to unleash a biological weapon to cause more chaos. And that's exactly what we'll say. It will be the easiest way to enforce curfews, take resisters into custody, quarantine people, and it will allow us to regain control of the cities and put down these rioters or any rebellion."

"Then you want me to order the suspension of the Constitution so we can announce a fictitious plague to aid our efforts at regaining control of the cities?" the president asked. "Why don't we just use our strategic superiority to regain control? I can declare a state of emergency, which is far less extreme."

"It won't be enough," the general said.

"Well, if it's not enough, *then* I can declare martial law," the president said. "Why don't we begin with a state of emergency?"

The general's expression revealed his annoyance. "Mr. President, we have riots of unprecedented scale occurring in seventeen major cities, and we have mobs assembling in at least thirty-nine smaller ones. Every fringe group and militia out there is now on the move."

"The president is aware of the situation, General," Fitz said dismissively. "Thank you."

General Imperia looked from Colonel Dranick to the Chairman of the Joint Chiefs, and then reluctantly sat back down, unable to wipe the scowl from his face.

"General Imperia is correct," the Chairman of the Joint Chiefs began. "Our country has never, including during the Civil War, faced this much unrest simultaneously, encompassing such a broad geographic area. We're talking about *every* region, and it's worsening by the minute." He stopped and made eye contact with the president. "Neither you, nor I, know what NorthBridge is planning to do next. They may actually unleash bioweapons that cause a plague, and if we've got hundreds of thousands of people dying, then martial law may not be enough. There are viruses that can do that. Let me show you the charts, we've run all the simulations."

"Well, let me give you some history Chairman," the president said. "We've never had full-scale martial law in America, including during the Civil War. Lincoln suspended some rights, and the courts later found he overreached. We don't run the government on hypotheticals. If we did, we'd be going to war every other week for some reason or another because we thought some country might do us harm, or that another might do things we don't like. Yes, this situation is really bad, but it could get a lot worse if we play into our enemies' hands. They *want* martial law."

"Mr. President, look at the screens," the Chairman began. "Let's get an update. Let's see how many more cities have fallen into the hands of rebels and gang violence. This is a coordinated attack on the country by a terrorist group. NorthBridge is the largest domestic terrorist organization we have ever known, and they have initiated more attacks on US soil that any other entity or country ever. In fact, all the attacks on American soil combined don't reach the level of NorthBridge. We are at war, and you are tying the hands of the military unless you give us the tool of martial law immediately."

"Is there consensus among the military?" Colonel Dranick asked.

"Yes," the Chairman of the Joint Chiefs of Staff said. "We have a consensus."

"And national security advisors?" the president asked, looking at Dranick.

"Yes, Mr. President. We have a consensus as well. All national security advisers are unanimously recommending declaring martial law immediately."

Hudson's gaze lingered with Dranick's for a long moment. "How is the National Guard doing?"

"Look for yourself, Mr. President," General Imperia said. "Not well."

"Surely there's another option," the president said. "We can send in the military without declaring martial law."

General Imperia let out an exasperated sigh. "Are you afraid to use force, Mr. President?"

"What did you just say?" the president asked, getting up and walking toward the general.

General Imperia glared at the president for a moment, then said, "I beg your pardon, Mr. President, my emotions got the better of me. I spoke out of turn."

"General, I understand these are emotional times. I was elected to protect those people," the president said, pointing at the screens filled with mayhem and flames. "I was also elected to defend the Constitution of the United States, and you can be sure that if I, or when I, give the order to suspend that Constitution, it will be because I see no clear alternative. This is not such a case, so I suggest you get your troops ready to go into those cities and restore order, because I'm declaring a state of national emergency. And if you don't like my decision, then General, I suggest you run for the presidency."

CHAPTER SIXTY-FOUR

Back in the Oval Office, where Schueller was waiting, Fitz and Melissa congratulated the president.

"Too soon for that," Hudson said. "We may lose this yet. I might have no choice but to declare martial law tonight."

"Let's hope not," Fitz said, opening a Coke.

"Melissa, you've practically been running the Office of Intergovernmental Affairs," Hudson said.

"Not really," the first lady protested.

"The OIA is responsible for maintaining the White House's relationships with state legislators, governors, tribal leaders, mayors, and other political leaders across the country."

"I know."

"And that's what you've been doing," the president said.

"To get them ready for Cherry Tree and Fair and Free. Are they ever going to happen now?" Melissa questioned.

"I don't know," the president admitted. "But I need you back on the phone with every governor. Find out what's happening on the ground, find out what they need, and most important, ask them how they can stop the trouble. They'll know better than the brass in Washington how to clean up their own backyards."

"Got it," she said, giving him a quick kiss before heading to her own West Wing office.

"Dad," Schueller said, "is it NorthBridge or the REMies?"

"I'm really not sure yet. It could be both, but it won't matter in a few more days if we don't stop it."

"We could easily lose control," Fitz said.

"We're alone now," the president said to Fitz. "Do you think I'm doing the right thing?"

"I have no idea," Fitz said, raising his Coke bottle in a salute.

Hudson allowed a smile.

"Dad, the REMies clearly want martial law," Schueller said. "They've been strengthening the president's ability to impose military rule through executive orders since 9/11. Look at this." He walked over and showed his father a list on his laptop. Schueller read aloud, "President Trump renewed an emergency proclamation continuing what was supposed to be a temporary state of national emergency after the 2001 terror attacks. The executive branch has ignored a law requiring it to report to Congress every six months on how much the president has spent under those extraordinary powers. It began with President Bush signing Proclamation 7463, giving himself sweeping powers to mobilize the military in the days following the 9/11 attacks. Bush and all the presidents since, including President Obama, have renewed that emergency each year. You've signed it, too."

"They told me it was a matter of national security."

"That's because presidents will do anything for national security," Schueller said.

Hudson nodded.

"Obama also issued an Executive Order that outlines an extreme level of communications preparedness in case of crisis or emergency, including the ability to take over any communication network and the internet," Schueller said. "And you all have kept renewing that one, too."

"Guilty again," the president said.

Fitz joined them. "Take a look at this," he said, holding up his tablet computer. "Obama signed another Executive Order. I remember Vonner telling me it was a REMie rule. You've already renewed it twice."

The president read it:

The authority of the President conferred by section 101 of the Act, 50 U.S.C. App. 2071, to require acceptance and priority performance of contracts or orders (other than contracts of employment) to promote the national defense over performance of any other contracts or orders, and to allocate materials, services, and facilities as deemed necessary or appropriate to promote the national defense, is delegated to the following agency heads:

(1) the Secretary of Agriculture with respect to food resources, food resource facilities, livestock resources, veterinary resources, plant health resources, and the domestic distribution of farm equipment and commercial fertilizer;

(2) the Secretary of Energy with respect to all forms of energy;

(3) the Secretary of Health and Human Services with respect to health resources;

(4) the Secretary of Transportation with respect to all forms of civil transportation;

(5) the Secretary of Defense with respect to water resources; and

(6) the Secretary of Commerce with respect to all other materials, services, and facilities, including construction materials.

"They weren't just getting ready for martial law," the president said angrily. "They've been looking for, and waiting for, the right moment to use operation Beta-Pi. They *wanted* it to happen."

"They *made* it happen," Schueller said.

CHAPTER SIXTY-FIVE

As the military moved into fifty-eight American cities, the president was repeatedly called back to the Situation Room.

"Fonda Raton and more than two hundred others are posting on various internet sites in support of the protesters," the FBI Director said. "There's a list on your monitor showing the others. We also have pirate broadcasters, such as Thorne, who are broadcasting."

"I know he's managed to get on some airwaves," the president said.

"His biggest reach is from streaming across the internet," she said.

"You should use the switch," the Chairman of the Joint Chiefs said to the president. "I'm sure the Director would agree."

She nodded.

The 'switch,' promoted as a countermeasure in case of a massive cyber-attack against the United States, was part of a Cyberspace Protection Act, signed into law by Hudson's predecessor, giving the president broad authority to slow, or completely shut down, the internet.

"Censorship, isolation, invasive tactics," the president said. "Using the kill switch is tantamount to martial law."

"We have evidence that the rebels and other groups are using the internet to plan attacks, avoid detection, thwart our troops, and perpetuate violence," the FBI Director said.

Hudson looked at Fitz. The Chief of Staff responded with a slight nod.

"Kill it," the president said.

Less than half an hour later, Fonda Raton called the president's private line.

"How *dare* you shut down the internet!" she blasted as he answered. "The REMies really picked a winner in you. Tell me this, did they finally get you on their side, or are you just too *stupid* to know they're using you?"

"Do you see what's happening out there!?" Hudson blasted back. "How many people are *dying* because of you?"

"You did this because you didn't act fast enough to end their empire!"

"Because NorthBridge won't give me the time I need! Your way or no way. I can still change this. *Stop* the uprising. Give me a chance, damn it!"

"Oh, yes, candidate Pound, 'we are the change.' But so far President Pound hasn't delivered."

"I don't have any idea how America got to this point," Hudson said. "Revolution, Civil War, fury in the streets, but I can—"

"Don't you?" Fonda asked. "Think about your history, history teacher. Think back to John Anderson's third-party candidacy in

'76, Perot getting almost twenty percent of the vote in '92, the surges of Howard Dean, Ron Paul, Barack Obama coming from nowhere, and Bernie Sanders almost taking the nomination from the Establishment's darling Hillary—of course they couldn't let *that* happen. Then, Trump . . . sixty-three million people voted for an arrogant, egotistical, trinket salesman because they were so desperate for something different. The momentum has been building for decades. The beleaguered 'voters' could tell something was wrong, that the country was way off track. They so badly wanted someone to fix it. A long string of politicians promised they would fix it, that they would make everything better, but each promise for change turned into another lie. Just. Like. Your. Promises."

"More rants," Hudson said. "Rants, guns, and bombs, that's not how to change things."

"Then why do we have so many followers? Our movement started during Trump. NorthBridgers supported him as one final hope, not because they agreed with him, but because they thought he really might drain the swamp and change things, make the REMies go away and give back the country to the people."

"Obviously Trump didn't do that."

"Of course not, because for all his blustery rhetoric, just like all his predecessors, the REMies also controlled him."

"We don't have time to debate history."

"Conservatives hated Bill Clinton, liberals hated George W. Bush, loved Obama, and then hated Trump even more than Bush, but they were really all the same," she said, ignoring his statement. "Clinton took plenty of military action, did massive pro-business trade deals like NAFTA and GATT, and led aggressive financial and telecommunications deregulation. Obama bombed more countries than Bush, and Trump kept it right on going, even after promising not to during his campaign. Each president does some cosmetic things to rally his base and infuriate the opposition party, but that's to keep up the illusion of two parties. It's only an illusion, yet few people question why, and the ones who do can't quite figure out it's the REMies who run the world!"

"I know all this," Hudson said. "That's what Cherry Tree was going to do—show the world the truth. We would force change without all the bloodshed and war."

"You had your chance. I bought you all the time I could. Now watch us bring down the empire."

"But the REMies aren't a united force. There are major factions fighting for control—banks and Wall Street, military leaders and defense contractors, multinational corporations—you know all the players. How is this uprising going to stop all of them?"

"It's all in the rebuilding," she said. "Time's up."

CHAPTER SIXTY-SIX

The crackdown was necessarily swift and brutal. With troops moving into dozens of cities, drones, air support, the need for increased border security and hundreds of other "threats" that needed to be neutralized, the military was spread critically thin. Non-essential personnel were recalled from around the globe, however, the international bases could not be depleted for long. The world was watching; terrorists and other enemies saw opportunity.

At the same time, infrastructure, utilities—including the power grid, seaports, and airports, along with a host of other sites —required added attention. The media and universities needed to be controlled. The 3D facial recognition system tagged anyone suspicious, allowed for easier enforcement of curfews, and rounded up those on government watch lists. Tens of thousands were arrested. Prisons filled beyond capacity, led to the opening of detention camps. A network of facilities that had been established by the Federal Emergency Management Agency in the preceding decades for other uses had now been converted to hold large numbers of dissidents.

In the ten days that followed the president's decision, North-Bridge seemed to have vanished into the shadows as the State of Emergency took hold and the military grabbed authority in all facets of American life. The shocking reality to the average citizen of how unstable their country had become over-shadowed what some saw as the greater issue—which was just how incredibly fast the military had taken over.

Vice President Brown stormed into the Oval Office while Hudson was meeting with his secretary and two legislative assistants.

"You want to tell me how this is any different than martial law?" the vice president demanded.

The president motioned to his secretary for the room to be cleared. "What are you even doing here?" he asked. "We're not supposed to be in the same building at the same time," he added firmly, "particularly in a crisis such as this."

"The line of succession is secure," the vice president replied. "The Speaker of the House is currently in his home district. President pro tempore of the Senate is at the Capitol Building. The Secretary of State is returning from Canada. But what's not safe is our country. I agree with you that martial law was too extreme, but you've done almost the same thing! A rose by any other name . . ."

"I've done what I've had to do," the president said.

"You may call this a state of emergency, but it might as well be martial law. You're in danger of losing what control you have over the government. You're ceding your power to the Pentagon."

"You saw those cities. I had to send the troops in."

"But you suspended the writ of habeas corpus without the consent of Congress. You've raised troops in every state. They're arresting people without cause, searching without warrants. I understand that today the Army occupied and closed several courthouses in New York and California, and that the military has taken over more than thirty local police forces who failed to act on your state of emergency orders."

"You weren't in the Sit Room," the president said. "Whatever you've seen on television is nothing compared to what's actually going on out there."

"How can I believe what I see on television when the military has taken over any stations and networks that were airing anything critical? It's martial law. You created a police state. How are you going to get out of this?"

"I. Don't. Know." The president stood up from the Resolute Desk and walked around the corner to stand right in front of the vice president. "The country was tearing itself apart. If I didn't take this action, we'd be in a full scale civil war. I'll figure out how to get out of it when I get there."

"But you *cannot* trust the military," the vice president said.

The president stared at her, surprised that she understood how precarious the relationship was with the Pentagon. "I know that," he said quietly.

"Then why are you letting them take control?"

"Because I don't have enough VS agents to keep order, and I can't spare the Secret Service to even take back control of Wichita, let alone Los Angeles, Chicago, Detroit, Houston . . . What am I supposed to *do*? What would you do if I were dead and you were the president? How would you have solved this problem?"

"We're trying to break the REMies' empire," the vice president began, "yet you're using the military, the very organization that's paid for and controlled by the REMies to keep their empire in power."

"And your point?"

"Maybe you should consider cutting a deal with Booker Lipton."

"He's the one who's *caused* all of this!"

"Is he?"

CHAPTER SIXTY-SEVEN

On the eighth day after the uprisings began, Melissa found Hudson in the Situation Room at three a.m. "You can't keep doing this," she said, stepping behind his chair and rubbing his shoulders.

"Doing what?"

"Working all night. You can't survive on an hour nap here, two hours of sleep there."

"It's the biggest crisis we've ever faced," he said, stifling a yawn.

"Imagine how much worse it would be if the president *died* during it."

"Maybe Celia could do a better job."

"I'll pretend I didn't hear that," she said. "Come to bed."

"Not yet."

"You've done all you could for today—or yesterday, since it's already tomorrow."

"The generals—"

"They're behaving," she said. "You've cut their authority every chance you got. There haven't been more than forty-eight hours where you haven't overridden them, reduced personnel, or had them pull out of a city. You've reinstated rights to nearly one-third of the cities and managed to close two FEMA camps already."

"It's going well, but we're not out of the woods. DIRT has been a huge help keeping the military in check. The biggest break may be the absence of any major NorthBridge attacks." He stood, leaned against the table, and brought her close. "And all your contacts in the state governments. I'm not sure what we would have done without the national guards and the state police. Those people haven't slept either."

"I've skipped a little sleep, too," she admitted.

"You're amazing. You've been on the phone every single day, with every single governor," he said. "I'm just trying to keep up with you."

"Then come to bed."

He didn't quite get three hours of sleep before they woke him for a call from Dranick.

"Secure line," the DNI confirmed.

"How bad?" the president asked impatiently, knowing Colonel Dranick wasn't calling with good news.

"Remember the couple?" Dranick asked.

"Of course," the president replied. They'd been following every moment of the lives of a man who worked for Coyne and his lover, a woman employed by Bastendorff. As best they'd been able to ascertain, neither REMie knew that the two underlings were involved in a secret romance. The rivals, each vying for the CapStone, would have forbidden any such contact. That is unless, as the Wizard had theorized, it was some kind of set-up. In the REMie world of MADE events, it could have been a trap for the couple, or a "dangle," what the CIA would call an agent sent to provide a stream of disinformation to the president.

"It looks like it wasn't NorthBridge," Dranick said.

"I'm exhausted Enapay, please just tell me."

"We've picked up from their conversations last night that this is all part of the CapWar. Coyne and Bastendorff are going at each other, and they're using the United States as their battlefield."

"*They* started this?"

"Yes, sir. They both want you out. They expected this to immediately bring you down. Apparently, they didn't count on the Pentagon to support you."

"You've clearly been helping with that."

There was a brief silence before Dranick responded. "I'm doing everything I can to help you get through this."

"Call the Director," Hudson said. "Get her to find a DIRT team that isn't vital to putting down the uprising. We need arrest warrants for Bastendorff and Coyne."

"Mr. President, excuse me," Dranick said, as if confused. "We don't need arrest warrants, we need a Dark Ops unit. It's time to take these two evil REMie bastards out."

CHAPTER SIXTY-EIGHT

Bastendorff cleared a table consisting of six elaborate Lego Star Wars sets, including a four-thousand-piece Death Star. As the multi-colored plastic bricks and assorted other pieces crashed onto the floor and ricocheted in hundreds of directions, the fat man bellowed as if he'd been knifed. "Why is Hudson Pound still alive!?"

An assistant, used to the billionaire's verbal abuse, reluctantly continued the briefing. He informed his boss of the progress being made by the administration against the riots and uprisings. Bastendorff interrupted the man continuously, interjecting profanity laced commentary on the reports. As the assistant proceeded, the outbursts worsened.

"Just three days ago Times Square was locked down!" Bastendorff barked. "The Pentagon had turned hotels in at least nine cities into temporary prisons, and now that's over?"

"Yes, sir. The president has apparently kept the generals on a tight leash. He's been undoing their measures swiftly. The public's view of the president is becoming more favorable as the crisis continues. The media and internet are still extremely limited. However, we've been able to gauge the population's sentiments through the normal government channels—"

"They're using Three-D and AI to assess and predict human behavior . . . "

"Yes, large scale Artificial Intelligence programs are interpreting the Three-D data with dramatic accuracy."

"And the data shows the president is winning?"

"Yes, the people are increasingly concerned and fearful about the Pentagon's power and the prospect of long-term military authority and occupation of their cities, towns, and even homes."

"Fear? I'll give them fear!" Bastendorff raged, clearing another table filled with Lego Ninjago temples and attack vehicles. "So they see Pound as a kind of hero?"

"That's what the data's showing, quite clearly. The public believes he's working to keep the Pentagon in check, that the system which ensures a civilian government in control of the military is more fragile and at risk than ever before in America."

"You know what happens to heroes? They have a fancy funeral, and then songs are written about them. Let the fools sing!"

The assistant nodded as if agreeing with his boss's statement, even though he always thought the big man was letting emotion warp his perspective. "They see Pound as fighting to preserve it while balancing the need for utilizing the armed forces during the crisis."

"*The* crisis? This is *my* crisis. *I* created it!" Bastendorff yelled. "And it should have grown from crisis to civil war by now. What the hell is going on over there? I've sunk billions into this war!"

His rage dissolved into another stream of expletives before he began calling in more of his lieutenants. After a group of fifteen of his top people had assembled, he gave new orders and revamped his strategy to destroy the president and create more trouble in America.

"I want him dead and the country left in shambles. Any and all means necessary are authorized. Ten million dollars to the one who gets it done!"

A more subdued Titus Coyne spoke with several elite financial leaders and four other REMies who were allied with his efforts.

"This is only round one," Coyne began. "While Pound has surprised us with his ability to handle the turmoil, this actually plays into our hands. Bastendorff may have chosen the complete destruction of the United States as his path to the CapStone, but I'm not interested in cleaning up that big of a mess. The president has done us a favor. Let him do the heavy lifting, I prefer not to get my hands dirty."

"But his popularity is increasing," a Federal Reserve Governor said.

"I assure you that he will not be the president for much longer."

"How long?" another REMie asked.

"Long enough to finish stabilizing things, he's good at that," Coyne said.

"Are we talking weeks or months?"

"Days," Coyne said, which created a murmur around the room. "Hudson Pound's time as president will be over in a matter of days."

The president had told Dranick he wanted assets seized and due process carried out. "Those REMies *will* be arrested."

"As if our justice system isn't part of their empire?" Dranick had questioned.

But the president already had a team of nearly two hundred lawyers working to restructure the entire system. The Gypsy program had identified a long list of judges and prosecutors who had "REMie tendencies," which meant they were knowingly or unknowingly working for the elites. "We won't sink to their level," the president had told his old army buddy. "They'll be put on trial. The world needs to see the full breadth of their conspiracy."

However, the appearance of justice and transparency for the REMies' great crimes wasn't his only motivation. REMies were not a unified force running the world, such as conspiracy theorists imagined the Illuminati were. Yet the REMies maintained power by abiding by a few rules, and the "RAT clause," as Hudson called it, was their most important, and the president's main concern. The REMie Asset Transfer, or "RAT" clause, stated that in the event of a REMie death, his wealth must pass to a family member or other REMie. This was one reason Vonner had researched his ancestry so thoroughly. REMies always knew to whom they were related. It was the RAT clause that had allowed them to keep and consolidate their wealth in the hands of so few families. New REMies, such as some of the tech billionaires of the past few decades, could trace their bloodlines to other REMies.

Hudson explained the decision to Melissa as they were grabbing a quick breakfast in the president's study.

"I understand the RAT clause is why you want to seize assets," the first lady said, "to keep them from passing their wealth. But won't all the possible heirs be indicted as co-conspirators?"

"No. These are going to be difficult cases. Even if we can get Fair and Free in place and level the playing field so we can be guaranteed honest judges, we'll be lucky to get all the REMies themselves in prison. Going beyond that to immediate family, let alone distant family members, will be impossible."

"I get it," she said. "But isn't the RAT clause what got Schueller his inheritance? What happens to his billions?"

"Schueller isn't a REMie. He won't be prosecuted."

"Vonner was."

"You can't prosecute a dead man."

The president took a call from Rex. "Thought you'd want to know," Vonner's old fixer began. "In the final wave of violence that hit Vegas, it seems a building belonging to a distant relative of yours got hit."

"Really?" the president asked. "Was anyone hurt?"

"Fortunately, most everyone was evacuated. However, there were numerous injuries. Most were nothing too serious." Rex rolled a handful of black dice onto a glass table. The rattle was loud enough that the president could hear them. "But the reason I'm calling," Rex continued, "is that there was one fatality."

"Sorry to hear that."

"Yeah, I knew you would be," Rex said. "It was your relative."

"Oh, no . . . are you sure?"

"Yeah. Tarka just confirmed it. Lester Devonshire is dead."

CHAPTER SIXTY-NINE

I took the most powerful military on the face of the earth just twelve days to completely put down the uprisings and restore order. Still, it had been an epic disaster—six thousand two hundred ninety-one dead, twice that many injuries, and property damage in the hundreds of billions. The cost to the economy was going to be in excess of a trillion dollars, maybe twice that depending on which economists were doing the figuring. The Federal Reserve had stepped in and was doing what some critics called "smoke and mirrors" to keep the economy afloat. However, as always after a war, the rebuilding would be a boon.

But the country was scarred. It would be a long time before anyone could know how deeply.

Hudson gave the speech of his life, declaring victory and thanking the brave men and women of the military and law enforcement, as well as the countless ordinary citizens who had acted with bravery and honor when called upon. To the portion of the general population who had not panicked and added to the mayhem, he offered deep gratitude and promised that this would not be allowed to happen again.

While the media was blaming NorthBridge, the president promised that a full investigation was underway, and he believed it would show that another group had created the catastrophe. "Outside forces are manipulating events and distracting everyone," he said in a thinly-veiled reference to MADE events, which he would soon be revealing as part of Cherry Tree. "They will not be allowed to win."

Privately, though, the president knew he and the country were in a weaker position than ever before. NorthBridge had mostly sat out the uprisings, perhaps knowing the REMies had been hoping to bring them into the mix. If they had, it would have led to the end of America.

But NorthBridge could strike at any moment. Fonda had made it clear that something was underway. The REMies had hardly dipped into their resources and still managed almost to ignite a civil war in the country the rest of the world viewed as the most stable, a safe haven for a century. No more.

If not for Dranick providing constant access to the full network of spy satellites, Hudson might have made a mistake, might have missed a trouble spot, might have messed up. Instead, by torturing his body with endless green tea and dangerously little sleep (and even a few of Fitz's Cokes) he was able to hold the Union together and prevent either rebels or the military from gaining too much power. General Imperia had led the operation, proving to be a brilliant tactician and demonstrating an uncanny ability at controlling civilian populations.

The president's popularity was at its highest point since the inauguration, but Hudson knew it would be fleeting. There were still thousands in prison and under house arrest, and the streets were filled with checkpoints and tension. Congress and the Cabinet were pushing him to restore normalcy as quickly as possible, but the president had other ideas. He had to act before the REMies or NorthBridge came back for round two.

The strategy now was to launch the enhanced Cherry Tree on Monday—three days away. The enhanced part of the plan included evidence of the REMies' involvement in the attacks that nearly destroyed the nation, combined with criminal charges filed against *all* the REMies for their long history of misdeeds and manipulations. Everything had been simplified and thousands of MADE events had been documented, linked back to the REMies, and illustrated. The cases were comprehensive and would shock the world, and the REMies had granted the president one important ingredient he'd been missing before—trust. A shaken public believed in him as a Lincoln-esque leader.

Late Friday night, Hudson was in the president's study working on more of the radical reforms and the new structure of government that would follow the REMies' demise. In his exhaustion, he kept losing his thought, envisioning the new wonderful era that would be ushered in with Fair and Free practices: an economy built on environmental concern instead of environmental exploitation, a healthcare system built upon health instead of care, and incentives for sharing wealth instead of hoarding wealth, for lifting people up instead of becoming the first one to get to the top, or maintaining a pool of corruption which kept others down. Yet even as he imagined all of that great promise, he worried whether Granger would be able to salvage enough from the collapsing central bank REMie financial empire to create a new one which would allow for all the exciting changes ahead. He had nightmares about the world collapsing into brutal anarchy where tens of millions died of starvation as everything crumbled.

A blinking on his computer brought him out of his worry. The Wizard was trying to reach him. After taking all the normal precautions that insured the communications would be secure, he opened the video window. Hudson could immediately tell something was wrong.

"Dawg, I just broke another one of Crane's encryptions."

"Crane?"

The president had almost forgotten that there was still data out on the DarkNet hidden by Crane, one of their best hackers. He had discovered a trove of secret information the night he was murdered. The earlier revelations that Booker Lipton, Fonda Raton, and Thorne were the leaders of NorthBridge had dramatically shifted the way they approached the terror organization. Ever since, the Wizard had put a team on the search—their mission: find the identity of AKA Adams, AKA Franklin, and any other possible AKAs.

"Have you found the other AKAs?" Hudson asked, his hopes surging.

"I've got Adams," the Wizard said, still looking grave. "Prepare yourself, Dawg. It couldn't be much worse. Are you alone?"

"Yes, tell me!"

"AKA Adams is Vice President Celia Brown."

Hudson felt the air sucked from his lungs. For an instant, his brain shut down, as if a circuit breaker had tripped. Searching for the words to respond, it seemed as if he didn't even know the language to speak them in.

"I've quadruple checked it. Adams is really her. No doubt," the Wizard said before Hudson could ask the obvious question.

"I . . . I don't believe it," Hudson finally said.

"Fine, but it's true. What the hell are we going to do?"

"How? Celia is antiwar, anti-violence . . . she's got a long history of seeking peace at every turn. This can't be right. She would never be affiliated with the terrorists."

"Are you going to arrest her?" the Wizard asked.

"Can't you hear me? Celia Brown is *not* a member of North-

Bridge, let alone one of its *leaders*. They've started a *war*. You know the vice president would rather jump in front of a speeding train than start a war."

"She may know how to find Booker, Fonda, and Thorne. I don't think waiting for AKA Franklin is a good idea anymore. You should get a DIRT team from the FBI to arrest the vice president. This might be our chance to stop NorthBridge before they strike."

"You're telling me you really believe this?" the president asked.

"I'm telling you with one hundred percent certainty that the vice president of the United States is AKA Adams, one of the leaders of NorthBridge." The Wizard stared at Hudson with the nearly four decades of their friendship in his eyes.

The president looked back, and although it was one of the most impossible things to believe he had ever heard, he no longer doubted it. "Damn," he said, shaking his head.

"What do you want to do?"

"I don't know. I'm heading to Camp David first thing in the morning. The vice president is in Texas right now. I think she'll be returning a few hours after I leave. You know it's always coordinated that we aren't in the same building at the same time."

"Yeah. She could have killed you by now."

"But she didn't," the president said, still trying to come to grips with the shocking news. "I'll have to check on her schedule to be sure, but I need to think about this. I need to strategize. You may be right that the best approach is to show up with a trusted DIRT team, question her, and see if we can get the locations of the others. She must know about AKA Franklin." The president felt his adrenaline flowing. "What the hell is she doing with NorthBridge? This is so insane. "

"Do you want to cancel Camp David?"

"No! You know we have to put the final pieces together for

Cherry Tree. And we can't arrest her before Monday. Can you imagine if we suddenly announce that the vice president is a NorthBridge terrorist after everything that's happened? Cherry Tree would be sunk."

"They don't know we know, so we could wait to arrest her until Monday."

"I'll need that long just to figure out how the world got so upside down," Hudson said. "And even then, her arrest would jeopardize Cherry Tree."

"Maybe we announce an illness and keep her hidden for a few days? Quietly detain her? Question her?"

"Risky. Maybe we do nothing. I'll put it into the mix with the others tomorrow. We'll come up with something."

After the call, Hudson wandered into the Oval Office. Only one dim light was on. He stood there absorbing the history of the room as he hadn't done since his early days in the White House. Silently, the president of the United States, facing a narrowing window to save the country, called on the wisdom of his predecessors, the real John Adams, Abraham Lincoln, and Thomas Jefferson.

What would make the vice president join NorthBridge?

He'd picked her with no influence—or at least he thought with no influence from Vonner or Fitz. Vonner had been so furious when Hudson had named her as his running mate, the first African American vice president. He wondered if the old man had known who she really was. He doubted it. However, Booker Lipton must've been laughing and toasting champagne when he heard that Vonner's boy had chosen a NorthBridge leader to be his vice president. And how had Fonda kept a straight face? He had trusted Celia Brown and believed in her, believed she was on his side. She had actually been the president during those nine minutes and for several days after the Air Force One attack. What if he had died for good? Celia Brown would've been the president. NorthBridge would have been in full control without ever having finished their revolution.

Why hasn't NorthBridge killed me? They could have so easily, and then they would have the presidency. Brown could appoint another NorthBridge member as vice president. They'd have it locked up by now.

He looked at the Resolute Desk in the fading light and whispered, "I don't know why I'm still alive."

CHAPTER SEVENTY

Only the weekend remained before their final chance to launch Cherry Tree and tell the world the truth about the REMies.

"We have forty-eight hours to get every last detail right," the president said, "because Cherry Tree isn't just going to change the future, it's going to shatter the past and change the present reality for everyone on the planet."

"Especially the REMies," Schueller said as the inner circle huddled in tense deliberations at Camp David.

It was a particularly heavy fog that morning; everything seemed eerily still. Even with the gravity of the times, an excited anticipation permeated the air as they finally felt the time for launch was here. Still, each of them knew that every single thing had to go right for Cherry Tree to have a chance at succeeding. The president had reviewed the list of problems they had to resolve before Monday morning. Then there were the wildcards: Would the uprisings stay suppressed? What would NorthBridge do?

The latter was made all the more unpredictable now that

they knew Vice President Brown was one of the founding members of NorthBridge and a part of the terrorist group's leadership.

"The vice president knows about Cherry Tree?" Schueller asked.

"Celia must be the leaker," Melissa concluded. "She's been undermining you all along."

"She'll be expecting an update this evening," Fitz said.

"I agree with the Wizard," Schueller said. "We should have a DIRT team quietly pick her up, now."

"Quietly arresting the vice president of the United States is not as simple as it sounds," Dranick said.

"Enough of this debate," the president said. "The vice president has no idea we're onto her. I'm scheduled to call her in about ten hours. We'll deal with it then."

"And what if NorthBridge attacks in the meantime?" Melissa asked.

"Then the vice president will be the least of our worries."

During the next six hours, they reviewed every aspect of Cherry Tree and made final decisions based on the latest intelligence provided by Dranick and simulations created by Gypsy. They held numerous video conferences with the Wizard and Granger about radical reforms. Progress was slow, but the looming deadline grew closer like a hooded executioner walking to the gallows.

The pressure mounting, their deliberations grew more heated. As they discussed what America's role would be in a post-Cherry Tree world, the tricky issue of the military rose to the fore. Fitz had just spoken about receiving some pushback from the Pentagon about closing bases and recalling troops.

"The Pentagon doesn't get to decide," the president said

bitterly. "The people elected me president and commander in chief of the Armed Forces. To quote George W Bush, 'I am the decider.'"

"Dad, I don't think you need to bring the Bushes into this," Schueller said. "Not in mixed company."

"We all know that you're the commander-in-chief," Fitz began, "but I think allowing the Pentagon to have a little more input wouldn't be such a bad idea, the Secretary of Defense said as much yesterday when you met. And—"

"Do you really think the Pentagon is going to act as fast and forcefully as we need them to?" the president asked, pacing at the window. "They'll drag their feet until the next election or until an assassin finally gets me."

"Hudson, please," Melissa said, aghast.

"Sorry Melissa, Schueller," the president said. "My point is this has to be done quickly, and I must act unilaterally, because otherwise it won't happen. You know this."

Melissa nodded.

"Let's ask Enapay," the president said. "His military back-ground, role as DNI, and dealings with the Pentagon during the uprisings gives him special insight."

"Mr. President," Dranick began. "I tend to agree with Fitz on this one. If we do the cuts too quickly, we leave ourselves vulner-able at some of the hotspots around the globe, and it will affect our foreign policy for decades. After the rise of NorthBridge and our recent domestic hostilities, I fear the timing is wrong and the outcome will be negative." Dranick paused to gauge the presi-dent's reaction.

Hudson stared attentively at his friend, waiting for more.

"At the same time," Dranick continued, "I see a substantial drawdown of troops abroad as a good strategy both to ease the deficit and to curtail our enormous national debt."

"The debt is unsustainable," Schueller said.

"Yes," Dranick agreed. "A drawdown also offers some stability here at home should we face renewed rioting and revolution. But I think your overall plan is too aggressive."

"Schueller, what do you think?" the president asked, sitting back down.

"I'm with you, Dad. We need those troops at home to combat NorthBridge and deal with the next wave of riots and uprisings that are definitely coming. We've been lucky that we were able to get that under control." Schueller had been suspicious, and even baffled by exactly how the military put down the uprisings so efficiently. He'd urged his father to appoint a committee to investigate, which he had, but those answers were a long way off. "Until we break down the rise and fall, we won't know when, but we can be sure it *will* happen again. There's too much discontent and divisiveness in the country. The REMies spent decades dividing us, and there are so many different factions of us versus them that we need all hands on deck here at home. I don't think your plan is aggressive enough. No offence, Colonel." Schueller nodded and smiled at Dranick, then continued. "That is to say nothing of the hundreds of billions of dollars we're wasting overseas for no reason, and as you yourself pointed out, the military has changed a lot just in the last few years. Wherever we face threats, we can get unmanned drones and other assets to hotspots quicker to handle any situation. We don't need all these bases and all those soldiers. They only serve the REMies. War sucks! Let's save the money and bring them home where we need them. The Pentagon routinely 'misplaces' hundreds of billions of dollars. They shouldn't be handling this—that's like asking the fox to clean up the henhouse."

"Good then," Hudson said. "Melissa, Granger, and the Wizard, also agree with me. I'm sorry Fitz and Enapay, you see it differently, but this is too important of an issue."

Fitz took a sip of his Coke and said, "I think it's a mistake."

Dranick nodded.

"Next topic, environmental protection agency," the president said. "I'm going to issue an executive order that's going to give them new authority. And Fitz, I know your reservations on this one, too, but we've got a couple friends in Congress to help us with this, and part of it no doubt will wind up in the Supreme Court, but by then—"

The door suddenly burst open and seven soldiers carrying MK416 assault rifles and 9mm pistols entered the room.

"What's this? What's happened?" the president asked, startled.

"Sir, my name is Major Anthony Miller, and my orders are to place you under house arrest."

"What? Who ordered you?" the president asked, astonished, as he jumped to his feet.

"Sir, unfortunately I am not at liberty to give you that information at the present time. Rest assured, no harm will come to you or your family. However, I must detain all of you here."

"Who the hell *are* you?" the president asked, not recognizing his own voice.

Fitz stood up. "This is unbelievable." He moved toward the soldier at the same time Schueller dashed to the door. Three soldiers immediately aimed their weapons at Fitz, one aimed at Schueller. The others kept their assault rifles trained on the president.

"Gentlemen, please return to your seats. You will not leave this room until we have an understanding," Major Miller said.

Fitz and Schueller each went back to their chairs.

"You are American soldiers, I am your commander in chief, and you will stand down *immediately*. I order you to put your weapons on the table and leave this room at once."

"No can do, sir," the major said. "You have been relieved from duty. You are no longer the commander in chief."

CHAPTER SEVENTY-ONE

The president stared out the window toward the woods that surrounded the cottages at Camp David. They were in the somewhat isolated Laurel Lodge. Hudson had chosen it for the final Cherry Tree preparations for that reason, as well as its three conference rooms, kitchen, spacious dining area, and other amenities. He hadn't expected it to become his prison.

Dranick had walked out of the building with the other soldiers. *He'd been in on it*, the president brooded. *How could he have done this to me? I saved his life and now he's thrown mine away.*

Hudson could see three soldiers between him and freedom. They patrolled the open area between the lodge and the tree line. As the others spoke their outrage, voiced their concerns not just for their own safety, but for the future of the country they loved, Hudson Pound stared out the window, unwilling to submit to this outcome. He'd been through too much to panic now, but his parental instincts took hold as he worried about Florence. The soldiers refused to give him any information about her or his siblings when he asked, and their cell phones had been confiscated.

Hudson wondered where Tarka was. *Has she also been arrested? Has she somehow escaped?*

His thoughts ricocheted off the questions bouncing around the room from the others.

What is the news reporting? How can I get word to Tarka? Did she know? Has the Wizard been arrested? Granger? How long are they going to keep us here? Where will they move us?

"Hudson? *Hudson?*"

Melissa was calling him back into the conversation. He reluctantly turned.

"Hudson, we have to figure this out," the first lady said.

"How can the generals think they can get away with this?" Fitz asked.

"Because generals always *do* get away with it," Schueller said.

"Not only that," the president said, "but there are very few times in history that the generals leading the coup have allowed the legitimate leaders to live."

Everyone looked at him and at each other with sober angst. They may have already had the same thoughts, but Hudson, with his boundless grasp of history, had been the first to voice it. They might be living their last hours.

"Sooner or later they'll have to dispose of at least me," Hudson continued. "And probably you all as well, lest there be any witnesses or anybody to contest whatever new government they have in store." His voice trembled for an instant as his eyes swept from Melissa's and lingered on Schueller. "For all we know, they've already told the public that we were killed by a NorthBridge terrorist attack or some horrible accident."

"And that's why the military had to step in," Fitz said. "Because if terrorists took out the whole leadership, the executive branch, and maybe even knocked off the Speaker of the House and the others in the line of succession, then anything is possible, and the military would be justified in taking over until order can be restored."

"So why are we still alive?" Melissa asked.

"Because it's early yet," Hudson said. "We probably don't have much time."

CHAPTER SEVENTY-TWO

"We need to change the narrative," Titus Coyne said to General Imperia as the two men walked along the deserted Vietnam Memorial. The entire National Mall area in Washington, DC had been closed off since the coup. Washington had always been a city full of power and history, but now the nation's Capital was full of military checkpoints, barricades, guard stations, and tanks.

"That damn rabble-rouser, Thorne, is still broadcasting somehow," General Imperia said. "It's outrageous that we haven't been able to shut down his signals yet. He's feeding into this anti-government fervor."

"The same anti-government sentiments that allowed you to take power, general."

"Pound was going to destroy our way of life," Imperia growled. "Might as well hand the country to the communists."

"Preaching to the choir," Coyne said, smiling.

Imperia continued his tirade. "Chinese, Russians, Islamic extremists . . . Pound was weak, and all he was doing was weakening us. Our system works. Greatest on earth."

"We designed an incredible system," Coyne agreed, "and it's been working for more than a hundred years. People may think it's easy having seven billion people on the planet, as if there's plenty of everything, or they imagine there's some better way to do everything. Sure, anything can be improved, but look how much our system has achieved. Look at the advances. I know there are people in poverty and all that, but we're slowly cutting that down. We're extending life expectancies—well, mostly. We're expanding the middle class around the world. Of course, it ebbs and flows in countries like ours, but overall it's expanding. With all that, people are still impatient. Everybody thinks there's another, better way. Well, there is no better way, general. If there were, we'd be doing it, and I—"

"Titus, do you mind saving your speech for somebody who gives a damn?" the general said. "I'm a busy man. I'm trying to keep this nation together."

"We all are, general. That's why I was saying we need a new narrative. The population is still getting information from pirated radio signals; and worse, somehow they're reaching nearly seventy percent of the population on their phones."

"I don't know how that's possible, we shut down the internet."

"*Nonessential* internet," Coyne corrected. "But there's still a lot going through, and Booker Lipton or somebody has figured out a way to get unauthorized sites and traffic through the channels."

"Then we'll just shut off the cell phones," the general said.

"Things are already shaky enough," Coyne said, momentarily distracted by all the names of the dead on the wall. "It's going to be hard enough to put things back together as it is, but we have to keep the country running. The economy will take years, probably *decades*, to recover from this. I don't want to put it all in the toilet just because we can't figure out a way to control what the people think, so I'm proposing we get our own agitators out there. We send in people who claim to be against the temporary military occupation of the government and we have them shift the narrative, move people's opinions in our direction slowly, subtly. Meanwhile, we work on jamming NorthBridge and find that dead man—Thorne."

"Sounds like the beginnings of a plan. I think it would be a good idea to use this opportunity to seize Booker Lipton's assets."

"That's a touchy one," Coyne said. "I'd like nothing more than to see just that. However, if people start seeing the military taking over nonstrategic properties, they'll think their homes are next."

"Hell, Booker Lipton's got nothing *but* strategic assets," the general said. "He's a threat to our democracy."

Coyne raised an eyebrow as if to say, *And we aren't?* "Let's put together a list of what we can do and get the boys over at the NSA to figure out how he's hijacked the cell networks and where that information is coming from."

"Each day is precious," General Imperia said. "As you know, there are hundreds of millions of guns out there. I don't want more guerilla fights in the streets than we've already got. Each day NorthBridge attracts more and more followers. Already people are saying they were right all along."

"Not everyone. Lots of people blame NorthBridge for the military having to step in since Pound couldn't keep things under control."

"Not enough of them know," the general said. "These are revolutionary times, and we just ceded that energy. People have less patience now. The changes come, and if things don't get better, they'll make another change even faster."

"Then we don't need Pound anymore, or the vice president," Coyne said with a firm nod. "Okay?"

General Imperia nodded, a smile forming on his lips. "I understand."

CHAPTER SEVENTY-THREE

The vice president had been in her West Wing office when the soldiers came. They quickly cordoned off the West Wing into four sections, leaving her detained with one other man, one of the president's senior aides who had been working the weekend to provide support to the president and his team at Camp David. The two of them were allowed to move to the southwest quadrant of the West Wing, which included the Chief of Staff's office (vacant since Fitz was at Camp David), the aide's office, and the vice president's office, along with a few other unoccupied rooms, a storage closet, and a restroom. Guards were posted outside the hall leading to the National Security Adviser's office, the two doors to the outside, and the hall leading to the Oval Office.

They told her only that the president had been arrested and that the Chairman of the Joint Chiefs was now in charge. When she demanded more information, she was informed that General Imperia would be there at five p.m. to brief her. Thirty minutes after the takeover, she took the aide into her confidence and told him she had a way out, but needed him to remain.

"I'll be back for that meeting," she said. "Be ready to go."

He nodded, too stunned to question her about anything.

A few minutes later, she was down in the tunnels. The president had showed her a secret entrance between the Chief of Staff's office and hers. It had long been concealed after several renovations, and involved some tricky maneuvering in the back of a closet to reach. The steps down were narrow and creaky, but solid.

From there, she made her way through the tunnels, and after a series of unmanned security electronic doors, for which her passcode gave entrance, she made it to the Treasury Building and reached Booker on a landline.

"It's a coup," he told her. "Full military takeover. Well planned."

"Damn it, they did it!" she said. "Is the president okay?"

"We're still trying to find out," Booker said. "Either way, our next move must be perfect or we'll be in an all-out war."

"Neither side can win that."

"We knew the uprisings were only the first step to this. It gave them perfect cover to blanket troops across the country with no objections. They were welcomed in most cities. And it was an easy leap to install military officers at all levels."

"And, as expected, they're blaming it all on us," she said. "Have they implemented Beta-Pi?" she asked, trying to figure out if her plan could work.

"Not yet, which means they're getting little resistance, but that will change, and within a few days we'll no doubt hear the media announcing that we've unleashed a bioweapon. Viruses will be detected wherever they're having trouble subduing the population."

"Has Congress been dismissed?"

"They're calling it a 'temporary suspension'," Booker said, and then read from the Pentagon's official declaration: "'Entire

Constitution on hold until we eradicate NorthBridge from our country. When that mission is accomplished, the Constitution will be restored, and new elections held.'"

"New elections?" the vice president asked.

"Yes, because you and President Pound were killed by North-Bridge agents today."

"I see," she said, knowing she did not have long to live. She told Booker her plan.

"It could work, assuming we get through security at the entrance . . . but that's doable," Booker said. "Still, why don't we get you out of there? I can have someone get to you in fifteen minutes, and we have ways around the checkpoints."

"No, I want to do this," she said.

"You're not an operative."

"No, I'm the vice president of the United States, and until we know the fate of the president, I am the acting president. The REMies may have rigged the system, and America may only be a part of their empire, but I'll be damned if I'll let them take it."

Booker was silent for a moment. "Okay," he finally said. "Sit tight. I can get a package to you in less than an hour. That will give you plenty of time to make the delivery. Celia . . . are you sure?"

"I'm not sure," she admitted. "But AKA Adams is positive."

CHAPTER SEVENTY-FOUR

The president, first lady, Schueller, Fitz, and several aides, sat around the conference table at Laurel Lodge, all in a state of shock. Two Secret Service agents, having been relieved of their weapons and communications devices, sat by the window, continuing to search for ways to fulfill their assignment of protecting the president.

"I never could have guessed that Dranick would have helped orchestrate a coup in America," the president said. "Let alone betray me."

"He said that his actions might not immediately make sense, but that eventually they would be understood," Melissa said. "Do you think it's possible he thinks he's somehow helping you?"

"How is this helping anything?" Schueller asked.

"I have no idea," the president said.

"He said that as he was walking out of the room with the soldiers who are holding us here," Fitz said. "I think he was attempting to prevent one of us from taking a swing at him."

"Maybe," the president said. "Dranick is a tough guy. I don't think all of us combined could take him."

"I'd like to take a shot at him," Agent Bond said from across the room. "If you'll excuse my intrusion."

Hudson smiled for the first time since they'd been arrested. "I stand corrected, 007. I have no doubts that you could handle the colonel." His smile faded. "But right now, I can't think about it. Nothing matters more than defeating this coup, reestablishing democracy, and restoring the duly elected president."

"Hell yes!" Schueller said.

"I have sworn to uphold the Constitution," Hudson said. "What the soldiers and their superior officers have done here today is unconstitutional. There's no excuse for their actions, and no reason good enough for what Colonel Dranick has done."

Two soldiers entered the building carrying a brick-sized black box. "Sir, we have a phone call for you."

They all looked at Hudson. He shrugged. "Apparently someone knows I'm alive."

The icy voice of General Imperia was unmistakable as it came over the speaker. "Hello, Hudson. Of course I know you're alive. I'm the one who's keeping it that way."

"Imperia, I should have known," Hudson said, seething, as if trying to find a way inside the black box to strangle the general. "Have you forgotten this is America?"

"Save your patriotic history lesson, Hudson. I'm preventing the country from enduring any more of your incompetence."

"That's not how it works!"

"Really? It seems to be working just fine," General Imperia said. "Although, San Francisco is proving to be a hassle. I've tried to keep casualties down, but you left people with the impression that the military was weak."

"Do you think the public is just going to—"

"That's the reason for my call," Imperia said. "One of my officers will be bringing around a document I'd like you to sign. It's an admission of your inability to govern during this crisis, and a statement that you have voluntarily relinquished control to the military until NorthBridge is defeated."

"I'll never do that," Hudson said bitterly. "Maybe you should ask Colonel Dranick to sign it."

"Fine. Later you'll recall this as another one of your great mistakes. Meanwhile, I'll be in charge and doing what you couldn't: protecting the American people."

"Protecting? You're *murdering* people!"

"In times of war, it's not called murder. I'm fighting the enemy."

"That's what the Nazis said."

"Do you know how many lives we'll save if we stop North-Bridge now? Something you were unable to do."

"That's how Truman justified dropping the atomic bomb on civilians."

"History proved him right."

"Only the history *we* wrote—that doesn't make it true," Hudson said. "Tell me, why did he have to drop the second bomb, then?"

"He didn't."

"That's my point."

"A debate for another day," General Imperia said. "This is a revolution."

"A revolution *you* are leading!" Hudson yelled.

"No. No, I'm stopping the revolution *you* allowed. A few more days, and NorthBridge would be occupying our cities."

"Instead you're doing it. You're power mad."

"No, don't paint me a villain," General Imperia said. "I can't make you understand this, but the future of our country is at stake if we allow you to continue down this path."

"My God, who put you in charge?"

"The United States Army and God."

"You're a sanctimonious tyrant, Imperia. It wasn't God or the

Army—the REMies made you! You're nothing but an errand boy for the elites, and you don't even realize that you're already dead, because when the dust settles, the REMies will need someone to blame for mishandling the situation, and that's *you*. I've seen this before. You have the two great traits of a fall guy—you know too much, and you're dumb enough to believe you're important to the boss."

"We'll see about that, Hudson. Your arrogance is amusing . . . that you somehow think I won't be at your funeral—"

"You've threatened me in front of witnesses."

General Imperia guffawed a laugh. "Oh, there won't be any witnesses."

CHAPTER SEVENTY-FIVE

After the call with Imperia, the mood in the room turned desperate and depressed. Each of them knew at any moment the soldiers could return to execute them.

"No one thinks this can ever happen in America," Fitz said. "Vonner always said, 'At any given time, we are only three days away from the end of the world as we know it.' But everyone just pretends it'll always be this way. One bullet, one nuke, one virus, one natural disaster, one mad man . . . "

"One conspiracy," Hudson finished.

"Exactly," Fitz said.

"But there's always a way," Agent Bond said.

"Do you have an idea?" one of the aides asked.

007 shook his head. "Not yet, but there *is* a way. We just have to find it."

"We're smarter than they are," Melissa said. "We need to get word to the outside world. The Wizard, Granger . . . "

"Booker, Fonda," Hudson added.

"Would they help us?" another aide asked.

"I bet they would," Schueller said. "They hate the REMies more than we do."

"I know they would," the president said.

"But how can we reach them?"

"Maybe there's a way."

"We've already talked about trying to escape," Schueller said. "It's way too risky. Even if by some miracle we could get past all the soldiers, we don't know what's going on out there, and how do we get transportation?"

"No, nothing like that," the president said. "But we need to get them to move us to another building."

After huddling with Fitz, Schueller, Melissa, and Bond, the president asked his other aides to trust him.

"It's better if you don't know the plan."

They were all members of his inner circle. They knew the stakes, and agreed.

Soon, one of the Secret Service agents went to the door and asked the soldiers if they could be moved to Aspen Lodge or Holly Cabin—the only other two single buildings large enough to accommodate the group. The soldiers came in and inspected and found that the agent had been telling the truth. The heat was no longer working in the lodge, and with snow on the ground and outside temperatures already in the twenties, the drafty lodge was no longer comfortable, and definitely wouldn't be adequate overnight.

After checking with their commanding officer, who was using Aspen Lodge—formerly the president's private residence—as his headquarters, approval was obtained. The soldiers spent an additional twenty minutes searching and securing Holly Cabin before moving the eleven-member presidential party into their new lodgings.

The president waited by the window, watching to make sure the soldiers weren't coming back inside. Schueller and Melissa joined him after a few minutes.

"Are you sure we can get there from here?" Melissa asked in a hushed tone.

"I was told about the entrance, but I never saw it," Hudson whispered. "And I haven't been in the passageway. It's possible it could be blocked, but allegedly it's connected to the safe room."

Built during the first year of the Kennedy administration, directly under the president's residence, Aspen Lodge, was a secret safe room where the president and his family could escape to in the event of danger or attack. The existence of the room was highly classified, with only a few people other than the president knowing about it. While it could not withstand a direct nuclear strike, it had been designed to keep the president safe in the event of a nuclear attack on Washington, DC, some sixty-two miles away.

The president had thought of the safe room, but upon learning that the occupying military unit had assumed Aspen Lodge as their headquarters, he knew getting there would be impossible. He'd forgotten about the existence of an old underground passageway from Holly Cabin, which used to be the main meeting facility until the newer Laurel Lodge was built, to the safe room.

"Even if we find the entrance, and the passageway isn't blocked," Schueller whispered, "they must know about the safe room."

"Maybe not," Hudson said quietly, still watching the soldiers out the window. "As you know, Camp David isn't just the presidential country retreat. It's actually a military installation officially known as Naval Support Facility Thurmont. The Commanding Officer is the only one, outside of the head of a handful of the Secret Service, who knows about the safe room. I doubt he's given that information to these traitors. He's a career officer, a ringing patriot, and the thought of a coup destroying nearly two hundred fifty years of democracy will sicken him."

"Then we have a chance," Schueller said.

The president went over their plan again with Fitz and 007, the only other two who would go with the first family, while the others stayed behind and made sure to be seen regularly moving about the cabin.

Trying to hide his anguish over abandoning them, Hudson thanked each of them personally, knowing he or any of them could be dead in minutes. He didn't want to leave them behind, but the safe room only held four people. They were already pushing it with five; they didn't know how long they would be forced to remain inside the bunker.

Hudson and Schueller went into a large storage closet and checked his memory.

"Look here," the president said. "If we pull this lever, this whole shelf will move to one side."

"What lever?" Schueller asked, straining to see anything mechanical that could open a door.

His father pointed up to a piece of painted wood molding that seemed to have been there for a hundred years. "Impressively concealed, isn't it?"

Schueller nodded, still not believing the molding would move or open anything. "What about all the stuff on the shelf?" Schueller pointed to the shelves full of plates, glassware, table linens, serving platters, candlesticks, and other banquet related items.

"It's all with hydraulics or something," the president said. "We open it slowly and none of it moves or falls off."

"Then let's do it."

CHAPTER SEVENTY-SIX

The vice president grew increasingly impatient while waiting for the package from Booker. She sat in a corner of the empty office reviewing every detail of her plan. *If the package doesn't arrive in the next seven minutes, I'll miss the window,* she thought. *Then what will I do? I can't go back to face execution.*

Just then, the phone rang.

"It should be there in ten minutes," Booker said after she'd answered. "The security and check points in and around DC have proved more difficult than I'd hoped, and, of course, there's no non-military air traffic allowed."

"I don't have that much time."

"Then get out of the building with the messenger. He'll be able to move you to a hidden location inside the city."

"I'd be recognized."

"It'll be dark. I can protect you."

"No," the vice president said. "I'm not going to let Imperia get away with this."

"Think about it. I'll call back when he arrives."

The package arrived six minutes later. The man gave her a

few brief instructions and a secure cell phone. As she headed back into the tunnel. Booker called a minute later as she was breathlessly running back to the White House.

"You have to be careful," Booker said.

"Too late for that," she said, panting.

"I mean it," Booker insisted. "You dead doesn't advance the cause, understand?"

"The messenger told me what to do," she said. "He offered to go instead."

"I told him to."

"I told him *not* to!"

"One day we'll laugh about this."

"I doubt that," she said. "Either way . . . get the truth out."

"I will. Talk to you soon."

"Booker, one more thing," she said, dashing through the dimly lit corridor.

"Yeah?"

"Just in case, tell my husband I love him."

Vice President Celia Brown hurried down the winding tunnel under the White House, being careful not to trip in the faint light. The package in her hand could save the country and restore democracy, although, at that moment, she didn't know if it would be her or Hudson who would be president—or neither—because she didn't know if he was still alive. However, if she delivered the package and accomplished her task, the vice president felt sure that the generals could be toppled.

For that to happen, though, much still had to be done, and she was almost out of time.

General Imperia will not leave the White House, she thought. Then she went over the brief instructions the messenger had given her. "Simple and deadly dangerous," he had warned.

The vice president entered the passcode with trembling fingers and climbed the creaking wooden steps with less than two minutes to spare. She emerged from the tunnel entrance as the president's aide paced nearby.

"I didn't think you were coming back," he said, exhaling deeply.

"Get to your office, hide under your desk," she said. "Go now!"

Vice President Celia Brown ran into her own office.

General Imperia, accompanied by four military aides, arrived nine minutes late. The five uniformed men entered her office without knocking.

"Ms. Brown," the general said. "You have officially been relieved of your duties."

"By whose authority?"

"The Chairman of the Joint Chiefs will be sworn in as president in the morning," Imperia said.

"What about President Pound?" she demanded.

"He is no longer," Imperia said with a sly smile.

Her wide-eyed expression made him laugh.

"No longer president, I should say." He looked to his subordinates. "Let's just leave it at that."

"How do you plan to sell this military takeover to the American people?" she asked, hoping his answer would lead her closer to her goal.

"The American people, in case you haven't noticed, aren't really interested in details," he said. "This is all NorthBridge's doing."

"Then you'll be happy to know that we've identified the leadership of NorthBridge," the vice president said.

"Really? I don't think so."

"I have the proof."

"Show it to me."

"It's in Fitz's office. I can get it."

Imperia narrowed his eyes. He needed that information. "Fine." He turned to one of the aides. "Go with her."

The vice president pressed a hidden button under her desk, got up, and led the man toward the door. But before she could get out of the room, General Imperia got up and walked around to the other side of her desk.

"Ms. Brown, wait."

For a split second she considered running from the room, but for some reason she turned and calmly answered, "Yes?"

"When did you obtain this information?" He sat in her chair, putting his feet up on her desk. "And why would the Chief of Staff keep it in his office?"

"The source came through Fitz," she said. "He got it last night. The president, Fitz, and some others are deliberating this weekend at Camp David, deciding on the best strategy to use the data and what course of action to take."

"I don't think so," the general said.

"It's the truth," the vice president insisted.

"Tell me the names," Imperia said.

"I don't recall them at the moment, but it's all in Fitz's office."

"Yes, I'm sure there's something in there, but not the names of NorthBridge's leaders, because Colonel Dranick, the Director of National Intelligence, was at Camp David with the president, and I was speaking with the Colonel on my way to meet you," Imperia said, a suspicious, sinister tone in his voice. "Don't you think that Colonel Dranick would have mentioned this piece of vital information to me?"

"Perhaps Colonel Dranick is loyal to the president you just overthrew," the vice president said calmly.

"Perhaps he is not," the general said emphatically.

"Whatever," the vice president said. "Decide for yourself after you see the report." She slowly walked out the door. The aide hesitated a second, looking back to Imperia for guidance.

BOOM! BOOOOOOOM!

The massive explosion shook the entire building.

CHAPTER SEVENTY-SEVEN

The president asked Melissa, Schueller, Fitz, and Agent Bond to wait while he went back one more time to check that the guards were still outside and not suspicious. After a quick final 'thank you' to his aides and the other Secret Service agents who were being left behind, Hudson joined the others at the now open entrance to the passageway.

They estimated it might take ten minutes for them to get from the tunnel at Holly Cabin to the safe room door under Aspen Lodge. The steps down were wider than Hudson had expected. As soon as they reached the passageway, lights embedded in the smooth tiled walls came on automatically.

"Let's hope they don't know about the safe room," the president said, estimating there was only about five feet of earth above the ceiling of the tunnel, "or this will be a short walk."

They hurried at a steady jog.

"We don't know how many soldiers are with them," Fitz said. "They just pulled off a *coup*. What are they telling the American people? If they got your pal Dranick to go along, they could have the entire military."

"The REMies may have produced a video with me agreeing to give Alaska back to the Russians, for all I know," Hudson said. "I'm sure they did something to make me look like a traitor."

"The American people will believe whatever the government tells them," Schueller said. "Especially if it's on TV."

They rounded a sharp curve and noticed the passageway started climbing gently. A minute later, Hudson, still in the lead, stopped at a fork.

"I didn't know about this," he said.

"Which way?" Fitz asked urgently.

"Left," Melissa said.

"We're probably under the main pathway," Agent Bond speculated, "so it would be my guess that the right passage would go off to the Barracks or Hickory."

"Then left it is," Hudson said. The five fugitives resumed their jog.

"What are we going to do in the safe room?" Fitz asked.

"There's a satellite phone, computer, communications link . . . " the president said.

"What if it doesn't work?"

"It'll work."

A few minutes later, they came to another fork.

"Now which way?" the president asked.

"It looks like the left one goes in a wide sweep," Agent Bond said after checking it out. "Visualizing the layout of the area, the right passage is more likely to go to Aspen. In fact, we should be close."

"Where does the left one go, 007?" Schueller asked.

"Probably to the helipad," Agent Bond replied.

"Helipad? Why don't we go there?" Schueller asked.

"Why?" Hudson said. "Do you have a helicopter waiting for us?"

"Marine One might still be there."

"He's got a point," Melissa said.

Fitz scoffed. "It's unlikely that they overlooked an obvious detail like that."

"They overlooked the safe room," Schueller said. "And these passageways."

"Let's hope they did," Fitz said.

"We could split up," Melissa suggested.

"Too risky," Hudson replied. "We're going to the safe room." He entered the right passageway. Melissa, Schueller, and Fitz followed, with Agent Bond bringing up the rear. Soon they saw a door up ahead.

"That doesn't look like the safe room," Hudson said as they approached it. "Hopefully it's on the other side."

When they reached the door, Hudson found it was secured with a double biometric security feature. A palm print was required at the same time as an iris scanner did a retinal read.

"I sure hope that's up-to-date," Schueller whispered. "It may be set for George Bush, for all we know."

Hudson moved his hand and positioned his eye, ready to try it, when they suddenly heard running feet coming from the passage behind them.

"Don't move!" a man shouted. "Stay where you are!"

CHAPTER SEVENTY-EIGHT

A s the gray, Washington, DC winter sky faded into that uncertain shade prior to nightfall, the White House complex appeared as if a missile had hit. A gaping, smoldering crater had torn through the West Wing after the southwest section of the building erupted into a fireball of flames. Acrid smoke billowed into a choking cloud of dust and debris. Twisting shrapnel and chunks of brick, stone, and mortar rained down in a lethal mix with shards of glass, splintered wood, and burning tar. The White House itself was on fire. Sirens, screams, and hundreds of soldiers converged almost instantly onto the chaotic scene.

Below it all, caught in a tangle of broken boards, hot metal, and thick, smoky air, Vice President Celia Brown coughed out dust and blood. "Thank God," she wheezed. "I'm alive."

She'd darted from her office to the hall and into the closet with the secret tunnel entrance a second before the bomb went off. As the blast reverberated outward from her desk, the vice president dove onto the old wooden staircase, which collapsed beneath her.

It worked, she thought. *General Imperia is dead. No one could survive that hell.*

As the vice president crawled out of the pile of rubble surrounding her, she whispered, "You screwed with the wrong vice president, Imperia, because I'm AKA Adams."

The package she'd asked Booker to get, which the messenger had delivered to her at the Treasury Building, contained Gruell-75, the top-secret military grade explosive made by SkyNok, a Booker-owned company which used a patented and classified manufacturing technique, combined with tactically engineered components, to produce the advanced, lightweight, and extremely pliable material which packed eighty-seven times more force than any prior forms of compound-explosives. There was enough Gruell-75 to blow half the building, which it did quite efficiently.

She stumbled to her feet and staggered down the tunnel, hoping to reach the Treasury Building before she collapsed. Her phone vibrated, which up until that moment she had forgotten she had. It took great effort to maneuver it from her pocket, and then she saw it was Booker. As soon as she answered it, she realized she couldn't hear.

"I'm deaf," she said as she kept pushing forward.

Seconds later, Booker texted her. ***How bad are you hurt? Where are you?***

"I have some blood," she said, unable to hear her own words. "Going to Treasury."

I'll have the messenger meet you there, Booker typed.

"NorthBridge strikes again!" she said.

We'll certainly get blamed, Booker typed. ***Especially when they find Gruell-75 residue. Fonda will have to do another piece about how suspicious it is that my***

hi-tech explosive keeps showing up in the damnedest places.

"Imperia's dead."

So are you, for the time being, Booker typed. *We still have a lot of work to do, and we don't have any good information on if the president is alive. But once we have you safe, we'll get you on the air, the internet, across the cell networks, the radio, everywhere. You can denounce the coup and tell the world the truth.*

CHAPTER SEVENTY-NINE

The biometric reader authenticated Hudson's identity and the lock released. The door opened automatically. He pushed Melissa through the opening and then grabbed Schueller's arm.

"You first, Dad," Schueller protested. "You're the important one."

"Not nearly as important as you," the president said, yanking Schueller through the door with him. They found themselves in a small foyer. Another door on the left wall most likely lead to the stairs up to Aspen Lodge, and across from them was the vault-like door to the safe room.

As shots ricocheted against the walls of the passageway, Fitz dove into the foyer. Another shot bounced off the floor near the door.

"I'm hit!" Fitz yelped.

The president was going through another biometric screening at the door to the safe room. Schueller and Melissa pulled Fitz to his feet. The chief of staff moaned in agony, blood on his hands. They helped him down onto the floor of the safe-room.

"Where's 007?" the president asked as the safe-room door opened.

"Still in the passageway," Schueller said, running back. "Dad, he's down!"

"Stay here," the president told Melissa. "That closes the door," he said, pointing to a red metal button on the wall. He headed back to the passageway where Schueller was hesitating at the entrance.

The passage was filled with soldiers. Agent Bond was slumped on the floor, blocking the door. Two of their pursuers aimed rifles at the door where Schueller and the president now stood.

Agent Bond reached in his coat as if going for a weapon, then pointed his hand at the soldiers like it was a pistol. The men went for the floor and took cover.

"Go!" 007 shouted to the president. "Leave me, I'm doing my job. *Now!*"

Hudson grabbed Schueller and they made a dash for the safe room. Melissa hit the button as soon as they were over the threshold. A spray of bullets hit the closing door.

Then, suddenly, they were in a vacuum. No sound. No danger. As if the outside world had vanished.

"We're safe!" Melissa cheered.

"At least for now," Fitz said, his leg bleeding.

Melissa grabbed the first-aid kit. "I wish Florence were here." Then she thought better of her words. "Not really, I mean . . . "

"We know what you meant," Hudson said.

"I do know how to tie a tourniquet around it."

"Someone always seems to shoot at me when I'm with you, Mr. President," Fitz said wearily.

"Sorry about that, Fitz. You'll be all right,"

"What about 007?" Fitz asked.

"It didn't look good," Schueller said.

"Where'd he get hit?" the president asked. "I couldn't see."

"Neck," Schueller answered.

"We can only hope they get him quick medical attention," Melissa said.

"We can only hope they didn't shoot him," the president said. "He pretended to pull a weapon."

They were all quiet for a moment.

"In case they do figure out a way into here," the president said, "let's get to the communications."

Schueller, who had been rummaging around the windowless twelve-foot by fourteen-foot room, held up two cell phones that had been charging on a cradle attached to the concrete wall. He handed one to his father, but neither worked.

"There's supposed to be a secure satellite phone in here," the president said.

"Here," Melissa said, handing him the unit.

Hudson immediately tried to reach the Wizard. "No answer," he said after a minute.

"They probably arrested him," Melissa said.

"That would not have been pretty," the president said, dialing the number to another man who had saved his life before. "Ace," Hudson said when his brother answered, so relieved that his eyes filled with tears, "I don't have much time."

"Hudson?" Ace asked, disbelieving. "They said you were dead."

CHAPTER EIGHTY

Hudson quickly explained to his brother what had happened. Ace told him there was spotty cell coverage, and that the internet was mostly down everywhere, even on phones, except somehow the Raton Report and some other alternative sites were still coming through on cell phones. Land lines were still up.

"How can I help?" Ace asked. "Where's Schueller and Florence? Is Melissa with you?"

"Schueller and Melissa are with me. They're fine. I want you to check on Florence. I also need you to keep trying to reach the Wizard, but they may already have him." Hudson gave his brother the number. "And it's vital that you call the Inner Movement. They're based out of San Francisco. Make sure they know that you're my brother, and you need to speak to Linh. Tell them you're calling with an urgent message from me."

"Okay, okay, I'm writing this down. What do I tell her?"

"Tell her what's happened, and that I need Booker Lipton." Hudson would try to reach her himself in a few minutes if the SAT phone held out, but that was far from assured. The military could easily and quickly reposition or destroy the satellites that were making this, and any other call, possible.

"Got it."

"Ask her to get Booker Lipton to rescue us."

"He can do that?"

"Booker Lipton can do anything he wants." Hudson met Melissa's eyes with the irony of what he was asking—for the head of NorthBridge to save him from his own military. She gave him a reassuring look.

"And the Wizard, what do I tell him?"

"Make sure he knows exactly where we are and what's happening to us. He'll know what to do." Hudson went on to explain in detail what he knew about the soldiers, named General Imperia as the coup leader, then gave him the location of the safe room. Ace promised he'd make all the calls and make sure Florence was safe.

Hudson's next call was to the vice president. No answer.

"No surprise," he said to Schueller. "I'm sure they couldn't wait to arrest her."

"We've got the bleeding stopped," Melissa said, finishing up first-aid work on Fitz. "At least I think it stopped . . . this really isn't my thing."

"You did great," Fitz said. "We can't have Florence with us every time we get attacked, can we?"

Melissa patted Fitz on the shoulder and smiled.

"The news media is about half of what it was," Hudson said. "But they're clearly part of this, which means the military is acting with the REMies approval."

"Would the REMies really want this?" Melissa asked. "A coup in America kind of breaks their system, when you think about it."

"Hard to say," the president said. "This could be the final play for the CapStone."

"Which REMie would be powerful enough to make this happen?" Schueller asked.

"The military has probably taken over all the major media outlets in the country," Fitz said, sounding weak. "That's hard to do."

"I don't think Bastendorff has the connections within the military to get this kind of radical move done," the president said. "Maybe Titus Coyne."

"What if it's Booker?" Fitz asked, grimacing as he repositioned himself.

"Then God help us," Melissa said.

"Better try the Wizard again," Schueller suggested. "He might be our only hope."

"How long can we stay in here?" Fitz asked.

"I think we're good for a year," Hudson said as he dialed the Wizard's number again.

Fitz looked down at his blood-soaked pants. "Maybe *you* all can last a year. I may actually need medical attention before then." He'd already forced himself to feel the area around the wound. There was no exit hole. The bullet was still in him.

"Don't worry," Hudson said as he waited, hoping the call would connect. "I'm not gonna let you die in here."

"I have no doubt there are a dozen soldiers on the other side of that door, just waiting for us to open it," Fitz said. "Getting me to medical attention is the same thing as surrendering."

"Let's hope it doesn't come to that then," Hudson said, realizing the Wizard was not answering.

"Dad, there's a radio set over here," Schueller said. "I think it's a shortwave. I can probably figure it out. You want me to try?"

"Yes, please!" Hudson said, disconnecting his attempted call to the Wizard and trying Fonda. "Broadcast out to the entire world if you can."

"Is that wise?" Fitz asked.

"Why wouldn't it be?" Hudson asked.

"Remember the end game," Fitz replied. "You want to take out the REMies. I'm assuming the world doesn't yet know you're being held prisoner. If they find out, there could be the kind of chaos the likes of which the world has never seen."

"Let me think," Hudson said.

"Look what I found," Melissa said, holding up a six pack of Cokes. "They're warm, but they're real Coke."

"Warm or not," Fitz said, "they're the medicine I need, and you're an angel."

"I wish I knew how to reach Rex," Hudson said. "We need Tarka and Vonner Security to storm this place."

Fitz looked at Melissa. She shook her head slowly. Hudson missed the exchange, but Schueller had seen it.

"What?" Schueller asked Melissa.

"Nothing."

"What nothing?" Hudson asked.

She shook her head more firmly to Fitz. "Nothing," she repeated.

Hudson looked at Fitz, and then back to Melissa. "What's going on?"

Silence.

The president, looking like he was ready to blow a kidney, more serious than ever in his life and wondering in the last nanosecond just who he was captive with, lowered his voice as if issuing life-saving instructions to a surgeon.

"We are sitting here in an underground concrete box with half of the most powerful military in the history of the world trying to figure out how to get us out." The president's gaze lingered on Melissa, and then turned to Fitz. "Ever hear of the GBU-43/B? It's a Massive Ordnance Air Blast, but most people call it the 'Mother of All Bombs.' It's an eleven ton, large yield bomb that will instantly transform us into fossil fuel. No one will ever know we were here. I have no doubt they're fueling up a C-130 Hercules right now to drop it on us, so if you have any information that can help us get out of here, *anything* at all, then tell me now."

Fitz looked at the first lady. She remained silent.

"Melissa can reach Rex," Fitz finally said. "She has a number that will forward to him anywhere in the world via satellite."

"Great," the president said, clipped. "Give it to me." He turned to Melissa. "And then explain to me why you have such a number."

She gave him the number, but said nothing else. Hudson looked back to Fitz. He shook his head. "Her story to tell."

The president dialed the number into the SAT phone. While he waited, he stared at his wife. "Somebody'd better start talking."

"Yeah?" Rex answered after a few minutes.

"Rex, it's Hudson. We need help."

CHAPTER EIGHTY-ONE

"Resurrected again, hallelujah!" Rex said.

"'The reports of my death have been greatly exaggerated,'" Hudson replied.

"Seriously, you're alive? I really have to stop believing the media."

The president told him the situation and where they were.

"I'll get Tarka and a team ready, but it'll be morning before we can get there."

"Morning?"

"We're up against a little more than a corporate security firm or a two-bit military of some little country no one can spell the name of," Rex said. "It's a lot to get together. Got to make sure we bring you out alive."

"They may blow this bunker before then," the president said. "There may be nothing left of us in the morning."

"They know where you are, and they know you can't go anywhere. I doubt they're worried. I expect they'll cut your communications pretty soon, though."

"Then tell me what's going on out there."

"It's ugly. The CapWar overflowed into the real world," Rex said. "Door-to-door searches, mass arrests. There's just been reports that the military is investigating biological warfare strikes from either NorthBridge or a foreign terrorist group. At the same time, the Pentagon claimed that a cyberattack had taken out most of the internet. They've warned citizens that the power grid may go next."

"They've implemented the Beta-Pi plan," the president said. "It's just another false flag, another MADE event."

"There's got to be a way to get word out," Fitz said from the floor, voice strained by his injury. "Right now, everybody thinks the military is their savior."

"And maybe the military believes that themselves," Melissa said.

Hudson looked at her, bewildered.

"They've obviously portrayed you as a weak leader unable to stand up to NorthBridge, unable or unwilling to protect the country," Melissa said. "That's how they've gotten all those enlisted men to act against their commander-in-chief and their fellow citizens."

"I'm sure you're right," Hudson said. "I remember asking the question during the uprisings when they proposed implementing Beta-Pi about how they would get troops to act against their own neighbors. They deploy troops as far away from their hometown as possible. Computers crosscheck Facebook and other databases to make sure they have no friends or relatives near their deployment. Their commanders give them strict orders and false narratives claiming NorthBridge members are in the area ready to spread a virus."

"In this case, they said NorthBridge killed you and the vice president," Rex said. "Apparently a missile just hit the White House, but who knows if that really happened."

"The vice president was supposed to be at the White House," Fitz said.

"Remember, Brown is AKA Adams, so . . . " Schueller ventured.

"So she probably knows a lot more than us," Hudson finished. "My brother said that the power has been going out for a few minutes every hour where he is, which was also part of Beta-Pi. It keeps the population in the dark, quite literally, wondering if the power blackouts will last, when they'll come again, and not being able to count on electricity at all. Plus they'll start having troops stationed around every hospital in the country."

"That's happening already," Rex said.

"They'll claim it's to protect doctors and medicines from unruly gangs, but that's just the cover story," Hudson said. "What they're actually doing is making sure nobody can verify the amount of, and extent of, the injured or quote-unquote infected. It sounds like the Pentagon is going with the Beta-Pi virus lie, which means they're already getting lots of resistance. We can use that."

"Already formulating a plan," Rex said. "I've got Tarka. I'm going to patch her in."

"Mr. President," Tarka greeted.

"Alive and well," Hudson said. "Now, listen, this isn't just about a rescue mission. We've got to figure out a way to get me in front of a camera broadcasting to the whole country. Scratch that, the entire world. The scenarios I can think of with what could happen now that the world sees us in total meltdown . . . "

"I can get you on every ready device, but we might need some of Booker's satellites," Rex said.

"I've got a call into him," the president said, "but that may never happen. Tarka, you try to reach him, and Rex, we'll need a contingency plan in case we don't get his satellites. Also, can you find out if the Wizard is okay and track down Granger? And—"

"There's something else you should know," Rex said.

"Go ahead."

"The REMies have—"

The line went dead.

CHAPTER EIGHTY-TWO

Bastendorff stood in his office, watching eight large screens at once, walking back and forth among them, trying to get a closer look at some of the scenes.

"What the hell is going on in America?" the REMie asked.

"It's difficult to tell," his top lieutenant replied. "But our best assessments are that it appears to be either a coup and Pound is no longer in power, or more domestic crises, possibly new uprisings, NorthBridge attacks, or other issues, and this time the president has decided to actually declare martial law instead of a state of emergency."

"Who's behind it?"

"We're still trying to determine that, but it could be Booker Lipton."

"No, not his style," Bastendorff said. "I'll wager it's that weasel, Titus Coyne. He's in tight with some of those Pentagon bigwigs. Damn, damn, *damn*!" Bastendorff threw his hands up in the air and shook his fists. "What a way to the CapStone . . . "

"Sir?"

"Take control of the United States, including their military—boom, you got the CapStone."

"You think Coyne did all this?"

"Titus may have just won the final CapWar, and what the hell are we doing here?"

"Is a coup really going to hold in America?" the lieutenant asked. "Aren't there hundreds of millions of guns? How can they control the civilian population?"

"It depends on why they told the stupid masses that the military was totally taking over."

"We have early reports of a plague virus running out of control. Haven't been able to confirm that, though."

"Brilliant, that'll scare the hell out of anybody."

"So the—"

"How can we stop this?" Bastendorff interrupted as he jiggled a few loose Legos in his hand.

"Obviously we can't take on the US military. However, as we've all learned in the last twenty years, information is the real power, and the ability to reach millions at a time."

"Yes," Bastendorff said, seeing where his lieutenant was going. "We have to broadcast to the American people. Tell them what's really happening. Can we do that? Is there a way?"

"I think we could certainly get in from the Canadian and Mexican borders, and we can reach facilities quickly off the West Coast and off the northeast," he said. "Perhaps even Florida. We can cover probably sixty percent of the population . . . though, knowing they'll be jamming satellite signals, we'll have to get in through the old-fashioned frequencies."

"Then get on it," Bastendorff said, returning to his desk. "I'll get to the scripts."

Bastendorff hit a button as his lieutenant was leaving. A woman came in immediately.

"Judy, we need to write some news," Bastendorff said, smiling while scooping a few chocolates out of a bowl on his desk and pushing them into his plump mouth.

"What are we wanting the news to be?" she asked.

"Start with the real stuff—markets around the world in turmoil and closed, banks collapsing, world economy in worst crisis ever, blah, blah, blah, and then hit them with the military taking over America by claiming a fake plague." He smiled. "Brilliant idea, that slimeball, Coyne. We may be too late," he muttered to himself, then continued dictating to Judy. "The idea is that the poor dumb bastards in America will think they're picking up international reports, so talk a lot about how the Pentagon has taken control of the US media and so on. Then tell them about Operation White Flag."

"White Flag?"

"Yeah, I just made it up. Catchy, huh? Anyway, secret US government plan to disarm the public—*they're coming for the guns!* Fake plague. Taking guns. All linked to the Illuminati."

"Sir, there is no Illuminati," she said.

"No, but the conspiracy nuts always think it's the Illuminati that's going to enslave them. Ha! Fools. They don't realize they've been slaves to the REMies for more than a century."

CHAPTER EIGHTY-THREE

The president briefly speculated as to what Rex had been about to tell them before the line failed, but their attention quickly shifted to connecting to the outside world. After some time, trying all modes of communication in the safe room, the president, first lady, Schueller, and Fitz were forced to realize they were completely cut off.

"We just have to hope Rex and Tarka can devise a plan to get to us," the president said. "And that Ace gets word to Booker through Linh."

"It's a tough one," Fitz said, sounding weaker. "Camp David is no easy target even during normal times, and I imagine they have all kinds of extra heavy protection now."

"I wonder how 007 is," Schueller said.

Hudson nodded silently.

"Can we really trust Booker?" Schueller asked.

"I don't know," the president said. "But we *can* trust Linh."

No one said anything for a few minutes.

Finally, Hudson sat next to Melissa. "Want to tell me what that was all about with your having Rex's earth-line?"

"No," Melissa said. "No, I don't."

He stared at her as if trying to read her secrets. "You have to."

"I know," she said. "But not here."

"There may not be another chance."

Melissa nodded, wiping a tear as it formed. She looked at him, a soft, pleading look, desperate almost, begging forgiveness for what she was about to tell him.

Hudson felt the implications of her wordless plea and gasped softly, bracing himself for what he suddenly feared was something horrible.

Melissa took a deep breath. "Rex and I have been working on a plan . . . taking steps to put Schueller into position to get the CapStone."

Schueller looked over in surprise, but said nothing. He had found some painkillers and was handing them to Fitz.

"I don't understand," Hudson said.

"I know you don't."

"Why?"

"The odds of your successfully defeating the REMies . . . Look where we are. We're as good as buried alive in a concrete vault. The REMies are too powerful. All along, I've tried to make that clear to you; that the REMies don't just run the world, they *are* the world. You've been trying to conquer the world all by yourself. It's an impossible task. If I'd thought there—"

"Wait, I thought we were doing this together. I wasn't alone. I had you, Schueller, Florence, the Wizard, Fitz, Granger, Rex—at least I *thought* I had Rex. Apparently, *you* had Rex. Tell me exactly what's been going on."

She looked at Fitz. "I can't."

"Have you been sleeping with Rex?"

"God, no!" She looked from Hudson to Schueller, shaking her head. "No, I just . . . wish it were that simple."

Hudson felt his stomach tighten. *Worse than an affair?* His brain swirled. "Are you an AKA?"

She laughed. "I wish." Her laugh collapsed into a moan. "Hudson, I need you to believe me. I love you so much. I fell in love with you during the campaign. Your determination, conviction, your sense of right and honor—you're an amazing man, and you dazzled me. Everything—"

"You fell in love with me *during* the campaign? We were together two years *before* the campaign. We were married *before* the campaign! Why did you marry me if you didn't love me yet?"

She stared at him for a long time, teary eyed, with the same pleading, desperate look from before.

More than two minutes passed. Hudson never took his eyes off her, but his mind was replaying the past five years, reviewing details, putting pieces together. The crushing tension in the small room was suffocating. Fitz had closed his eyes. Schueller, a totally perplexed expression on his face, was trying to figure out what this was all about, at the same time wondering if they could possibly escape, and what was happening up there across the country; a country no longer like the United States of America, instead like a South American nation riddled with coup attempts.

Finally, Hudson understood. "Tell me you weren't working for Vonner."

Fitz opened his eyes. Schueller stretched so he could see Melissa's face.

CHAPTER EIGHTY-FOUR

Melissa reached for Hudson's hand. He pulled back.

"Yes," she said, almost in a whisper. "I was working for Vonner."

Hudson felt dizzy, almost faint. "For how long?"

She shook her head. Her eyes filled with tears.

"How long?" he asked angrily.

"Since before . . . before we met."

"Ohhh no!" Hudson reeled around, hitting the wall with the side of his fist.

Fitz closed his eyes again.

Schueller looked at Melissa as if she'd just stabbed his father.

All Hudson wanted to do was to get as far away from her as possible, but they were trapped, possibly forever, together.

"Hudson, please listen to me," she tried.

"No!" He turned back to face her. "What could you possibly say to fix this?"

"Please let me try to explain."

"Explain? Explain what? That Vonner hired you to marry me, to keep an eye on me? What else did he pay you to do?

There's no way to explain . . . you can't make this right Melissa. How do you live with yourself? What kind of a person . . . ?"

"There was no malice in what I did. Vonner always intended you to be the one who could change things, but he knew you didn't know enough in the beginning, that you would stray, make mistakes, and he needed to know because, as you've learned, there's no room for error when dealing with the REMies. But, Hudson, I really did fall in love with you. I love you so much."

"So you keep saying, but, Melissa . . . is that even your real name?"

"Of course, it's my real name."

He shrugged. "How would I know?" Then, remembering how close Schueller and Melissa had been, he turned to his son. "Are you okay?"

Schueller's dry response came out as almost a croak. "Unbelievable."

"I'm sorry, Schueller," Melissa said.

"How do you apologize for being a spy, a double-agent, a whore!?" Schueller screamed at her.

"Schueller," Hudson said. "Easy."

"Why?" Schueller's response filled with even more fire. "Vonner *paid* her. I'm pretty sure you two had sex occasionally. Was that part of her deal? What do *you* call that?"

"Vonner, like you, wanted to change the world," Melissa said to Hudson. "He wanted to bring down the REMie empire, but believed in a slower approach than you, and I agreed with him. I think time has proven we were right. Look at what's happened. The country is under military control. It's safe to assume economies around the world are collapsing. For all we know, it's anarchy out there. You were going too fast."

"You were the leaker, too, weren't you?" Hudson asked, suddenly seeing it all.

"I never leaked anything to hurt you. I was trying to steer you in the right direction."

"Incredible!" Hudson yelled. "Who *are* you?"

"We wanted the same thing—Vonner, you, me. We all wanted to end the empire."

"Hold on," Hudson said, turning to his Chief of Staff, still laying on a foam mat. "Fitz, did you know?"

Fitz opened his eyes. "I did," Fitz answered in a scratchy voice.

"It keeps getting worse," Hudson said. "You were supposed to have my back."

"I did what I thought was best. She wasn't trying to hurt you."

"Wasn't hurting me?" he said incredulously. "This is way beyond hurt, this is Greek tragedy. You don't think being cut in half is hurt? In *half*!" He stood as if he might hit someone, his hands shaking uncontrollably. Melissa reached for him again. He recoiled, more to prevent his fury from taking over than to get away from her. "But set aside the personal treachery of this acid attack . . . she was leaking, counter to all we were trying to do—"

"I didn't know about the leaks," Fitz said. "I knew it could have been her, but it could have been any of us."

Hudson shook his head, a vile expression on his face, head pounding as if he'd been hit with a two-by-four. "Here we are then," he said, waving his arm around the room. "What about this? The poetic irony here . . . Vonner must be laughing his ass off. He hired Melissa to watch me, then hired me to become president, then hired Fitz to watch it all, and finally, he gave all his money to Schueller. The four of us, Vonner's puppets, trapped in a presidential tomb where we'll probably all die."

CHAPTER EIGHTY-FIVE

Coyne stood at the window of a high-rise on the Virginia side of the Potomac River, where he could see the small plume of smoke rising above Washington. "Was it a missile?" he asked.

"We don't think so," a man in a military uniform answered.

"And you're sure General Imperia and Vice President Brown are dead?" Coyne asked as he turned away from the window and back to the men gathered—a mix of bankers, military, and a few of his top assistants.

"No one could have survived."

"Well, I'm sorry about the general, that's quite a loss for our cause, but at least the vice president is one less headache we have to deal with."

"Yes, sir."

"Who did it? NorthBridge, or another REMie?"

"It's still too hot to really get in there, but we do have an F-team on site, and I've just been told that there are reliable indications it was Gruell-75, but we won't know for sure until the tests—"

"Damn it," Coyne said. "It's Booker. He's going for the CapStone."

"You knew it was a risk when you opened this up," a Federal Reserve Governor said.

"*I* didn't open this up, it was Bastendorff and his insurgents trying to bring on the chaos when they launched the uprisings."

"This was already planned before they started the riots . . . and they were over already," the man said.

"It was the only way," Coyne admitted.

"Apparently, others agree with you."

"Whatever, we're still in charge."

"The Chairman of Joint Chiefs has assumed command," another military man said, his chest full of decorations.

"What's going on out there?" Coyne, annoyed, asked the man.

"Travel restrictions have been instituted. Road closures. Large quarantine zones. FEMA camps reopened in every geographic region."

"Excellent," Coyne said. "Curfews tonight?"

"Yes. Mandatory curfews, strictly enforced."

"Guns?"

"We're making progress seizing them in door-to-door raids, but, as you know, this will take up to eighteen months to accomplish."

"We've announced that everyone is subject to search and seizure," another military man added. "The Constitution has been suspended for the general good. Identification is required for all travel outside the home. Firearms are being confiscated, but we're maintaining a low profile with that one."

"Resistance?"

"Skirmishes have broken out with people trying to protect their guns. They were treated as criminals. Killed, or captured and imprisoned. Fewer than four thousand today, but the situation has substantially shifted since Beta-Pi was implemented."

"Yeah, I'll bet," Coyne said. "The prospect of a rapidly spreading fatal virus tends to make people docile."

The man nodded. "We've dubbed the virus 'Masama,' which is Filipino for evil."

"Filipino?"

"We're saying the virus originated in the Philippines."

"Nice touch," Coyne said.

"There were some demonstrations prior to the news of the virus against the suspension of civil rights, including freedom of speech, freedom of assembly, and freedom of the press, but we've made it clear that we still don't know if the weaponized virus is part of a foreign invasion, NorthBridge, or some other terror group. Just that it's spreading fast, and with the president and vice president dead, the Pentagon is acting to protect the population, and the loss of basic rights will be only temporary."

"The troops are there for your protection, the loss of rights is temporary," Coyne mocked. "It's all only an extreme measure to regain control since the civilian government had broken down, only until the threat is neutralized and the insurrections put down."

"Yes, sir. We've announced that food is expected to be rationed and could even be confiscated if hoarding takes place. All large grocery stores and distribution centers are now under military guard."

"Sir," another man in uniform said, "you said the president is dead, but—"

"I know." Coyne held up a hand to silence him. "It's under control."

"Yes, sir."

After the briefing, Coyne quietly took a few key people aside and told them that the president had locked himself in an underground safe room with no way to escape. "We've cut off all his communications. He can rot in there. No one will ever know that he didn't die as we said he did—in an earlier attack. Hudson Pound is no longer a problem."

CHAPTER EIGHTY-SIX

The vice president crawled out of the false bottom section of the SUV that NorthBridge had previously used for smuggling weapons. Inside the garage of an $8 million Georgetown mansion less than three miles from the White House, she stretched her legs. The messenger escorted her inside. The home was anything but a residence. Although the first floor appeared to be an upscale living area, on the upper floors were extremely advanced communications equipment and a large store of weapons.

A doctor was waiting to examine her. A few cracked ribs, contusions, and some bad gashes requiring stitches, but otherwise she was in seemingly good shape. Her hearing had improved enough to converse. The doctor did warn there might be some permanent loss. After getting cleaned up and downing a bowl (soup, she was ready to take on the world again.

It was in a small upstairs room, layered in hi-tech shie¹ that Vice President Celia Brown learned the full extent coup. She listened to uncensored reports coming in fror Bridge operatives and BLAXer units around thҽ

Another channel was summarizing international reporting. Forty-five minutes after her arrival, she joined a secure multi-encrypted video conference with Booker, Fonda, Thorne, and AKA Franklin.

"I've spoken to our people inside," Booker said, referring to people on his payroll who worked in the upper levels of the CIA and NSA, as well as several within the hierarchy of the US military intelligence agencies. "This coup is extremely fragile. It's being pushed by Titus Coyne and a handful of other REMies he's roped into a cartel."

"So we can break it?" Thorne asked.

"Yes," Booker said. "And that's exactly what we're going to do."

"And then what?"

"It depends on whether President Pound is still alive."

"Why? Either way, he's finished."

"I don't think so," Booker said. "Vonner Security is mobilizing. I believe he's alive and they're going to rescue him."

"And he's our best chance," Fonda added. "The revolution needs stability and legitimacy."

"I disagree," Thorne said.

"We all want the *empire* destroyed," the vice president said. "Not civilization. We need to compromise, work together. It's our only chance."

"What about you, Franklin?" Thorne asked. "Are you with the wimps?"

"I am," AKA Franklin said. "Picking up the pieces is going to be a big job. Pound's Fair and Free *can* work, but not without him, and if for some reason he doesn't make it, then Adams will carry the flag."

"You all wasted my time!" Thorne said.

"Think about it," Fonda said. "The REMies have it all. They

can battle out of this chaos, rebuild their empire. Money, weapons, resources, they'll kill millions to win . . . *billions.*"

Thorne nodded. "Yeah," he muttered bitterly. "They always win."

"Let's try it with Hudson," Fonda said. "If it doesn't work, NorthBridge 2.0 will rise from the ashes and start again."

"Okay," Thorne said. "But he has to go after every REMie on the list. Prison or death."

Everyone agreed.

"Then the rebels are united," Fonda said.

"Yeah," Thorne said. "Until the empire falls."

CHAPTER EIGHTY-SEVEN

The Wizard had gone into hiding at the first sign of trouble. Gypsy had picked up a major coordinated domestic move by the military before the internet went down. He'd tried unsuccessfully to warn the president, and then fled. The Wizard had contingency plans as back up and fail-safes on top of that. In the event of a sudden attack with less than a few minutes' warning, he had already set up a temporary storage shed in the woods behind a church up the road from the Hunter Mill mansion. He'd equipped it with a Tesla wall-mounted battery and had a buried electric line he could easily connect to a box at the church.

As soon as he was settled, he began working the DarkNet, which was still up, accessing international servers to get on the regular internet. However, his biggest source of hard data came from the Defense Information Systems Agency, or "DISA", a collection of secret internets for the military and intelligence agencies.

Unsure if the president was alive or not, the Wizard was determined that, one way or another, he would still launch Cherry Tree. He worked through exhaustion until he could hardly feel his cold, stiff fingers, tracking everything, programming Gypsy to identify every coup conspirator, locate all the REMies, and track them. At the same time he tried to glean information about what was happening at Camp David and the White House. His attempts to reach Rex and Granger failed.

"Don't be dead, Dawg," he whispered a hundred times in the dark, cold storage shed as he searched for any way he could help. "Live again, my friend." But he knew the generals who'd orchestrated the coup would be smart enough not to leave the president alive, especially when they could so easily blame NorthBridge. "Damn, why didn't we see this coming! Dranick should have picked up some kind of warning."

The only activity that night were soldiers and armored vehicles patrolling the deserted streets. Any attempts at resistance were met with a swift and overwhelming response. Limits had been placed on ATM withdrawals to no more than one hundred dollars. Gas stations had all been placed under military control.

What information got through, on occasional bursts, did not mention the coup. Instead, the reports were about the crackdown on corruption in the face of a horrific worldwide pandemic. Stories were filled with the gruesome details of the deadly Masama virus and the sufferings of its victims. There were also many official announcements about the threat of NorthBridge, whom the government was blaming for the spread of the virus and the violence in different regions. The public was encouraged to report anyone not complying with the new restrictions as a rebel, a NorthBridger.

The US military brought overwhelming force into regions in what appeared to be a well-planned operation. The Chairman of the Joint Chiefs, as acting president, had ordered that no resistance would be tolerated. At the first sign of unrest, elite units would level an entire block. "All in the defense of the country," survivors were told. "Dangerous NorthBridge rebels were taking refuge there," in the obliterated area.

Most state and local officials had come out quickly in full support of the military. They gave soundbites about the horrors of NorthBridge and how "the good men and women of the American military were protecting the population." Others decried "the military's greatest mission to save us from the horrific Masama virus."

But the Wizard knew that this was not a coup in the traditional sense of military takeovers seeking to remove a leader. This coup would have happened despite whoever was in office. It was a direct result of the CapWars. The military was taking over at the behest of the REMies, making a bold grab for the CapStone.

Key people in the government, the media, the military, and many in business and industry were arrested. The arrests had the effect of sending a message to anyone considering opposing the military. They also removed anyone who could challenge the REMies. It was one sweeping purge.

Above all, the Wizard knew one thing for sure. In order for a coup to be possible, the right conditions must exist, and the most important requisite is some form of major instability. As Vonner once said, '*At any given time, we are only three days away from the end of the world as we know it.*'

CHAPTER EIGHTY-EIGHT

The night in the safe room seemed to drag on in an endless combination of fear, frustration, anger, and sorrow. An oppressive heaviness weighed on them; each felt their own mix of death row inmate and being on the boats ready to hit Normandy Beach on D-Day. Making it worse was the absence of any details about what was happening on the surface and across the country, and the acid burn of Melissa's betrayal. At times the room was consumed by silence, an absence of sound so intense that it might have weight and dark shades of color.

Hudson wrestled with worry about Florence, his siblings, and all the innocent citizens who had no idea they were caught in the biggest MADE event since World War II, that they were all victims of the final CapWar. He also felt displaced, his life suddenly foreign to himself. Melissa continually distracted his thoughts away from strategizing, even from hope. The burden of it was unbearable.

She tried several times during the long sleepless hours to talk to him. Each time he reacted with different emotions—rage, mourning, disgust, deep sadness. "I can't," he said each time. "I'm not strong enough to deal with you *and* survive this night." But he had told her "If we somehow miraculously get out of the safe room and regain power after all this, the country won't be able to handle a divorce between the president and first lady. So, I'm asking, for the good of the country, if we get there—and there are a truckload of 'ifs' between now and then—but if we do, then at least agree to that. To play at being the first lady for a little longer so I can try to rebuild the country. But it's only an act."

She had not responded, and he really hadn't wanted her to.

Fitz was holding on, but they were all concerned that if they didn't get out soon and get him to a surgeon, he wouldn't make it. Hudson, who'd seen plenty of gunshot wounds during his time in the Army, and more since he'd run for president, confided in Schueller. "Fitz won't make it another night."

"Tarka will come," Schueller said.

"Can she get in? Past the Revolutionary Guard up there?"

"Take Delta Force and throw in a few Navy Seals against Tarka and her VS . . . it's going to be a death match for sure," Schueller said. "But my money's on Tarka."

Hudson thought back on everything she had done, all the times she'd saved him. He couldn't bet against her either, but this time the odds were far worse than ever before. "I hope you're right."

"I am." Schueller leaned in close to his father and whispered, "I'm gutted by Melissa, so I'm amazed you're still standing. You never stop impressing me, Dad."

"It's shock that's keeping me going, and being numb," he whispered back. "Plus, I'm trapped, so there really isn't anything impressive about it. I simply have no choice."

Melissa, on the other side of the room, pulled another blanket around a shivering Fitz. "Dranick betrayed him," she whispered to Fitz, who couldn't hear her. "I didn't. He may not agree with my methods, but I've done nothing but try to help him since the day we met." She mopped Fitz's feverish brow with a cold, wet washcloth. "He never would have made it this far without you and me, Fitz."

She realized he hadn't heard a thing she'd said.

"Hang in there, Fitz. There's still hope. Rex and Tarka aren't going to let us die in here."

And she believed that. Melissa always thought there was hope. However, she was a practical woman, and knew that Dranick would have told his superiors about Rex, Tarka, the Wizard, and Granger, which meant the ones they were counting on to save them could all already be dead.

CHAPTER EIGHTY-NINE

The next morning, the president and Schueller stumbled around the safe room, exhausted after little sleep. Schueller served canned fruit and granola bars for breakfast.

"How is he?" Hudson asked Melissa, who'd spent the night next to Fitz.

She shook her head. "We've got to get out of here."

"We may have to surrender then," Hudson said.

"No," Fitz moaned.

"Glad to see you're still among the living," Hudson said, kneeling next to his chief of staff.

"Coke," he said.

"I don't think that's a good idea," Melissa said. "How about some water?"

Fitz made a face, but took a sip.

"You need a doctor," Hudson said. "I'm not going to watch you die."

"Surrender," Fitz said weakly, "and you'll be the one dying. That's no fun either."

"Trust me, I know," Hudson said.

The SAT phone rang. They all looked at each other for an instant before Hudson answered.

"Mr. President."

"Rex?"

"Would you mind opening the door and letting Tarka in?"

"Are you kidding?"

"Does that sound like a joke I would tell?" he asked.

"Open the door," Hudson said.

Melissa pushed the button.

Tarka, dirty, sweaty, and bloody, stood on the other side holding an assault rifle, with another one strapped to her back. Twenty or thirty VS agents crowded the corridor behind her.

"Amazing," the president said, hugging Tarka.

Tarka looked down at Fitz and called for a stretcher. "Sorry it took so long to get here," she said to Hudson. "It seems we hadn't been invited."

"What's it look like up there?" Schueller asked.

"Unrecognizable," she said. "We need to go."

"Where are we going?" Hudson asked.

"Home," Tarka said.

"Ohio?"

A quick smile formed. "The White House."

"Is that wise?" Melissa asked.

"Booker's BLAXers have secured it. Safe as anywhere right now."

During the helicopter ride back to Washington, the president thought about all the bodies he'd seen at Camp David. Servicemen who had just been following orders, told lies, and given commands to do the wrong thing, lay dead or injured for the same old reasons: greed and fear. Dozens of Secret Service and VS agents had also died, none more upsetting to him than 007.

Tarka informed him that Florence had been taken to a safe place by VS agents. He'd have to tell his daughter about Agent Bond, but that could wait. There was already plenty to mourn.

The White House, with its cratered and partially destroyed West Wing, along with more than a thousand armed military loyalists, BLAXers, Secret Service, and VS agents, resembled a front-line Army base more than the executive mansion. Hudson had been told that the vice president was alive and, as a safety precaution, remained under heavy guard at her official residence located on the northeast grounds of the US Naval Observatory a few miles away. He looked forward to speaking with her later.

A surprise guest was waiting for him in the White House Library, which had hastily been converted to the president's office after the Oval Office and President's Study had sustained damage.

"Colonel Dranick," the president said. "I didn't expect to see you again." He gave his friend a hard look. "Enapay, you betrayed me."

"It was never my intent."

"Nevertheless, even if I can forgive you—and after spending nine minutes in the stars and a night in a tomb, I'm sure I will eventually be able to—the families of all those who died as a result of this coup . . . I doubt they will."

Dranick nodded, handing the president a folder. "It's a complete list of all the people involved, at every level."

"Thank you. This will help us end this disaster a little faster." Hudson picked up a phone and muttered a few words into it. Two soldiers came in and arrested Dranick. He went quietly.

A few minutes later, Tarka came in.

"I see you've gotten cleaned up. Are you okay?" the president asked.

"Never better."

He gave her a doubtful look. "If you're up to it, I'd appreciate your overseeing this." He handed her the folder Dranick had just given him. She opened it and scanned the pages. "They all need to be arrested immediately."

"Big job," she said. "I thought we were going after REMies."

"They're next."

"Then I'll make sure this gets done by the end of the day."

The president smiled. "I bet you will."

She turned to leave.

"Tarka," the president called when she was at the door. "Thank you."

She nodded, smiled, and left.

CHAPTER NINETY

The president used the BLAXers, Vonner Security, Secret Service, and military loyalists to retake the Pentagon. It helped that Booker's companies had supplied many of the computer components and chips that went into the security and defense systems. Once the enlisted men and women realized the president was alive and had been the victim of an overthrow plot rather than a successful assassination, they were quick to fall into line, and the proper chain of command was rapidly reestablished, ending with Hudson as commander in chief. The Chairman of the Joint Chiefs was taken into custody and would never know freedom again. Tarka and other elite teams moved swiftly to arrest all of the coup participants as opposition collapsed breathtakingly fast.

A few hours later, the president ordered the internet turned back on, reestablished the full cellular networks, and, temporarily, nationalized all radio and television broadcasts. Then he gave a simple speech that would change the world.

"This was no simple coup d'état by rogue forces," Hudson began as his speech was broadcast to the world. "Elements in the US Military were part of a deep state that has been protecting the interests of the corrupt elites, specifically a cartel known as the REMies."

He went on to explain exactly who they were and how for more than a century, this cartel had been ruling the world and controlling the population through MADE events.

"In the past, Democrats and Republicans blustered whenever their team wasn't in control, but it was never more than a distraction. The Wall Street bankers were still in charge of the fiscal policy, the defense contractors still ran the Pentagon, the pharmaceutical and agrichemical companies ran their respective government departments, and the Federal Reserve Board bent the economy to the will of its owners. Every election we are promised alternating doses of hope and change. It never comes. We only thought there was a difference . . .

"Today, we are launching Cherry Tree, a program which will prove the hellacious crimes of the REMies to such an extent that they attempted the coup to suppress these findings. Cherry Tree was named for America's Founding Father and the story of how, as a boy, he admitted to chopping down a cherry tree with the famous words, 'I cannot tell a lie.' Cherry Tree, then, is a metaphor for truth, and that is exactly what this initiative does. It presents the facts about the REMies and recasts the past century in a new light based upon those facts. The truth must finally be made real, for only the truth can bring the promised change."

Cherry Tree's deep trove of verified information was instantly available on every linked device on the planet. The Kennedy papers were quickly confirmed by historians and scholars. The public was predictably outraged. They may not have known the exact participants and the precise steps taken that led to the Dallas ambush against JFK, but finally the conspiracy was no longer a theory.

Arrest warrants were issued not just for the REMies themselves, but for everyone who had knowingly participated in MADE events. Thousands were arrested, and trillions of dollars in assets were seized. Between the coup and the REMie purge, the economy was no longer functioning. Right on cue, Fair and Free was introduced with a host of other radical reforms. So many members of Congress had been arrested that the president had to act on executive authority until the new elections could be held—now with term limits.

Hudson had moved into the Lincoln Bedroom for the time being, but went to the first lady's suite to get an update on Fitz. Melissa had just been to the hospital to see him.

"The doctors say he's doing well. He'll have a limp, probably worse than yours, but otherwise they expect a full recovery," Melissa said. "He told me to tell you it was a great speech . . . I thought so, too."

"Thanks," Hudson said. "The REMies are running and scattering like scared rats, but the Wizard has been tracking them, and every single country has agreed to extradition."

"Because you've been seizing assets."

"Right, everyone wants a share of what the REMies looted."

"A lot of work ahead, but congratulations. It looks like you've done it." She smiled, a sad, Mona Lisa kind of smile. "I may not have thought you could beat them, but that doesn't mean I didn't believe in you."

He nodded, not sure what to say.

"I'm sorry, Hudson. I'll stay, I'll do whatever you need me to do."

"Thanks."

She nodded. "I guess, there isn't a chance that—"

"No," he said, a lump in his throat. "We can't go back to good. Consider us one of the last casualties of the CapWar."

CHAPTER NINETY-ONE

S tanding on the broad wraparound porch of the vice president's official residence on the grounds of the Naval Observatory, Hudson stared at Celia Brown with a look that was a combination of awe and disgust.

"In a thousand years," Hudson began, "I never would have guessed that you were AKA Adams."

"I am so sorry to have deceived you," the vice president said. "I did my best to never undermine your efforts."

"Celia, you're one of the leaders of NorthBridge, an organization that undermined me at every turn. Assassination attempts, threatening the security and stability of the entire nation—hell, they've been trying to overthrow the very government that you and I lead. You've been doing nothing *but* undermining me."

"We shared a common enemy, Mr. President."

"Now you sound like Booker. The REMies may have been NorthBridge's ultimate target, but in order to get to them, you and your band of terrorists had to trample over my administration, jeopardizing the stability of the entire world. And not giving my reforms any hope of gaining traction in the face of the chaos and violence you generated . . . " He stopped and looked at her with an expression of total exasperation on his face, still unbelieving. "And *violence*. How do you explain that? You've been antiwar your entire career, and yet your alter ego *has* been waging war, a bloody revolution, inciting civil war. I'd call you a hypocrite, but that just seems like a compliment considering your crimes."

"I can't tell you how many conversations I've had with the other NorthBridge leaders about your lack of understanding—"

"*My* lack of understanding? Are you kidding?"

"With your knowledge of history, how can you believe that the REMies could be removed, their empire broken, *without* a war?"

"I can list half a dozen peaceful revolutions—"

"The REMies weren't some aging dictator in charge of a bloated bureaucracy left behind by progress and prosperity," the vice president said. "They controlled everything across the globe —the money supply, the governments, the militaries, the media. You can't fight that with legislation, speeches, and press releases."

"Not with NorthBridge out there blowing things up and killing people."

"Dammit, Hudson, NorthBridge was the best chance against the REMies. Hasn't that been proven now? That's why I signed on. Booker originally recruited *me* to run for president. He wanted an antiwar president. A group of REMies planned a war with China, and he knew he could get their backing to put me in the White House."

"If they wanted war, why would they support one of the best known antiwar candidates there was?"

"His pitch to them was simple; the American people would never accept another war, especially with China. But if it was championed by me, a person who'd been against every war, *all* war, then the public could be easily convinced that it must be vital to our national security, like World War II."

"And you would sell out for that?" Hudson looked toward the steps leading off the porch, as if he might leave.

"I was never going to actually support the war," she said, her voice angry. "It was just to get me into office."

"So what happened?"

"You happened," the vice president said with a non-humorous laugh. "Vonner had a better candidate, and a better plan than Booker."

Hudson sat down in one of the big wooden chairs on the porch of the Vice President's Residence. He looked out at the Secret Service agents and thought of 007, a man who had, in the end, made the ultimate sacrifice to save the president.

"It wasn't just the candidate," Hudson said. "It was North-Bridge. Your friends caused chaos in the race, not to mention taking out quite a few candidates directly. Was that for you? Were those assassinations meant to get you into the White House?"

"I don't know," Vice President Brown said, looking off into the distance regretfully. "As you no doubt have learned by now, there's no single person calling the shots at NorthBridge."

"Surely you know who ordered those killings?"

She shook her head. "It's designed that way intentionally. I tried to find out, but even after the fact, it's kept secret."

"But you have your suspicions? You couldn't work with these people without knowing them, knowing which one of them would order an assassination. You may operate autonomously, but NorthBridge has a grand strategy. Whose grand strategy is that? Whose agenda does it advance?"

"You want me to say Booker Lipton." She glared at him as if insulted. "You think that because he's a REMie, this is a part of the CapWars?"

"I need to be sure."

"Because the FBI DIRT units are arresting all the REMies, and you have to decide if Booker goes down too?"

"All the REMies are going to prison." He paused and allowed a bitter smile. "As you know, there are countless wealthy individuals who are not REMies whom we can't arrest and don't *want* to arrest. But I do believe we'll get the new billion-dollar cap on personal wealth enacted into law across the globe within months, and it'll be retroactive, so they'll be forced to divest." Part of the radical reforms called for international legislation capping the amount of personal wealth at $1 billion. Any excess would have to be distributed to non-profits. "Charities are going to be able to change the world with that flood of money. The start of the great realignment." Hudson looked into the sky for a moment. "But Booker is a REMie and he led NorthBridge. Those are both reasons to lock him up."

"He's not one of them."

"I know, but people died in those attacks."

"It's not very different from the American Revolution which created this nation," she said. "Or that people—*good* people— died in saving you! Who got you out?"

"It is *very* different," Hudson protested.

"Please, let me finish. You cannot deny, after all that's happened, that there was any hope of bringing down the empire without what NorthBridge did. We would have had another corrupt president in the White House, and the CapWars would have finally been won. Either Bastendorff or Coyne would have the CapStone, and the world would be in for another century, or more, of greed, consumption, waste, poverty—"

"I do know."

"Then?"

"If I let Booker off the hook, there's a chance that this was all just an elaborate and brilliant play for the CapStone. Don't you see? If he remains free, Booker has won the CapWar."

"But the billion-dollar cap on personal wealth will take care of that," the vice president said. "No more REMies, no more CapWars. The CapStone doesn't matter if the empire is over."

"Perhaps you're right," Hudson said. "The only thing is Booker's smarter than the rest of us put together."

"My point exactly."

CHAPTER NINETY-TWO

Granger and the president stood on the still-damaged White House roof. Lately, it had become one of Hudson's favorite places. It was as if he could escape his marble dungeon filled with antiques, history, and stress, to get out and see the sunshine or the stars. He loved the view of the city as it expanded out into the country. Washington was filled with a vibrancy common in international cities, steeped in secrets, mystery, power, beauty—both lost and won, and some yet waiting to be discovered.

"I think it's going to work," Granger said. "So far over eighty-three percent of all funds held by the lower ninety percent of the population have been exchanged for digiGOLD."

Hudson smiled and let out a sigh. "I cannot thank you enough, Granger, for lending your immaculate mind to this greatest of challenges."

Granger bowed his head slightly.

"And what of the top ten percent?" Hudson asked after a pause. "You had a lot of chips in this game." The two men stared at each other knowingly. "There were times when I didn't know for sure whose side you were on, the REMies, NorthBridge, or the people's. But in the end, it was the very fact that you had feet in all three of those worlds that made you the perfect architect of the new system."

"None of this would have happened without you, Mr. President. I don't think I've ever known a braver man. And if it's time for confessions, I must admit there were times when I thought you a coward, maybe even a fool, and certainly not up to this monumental task. But now that it's done, I see it was you who made it happen. You brought together just the right mix of innocence, courage, knowledge of history, an ability to handle people —the good and the bad." Granger nodded his head, held out his hand, and shook the president's firmly. "It's been an honor to play a part."

"Thank you. Still a lot of work to do, makes me tired thinking about how much, so I hope you're not going anywhere. I still need you. The world needs you."

"I'll be here until we get it just perfect."

"Perfect?" The president looked out over the city's monuments. "Isn't that impossible?"

"Perfection is all I live for."

"You and Rex and the Wizard . . . bunch of freaks," the president said with great affection.

"And the freaks shall inherit the earth," Granger replied, smiling broadly.

The president nodded. "I certainly hope so. And what of the other ten percent?" he asked again.

"I think after the review boards get done with them, the ones that don't go to jail will be in one hundred percent compliance."

Impartial review boards had been appointed to analyze the holdings of the wealthiest ten percent of the world's population to determine if any of it was obtained by means that would be possible under the new system. It was doubtful much of it would fall into the new guidelines. Some would be prosecuted, a few might be allowed to keep a little. The rest would be given a stipend in an amount of digiGOLD held by the average citizen— a rude awakening for the elites.

Granger paced to the edge of the roof, looking down to the South Lawn. The two men stood there silently for a few minutes, both locked in their own reflections. Finally, Granger walked back to Hudson. "Can I ask you something, Mr. President?"

"Of course," the president replied, already guessing what Granger might ask. He'd made a wager with himself on how long it would take for the brilliant technologist to ask, knowing that curiosity was a genius's greatest fault, and his most important asset.

"How long have you known?" Granger asked.

"About Franklin?"

"Yes."

"A couple of months."

Granger's eyes widened and his mouth fell open slightly. "Really?"

"Yep," the president said, enjoying the moment.

"Then why didn't you bust me? Why did you continue to let me work on Fair and Free?"

"Because you may have been the only person in the world who could've pulled this off. I needed you," the president said. "And I counted on your mind; not just to create the new system, but I believed that your great intellect would surely detect that I was doing the right thing, that my path was viable."

Granger stared, speechless.

"You had already passed up the opportunity for REMie-like riches," the president added. "You knew that this had to be done. We needed to be fair and free for the first time in human history to break the shackles of greed and corruption. A mind such as yours would see even better than the rest of us which way was the right way, so I had to believe you were on our side."

Granger stared at him quietly for several moments. "Even as impressed as I've been by you, I've still underestimated you, Mr. President."

"Well, I'll take that as a great compliment, AKA Franklin. And who else could have justified taking the alias of Benjamin Franklin?"

"I aspire to his greatness," Granger said. "I still can't get over that you risked NorthBridge infiltration into the very plan to save society. That was a real tough-guy move."

"Not really," Hudson said. "Booker and Fonda were right all along. NorthBridge and I wanted the same thing, we just went about it in different ways. Looking back on it now, it's easy to see neither one of us could have gotten here without the other."

"Now that we've fixed it," Granger said, "made everything Fair and Free, I have one worry, one terror that keeps me up nights."

"What?" Hudson asked, concerned.

"That it will all start over again," Granger said, looking off to the setting sun. "Someone once warned, 'Slaves dream not of freedom, but of becoming masters.'"

EPILOGUE

A year after the coup, the world was a very different place. The Federal Reserve and all other central banks across the globe were gone. The new cryptocurrency, digiGOLD, was the international standard, and the Automated Payment Transaction tax had also been adopted in every country. Much stricter laws were introduced concerning corporate governance. All corporations with a market cap exceeding $100 million were required to have regard to the public good in all major corporate decision-making. The fiduciary responsibility of their boards now went beyond shareholders. Standards were established for pollution, recycling, consumption, human rights, employee relations, community involvement, and philanthropy.

Coyne had been arrested in South Africa. Bastendorff had been tracked down in Monaco. Both were serving life sentences without the possibility of parole. Thirty-one other surviving REMies had also been tried and imprisoned. Booker, the last REMie, had been pardoned, and agreed to give up all but $1 billion of his wealth, although there were grumblings inside the administration that Booker had hidden billions that people would never find. He had, after all, been one of the creators of digi-GOLD. Still, he agreed with the principle, saying, "Why would anyone need more than a billion dollars while there is still one person in the world living in poverty?"

Schueller had also retained $1 billion of his inheritance and turned over the rest to his various charities and foundations. ZAP had become a world leader in alternative energy. MEDs had expanded around the planet as universal healthcare was provided to everyone. The Free Food Foundation, now run by Melissa full-time, was making tremendous headway in its goal of one hundred million gardens planted in three years. With the sudden influx of REMie cash, it had also gone beyond its original mission and in addition to providing free seeds, garden tools, and supplies, it was working to restore soil and groundwater to organic and pristine states. Other non-profits had tackled mandatory recycling and pollution. It looked like millions of new jobs and explosive economic growth were going to be part of a very bright future, since the reins had finally been lifted.

The B-4 members who lived through the coup, as well as seventy-three other military leaders, were court-martialed and enduring life sentences in military prisons, including the former Chairman of the Joint Chiefs. Hudson had offered Colonel Enapay Dranick a pardon, but his friend had refused to accept it. His sentence ensured he would die in prison. Hudson was torn; the emotional displacement of a great friend would always haunt him.

Thorne declared his candidacy for the US Senate—there were plenty of vacancies. Fonda still ran the Raton Report, which was more popular than ever. Hudson had not spoken to her since before the coup, but on the one year anniversary of the military takeover, he granted her an interview in the Oval Office.

Hudson, more popular than any US leader in history, with one year left in his term, riding approval ratings in the nineties, shocked the country, and the world, by announcing his resignation. He'd taken a teaching position at Reed College in Portland, Oregon. He'd also accepted an offer to sit on the board of the Inner Movement. The Wizard would be leaving Washington at the same time to join Linh's staff.

In the statement released by the White House, Hudson had expressed his full confidence in Vice President Brown assuming the presidency, and offered his complete endorsement and hope that she would run for reelection at the end of the term.

During his interview with Fonda, they discussed his thoughts on the coup, its part in bringing about the fall of the REMie empire, the dissolution of NorthBridge, and the many radical reforms which were now law.

Fonda handed Hudson a gold CapStone she'd kept concealed in a large canvas bag. The gleaming, pyramid-shaped metal object was about ten inches wide, mounted on a polished-wood base. "It's from Booker," she said. "It's not real gold, just gold leaf. He's not as rich as he used to be, you know?" She winked.

Hudson smiled and read the engraved plaque on the base:

HUDSON POUND
WINNER OF THE FINAL CAPWAR

"I didn't win it."

"You most certainly did."

"There's still a REMie out there," he said, looking down at Booker's gift.

"Don't regret your decision to pardon him," Fonda said. "It was the right thing. Booker never really was a REMie, he just had so much money they had to let him in the club. None of them could ever stand him."

"I hope that's true."

"If Booker had been a real REMie, you never would have lived past the election."

Their eyes locked for a long, knowing moment.

"In any event," Hudson said, "I never really thanked you."

"Thank me?" Fonda said in mock surprise. "Whatever for?"

He thought for a moment. "For all your words, deployed at just the right time, to just the right people. You understand, better than anyone I've ever known, how powerful words really are."

She smiled. "I'm just glad I was right about you . . . or maybe 'almost right' is a better way to put it. In truth, you actually exceeded my expectations. And now, like your hero, George Washington, they would have made you king, but instead you're riding off into the sunset."

"My work here is done." Hudson looked around the restored Oval Office, absorbing his own history in the room. "Now Booker can finally have the first African American woman as president."

"Booker didn't want her to be president because she's African American," Fonda said. "Being African American himself, I'm sure he didn't mind that." Fonda smiled. "But contrary to what happened, Celia has a vision of the world without war that is so powerful, Booker always believed she was—*is*—strong enough to make it happen."

"I do, too."

"The three of us agree again," Fonda said, clapping her hands once. "So, Oregon, huh? What are you going to teach?"

"History, what else?" Hudson said, looking reflective. "But *true* history, about what the REMies did to the world for the last hundred and twenty years or so. I want to make sure it doesn't happen again."

"'Those who cannot learn from history are doomed to repeat it,'" Fonda said.

"Exactly. I never really wanted to be anything other than a history teacher," Hudson said, looking at the Frederic Remington sculpture, The Bronco Buster. "It's my job to make sure people learn the truth."

"Why Reed? You could have taught anywhere. Harvard, Princeton . . . "

"Too big, too old world, too everything," the president said. "I just want to make a difference, and my granddaughter will be born there."

"Florence?"

Hudson nodded, beaming.

"And it's about as far away as you could get from Melissa, right?" Fonda asked.

"No," Hudson said, looking sad. "It was you, Fonda, who taught me it's always easier to face the truth than to run from it." He grimaced.

"Just remember, wherever you go, there you are." She smiled genuinely, obviously from experience.

He let out a painful laugh.

"Make a difference . . . that's all you've ever done, Mr. President," she said, winking. "Fair and Free is working, billions around the world are leaving poverty, pollution is on track to be all but eliminated within a decade, so many improvements . . . " She leaned toward him, lowering her voice to a whisper. "You done good, Hudson." Then, speaking in a normal tone again, added, "The world is a better place." She took both his hands, gave them a squeeze, a quick shake, then tossed them loose. "Turns out **we really are the change.**"

END OF BOOK THREE

Want to read more of Booker Lipton's exploits? Try another one of my series. Visit BrandtLegg.com for your next adventure.

A NOTE FROM THE AUTHOR

- **_Thank you_** so much for reading my book!
- **Please help -** If you enjoyed it, please consider posting a quick review (even a few words) wherever you purchased this copy. Reviews are the greatest way to help an author. And, please tell your friends. Thanks!
- **I'd love to hear from you** – Questions, comments, whatever. Email me at my website, BrandtLegg.com. I'll definitely respond (within a few days).
- **Join my Inner Circle -** If you want to be the first to hear about my new releases, advance reads, occasional news and more, please join my Inner Circle at my website.

ABOUT THE AUTHOR

USA TODAY Bestselling Author Brandt Legg uses his unusual real life experiences to create page-turning novels. He's traveled with CIA agents, dined with senators and congressmen, mingled with astronauts, chatted with governors and presidential candidates, had a private conversation with a Secretary of Defense he still doesn't like to talk about, hung out with Oscar and Grammy winners, had drinks at the State Department, been pursued by tabloid reporters, and spent a birthday at the White House by invitation from the President of the United States.

At age eight, Legg's father died suddenly, plunging his family into poverty. Two years later, while suffering from crippling migraines, he started in business, and turned a hobby into a multi-million-dollar empire. National media dubbed him the "Teen Tycoon," and by the mid-eighties, Legg was one of the top young entrepreneurs in America, appearing as high as number twenty-four on the list (when Steve Jobs was #1, Bill Gates #4, and Michael Dell #6). Legg still jokes that he should have gone into computers.

By his twenties, after years of buying and selling businesses, leveraging, and risk-taking, the high-flying Legg became ensnarled in the financial whirlwind of the junk bond eighties. The stock market crashed and a firestorm of trouble came down. The Teen Tycoon racked up more than a million dollars in legal fees, was betrayed by those closest to him, lost his entire fortune, and ended up serving time for financial improprieties.

After a year, Legg emerged from federal prison, chastened and wiser, and began anew. More than twenty-five years later, he's now using all that hard-earned firsthand knowledge of conspiracies, corruption and high finance to weave his tales. Legg's books pulse with authenticity.

His series have excited nearly a million readers around the world. Although he refused an offer to make a television movie about his life as a teenage millionaire, his autobiography is in the works. There has also been interest from Hollywood to turn his thrillers into films. With any luck, one day you'll see your favorite characters on screen.

He lives in the Pacific Northwest, with his wife and son, writing full time, in several genres, containing the common themes of adventure, conspiracy, and thrillers. Of all his pursuits, being an author and crafting plots for novels is his favorite. (see below for a list of titles available).

For more information, or to contact him, please visit his website. He loves to hear from readers and always responds!

BrandtLegg.com

BOOKS BY BRANDT LEGG

CapWar ELECTION (CapStone Conspiracy #1)

CapWar EXPERIENCE (CapStone Conspiracy #2)

CapWar EMPIRE (CapStone Conspiracy #3)

The CapStone Conspiracy (books 1-3)

Cosega Search (Cosega Sequence #1)

Cosega Storm (Cosega Sequence #2)

Cosega Shift (Cosega Sequence #3)

Cosega Sphere (Cosega Sequence #4)

The Cosega Sequence (books 1-3)

The Last Librarian (Justar Journal #1)

The Lost TreeRunner (Justar Journal #2)

The List Keepers (Justar Journal #3)

The complete Justar Journal

Outview (Inner Movement #1)

Outin (Inner Movement #2)

Outmove (Inner Movement #3)

The complete Inner Movement trilogy

ACKNOWLEDGMENTS

It took a long time to finish this series. Many things happened along the way. I began the first book before the 2016 presidential election, and all the surprises that came with it, but there were personal matters that conspired to make this more of an odyssey, and I think the story is better for it. A special thanks to Marc, Germaine, and Bez, who were there in the mountains, on the coast, and other places where some of this series was written, and especially for being there in Los Angeles; your presence meant the world to me. Again, to Ro, for more than thanks and more than everything. Gratitude to my mother for all the hours of reading, and for trying not to worry. Cathie Harrison must be thanked again for reading faster than anyone ever. To Bonnie Brown Koeln, the Grammarian in Chief, who still reads the old-fashioned way—on paper. You're always up for a challenge, and you always inspire. My appreciation to Jack Llartin, for keeping me out of comma-trouble, etc. And, finally, to Teakki, who patiently waited to play cards until I finished writing each day.

Made in the USA
Coppell, TX
05 May 2022

77442533R00246